LEGACY
OF
VALOR

LEGACY OF *VALOR*

JED BABBIN

PENTLAND PRESS, INC.
ENGLAND • USA • SCOTLAND

PUBLISHED BY PENTLAND PRESS, INC.
5122 Bur Oak Circle, Raleigh, North Carolina 27612
United States of America
919-782-0281

ISBN 1-57197-213-7
Library of Congress Catalog Card Number 99-80018

Printed in the United States of America

O makin' mock o' uniforms
that guard you while you sleep
Is cheaper than them uniforms,
an' they're starvation cheap;
An' hustlin' drunken sodgers
when they're goin' large a bit
Is five times better business
than paradin' in full kit.
Then it's Tommy this, an Tommy that,
an' "Tommy, ow's your soul?"
But it's "Thin red line of 'eroes"
when the drums begin to roll.

—Rudyard Kipling, "Tommy."

For My Father
Harold H. Babbin
Captain, USMCR
Code Name "Black Bart"
Guadalcanal, 1942

For all of the fun I had writing this book, *Legacy of Valor* would never have been without the encouragement of my wife Sharon and the skilled advice and editing of my friend Katy Rehyansky who gave so much of her time. Technical accuracy must be credited to the help of three friends: Matt Keegan, whose encyclopedic knowledge of military technologies appears in many chapters; and two SEAL veterans, Al Clark, the Michael Jordan of tactical shooting, and Dale McClellan, grand master of the handgun. Heartfelt thanks to each of you from someone who is very lucky to have such a wife and such friends. I would also acknowledge the help of a very suave British gentleman, but for the fact that, as he admonished me, "The Regiment does not advertise."

PROLOGUE

JOB DESCRIPTION

27 April 1804
1110 Hours
Tripoli Harbor

The sand scraped under his boots as he paced the foredeck. He put his hands on his hips and stretched his head back to take a slow, deep breath, forcing his lungs to accept the hot, dusty air. At home, in the North Atlantic, there always was a morning wind stinging his face with the salt spray, cleansing his heart and mind. The cold winds of home always whispered to him, promising to carry him anywhere. But this North African wind had no voice. It brought no relief, only the heat, the sand, and the faint smell of rotting flesh.

He had taken his heavy coat off in the heat, but Murrow was still in full fig. Murrow's only concession to the heat was the scented kerchief held to his nose. The man would sooner faint from the heat than fail to wear every ornament of his rank.

"So you don't approve of my plan, Mr. Murrow?"

"No, Commodore Preble, I do not. It is far too much of a risk, sir. What you propose has never been done and cannot be done now. Look at the beach. There must be a thousand men assembled there."

The commodore obliged, raising his telescope. There *were* at least a thousand men there, parading back and forth in front of the city's gates. A small man rode a big white horse, prancing and galloping in front of the troops.

"Look, Murrow. That must be Karamanlis. We should be flattered that the Bey himself has come out to salute us."

"Commodore, we have time. Let us call another council of war and reconsider this plan."

"No. The time for talk is past. We have gone over the possibilities, and there is no good alternative. We have sailed these waters for three months searching for their fleet and have yet to bring them to battle. Our orders come directly from the president. He said ‘chastise the Tripolitan pirates,’ and that is what I mean to do.”

“With that lot, sir? With that Irish rabble? I doubt they could fight their way out of a straw basket. They’re nothing more than a bunch of wharf rats.”

“If you mean our little band of soldiers, I suggest that you not insult them too loudly. They may take offense. They do seem to be a rather dangerous bunch.”

On the deck below them, some forty men stood in ranks. To one side was a very large man wearing sergeant’s stripes. In front was a smaller, wiry man who paced back and forth, saying nothing, but looking constantly at the beach, at the commodore, and at the beach again.

The wiry man’s uniform hung on him like a sack. The commodore remembered how the young officer had looked, so smart in his new red uniform when they had left home six months before. Since then, it was all bad rations and severe heat. It had thinned them all.

“Yes, sir. And they are probably a greater danger to themselves than the enemy.”

“You must make allowances for them, Murrow. You know that every military force has its own tradition and customs. We borrow centuries of them from the British Navy. These men are only now creating their own.”

“But look at them, sir. Not a gentleman among them, least of all their officer. He seems to spend more time playing the fiddle than training the men. Not one proper uniform among them. Six months ago, half of them didn’t even know how to hold a saber. I dare say, none of them will make it through the walls into Tripoli itself.”

“We shall see presently. Our messenger returned only a few hours ago. We must await the Tripolitans’ reply. Shall they release the ships and men they have seized? If they do not, it is up to us to force the matter.”

The commodore had only three ships in his squadron. They sailed slowly, laboring back and forth across the mouth of the harbor in a rough triangle. At each turn they were ready to form a battle line left or right, or to turn in behind the commodore’s ship. By itself, each ship was not a formidable weapon, but the way Preble’s tactics combined their power, the squadron had the capability of sustained fire that was truly awesome.

Murrow dropped the perfumed kerchief from his nose. “Commodore Preble, you not only will break tradition, but we shall be violating every rule of war I know.”

“Mr. Murrow, you are within your rights in telling me of your disagreement. Now I have made my decision, and you shall do your best to carry it out. The rules of war be damned! We are a new nation, and we are entitled to write some of our own. Summon Mr. O’Bannon. I wish to speak to him again.”

The young lieutenant saw Murrow's wave and bounded up the ladders to the foredeck. His salute and the way he grinned at the commodore were a bit too much for Murrow.

"Lieutenant, you will button your coat and stand straight when addressing the Commodore, and—"

"Yes, *thank* you, Murrow." Preble's eyes bored into the young man. Who was he, really? What is inside the man? Is he truly ready for this mission?

"As for you, Lieutenant, you understand that you are to deliver the president's message clearly and without embellishment? You will have a terribly difficult time finding Karamanlis if he doesn't go straight to the palace when we begin the bombardment. I doubt you'll catch him anywhere else. You shall force the Tripolitans to surrender their captives without further bloodshed if possible. If not, the matter is left to your discretion. But do be discreet, Lieutenant. I mean to end a war, not start a larger one."

The lieutenant smiled a crooked smile. "Don't worry, sir. We'll get our people back, and they'll get the president's message straightaway."

Preble smiled his thin smile. "Off with you then, and good luck."

Murrow raised his telescope and scanned the beach. "Commodore, look at the Bey. He seems to be waving one of the flags they must have taken when they captured the *Algonquin*." Preble raised his telescope as well. The man on the white horse was waving an American flag, but as they looked on, a second man torched it, and the Bey rode his great white horse across the beach, waving the flaming pennant.

"I'd say that was a fair answer to our message, Mr. Murrow. Beat to quarters."

The drums beat the call to arms as the commodore's ship raised signal flags. The other two ships fell into line ahead. As the drums sounded, the men on the decks below pulled back their guns to load and prime them. In moments, the gun ports were open and the guns run out. The young lieutenant and his men had climbed into three whaleboats and were already rowing toward the beach. Preble raised his glass again and saw the lieutenant standing in the bow of one of the boats.

O'Bannon looked across to the other two boats. The men were grim, looking ahead to the beach. With a whoop, O'Bannon drew his saber and thrust it straight into the sky as if to pierce the sun. The saber's blade took fire, and for an instant an unholy light engulfed the sword and the man who held it. There was a roar from the men in the boats, and it echoed across the water.

The three ships had reached their stations and began a bombardment of the army on the beach and the walls of the city. Broadside after broadside they fired, tacking around a great circle. While one ship fired, two reloaded. After the first three broadsides, those left alive of the army on the beach had panicked and run into the city. By the time each of the ships had fired two more, the walls of the city were half-fallen and defenseless.

The whaleboats ground into the sand, and the lieutenant was the first out into the low water, tearing off his uniform coat. He looked at the city's walls. Where cannon had stood moments ago, there was nothing but smoking ruins. He had his pistols and his saber. And his men. He needed nothing more.

"All right, men. Form a skirmish line to the left. Double time. Follow me."

They trotted through the dead and wounded men who littered the beach. The proud man on the white horse was nowhere to be seen as they passed through the gates into the city. Now they marched side by side in a double column, the interpreter leading the way through the narrow streets. Thousands of eyes looked out at them from behind almost-closed doors and curtains.

They stood, all forty of them, at the base of the marble steps looking up. They had marched through the town without meeting any challenge. Now the beauty of the city first struck them, as they gazed on what seemed to be something out of a fairy tale. The white marble tower before them was so bright that it was painful to see. No matter.

"Fix bayonets." They moved, as one man, to the eighteen-inch short-swords on their belts as he pointed the saber forward. As he stared ahead, a death's-head grin came onto his face and a wild gleam into his eyes. "Double time. Follow me."

They ran up the steps toward the few remaining guards, who drew their swords at the advance. The man on the left swung his sword at them, missed, and was shot, along with two of the other guards who chose to stand their ground. The man on his right swung his sword high over head, but O'Bannon was younger, tougher, and quicker. The hilt of his saber caught the man square on the chin, and he dropped like a stone. The rest of the guards ran.

They ran down the hall, still in double file, to the main room. The fat man in the silk robe was babbling something in Arabic.

"What the devil is he saying?" O'Bannon demanded of the interpreter.

"He says, 'What men are these?' and 'How dare you approach me?'"

O'Bannon pressed the tip of his sword to the fat man's chest. "Tell him I am Lieutenant Presley Neville O'Bannon, United States Marine Corps. And I have a message for him from Thomas Jefferson."

The man in the silk robes was babbling an answer when O'Bannon cut him off. "Tell me where the captives are, or I'll cut out your heart and cook it for dinner."

As the interpreter talked, the small man's eyes grew wider. He was babbling again. The interpreter described the dungeon beneath them.

"Sergeant, take ten men and free everyone in that damned place. We shall hold our ground right here." The big man motioned to the first five ranks, and jogged off. They returned in a few minutes with seven dirty, beaten men.

O'Bannon turned to the man being helped along by the big sergeant. "Are there any more Americans here?"

"Sir, I am Joshua Tyler, captain of the *Algonquin*. These are all of my crew who remain alive. There are no other captives I know of, sir."

O'Bannon's eyes flashed again. "Sergeant, did your hear what Mr. Murrow called us when he was talking to the commodore?"

"No, sir. But one of the mates said he called us Irish rabble."

The lieutenant's grin grew wider. "Sergeant, Irish rabble such as we shan't get the message right. Let's take our fat friend to Mr. Murrow. He can make sure that we don't mess it up."

O'Bannon shoved the fat man toward the door with one hand and raised his saber in the other. The fat man screamed as the saber slashed down, slicing a neat cut down the center of the robe, just grazing the skin of his back. Karamanlis stumbled out of his robes and ran from the room. O'Bannon and his small band trotted after him, prodding him along.

The commodore was still pacing the foredeck, his telescope scanning the walls for a sign of the marines. "Mr. Murrow, I'll have a closer look."

"Please, Commodore, our men are inside the city. I suggest we retire a bit farther offshore to wait for them to come out. What if the enemy fleet catches us so close to shore? We can send one ship in to pick them up. If they ever come out."

"Nonsense. Have my boat lowered. I'm going to the beach. Stay here if you can't be parted from your perfumeries."

Murrow drew himself up ramrod straight. "If the commodore pleases, I should like to accompany him to the beach."

It was nearly an hour later when the commodore's boat ground into the sand where the whaleboats stood. He hopped out and was lifting his telescope to look at the city when Murrow caught up with him.

"Do you see them, sir? I cannot. We may not be able to wait much longer. The tide will change in the next half hour."

"I do see something, Murrow, but I can't see through the blasted dust blowing around. They can't be more than a few hundred yards off. Take a look yourself." He handed Murrow the telescope.

"I see them, sir. They appear to be in order but, but—" Murrow's face reddened.

"But what, damn it? Give me the glass."

The commodore looked, scowled, and looked again. The marines were in good order, but their prisoner looked very unhappy. The Bey of Tripoli was marching naked in front of the walls of his own city. Three minutes later, the small group paraded up to them.

Murrow's face grew redder by the moment. "Commodore, this conduct is contrary to the rules of war. I suggest—"

"I suggest, Murrow, that you send one of the men to the boats and have him get a piece of canvas to cover Mr. Karamanlis. And then you shall return to the ship while I have a brief conversation with our prisoner. The wind seems to be picking up, and I expect we will be able to leave shortly." Preble turned to the marine.

"Sheathe your saber, Lieutenant. I expect you'll not need it again today."

CHAPTER 1

AT THE POINT OF THE SPEAR

16 January 1991
0800 Hours
Outside Riyadh, Saudi Arabia

"Great place, Chief. No whiskey. No good movies. No place to do anything other than sit and fry in this goddamn desert."

"Quit yer bitchin', Franco. This is a Moslem country, an' we gotta respect the rules. Are you gonna bet or not?" Chief Perkins was a patient man. Especially when running his book.

The two looked at the objects of the bet. One, a tall husky blond kid, was stretching to warm up. The other, a shorter black man, stood with his arms crossed. He closely resembled a fire hydrant.

"You sure nobody ever beat Chief Wilson?"

"No, I ain't sure, and I also ain't sure that the record is twenty flips. An' guess who holds the record?"

"Okay, okay. I'll put five bucks on Tommy."

"Awright, ladies. The book is closed. We will now toss the coin. Tommy, as the younger guy you call it." He flipped a quarter into the air.

"Heads."

"Ah, the victim calls heads, and heads it is. Okay, master chief. On your face."

The stocky black man lay face down in the hot sand, a big shitty grin on his face. This was his game. One-armed pushups were his specialty. Other men were younger and more enthusiastic. But old age and treachery always beat youth and enthusiasm. Almost always.

The larger blond man lay face up on top of him.

"Okay, you know the rules for 'One Arm.' The bottom man can use only one arm to flip over. The top man can't do anything but balance on top, and hang on. You go until somebody quits. The guy on top when the bottom man wears out, wins. Ready? Go."

The blond man yelled "hooyah" as he was immediately flipped on his face, the other man now on top. About ten men were clustered around the contestants rolling back and forth, flipping over and over. . .

"C'mon, Tommy."

"You got him, Chief."

"He's wearing out already. Look how red his face is."

"He's black, you moron. Black people don't get red in the face."

"Like hell they don't."

"Go Tommy. Tommy, one more, buddy, an' you got him."

The blond giant was struggling. With Chief Wilson on top of him, every one-armed pushup was moving over 400 pounds. He pushed, pushed harder, his arm starting to shake. Then he collapsed amid shouts of "Aw, not again" and "Can't anybody beat this guy?"

The winner stood, counting his money slowly. The crowd started breaking up. Franco was back bugging the other chief.

"Hey, Chief Perkins, what's the dope? I hear we go tonight."

"Franco, whyn't you just go an' clean your sidearm? The LT will be back in a few minutes and maybe he'll have the orders for us. Just cool your jets, man. You read the warning order."

"Yeah, strike behind enemy lines. Capture or kill key government leaders and destroy high-value targets. So why the hell have we been sitting here for two weeks instead of doing the job?"

Master Chief Wilson raised his head from his counting exercise. "Boy, you ever heard of George Bush? When he says go, we'll go."

16 January
2045 Hours

They sat around the two large tents, reading, playing cards, and writing letters. Some cleaned weapons that didn't need cleaning. Some sharpened knives already sharp enough to shave with. Anything worth doing is worth overdoing.

The lieutenant walked in. Lieutenant (j.g.) Cullum O'Bannon looked like the rest of them, about five foot ten, muscular, with a swimmer's build. He held up a sheet of paper and said only, "Echo platoon, orders." He didn't need to tell them to gather around. One man ran to the other tent and returned immediately with its residents. There were thirteen of them sitting around the lieutenant, all eyes and ears. He pulled a large map out and spread it out on the floor.

"Okay, here's the scoop. We go tonight. The rest of Team 3 goes in by boat or helo drop. We'll do a medium altitude drop from about 15,000. No low opening tonight. We'll have to glide for about ten miles or so and then hoof it to the target.

"The target is a big office building, which just happens to be the headquarters of the Iraqi general staff. It's their equivalent of the Pentagon. We go to the top of this small building just under a half mile away. It's right there on the map. Take a look at the satellite photo. From there it's simple. We get up on the roof, set up the laser designators, and the bombers come in. They make their drop and TA comes in to pick us up."

"Hey, LT, that's awright." The mention of "TA" produced smiles around the group. Commander Tommy Atkins was a legend in the navy, the only helo driver who never missed a drop or a pickup.

"You bet your butt, fellas." Chief Wilson was smiling. "I been in this business longer than all a' you. Commander Atkins always gets in there. We're damned lucky he's our driver, 'cause he'll get us out, no matter how much shit is hittin' the fan."

"Yeah, but LT, what're they dropping? We're less than half a mile away."

"Good question. They'll probably hit the place with 2,000-pounders. Pretty big stuff. It'll be a little hairy that close."

"Okay, guys. We'll be feeling the blast, so keep your heads down. I don't want to lose anyone to some flying pieces of concrete. We also have to lase a second target, a SAM site right here." He pointed at another spot on the map. "TA can only get in if we hit these guys, too. We'll set up the second designator there. The fly-fly boys will hit that one with smaller stuff, probably 250-pounders."

"Hey, LT. Those weird-lookin' bombers we seen flying around last night. Your brother flies one of them, doesn't he?"

"Yeah. Don't remind me. I didn't come all this way just to be a spotter for my goddam big brother."

Master Chief Wilson looked at the lieutenant and muttered to himself. "Kids. Least he ain't a Goddam ensign with a drippy nose I gotta wipe."

16 January 1991
2355 Hours

The sky was crowded with aircraft orbiting inside friendly territory waiting for the signal to go. Layer upon layer were reflected on Iraqi radar screens scanning every altitude. The pilots were joking about frying eggs in all the microwave energy that swirled through the dark sky.

The big C-130 circled lazily at 18,000 feet. It had the radar signature of a Pennsylvania Dutch barn, but it was a great platform to launch jumpers. They might show up on radar like a flock of birds, but the enemy operators weren't nearly sharp enough to identify the Navy SEALs, Marine Force Recon, Army Special Forces, and British SAS units ready to take the war to the Iraqis.

The C-130 Hercules climbed through Saudi air space to join the three other transports and their fighter cover. Other formations turned south toward Kuwait, but the big Lockheed ship turned north toward Iraq.

With the jump ramp open, the noise was almost deafening. The C-130 Hercules is probably the toughest, safest aircraft in the world. It is also the most uncomfortable. Even with the ramp closed, the noise would leave your ears ringing for days after a long flight. But they were used to it, having ridden around the world in the Herky Bird more than once. They all had worn the issue earplugs, which were discarded as soon as the jump ramp opened.

A man a few places in front of him shouted above the roar of the engines. "You okay, LT?"

"Yeah, I'm okay, Chief. You know how much I love these goddamn night jumps. Jumping in daylight is cool, but this stuff. . . . Every time I do it, it scares the shit outta me."

"You're okay, boss. Just walk out the door."

"Right."

The jumpmaster had opened the door what seemed like an hour ago. Everyone was wearing the same MT1X parachutes they had practiced in over and over again. As usual, they were lined up not by rank but by jump order. The first man out had been shown in many a practice jump to fall slower than the others. Master Chief Wilson's weight and stumpy build gave him more than average wind resistance, so he was the slowest to fall.

Once they were out the door, the faster jumpers would spread their arms and legs to slow down and line up with Wilson. The platoon had done it dozens of times in practice jumps. This was not the same thing.

O'Bannon saw the dull green light go on next to the lowered ramp. The jumpmaster swung his arm, pointing out. Wilson went out, then a few others. O'Bannon stepped out into the black.

In free fall, the platoon looked for the small chemical light attached to the Wilson's pack and flew toward it. Soon all fourteen were in a rough half-circle formation arrayed on both sides of the chief. O'Bannon watched the altimeter on his wrist as it counted down the altitude. At 6,000 feet he waved another small chem light to signal the others and pulled his parachute open. Maintaining their silent formation, the SEALs floated toward their target, still ten kilometers away.

Baghdad was a city with a split personality. Their nation at war, the civilian population was off the streets after dark. But on the European side of town, the hotels were lit up like they were expecting the Shriners, and half the reporters in the world were wandering around—never too far from the hotel bar—aiming cameras and questions at anyone wearing a uniform.

The miniaturized radar detector O'Bannon wore sounded off in his earpiece. The distinctive raspy bleep of the SAM radar grew stronger on his right, so he pulled his control smoothly and guided his group in. Spotlights already lit up the sky, but unless the platoon was very unlucky they would pass far outside the lights and hit the ground about two kilometers from the primary target.

They touched down on the side of a hill, about a mile out of town, just beyond the lights of the city. Almost two hours to get to the primary objective and two minutes to secure it. The platoon formed up around O'Bannon and jogged off.

They all ran ten or twenty klicks a day, and the full packs they carried didn't even throw their balance off. Running in combat boots makes a lot of noise, but the SEALs had jump boots they designed themselves. They looked like a good pair of running shoes—which they were—sewn to the top halves of combat boots—which they also were. They were a bunch quieter than regular boots. The platoon could have run the two kilometers in ten minutes, but jogging was for the beach, not for patrolling hostile ground. You figure one mile per hour patrolling, so two klicks was about an hour and a half. They had two hours. Plenty of time to do it right.

They communicated with hand signals or brief, plain-English phrases in the clear over their short-range radios. Guys in the movies could signal by clicking their microphones. In the real world, using words reduces confusion. The bad guys are almost never listening and can't figure out that they have a problem until way too late.

They were moving out of the comfort of darkness as they neared the target. O'Bannon could see the cluster of tall buildings to his left about another half mile away. Like everything around them, the three buildings were lit up. The blackouts, which no civilian obeyed, were also ignored by the Iraqi military. Their headquarters buildings should have been concealed, or the headquarters moved. Right now all the Americans had to do was pick the right buildings to hit.

O'Bannon slowed their pace as they got to the edge of the block, street lights beginning to cast their shadows. A moment later he stopped short, keyed his microphone, and said "Fade." Without a sound, the entire platoon melted into darkened corners and doorways.

The Iraqi patrol casually strolled around the corner, their rifles slung over their shoulders. Hometown duty was good for them. They could smoke cigarettes at night without incurring the wrath of some front-line noncom. O'Bannon drew his Sig Sauer pistol, his two-handed grip close to his chest, ready to shoot. He sensed his partner coming up on his left. When the Iraqis were fifteen feet away, he took one step forward into a kneeling position and fired two rounds into the chest of the farthest man, and one shot into his head. The supressor and the subsonic rounds combined to make the shots sound like flies buzzing through the air. O'Bannon heard one more as his partner stood next to him and shot the other soldier. "Took ya three, lootenant," whispered the other man.

Team members instantly dragged the dead men into the shadows.

The junior chief, Perkins, spoke softly. "LT, we both know what we gotta do now." Wilson looked worried, but stayed quiet.

"Chief, if you think we're stopping here—"

"Boss, doctrine is clear. We've been engaged. We gotta extract."

O'Bannon looked at Wilson with a crooked smile. "Master chief, I'm told we are required to abort." He looked at the others, still spread out in their tactical formation.

"Chief Perkins, we are one platooon out of all of Team 3. You realize how much shit we're gonna take from the rest of the team if we punt?"

"I know, boss, but doctrine—"

O'Bannon looked at the others. "Anybody else want to punt?" He knew that calling a SEAL a quitter was worse than anything you could say. The hint was enough. There were no takers.

"Okay, let's get moving."

Five more minutes and O'Bannon drew the team up behind the objective, a building across town from the target, and about twenty stories shorter. As usual, it looked just like the satellite recon photo they all had seen. Another high-low pair led them inside, quietly ending the career of one more Iraqi standing guard. The SEALs walked up the three sets of stairs and stopped behind the door to the roof for two minutes. The only one panting was behind O'Bannon. The man was a few inches shorter than he, and quite a bit wider. When he moved, his block-shaped torso seemed to overbalance his short legs.

"You a little out of shape, master chief?"

"Yeah, boss. But I can still nail 'em with one shot." O'Bannon turned and said, "Five minutes 'til show time. Let's get the stuff set up."

Four SEALs laid down their packs and went through the door before O'Bannon finished his sentence. They went low, and secured the unguarded roof immediately.

O'Bannon and the other four followed and set up the laser target designators and the secure radio in two minutes. He looked at his watch. One minute to two. Time to tune in, turn on, and get out. O'Bannon reached for the microphone to the big radio.

"Goblin, this is Flashlight 1. The gadgets are on. Say your time."

"Flashlight, this is Goblin. Ninety seconds. That you, Cully? Get your head down, numb nuts."

The Lockheed F-117A was about as secret a machine as had ever been built. Conceived and built in a huge hangar in Burbank, California, it had gone to war only once before, in a little fracas in Panama. The pilots of the 37th Tactical Fighter Wing lived and breathed the bird the generals wanted to call the

"Wobblin' Goblin." The pilots called it the "Surfboard" for its slippery handling. If you didn't pay her constant attention, she'd slip out from under you and spin into the ground in seconds. For all the aircraft's problems, they knew it could take them where no one else could go—into the most intense anti-aircraft defenses manned by the most scared, trigger-happy bunch outside of L.A.

They called themselves the Vampire Squadron because they almost never flew in daylight. Their body clocks were inverted, like a night watchman's. They lived at a place the inventor of the '117 called "Paradise Ranch." It was anything but a paradise—just a few thousand acres of desert dust and a couple of runways near a town called Tonopah. Not too many married men lasted more than a few months with the outfit.

This raid was led by the one of the few guys in the outfit who really loved their spartan life. He liked Paradise Ranch more than any place else in the world: his engineers, his pilots, and above all, his squadron. Major Matt O'Bannon had spent an entire week hiking around the base of a mountain where one of the developmental versions of the '117 had crashed, looking for a piece of the secret radar-absorbing skin that had been lost. He'd found it, too. Flying was his life, and everyone he flew with would follow him into a dogfight in hell. All he had to do was fly the first bird in. He always did.

Matt O'Bannon keyed his mike once more as he reefed the F-117 through a shallow turn at the initial point on the bomb run. "Hey, numb nuts. We be here. IP."

Cully turned his head to the west and listened. The SEALs ducked as they heard the fighters approach. It sounded like a very small jet coming closer, then the sound disappeared entirely. The four 2,000-pound bombs fell silently, guided to within inches of their targets by the laser designators. He keyed his radio as the bombs fell, switching back to the Navy frequency.

"TA, come in TA. Time to leave." The chopper pilot heard the call and turned the Sea King helicopter toward the building in the distance where the SEALs sat. He saw the flashes as the bombs hit.

The SEALs had ducked down next to the low wall closest to the target building as the bombs hit, but even at a half mile, the blast was deafening, and the concussion was like a punch to the chest.

As they recovered from that blast, the second wave of bombers took out the nearby SAM site. One hit to the control van with a 250-pound bomb was all it needed. Pieces of the building and the SAM site rained down on them, and two were injured. The platoon medic, the burly blond kid who had lost the game of "one arm," quickly checked them over and pronounced them ready to move.

Commander Tommy Atkins had been flying choppers since the early 1980s and was the old man of his group. He outranked all of his SEAL platoon. Flying for the navy was his life, but his permanent station for almost three years had been with the Army's Task Force 160, the Night Stalkers. Their special ops expertise was unequaled. Now he was back home, driving the SEALs into and out of trouble.

Atkins flew his chopper at rooftop level. After the first bombing run by the F-117s, every gun and missile emplacement in the Iraqi air defense system was firing as fast as its crew could load it. But the F-117s were long gone, and the sky was empty except for the anti-aircraft fire. Flying low and fast was not a new game for Atkins. When he reached the extraction point, he popped up and saw the SEALs huddled against the wall. Their position was now lit brightly by the fires in the city, and the burning SAM site.

"Hey, Cully. You waitin' for an engraved invite?" Atkins shouted as O'Bannon ran up half-carrying one of the wounded men. His South Philly accent came through even in combat.

"We got two guys hurt, Tommy. Let's get back to the base fast. Perkins got hit pretty bad."

"Rog. We be gone." The chopper lifted off as the last SEAL dived in. Atkins took it up off the roof, and then down fast, practically to street level. He pressed the cyclic control forward and the Sea King roared off out of the fight.

CHAPTER 2

AT THE HEART OF FOREIGN POLICY

22 June 1993
1505 Hours
Istanbul, Turkey

"Prime minister, the hospital just called. Mr. Ozal died a few minutes ago."

The man behind the desk raised his very head slowly, as if his huge mustache was too heavy to lift. Suleiman Semret was almost six foot seven, and as bald as a cue ball. His smoldering eyes often seemed to burn right through his political opponents.

The news of Ozal's death was expected, but no less sad for that. To most of the world, Turgut Ozal was the face of Turkey. His leadership made his nation a foundation on which much of the Western Alliance rested. Yes, Ozal feuded with the Greeks as every good Turk would sooner or later. But the Soviets knew their route to the Middle East was never secure as long as Ozal kept Turkey free. And that he did, for more than two decades.

"Thank you. Call the minister of state. The plans he has made for the funeral should proceed as soon as possible." With a brief bow, the other man withdrew. Semret picked up the telephone to call the NATO allies who would come to the funeral. The operator came on the line.

"Yes, sir?"

"Place calls for me immediately to the president of the United States, the prime ministers of Britain, France, and Germany. Then Japan, Italy, and any of the NATO prime ministers I haven't already listed." He hung up. A few moments later the phone rang.

"President Brandon of the United States will be on the line in a moment, sir."

"Hello? Mr. Semret? How're you this bright cheery mornin'?"

"I am well, Mr. President, and I hope you and your family are well. But I bring sad news. A few minutes ago, former Prime Minister Ozal died. The funeral will be in one week. I wanted to call you first to see if we needed to accommodate your schedule in some way so you can attend."

In Washington, three twenty-something staffers sat in front of the president's desk, listening on headphone extensions plugged into the president's phone and typing notes to him on computer keypads. The notes were displayed on a monitor in front of the president in large type. Every time he hit the enter key, the next message appeared. A quick reader, the president tapped the enter key impatiently.

The first note said, "Can't do it next week. Big fundraisers in Denver, Cheyenne, and Chicago."

The president's voice accommodated the occasion. His sadness was palpable. "Mr. Semret, that is sad news, indeed. But I have some matters of state that will prevent me from coming."

"It is regrettable, but I understand, Mr. President. Then should I speak to Vice President La Guardia personally?"

The staffers were furiously typing in one note after another. One said, "Ozal kept Turkey in NATO for 20 years."

Another said, "La Guardia needs to stay here—Democratic Leadership Conference function Wednesday."

The third's note said, "He's just another raghead. We don't owe them a damned thing."

The president said, "I am not sure that Vinny La Guardia can come either, Mr. Prime Minister."

A small fire began smoldering in Semret's eyes. "Mr. President, I realize that you have many pressing duties and so does the vice president. But surely Turgut Ozal, your most faithful NATO partner since World War II, should have some personal consideration in this time of our national mourning."

The note writers were going wild. The president's eyes scanned the screen to see, "We can't piss these guys off." Another staffer shook her head violently and typed, "Turkey and NATO are both irrelevant to our future. Pass this guy off to our ambassador." The third wrote, "Buy him off with a state visit next year?"

The president's words oozed through the phone. "Ah, Mr. Semret, I know of the long valued history of the relationship of our countries and Turkey's importance to NATO. But I regret that neither La Guardia nor I will be able to come."

"Even if we postpone the funeral? We could delay it for a few days, and—"

"I'm sorry. Our ambassador will certainly be there."

Three hours later, Semret finished his calls. The staffer reappeared at his door with the chief of staff behind him.

The staffer said, "Is there anything you need, prime minister?"

"No, not tonight. Have my car come around. Well, Izrik, have you tallied up the list for the funeral?"

"Yes, prime minister. Britain, Italy, Germany, and Spain are all sending their prime ministers. There will be either prime ministers or deputy prime ministers from every NATO country as well as Russia and most of the former Soviet bloc nations. China and Japan and both Koreas want to come."

"You are wrong, Izrik. Not every NATO country is sending their chief of state. There will be no one from the United States beside their ambassador."

"Surely you joke, prime minister."

Semret's eyes flamed again. "No. Even I could make a better joke. I spoke personally to President Brandon. It was humiliating to hear how casually he dismissed the idea. When I mentioned Ozal's name, it was like he was hearing it for the first time. It was as if he were trying to insult me."

"Do not take it so hard, prime minister. He is new to the job. He will learn."

"Perhaps he will, Izrik. But I will guarantee that Turkey will not pay for his education."

CHAPTER 3

AT ONE STEP BEHIND THE THRONE

30 January 1995
0810 Hours

The tall, skinny man with the Abe Lincoln beard rushed down the hall to the first lady's office. He had a stack of files in his arms, each of which bore a person's name and a label showing what job he or she was applying for. Appointments were slow in the Brandon administration, and there were a lot to be made. After the first few years in office, people were leaving in droves to make money as "consultants." Everywhere in Washington, former Brandon staffers were "consulting" on everything from peanut farming to foreign policy. In many cases, their advice on the former was indistinguishable from their advice on the latter.

"Sorry I'm a bit late, everybody." Dr. Steven Krueger wasn't speaking to the small group, just to his boss, First Lady Bella Brandon.

"That's quite all right, Steven," she said. "We certainly don't want to make the week's personnel decisions without you. The president wants us to handle all of the appointments that require Senate confirmation and all of the people who will be on the White House staff." Everyone in the room knew that when she said "us" she meant "me."

"Thank you Bella. I have a bunch of files here. Most of them are people you have already interviewed for jobs at the Cabinet level on down to the level of assistant secretary. Most of them are very capable and will take any spot we can give them. We also have a few new people who are being cleared for White House jobs."

"We'll take those first, Steve. What's the highest-ranking job we need to deal with today?"

"Well, Dr. Daniels, the national security advisor, needs a new deputy."

"Who does Anthony want?"

"He has proposed several names from, ah, a rather unusual source. He says that he has been under intense pressure from the Pentagon to have one of their people here."

"Couldn't he find anyone at the institute?" A couple of the staffers shuffled through their notes. Dr. Anthony Daniels, along with Dr. Steven Krueger and several other White House staffers, had been appointed from their senior fellowships at the first lady's favorite think tank. The World Institute for a Modern Peaceful Society had provided her husband's administration with three cabinet members and dozens of key staffers in many agencies. There was an unspoken rule that any appointments in national security or economic policy would be filled with someone from the institute.

"Dr. Daniels asked me to convey the bad news to you, Mrs. Brandon. The institute may have to take a back seat on this one. They really don't have any good candidates left. Besides, he feels that we should placate the Pentagon by putting one of their people in this job."

"Oh, dear. Okay, it might be good politically. The photos of the president with his staff are a bit too uniform. How about someone in the pictures who really does wear a uniform?" All of the staffers smiled at her quip. "Who does Anthony want?"

"He has three candidates. One is a career Pentagon civil service type. He's a graduate of MIT and the Kennedy School of Government at Harvard. He has published several books on national security and specializes in Middle East policy. Now he's a part-time professor at the Georgetown Foreign Policy School.

"The second is an army one-star general, the first ever of Chinese American descent. He has a Ph.D. from the University of Texas in foreign policy and is supposed to be the quickest mind in the whole military establishment. Of course, that's a relative comparison." There were judicious snickers among the staff.

"The third is a marine brigadier general, and he's probably the least qualified of the lot. He has no formal education at all, just a degree from the Naval Academy. He's an old Vietnam-era war horse. He spent a lot of time in combat, was wounded several times. More recently this fellow was a test pilot and managed a big procurement program."

"That doesn't sound too good. If he were working here, how much trouble would he make? I don't know if he could get along with Ike at all. How would he feel about working with a president who protested against the war and refused to be drafted?"

"I don't know, Bella. But you're right. Don't we really need someone who has better academic qualifications?"

"How old is this man, Steven?"

"About fifty-two. He has a reputation for intensity, but he may be pretty burned out by now. And you know how those people drink. He may be a closet alcoholic, for all we know. "

"Well, that could be perfect. If he's disabled like that we can put him to work elsewhere, too. How about using him to showcase our alcohol rehabilitation initiative? Sort of 'president helps the country by adding a soldier with a disability to his staff'?" This time the staff nodded to each other.

"Bella, he's used to following orders. Once he's here, we can showcase him with the president on a whole raft of issues," said Krueger.

"Should I bring him in for you to interview?"

"No need. I think we should all feel grateful that such people are available to serve our administration and its agenda. Anyway, the national security advisor isn't as important as he used to be."

She looked around the attentive group. "Now we've all got to understand him and try to help him work with us." She mirrored Krueger's professorial smile.

"The old burned-out marine it is, Steven. Inform Dr. Daniels of my choice. And I expect all of you to make this man feel right at home when he gets here. Just keep in mind that someone from the military culture won't understand us very well. It will be up to all of you to make sure he knows how we run things in this White House."

CHAPTER 4

AT THE DEFERENTIAL PALACE

Same Day

The DIB—the CIA's daily intelligence briefing for the president—used to be given first thing in the morning. Ike Brandon had changed it to the afternoon, just after lunch. Some topics repeat themselves over and over. The briefers tried not to repeat topics more than weekly, because the president got bored. But the issue of the poison gas and biological weapons in Iran and Iraq kept coming back.

For weeks, the chairman of the Joint Chiefs of Staff had been begging for a meeting with the president specifically to talk about those weapons. Finally, the president's staff relented and scheduled it for the slot reserved for the DIB. When the CIA found out about this, the CIA director, Dr. Harvey Miter, got himself invited. He would give the briefing. Preserving the time slot for CIA's disposal was important.

Now the players were filing into the secured conference room in the White House, a floor below the Oval Office. The president looked around. Everyone he wanted to be there was, except his wife. Oh, hell. He was tired of waiting.

"Okay, let's get this going."

"Mr. President, isn't the national security advisor coming?" asked the chairman of the Joint Chiefs.

"Ah, no, general. I didn't see the need to invite him. I'll tell him about it later. Harvey, go ahead. Let's get on with it."

"Yes, Mr. President." Miter turned on the inevitable viewgraph machine and put the first slide up.

"Mr. President, this is a satellite photo of the anthrax site we suspected twenty miles from Baghdad, and which we addressed in the briefings to you over the past couple of weeks. If you look at the upper right-hand corner, you can see the building where the missile delivery pods are being loaded. The trucks in the middle right part of the picture are there to take the missile pods to the final assembly area.

"This picture is of the missile assembly area north of Tehran. We have dozens of pictures and reports that the missiles being assembled here are short- and medium-range ballistic missiles. We have the same sort of anthrax growth areas here as we see in Iraq. We suspect that there are other infectious strains being grown there that may include smallpox. Also, we see the same missiles being assembled in Iraq as we do here.

"What's important about this is the apparent readiness of both countries' systems. We estimate that in as little as a few weeks, and no more than two months, both countries will have operational missiles with biological weapons in place. You may remember that they both have had nerve gas and other poison gas weapons for some time. Now, with the new missiles coming in from Korea, they have the means to deliver them.

"Okay, Harvey," said the president. "But what's the rush on this? Nobody is at war."

"Not only is nobody at war, there are no prospects for war. The Middle East peace process is proceeding quite nicely," said Blaine Graham, the secretary of State. His small, cold eyes looked at Miter from across the table. "These weapons are terrible. But what is to say that they are not defensive, just like our nuclear weapons were in the Cold War?"

"There are two differences, Mr. Secretary." Admiral Halett, the chief of Naval Operations, spoke with an intense voice that commanded attention. "The first is that our deterrent was deployed in response to a similar threat, with very tight safeguards against its accidental use. The second is that these people have already shown a taste for using these weapons. Don't forget, Hussein used chemicals against Iran and again against the Kurds. What's more, these guys may be testing their missiles soon. The only test range they have available is the Persian Gulf, or straight back into their own territory."

The president stirred again. "So what's the big deal? We test missiles, they test missiles. The Chinese and Russians test them all the time. Our diplomatic efforts show some promise. Maybe we should agree to let them fire a few shots per year. What do you think, Blaine?"

"It's a good idea, Mr. President. Maybe we could get them to agree to a specific path for any missiles they test fire. That way, we could avoid a war breaking out over some tests."

Miter's eyes drooped. "Mr. President, the whole idea of these tests would be to make the Iranians or the Iraqis more ready to shoot for real. If they test the systems, they train their people to do it right."

"But Harvey, if our push for the peace process succeeds, we may see them disarm those missiles. If they have these missiles ready to go, they'd be giving up something bigger than just a few boxes of missile parts. It could be a real success for us."

Halett butted back in. “Mr. President, we may or may not succeed diplomatically. Shouldn’t we try to keep them from increasing the threat now, rather than having to deal with it later?”

“Admiral, I appreciate your point of view, I really do. What you say has a lot of merit. But our objective is somewhat more limited.”

“Sir, you’re the only person who can decide what our objective should be. But, respectfully sir, we’ve gone a long way from the policy we started with. In 1991 we said we’d prevent them from having *any* of these weapons and insisted on on-site inspections to be sure of it.

“After that, we’ve said that maybe we don’t need to inspect all the sites. Now, you told the press yesterday that all we need to do is substantially reduce their ability to make and deliver these weapons. The Pentagon wants to carry out your policy in the most effective way possible. But we don’t know what it’s going to be.”

“Admiral, you clearly don’t see the benefit of keeping them off balance,” said the secretary of State. “If they don’t know whether we’ll insist on a total ban, they may be willing to give up something else.”

“This threat, as you call it, Admiral. What’s the big deal?” asked another figure. Vice President Vincent La Guardia was seldom silent in meetings like this. Or in any other kind of meeting. “Why can’t the Israelis shoot down anything coming their way? You’ve told us time after time that they have the ability.”

“Mr. Vice President, they do have a good system, but it won’t necessarily protect them fully. What if one missile gets through? You could have a whole city wiped out in the most horrible way imaginable.”

“And more than that, sir. The Kuwaitis have almost no antimissile defense, just a couple of Patriot batteries. Even worse, our ships in the Gulf have only the most basic protections against low-flying missiles. Nothing we have can protect against a high-altitude nuclear burst or most low level attacks with chemical or biological weapons.”

“We estimate that the Iranians have about seventy-five missiles with warheads capable of delivering chemical or biological weapons. The Iraqis have about twice that many.”

“So we’re talking about more than two hundred of these things,” said La Guardia. “ Tell me if I remember right, Harvey. These missiles can hit targets like Tel Aviv in Israel or King Saud City in Saudi Arabia. And Saddam can wipe out Kuwait in about fifteen minutes with these things, right?”

“Yes, that’s all true.” Miter sat down while La Guardia stood up and paced around the room. The president had a bored look. He wished there were a window he could stare out. But the vice president was just warming up.

“General, what do we do to prevent these things from killing people?”

General Stoneman, the chairman of the Joint Chiefs, was an old army tank commander. “Mr. Vice President, the best thing we can do is to make it damned clear that if these guys use those weapons on us or our friends, we will obliterate them.”

“With nuclear bombs? That doesn’t *prevent* it from happening. How do we prevent these damned things from killing thousands of people in the first place?”

“Sir, we could bomb all of those sites tomorrow. But our understanding of what you and the president wanted was for us to let the U.N. military command take the lead on this. They have control of our airborne reconnaissance forces. I don’t think the United States wants to declare war all by ourselves.”

“That is precisely right, general,” said the president. “And we should all remember this. I have promised the secretary general and many of our allies that we won’t act unilaterally, and I mean it. You all know as well as I do that there is no consensus in the Security Council for military action against Iraq and Iran. We can’t act without that consensus.

“I will *not* be the man who breaks the peace in the Middle East. I also will not be the man to put America back on its high horse. Our go-it-alone days are over, ladies and gentlemen. Before we waste any more time discussing fights we don’t need, I suggest we press on to other subjects.”

“I’m sorry, Mr. President, but could I make one more point on this subject?” Admiral Halett’s commanding voice was much softer now. “I think that we have a real dilemma. With all due respect to the State Department, they seem to be saying that we either negotiate the bad guys out of their favorite weapons, or we wait for them to use those missiles on us or Israel or Saudi Arabia, or somebody else we like, and then we nuke ’em. Mr. President, I think that poses an acute moral dilemma. Do we have to wait for the Iraqis or the Iranians to kill a few thousand people before we take matters into our own hands and make sure they don’t have the means to do that?”

Blaine Graham’s voice was rising. “We need no war-mongering from the Pentagon, Admiral. The president is right about this. Unless and until we get a go ahead from the Security Council, we shall not move. We shall continue the peace process. I’m sure neither Iraq nor Iran want to kill thousands of innocent people. We must have faith in the process, gentlemen.”

“Okay,” thought Halett. “I just don’t want to be at ground zero when this ‘peace process’ goes tits up.”

CHAPTER 5

AT THE TAIL OF THE DOG

12 February 1995
1030 Hours

The Senate Armed Services Committee meets privately in the elegance of Room 224 of the Russell Senate Office Building, named for one of the committee's revered former chairmen. Senator Richard Brevard Russell served his country for decades, building on the trust and respect the nation shared with its military. The new chairman was of a much different breed.

"Admiral, you don't need to snow me. We all know the Cold War is over. Look, this is a private hearing. You can level with us. We all know that the end of the Cold War ends the need for most of our forces." Senator Michael Porter sat back in his chair and glanced over the rims of his reading glasses. He thought it was his most professorial look. "Why not just admit it? We're not here to take the navy apart, just modernize it and inject a little reality into your budgeting."

"Mr. Chairman, I don't know where to begin. What my testimony shows, and what my staff has presented to your staff in classified briefings, proves that this nation still faces a nuclear threat from several nations. More than that, the breakdown of the Warsaw Pact leaves us with any number of contingencies that pose real threats to our interests at home and abroad." Admiral Tom Pierson was known as "Long Tom" not only for his height but also for his marathon lectures about the design and performance of the aircraft he and the men he commanded flew. Before asking Long Tom a question about one of those birds, you'd better pack a lunch.

Pierson never flew an aircraft before he'd learned the science of it. More an engineer than a flier, he was pushed by his superiors to be a test pilot, but gave it up when offered a combat command in Vietnam. He hadn't flown much in the few months since being appointed to his new post. Now vice chief of Naval Operations, he was stuck with the budgeting process and the politics that went with it. Every time he had to duel with the politicos, he knew he lost something. Sometimes it was only his peace of mind.

"Mr. Chairman, the cuts you and some of the other members of the committee have proposed would do two things. First, they would so severely reduce our op tempo that I couldn't guarantee the combat readiness of even a single air group. Second, these cuts would require me to eliminate two to four of our eight SEAL teams. I submit, sir, that we cannot guarantee America's safety without those forces."

"Admiral, let's explore that a bit." The junior senator from California smiled down from the dais. Senator Pete Manfredi had served in the House for six years before winning his Senate race. His House career had been typical for an up-and-coming California Democrat. While representing a district with many defense companies, Manfredi had voted against every military budget and every weapons program that came up for a vote. Pierson's assistant, a captain from legislative liaison—"L & L"—leaned over and whispered, "Go easy, Admiral. Watch this guy." Pierson frowned his answer. He hated dealing with professional "handlers" almost as much as he hated these hearings.

"I don't think we need so many flying hours. Why can't we survive on the hours the British or the French train?" Manfredi was smiling again, because he knew that his question, and whatever the admiral's answer was, would be leaked artfully to the *Los Angeles Times* and CNN in time for the evening news.

"Senator Manfredi, the simple answer is that we don't train like the French because we don't want our pilots to have the skill levels of the French. I hate to put it in those terms, sir, but any two of my boys can smoke any ten of theirs. And that's not just because our aircraft are marginally better. Our guys win because they train to win a lot harder than anybody else does, and that takes a lot of flying hours. They're not just sitting in the cockpit cruising around. That doesn't teach you much. The time they spend is in yankin' and bankin'. Air combat maneuvering. What our boys do is train hard to build and keep the skills to win." Long Tom looked Manfredi straight in the eye without, he hoped, too much hostility.

Manfredi smiled again, thinking about how he would tell the French ambassador about the navy's low opinion of our allies. "Admiral, that may be so. But we're not about to fight the French. How hard do we need to train to beat the Haitians? I think we can safely cut twenty or thirty percent of the flying hours, and I will offer an amendment to that effect." A red light went on in front of the chairman's desk signaling that Manfredi's time was up for that round of questions.

The chairman turned to the left again and found another ally. "The chair recognizes the junior senator from Oregon."

Barbara Berkely smiled. After ten years of opposing the military budgets from a seat in the House, she too had graduated to the World's Greatest Deliberative Body.

"Admiral, I think Senator Manfredi has got it all wrong. Sure, the Cold War is over. But not only do we not need so many flying hours, we probably don't need the SEALs at all. Now if I've got it right, they've been doing essentially the same thing since World War II. We still have the Army Special Forces. They have the Delta Force to deal with terrorists. Why do we need the SEALs, too?"

Pierson sighed a long sigh. "Senator, you and I have had this same disagreement ever since I came to Washington two years ago. The simple answer is the SEALs are needed because the threats they answer are still there, and no one else can do what they do. What you're implying is that we should do away with the SEALs as a unit, and zero out Marine Recon and Army Special Forces as well. I can tell you here and now that, if you do, we cannot guarantee the safety of our civilian population."

"Well, Admiral, we can probably do without all that melodrama. I guess we're lucky that you alone don't have to give us that guarantee. We have almost two thousand SEALs spread around the world in eight teams. I just don't believe we need them, far less in those numbers."

As Pierson started to respond, another senator stirred. He looked as tired as Long Tom, and twenty years older. "Mr. Chairman, I have to attend a meeting with the Judiciary Committee in a few minutes. May I have my time questioning the Admiral out of turn?" Manfredi grimaced as Porter said, "You may indeed take your turn, senator. The chair recognizes its good friend, the senior senator from Missouri."

The old man pushed himself erect in his chair. He looked a bit rumpled, but his sharp gray eyes riveted the attention of anyone he looked at. Senator Nathaniel Barrett dated back to the days of Barry Goldwater and Henry "Scoop" Jackson. His status as dean of the Senate gave him privileges like the one he had just exercised.

"Admiral, you said that the proposed cuts in the navy budget would substantially reduce flying hours, and I accept that. I'm just an old mud marine from Korea days, and I may not have the same understanding as some of the newer committee members. Senator Manfredi and I will have to debate that one in executive session, and perhaps on the floor." Pierson caught a glimpse of Manfredi out of the corner of his eye. The man was obviously enjoying himself. "What does that little bastard know that I don't," the admiral thought. It would not be the last time he had that thought.

Barrett continued. "But what troubles me even more is that you say we'll have to cut two of the SEAL teams. I don't suppose anyone would seriously propose to do away with the SEALs altogether." Barrett caught Berkely's eye and winked at her. She looked as if someone had dumped a bucket of cold water in her lap. Barrett went on without missing a beat. "How is cutting four teams possible, and which ones will go if we have to cut?"

"Senator, the cut proposed by the chairman and Senator Manfredi would reduce special operations funding by at least fifty percent. You know that the biggest cuts we had last year were in that area as well. Senator Berkely wants to do away with the SEALs. If there's another fifty percent cut, we'll have to choose between retiring the last submarine equipped to insert covert teams on hostile shores and cutting half the SEAL teams altogether. Sir, if I have to make that choice, I'll scrap the sub. Our teams will still get where they need to, but it will be riskier. To answer the other question, sir, I just don't know. I guess we'd keep Teams 6 for counterterrorist operations, Team 3 for desert ops, and Team 4 for other covert operations. The others could be fair game."

"I see. Well, I hope that when the committee votes, we can agree that fewer flying hours can be cut and that we need all eight of the SEAL teams. It seems little enough expense for the capability they provide. Thank you, Admiral, and I thank the chair."

"The committee is adjourned," said Porter and he and Manfredi scurried out without a glance at the Admiral.

Pierson turned to the captain from L&L. "You've got a mission, Captain, and I want it carried out immediately. We have a real sales job to do on some of those senators. I want you to get an aircraft and take a staffer from each of their offices down to Little Creek for an orientation. I'll get it up with CINCLANT. But get it done before the committee goes into markup."

"Yessir," smiled the L&L man, thinking, "Road trip."

CHAPTER 6

DEFENDING DEMOCRACY ON THE FAR-FLUNG FRONTIERS OF FREEDOM

The headlines told of the brief engagement between the U.N. peacekeeping force and the Somali warlord's troops. The American army platoon had been left at their outpost by their U.N. commander, a Belgian colonel who thought there was little danger of attack. When the attack came, the Belgian didn't think things were serious enough to send the armor and other reinforcements the Americans called for. The chain of command was confused, and by the time the American local commander got wind of it, the fight was over.

They sat in the White House Oval Office, watching the CNN reports. They were faster than the CIA or military intelligence. The president turned away when the camera showed an American soldier's body being dragged through the streets of Mogadishu behind a car flying the warlord's flag.

"Mr. President, we need to issue a statement on this immediately. We need to emphasize your commitment to the peace process and U.N. control of the situation," said the White House press secretary. The press secretary was at the meeting, along with the president's personal pollster and media consultant. They were at all important meetings.

The president's entire national security team had gathered to listen to the reports and confer with their U.N. counterparts. The secretaries of state and defense, the director of Central Intelligence, and the first lady were there. Dr. Frederick Touchman, the secretary of defense, spoke quickly. He knew where his president wanted this to go.

"I agree, Mr. President. We should contact the secretary general immediately and indicate our continued support for the U.N. presence in Somalia. Furthermore, we should indicate that the chain of command is not the issue."

"Okay, boys, I like that idea," said the commander in chief. "You know, I think we should always seek consensus of the U.N. and its leaders before we act in situations like this. We can get more agreement from them than we can from the Congress. All the Republicans want to do is bitch about how much authority we're giving old 'Boolah Boolah' over our troops." The Yale-educated president insisted on calling the U.N. secretary general "Boolah Boolah." His real name was Doctor Professor Boolwah-Boolwah Gemali.

"You're sure right on that one, Mr. President." The White House Chief of Staff was always eager to echo his boss. "Shouldn't we put the word out that he's doing what we want, anyway?"

"You're right, Mac. Let's get the word out that we're in the peace process for the long haul. But we need to do more than just shore up old Boolah Boolah. I think the time has come to really turn our armed services around. Freddie, I want you and your people to come up with a comprehensive plan to maximize our armed forces training and equipment for peacekeeping missions. If we need legislation, I think we could get Pete Manfredi and his committee to support it."

"We'll get on it right away, Mr. President. I think we should emphasize the training and preparedness for peacekeeping missions. I'll tell the Joint Chiefs to get something going. Our troops should be saving lives, not taking them."

"Right you are. Go to it, Freddie."

"Ah, one more thing, Mr. President. We should issue a statement about your sadness at the loss and the necessity for maintaining our presence."

"Huh?"

"The soldiers that were killed, Mr. President."

"Oh, oh, sure. Tell you what. When they bring the bodies back to the States, where will the plane land?"

"Probably at Dover, Delaware, sir. The big air force base there has facilities for that sort of thing."

"Okay, Freddie. Have them brought back there. Bella and I will go to meet the plane, and we'll bring the press plane with us. Not just the networks and the pool guys. The whole bunch. We should have photos of us walking behind the coffins. It will be a very sad day. Let's have the wives and parents of the dead boys there. I want to be seen grieving with them. It's the least I can do."

CHAPTER 7

TOOTH TO TAIL

28 February
0600 Hours

"Mr. Forsythe. Wake up, sir. Time to turn to," said a young sailor in combat fatigues.

Jonathan Forsythe, Harvard graduate and, at twenty-six years of age, senior military advisor to Senator Manfredi, said, "Huh? What? Oh, sure." Of the seventeen senators on the committee, only ten had bothered to send staffers to the SEAL orientation, and only one of them had insisted on joining the SEALs for their morning PT. Forsythe was a marathoner and wanted to be at the orientation because he wanted to prove he could do whatever the SEALs could. But more than that, he knew Katherine Reilly from Senator Barrett's office would be there. He had been trying to get into her pants for six months with a resounding lack of success. He had flown down the night before and stayed in the VIP quarters in Admirals' Row, far from the SEALs' barracks. Now he had to get moving.

The team had been standing there for ten minutes when the staffer finally scrambled up to the formation. Cully O'Bannon introduced each of the team and announced the schedule. Normal stuff—warm-up exercises, a three-mile swim, and a five-mile run. And the abnormal stuff.

"Gents, our favorite geezer, Master Chief Wilson, sprained his ankle in yesterday's jump. He can swim, but he can't run."

"He couldn't run even if his foot was okay," one man grumbled from the back row.

"Right again, Duke. So you and your low man take the first turn carrying him on the run." A chorus of groans came from the rest of the team.

Duke Jamison, a wiry surfer from Laguna Beach, usually loved the swim and hated the run. The thought of carrying Wilson, who weighed a lot more than he did, didn't seem to worry him as much as it should have. He looked over to his low man and shrugged. The low man smiled back at him. Vince Franco was the SEALs' unofficial weight-lifting champ. He could probably run with Wilson tucked under one arm.

"Macho male bullshit," muttered Forsythe, as they jogged down to the lockers to put on their wetsuits and grab fins, masks, and snorkels.

"Why all the gear?" he asked. "Sir," said Chief Wilson, "It's 28 February. This may be southern Virginia, but the water temperature is about fifty-five degrees." Forsythe struggled into the wetsuit fitted to him the night before. Then he put on his dive boots.

"Okay, Lieutenant." All eyes turned to Forsythe. "Are we gonna talk about it or do it?"

"Mr. Forsythe, we do things a particular way around here, and we're delighted to have you join us." Cully had clear orders to placate Forsythe. CINCLANT had himself made the point on the telephone the previous afternoon: "DFU, Lieutenant. Don't give this bastard any ammo to take back to his boss." DFU was navy for "don't fuck up." Cully half expected Forsythe to show up wearing a T-shirt that said "Make Love, Not War." Actually, it said, "Save the Rain Forests."

"Our custom, Mr. Forsythe, is to have our fastest runner and swimmer set the pace for the team. Master chief, whose times were the best in the individuals last week?"

"Mike Rigazzi on the run and Charlie Scott on the swim, for the fifth week in a row."

"Way to go, Charlie," said Cully.

"Okay, move out."

CPO Scott led them down to the water's edge where they donned their fins and waded into the water. When everyone was in deep water, Scott led them off at a fast pace. Everyone tried to keep up or pass, and after ten minutes, Forsythe was gasping for breath.

Cully had lagged behind with Chief Wilson to keep track of Forsythe. "Are you okay, sir?"

"Sure I am," said Forsythe, "I don't need any help. Goddamn it, I can do this."

"Suit yourself," said Cully, thinking, *Maybe I should just drown the little prick.* He nodded to Wilson to keep an eye on Forsythe and swam ahead to join the team.

There was a quick gear change, and then the run. The run was even worse. Forsythe's best pace barely kept up with the unlucky pair lugging Chief Wilson. Running on sand was different than running on an asphalt track. And the SEALs were running in jump boots. By the end, he was exhausted and angry.

The run ended in front of the SEAL barracks. When Cully ran up with the team, he noticed a group waiting for them. All twenty-somethings wearing jeans or sweats. Great. The rest of the staffers. He led the platoon through an entryway where they each strapped on a low-ride leg holster with a Beretta 9mm automatic in it. Still breathing hard, he walked up to the staffers.

"Hi. Welcome to Little Creek. I'm Cully O'Bannon, commander of Foxtrot platoon of Seal Team 2. I'm also executive officer of Team 2. I'll be your host today. I've been advised that all of you hold current security clearance at secret or higher levels. Please remember that everything you see or hear from now on is classified at the secret level."

Just then Forsythe jogged past, red-faced. A tall woman among the staffers said, "Jonathan, couldn't you keep up with these guys?"

Forsythe snorted and walked quickly past the group, headed for the locker room. Cully looked at the woman, and did a double take. She was very tall, maybe five-ten or five-eleven. Short brown hair. Great face. Great body. And dark blue eyes. The darkest, bluest eyes he had ever seen. Gun-metal blue. Navy blue. Can't be that blue for real. He realized he was staring.

"Hi, Lieutenant O'Bannon. I'm Kate Reilly. I work for Senator Nate Barrett. And yes, my eyes really are this color. I don't wear tinted contacts." She gave him a smile that practically melted his knees.

"Sorry for staring. Pleased to meet ya." He looked at Forsythe's back. "Friend of yours?"

"He wishes. Just like most of the other guys I know in Washington. All show and no go." She smiled again. "Do you always strap on a gun after you run?"

"Most days, ma'am. We have one more thing to do before our breathing and pulse rates drop to normal. If you follow Seaman Jackson, we'll show you."

The team had stopped to wait for him, jogging in place. The guests were walked around the back of the building and down a path. Each was handed a set of headphone-style ear protectors. What they saw was a ten-foot-high sandbank and, in front of it, what appeared to be a clothesline hung at about five feet off the ground. Clipped to it were a dozen or so playing cards, spaced at two-foot intervals.

Just as the guests took their places, the team came around the building at a trot. Each drew the Beretta from the holster and pointed it down and out. As the first man reached the middle card, the team started shooting sporadically, still maintaining their jogging pace and interval. The shooting stopped as the last man passed the last card. Cully led them up to the staffers while Jackson gathered the cards and handed them to him.

"Ladies and gentlemen, the object of your visit with us today is for us to show you some of what we do. My job is to tell you just about anything you want to know about our job and how we do it." The questions came out in a flood.

"Okay, so what's with the trick shooting? Did any of you guys hit any of the cards? And who cares if you did?"

"Sir, every SEAL team is qualified for hostage rescue and covert operations, among others. It's no secret that when one of those jobs goes down, the objective is to kill all the bad guys, as quickly as we can. The best way to do that is to shoot every terrorist twice. Preferably in the head. Our card game is part of the training for that."

Cully handed the cards to the staffer who, six months earlier, had been handing out campaign brochures at shopping malls. "Jesus. Two holes in each."

"And we do it after the swim and run. Take it from me, sir. It's harder to do when you're out of breath."

"Why kill everyone in a room? Why can't you capture people? If you guys are as good as you say you are, why can't you catch the terrorists and bring them to justice?"

"Sir, we're not policemen. A cop is supposed to restore order. Quiet people down. Use the minimum amount of force necessary to do the job. Our job is different. Our job is to fight and win. We define winning as achieving our objective and getting out alive. To do that, you don't try to negotiate with some punk who's holding a gun to the head of a ten-year-old girl. You shoot him in the head. Twice."

The short blond woman sounded off. "Okay, O'Bannon. We know your cowboys-and-Indians view of the world. But every expert on counterterrorism says you guys should be primarily a threat negotiators use to leverage a peaceful settlement."

"Ma'am, I can't argue with your experts, whoever they are." There were a few snickers from some of the other staffers. "All I can say is if the bad guys know we're coming, we can't do the job, or at least can't do it as well as we can when we hit without warning. When our team goes in, we're in control of the situation. If I have to stop to negotiate what we're going to do next, I give part of that control to the person I'm negotiating with. I know we win if we have the initiative and control what happens next.

"Well, if there are no further questions, I'll turn you over to Master Chief Wilson, who will escort you into the briefing room. Captain Schaffer is there and will conduct the rest of the briefings."

"Thanks, Mr. O'Bannon. This way, folks." Cully led the team off to the showers while the brass took over the show.

The briefing room was like every other the staffers had been in. Plain walls, and a screen. Some of them groaned when they saw the inevitable overhead projector. Someone said, "Oh, no. Death by viewgraph." A slim navy captain was waiting for them. Forsythe was back after a quick shower, in jeans, and shivering. He headed for the coffee.

"I'm Stan Schaffer, commander of SEAL Forces Atlantic. Welcome to Little Creek. Grab a cup of coffee or a soda and have a seat. We'll be with you all day today, so let's keep it informal. Ask whatever you'd like.

"What you saw outside was just one of the flashy parts of what we do here. The point we want to make to you today is that we do things that no one else can, and we do them very well.

"What you saw was not something anyone else sees. We try to keep most of our training and techniques as secret as we can. There's a simple reason for it. The essence of special operations is stealth—concealment. The way the SEALs succeed is by achieving surprise. We get in before anyone knows we're there, do the job with the minimum of exposure, and get out quickly. The fewer people who know how we do it, the greater chance we have to succeed. We've learned this over fifty years of doing these jobs.

"The SEAL teams are far older than you may know. SEALs were organized formally on the orders of President John F. Kennedy. But we go back a lot farther. In World War II, when the Marines landed on the island of Tarawa, they had to wade about a hundred yards through chest-deep water and machine gun fire to get to the beach. Hundreds were killed. That landing was based on inadequate intelligence. As a result, the Navy formed its first swimmers unit, known as "frogmen." Their mission was to land on the beaches ahead of time and scout out a path for the jarheads. They were the Underwater Demolition Teams—the UDTs—and they were the predecessor to the SEALs of today.

"Now, thank God, the world seems to have evolved away from the mass destruction of the last half-century or so. Smaller wars, terrorist threats, and the short but extremely bloody conflicts like the Gulf War a couple of years ago seem to be the norm. And that's where the SEALs can do the most, in the least time.

"Our British counterparts, the Special Air Service, and the Special Boat Service, have a couple of mottos that say, 'Who dares, wins,' and 'If not by strength, then guile.' We'd never admit it to the Brits, but if you combine the two, that's as good a statement of our philosophy as you can get. Questions?

"Right now, we have seven SEAL teams, each with about 200 active SEALs. We also have a bunch of guys we call the 'injured reserve' just like in baseball. All told, we have about 2,000 SEALs.

"You may have heard how they're spread out. The odd-number teams, 1, 3, 5, and 7, are based on the West Coast. Their operations range west from California to Asia. The even-numbered teams, 2, 4, and 8, are on the East Coast."

"What about Team 6? I thought they were your best antiterrorist guys?"

"Sir, Team 6 no longer exists. We have a group called 'development group' which contains many of the old Team 6 gang, but they're assigned to research and development. You know, new weapons and tactics and that sort of thing."

"Oh, come on, Captain. That's not what the classified annex to the DoD appropriations bill says."

"Well, that's all I can say. Maybe another day, we'll all take a trip down to Dam Neck where the, ah, 'dev group' is based.

"Anyway, like I was saying, some of the teams are a bit specialized. Team 3, for example, is the desert warfare experts. Team 8 is usually stationed with the Atlantic Fleet. They spend a lot of time at sea. If there are no more questions, let's go back out for more of the demonstrations."

The rest of the day was a blur for the staffers. They saw SEAL insertion techniques. SEALs jumped into the water from low-flying helicopters. SEALs jumped from a C-130 passing high overhead and "halo'd," opening the parachutes and, at almost the same second, slipping out of their parachute harnesses just as they hit the water.

"Most of the time," said Schaffer, "we hit the beach in rubber rafts launched from a submarine, but sometimes we launch or recover from surface craft. If you'll follow me, we'll board one of those craft now. "

Schaeffer led them out and onto a large river boat, about fifty feet long. Its rear deck sloped down into the water. When the last staffer was aboard, the craft roared out into the river, accelerating to about forty knots. Schaeffer shouted over the engine noise.

"Sometimes, we have to leave in a hurry. The boat we're on is a Mark 8. It can do over sixty knots. Watch the shoreline on your left."

The staffers turned and looked. Some of the bushes along the shore suddenly turned into fourteen men in two Zodiac rubber boats. They caught up to the big boat in a sudden burst of speed. In another ten seconds, the two boats had driven up the aft ramp of the boat, which then turned away from shore and accelerated away. Still dripping wet, Cully leaned over Kate Reilly and shouted, "These boats are fabulous. I get a real rush driving up onto that ramp." She smiled back.

One of the staffers, obviously one who hadn't been coached to be aloof to all around him piped up with a question.

"Hey, I saw a film on you guys. One part of it showed a bunch of guys running around carrying these rubber rafts everywhere they went. The raft was on their heads when they ran, they pushed it along when they swam. They even ate holding the damned thing. They really looked dumb."

"Sir, those people must have been SEAL applicants, in their fifth week of the first phase of SEAL school. It's called 'BUDS' for Basic Underwater Demolition School. You may be aware that we get hundreds of applications for the SEALs every year, and we usually have only a handful of openings. Our school is very tough, and the last week of BUDS is designed to weed out the quitters. We want to know now, not later, who's gonna quit when the going gets tough. We call it 'hell week.' The applicants are kept awake for five days straight. They keep up a full training schedule, and we test them for their ability to function under stress and extreme exhaustion. You may be aware that the

SEALs work as two-man pairs called swim buddies. Two men are a shooting pair. When we attack, one goes high, and the other goes low. One sweeps left while his partner goes right. This enables them to clear an area, shooting freely, without hitting each other.

"During hell week, we assign the applicants to each other in pairs. Then they get a 'IBS,' as we call them. An IBS is an 'inflatable boat, small'. They're the Zodiac inflatable boats you all have seen. They weigh about 150 pounds. The two applicants take their IBS with them everywhere they go. Eating, swimming, running, and shooting, their IBS is always there. It makes for some pretty tired guys after a day or two."

And there were the briefings and the Q&A. As the day wore down, so did everyone's stiffness. Even Forsythe seemed to be warming up a bit after the humiliation of the morning. They had a final session at the bar CINCLANT had set up in the "tank," a secured conference room where classified topics could be discussed. The booze flowed freely, and the conversation rambled on.

"Okay, Cully. I'll buy that you guys can do things that others can't. I'll buy that even in peacetime we need to be able to put tough guys into dangerous places. But what I don't get is what we need *all* of you for. And all your special toys. Yeah, you look really cool with your guys driving your rafts up the back ramp of those boats, but those damn boats cost a cool $4 million apiece. My boss can build a new post office for that money and create a bunch of union jobs."

"I suppose so, Jonathan." Cully was actually beginning to like this guy. "But there's other ways to mail letters. It's not like they're gonna stop delivering Christmas cards because we ride fast boats."

Schaeffer jumped in. "I think what Cully is trying to say is that the SEALs are unique."

"Oh, yeah, sure, Stan. Can you guys really believe all the crap about that?

"I hear the same crap from the air force fighter pilots, from the navy submariners, and even from the goddamn coast guard drug chasers. Every bunch of guys with guns thinks they're God's gift to national security. Everybody is impressed with you guys, but I think we agree that there are a whole lot of better ways we can spend the country's money."

"Jonathan's right." Tonya Johnson, the short, attractive blonde woman from Senator Berkely's office, had been quiet since morning. "My boss has a program for preserving the Pacific Coast wetlands that can be fully funded with the money we can easily cut from your program. Even the White House says it's a priority to save those wetlands."

Kate Reilly almost laughed. "Tonya, we can't fund every pet project our bosses have out of the SEALs appropriation. There's not enough to go around. That 'peace dividend' we keep talking about isn't a bottomless pot of gold. Sure we can spend less than before, but we can't stop defending the country altogether."

Schaeffer leaned forward to speak. "Ms. Johnson, we aren't the only game in the business, and maybe some things can be cut back. But we're an essential part of a whole team. What people aren't saying here today is that to defend the country, *all* of the pieces have to fit together. There's a reason we have an army and navy and an air force. If you want to win a war you have to have all the parts, and they all have to work together in the right way in the right time."

"Captain, you make war sound like some goddamn kabuki dance. You don't really believe that, do you?"

"Yes, ma'am, I do. It's not a dance. It's more like a football game. If the blockers don't hold the defensive rushers, the quarterback gets thrown for a loss. If we don't work with the army, the air force, and the marines, they have to spend a lot more time and lives to do their job. That's why we train so much on joint operations. Whoever said, 'the more you sweat in peace, the less you bleed in war' really knew what he was talking about."

Cully jumped back in. "You guys are making decisions to move money around. Fine. But be damn careful when you do it, or the 'peace dividend' you want to spend so badly may not be a dividend you can spend. That 'peace dividend' may be a war we can't handle."

"You can't really believe we don't need special operations forces. Don't you read the newspapers? The Indians and Pakistanis are going at it right now. The secretary of state says we won't let Iran complete the missile tunnels they're building right now. Libya is building a bomb-proof chemical weapons plant underground, which the president says threatens our security right now. How do you plan to deal with those situations without us?"

The blonde took immediate offense. "You may think you know more about the world than we do, Mr. O'Bannon, but we're the paid experts. You're just protecting your rice bowl, and it ain't selling. Anybody knows we can knock off the missile tunnels or the chemical plant with cruise missiles."

Cully shook his head in disbelief. "Ms. Johnson, if you believe that you're not qualified to advise anybody. You really think cruise missiles will handle that?"

"Yes I do, and I've written a definitive report on the subject, which my boss is presenting to the secretary of state tomorrow."

"Well, your 'definitive' report ain't worth a damn. Cruise missiles will handle the job only with nuclear warheads. You really want to launch nukes against Iran? If you don't, we're the only other choice."

"Here you go again with the 'only we can save the world' bullshit." Forsythe was building up a head of steam, too. "Come off it. America survived for almost two hundred years without you guys. It can do fine without you again. My boss doesn't care if Iran builds those tunnels, anyway. They won't dare use 'em for anything that threatens us."

Schaeffer tried to calm the waters. "That may or may not be true, Mr. Forsythe. Wouldn't we be better off preparing to meet the threat than have to face it without being ready?"

Wilson appeared at the door. "Captain Schaeffer, the bus is here to take them back to the aircraft."

Schaeffer wasn't sure if he was relieved or frustrated that the conversation was cut off. "Thank you all for your interest in us. We hope you have come to understand what we do and why we do it."

CHAPTER 8

AT FORT FUMBLE

1 March
1000 Hours

The day was slipping away from them. The Joint Chiefs usually began their daily meeting at 0715 and finished by 0800. This session was taking far too long.

One of General Stoneman's aides, an air force brigadier who looked like Robert Redford, smiled at himself in the mirror. Four more months of pouring coffee for Stoneman, and he would get a second star, and probably the exec's job at a major command. Life was good. With any luck, he'd be back at Hickam AFB in Honolulu pretty soon. But all those Congressmen and senators had to have their calls returned today, not to mention the pressies. The chief better get back damned soon.

But the meeting was far from over. Touchman had seen heated debates before among his staff. But his temper grew shorter as the debate went on today. His mind saw it growing by the minute. He was going to put his foot down hard. How dare they challenge what the president had said?

"Just what the hell do you mean by that remark, Admiral?" Touchman's wrath was aimed at the CNO, Admiral Freeman, who pointed out that the training being proposed was inconsistent with the navy's mission. "Sir, all I meant was what I said. Our troops and sailors need to train to win battles, not to restore civilian governments in places like Somalia. We have to have people who can win battles. We won't have them if we train our people to be a bunch of heavily armed social workers."

"Admiral, maybe you haven't heard what I've been saying. This comes directly from the president, and it's an order, not something we're going to debate. Brandon has committed this nation to a peace process through the United Nations. That means that your mission is changed. You will prepare your people to sustain the peace, to build governments, and to protect the environment. Don't you get it? The Soviet Union doesn't exist anymore. We can't afford any more Cold War paranoia. Our resources—and I mean all of our people—are going to be redirected and retrained for new missions."

"Sir, that's what we'll do if we're ordered to, but I have to give you my best advice on it. We don't want to train our people to do two very different jobs. You can't train a priest to be a gunfighter. You can't cross-train a doctor so that he'll kill people instead of saving them. If a person is confused about his purpose in this business, he'll probably get himself and his people killed."

The chairman sat through this exchange quietly, knowing the battle was lost. He had come up from West Point, and after thirty years in the army, his job as chairman of the Joint Chiefs of Staff was secure for only two years at a time. He saw no benefit in resisting the president's ideas.

"Mr. Secretary, I think Admiral Freeman is justified in his skepticism. But he forgets that the kind of people we get these days are a lot smarter than when you and I joined up, Admiral." The chairman smiled and nodded knowingly at Freeman. "What I mean is that our enlisted people, both men and women, can handle this. We don't need to keep them on edge to defeat the Soviets, because the Soviets are out of business. We need to teach them other skills."

The lone marine in the room could read the way the wind was blowing as well as the chairman. The commandant saw Touchman putting his foot down. But he had to do the same thing. So far, the marines were the only service to keep the sexes apart in basic training. Hell, it had worked since 1775. He'd won that battle, so far. But the price was high. His threat to resign over the issue put the defense secretary in a God-awful position. Touchman had backed down, but Dunham had made an enemy.

"Mr. Secretary, I think General Stoneman is right," said Dunham. "Our people are better than they used to be. But I still worry about this peacekeeping mission. I worry about those nineteen-year-old marines following a twenty-something sergeant into a hot landing zone. If that sergeant is trained to yell, "halt or we'll shoot" when he should yell "fire," we don't win the fight. A lot of those kids are gonna come home in body bags."

"General, you said the same thing two years ago when we changed the policy on homosexuality in the military. You said the same thing last year when we began sexually integrating the combat forces. If I believed you, I'd see things falling apart around here. We haven't lost any wars lately, have we?"

"Sir, I mean no disrespect, but we haven't fought any lately either, and that's a very good thing."

"I never thought of you as a pacifist, general."

"No one has ever accused me of being one, sir. But I think if you take a poll of everyone in the Pentagon, you'll find that the only people who are looking forward to the next war are those who won't have to grab a rifle and go fight it."

"Meaning precisely what, general?"

"Just that we may want to go slowly with this flood of changes, sir. It's still a dangerous world out there. We need to keep the edge if we're gonna deter a war or win the next one."

CHAPTER 9

AT THE CENTER OF THE UNIVERSE

2 March
0830 Hours

He kept telling himself this was a good job. Deputy to the national security advisor, contact with the president nearly every day. Telephone calls from the Joint Chiefs every night. Calls from senators sucking up to him. Calls from reporters. Those were the easiest. Everyone else said, just give 'em the mushroom treatment: Keep 'em in the dark and feed 'em bullshit. He wouldn't lie. So he just didn't return the calls. He knew this job would be a nightmare, so he didn't volunteer, but when the commandant himself says do it, you do it.

This was different from what everyone, including Henry Kissinger, had told him. In prior administrations, the national security advisor was an intimate of the president, involved in all major, and most minor, strategic decisions. But with President Brandon, everything was different. Now, the NSA was an afterthought. Dr. Anthony Daniels was usually not even invited to key meetings. The meeting Hunter was hustling down the hall to join had been going on for five minutes before the president remembered to invite Daniels who, as usual, was off writing some intellectual analysis of something or other and wasn't available.

He straightened his shoulders. Even with this job, he still managed to run two or three miles a day. He still looked like the skinny kid from Montana who found his way to Annapolis more or less by accident. A wild kid, who no one thought would make it to college after all the trouble he'd been in. There were three times in his past when people had left him for dead. But he still did his push-ups like they taught him to almost thirty years ago. Jim Hunter, brigadier general of Marines, nodded to the Secret Service men guarding the door, knocked once, and entered the Oval Office.

"Good morning, Mr. President, Mr. Vice President, Mr. Secretary. Dr. Daniels asked me to sit in this morning if I may." Every head in the room turned to the sound of his voice. It was strange. It happened every time. No matter how hard they tried to ignore him, that soft, slow western drawl commanded their attention.

"Hello, Jim." The president was a big, affable guy who always smiled the same toothy grin. "Glad to have you. We were going over the budget questions before Freddy testifies in the House hearings today. Continue, Freddy."

Defense Secretary Frederick Touchman looked at Hunter over his professor's half-glasses. "As I was saying, Mr. President, the Senate leadership is quite convinced that we can impose significant cuts on special forces and save enough for the increase in the environmental cleanup program you wanted. By making that thirty percent cut, we lose only twenty percent of the force structure, which seems redundant anyway. Most can come out of the navy, with the SEALs and Marine Force Recon absorbing almost all of it. That leaves us with Army Special Forces, albeit without Delta Force and some of its other units. I believe we'll be able to handle any contingency with the remaining people."

Hunter began a slow burn. He couldn't blatantly contradict Touchman, even if he was the deputy national security advisor. But he also couldn't let this continue. Another voice opened up before he could.

"Where the hell did you get that, Freddy? Even from you, that's incredible bullshit." The vice president stood up. At his full height, all five feet, six inches of it, the man was an imposing figure. Vincent La Guardia was the first Italian American to hold national office. A descendant of the famous New York mayor, he never ran from a fight. He couldn't, on those short legs. He also couldn't because he started so many of them, and was always right in the middle.

Most people only knew the man for the bare-knuckled energy he brought to every job he took on. What few knew was his past. Unable to learn, he was labeled retarded at the age of eight. After barely scraping through high school, he joined the union and got a job as a garbage man. Three years later he began to date a girl whose father was an optometrist, and whose diagnosis of La Guardia as dyslexic proved right. His career in garbage ended, and the little man proved to be a certified genius. He entered politics with a Ph.D. in political science from Harvard and an abiding dislike for neckties.

"I neva heard such crap. Yeah, we stand for the little guy. But don't give us this guns-or-butter bullshit. We keep hearing about the Iranians trying to slip bombs into New York. We got nutty mountain men threatening to blow us up. The goddamn FBI can't even find the guy who's been sending mail bombs to federal judges. You wanna scrap our anti-terrorist forces? No way."

The president waved him down. "Easy, Vinny. Freddy has a point. We don't need the military to attack some nutty mail bomber. If we ever figure out who he is, a couple of sheriff's deputies will be enough to get him. Why do we need all of these different groups spread all over the military? We've got Delta Force, the SEALs, Force Recon, and probably several others. Why not drop a few? After all, the Soviet Union is gone. We're as safe as we're ever going to be."

Hunter sat back and breathed slowly and deeply. None of this talk made sense in his mind. Hunter had been there, in the mud in I Corps. His rifle company had taken thirty percent casualties in one day. When his time came, it was in the form of two AK-47 slugs in his chest. The medics said he would die and called the priest who served the evac hospital to give him last rites, but Hunter waved him away with the one hand he could move. Then the docs told him he'd never walk again, so he started to run. They said he was in no shape to be a mud marine any more, so he learned how to fly. This stupid job came after two tours as chief test pilot of the Marine Corps. Those air force pukes really hated it when he graduated first in his class from their test pilot school. They stopped hating it as soon as he bought the first round at the O-club that night.

Hunter looked at the president. He didn't resent him and his crowd, he just couldn't understand them. To him, these meetings seemed like the bar scene from *Star Wars*.

"Please, Mr. President, if I could interject one thought. It's true, some of the forces seem redundant, but take it from me, sir, they each do things that none of the others can do. These men are very well trained."

"Yeah, Jim, I know they are. But that raises another problem itself. How can these guys live useful lives in peacetime? Aren't they walking time bombs in our society?"

Hunter took another slow deep breath. *Careful. If you say it with humor, you can get away with it.*

"Sir, these men are a lot like me. I've trained a bunch of them myself in the two years I commanded Force Recon. I can use the right fork at a state dinner, and I haven't killed anybody in at least a coupla days."

The president smiled again. "Jim, don't take offense. But you have to admit, some of these guys have a hard time adjusting."

"I'm sorry if I overreacted, Mr. President. But the people you're talking about are my friends. I've trained lots of them myself. Dr. Touchman has a point, but can't we find the dollars to cut elsewhere?"

The VP sat down. "Jim is right. We can make the cuts elsewhere in the DoD budget and still get the peace dividend to pay for school lunches. Let's get back to work."

2 March
1140 Hours

"We work in a very politically charged environment," said Defense Secretary Touchman to his military aide. Touchman was good at many things, especially demonstrating his powerful command of the obvious. "Therefore, we must always be concerned about appearances. I am proud of the fact that every one of my staff is a woman or a minority."

His military aide nodded wisely. Army Major General Barbara Gensler had been a college friend of the first lady. She was the first woman to be the mil-A for the Secretary.

"I agree completely, Mr. Secretary, but appearances don't mean as much around here as you may think. I sense it in every meeting. There is enormous resentment toward me from the military establishment around us."

Touchman blinked at the thought that his military aide didn't think she was part of the establishment. "No, Barbara, I can hardly believe it. Why do you think they resent you?"

"Very simple. It's because I am a woman, and because I have never been in combat. One of those old Popeye admirals had the nerve to tell me off on that score. He said that we were breaking an unwritten rule in the Pentagon—"

"Tradition be damned," grumbled Touchman.

"Well, tradition says that when we have a secretary of Defense, or of one of the military service secretaries that hasn't been in the service, they get a mil-A who has actually been in combat. It's supposed to give you a better view of the world. The guy had the balls to tell me that these 'war fighters' had actually kept us out of a few small wars. Can you believe that? Any of these cowboys trying to keep us *out* of war?"

"Barbara, we really need to understand those people, and bring them around. You and I are the point guards for the president's efforts to reform the military. We'll have many conversations like the one you had with Admiral Popeye. They don't get it. Their way of doing things is over, and they just don't see it yet. The president has an agenda for social change, and he and Mrs. Brandon expect you and me to see that it gets done."

"Mr. Secretary, I have the report on the aircraft accident that killed the navy woman fighter pilot and her back seater. I was just going to deliver it to the chairman's office, but I wanted to talk to you about it first."

"What's the bottom line?"

"They say that there were two causes. First is pilot error. She apparently turned the wrong way when one engine flamed out, and that caused the plane to spin into the side of the carrier. Second, there may have been a fuel pump malfunction."

"You know what to do with that report. I'm sure it can be rewritten just a bit. I'm sure the accident investigators had some doubts about the causes. If there was an engine malfunction, there may have been a cascade of failures through the craft."

"There are other problems with the report, though, sir. The pilot apparently was about to be grounded when the accident happened. She had been given poor marks for her flying over a period of several weeks."

"Why is that even relevant? Such massive mechanical failures would have brought even the best of pilots down, wouldn't they?"

"Yes, sir. I'll make sure Mrs. Brandon knows about the, uh, modified findings. I'll also let Senator Berkely know about it."

"You do that."

Down the hall from the defense secretary's office, the office of the chairman of the Joint Chiefs is as ornate as any in the Pentagon. General Stoneman looked around. The fancy surroundings were often depressing. What depressed him was how little it all meant when things went badly, like now. The report of the carrier accident had been delivered by the Secretary's military aide. Being army herself, she drew the honor of dropping the report off for Stoneman to read.

Stoneman couldn't stand to read another one of these reports. What Dunham had said about the flood of changes affecting the combat capabilities of the army, navy, and air force was right on the money, but Stoneman couldn't bear to hear it, much less agree with it. Like every other chairman of the Joint Chiefs, he served at the pleasure of the president. That meant that, before he got the job, he had to be someone the president liked and trusted. In the Brandon administration, it also meant that he had to pass muster in interviews with the President and the first lady as well.

It had been shortly after the inauguration when he first went to the White House. He had been there before, of course, but not to meet the president in an interview. They had talked for a long time, mostly about personal likes and dislikes. They talked about golf, which they both played avidly and at which neither was very good. They talked then about the president's plans for changing the policies on gays being dismissed from service and plans for making combat jobs available to women. Stoneman had swallowed hard. The message was driven home in the hour-long inquisition he had suffered at the hands of the first lady when the president had left the room. She had made it very clear that the job was his if he supported the changes, and it was somebody else's if he didn't.

But the evidence was mounting that maybe all of these changes weren't good for the forces after all. Integrating women in the combat arms sounded good in theory. If you don't change the standards, if the women can qualify the same way as men do, why not? The argument seemed logical enough. But there were changes. There always were changes. A woman who wanted to graduate from West Point had to do only fifty sit-ups in a minute and run a mile in seven minutes. If a man wanted to graduate, he had to do seventy-five sit-ups in a minute, and run a six-minute mile. In the other services, there were similar differences, but no one would admit to them.

A marine was expected to hump a sixty-pound pack over twenty miles of mud and then jump up and put metal on the target. There probably were women who could do that. But there weren't women, or men, who could do it side by side with the other sex. The costs of gender integration were growing, as proved by the navy aircraft accident report he just read. The navy's workhorse fighter, the F-14 Tomcat, is a big, heavy, unforgiving beast. Flying it is an art, not a science. There were precisely two female F-14 drivers in the navy, until three weeks ago. Three weeks ago, one of them had been killed when her $35 million machine hit the side of the carrier *George Washington* while practicing landings.

The public story the navy put out was that the left engine had flamed out at the last instant, slewing the aircraft around to the left and causing the crash. But the classified report Stoneman just read told a different story. In naval aviation, student pilots and junior operational pilots were given "down checks" if their flying was subpar. One down check resulted in the pilot being grounded until an instructor had flown a lot of hours with the pilot and had signed his name to an order canceling the down check. The woman who had crashed had three uncorrected down checks on her record, but the navy had let her keep flying for fear of the political impact of grounding her. Now she and her backseater were dead. One hell of a price to pay to be politically correct.

The report Stoneman read had never been passed on to the Senate and House Armed Services Committees. They only got the sanitized version Touchman had authored, and God only knew what they would do with it.

Barbara Gensler knew what they would do with it. To stack the deck, she had discussed the report with Dr. Krueger, the first lady's chief of staff, as well as with her friend Senator Berkely. They were all prepared to condemn the swirling rumors of pilot incompetence using some instructors' reports from early pilot training that had praised the now-dead woman as a promising future fighter jock. It helped to have the records handy like that.

CHAPTER 10

TOO NARROW, TOO SHALLOW

3 March
0615 Hours

The chairman of the Joint Chiefs sat at his bedside, talking into the secured phone. "Are you sure this is a launch?"

"General, CINC NORAD is sure. He's on the line now, and we're ringing the president."

Stoneman cradled the phone in the crook of his shoulder while he reached for his glasses. He was fully awake, dressing for a day in the office.

"Hi, generals. What's the problem?" The president's tone never varied. Cheerfulness would prevail even in a nuclear war.

"Mr. President, this is General Walker at NORAD. Less than a minute ago, we picked up and confirmed missile launches from sites three, five, and six in Iraq. From what we read them now, they are ballistic missiles that are going to fall at very short range, over the Persian Gulf at or near the point where the *Eisenhower* task force is right now." "

"Okay, but the Iranians told us yesterday that they were going to test fire some missiles over the Gulf today, didn't they?"

"Yes sir, they did, and I thought you issued a statement telling them we would not tolerate it."

"Yeah, but so what? Maybe they're just testing them anyway. I'm not sure we have the right to stop them."

"Yessir, but our ships are right on their flight path. If they're not tests, we could have a lot of dead sailors in about three minutes."

"So what can we do about it?" The president, now fully awake, was silently calculating the poll results from a missile strike on U.S. ships. Probably no effect at all, so long as nobody was hurt. If there were casualties, a counterattack would be a big boost in the polls.

"Gentlemen, our people will only fire if fired upon. I expect you to call me *immediately* if one of those missiles is real and not a test." The president hung up his phone. The first lady rolled over.

"What was all that about?"

"Nothing, dear. What's for breakfast?"

Aboard the U.S.S. City of Corpus Christi

"Captain, we have flash traffic from CINCSUBLANT."

"Okay, whaddya have?" The seaman handed him the short message.

"Sound general quarters. Sonar, give me all contacts. Make your depth seven zero feet." At that depth, only a few feet of periscope would break the water. *Options, options,* he thought. *That's what we need now. But what options? If it's a nuclear strike, we've had it anywhere close to the surface. A biological strike will hurt the surface guys badly. Corpus Christi* was part of the battle group accompanying the carrier *Eisenhower* in these exercises.

"Skipper, we have *Ike* and the rest of the group as normal. The three contacts we have tracked for the last several hours are still there."

"Are they still the same ones we've been tracking?"

"Yes sir, I have the two Iraqi frigates, which are now at twenty thousand yards. The third contact is a possible sub, probably a diesel-electric boat. Can't quite get her, sir. She's pretty quiet."

"Dammit. Go to silent running now. XO, this message confirms launch of three missiles from a site in Iraq. They are headed straight for us. What's max depth here?"

The XO took a quick look at the charts, comparing them to the last reading from the global positioning satellite.

"Skipper, we have only about four hundred feet under the keel."

"Shit, not enough to go deep."

"Skipper, the frigates have increased speed. They're headed for us now. Sounds like they're balls to the wall."

"Where's the sub?"

"I still can't confirm, sir. He may be about ten thousand yards, bearing 035."

"XO, take her down to 350 then go right ninety degrees. Chief, contact *Ike*. Confirm frigates coming in. Request weapons free. Sonar, find that goddamn sub."

At the White House

The president was seated at a small table in the sitting room next to his bedroom. His usual breakfast was in front of him, along with the five principal U.S. daily newspapers, which he scanned every morning. He held *The Dallas Morning News* in his left hand. *The New York Times*, *The Chicago Tribune*, The

Morning News in his left hand. *The New York Times*, *The Chicago Tribune*, T*he Wall Street Journal*, and *The Los Angeles Times* had all been read when the phone rang again. Stoneman's voice was almost frantic.

"Mr. President, we have the two missiles now downrange, over the top of their arc. They're coming down. Right over the *Eisenhower* and her battle group."

Stoneman grabbed a note from another aide. "Mr. President, the *Eisenhower* battle group reports two Iraqi frigates closing fast on them, possibly accompanied by a sub. They want to be able to shoot if the Iraqis get within ten miles."

"Tell them not to fire unless fired upon. We're not going to be the ones to start a war."

"Mr. President, please! They are shooting missiles at us, not the other way around."

"All right, tell them to shoot down the incoming missiles."

"Mr. President." General Walker's voice had sunk to a whisper. "They don't have the ability to do that. All they can do now is sit back and take whatever is coming."

Aboard the Corpus Christi

"Skipper, from the *Ike*. Negative on weapons free, and they say that's from the president. The missiles nosed over, sir. We should have impact in under thirty seconds."

"Skipper, what about the guys on the surface?"

"You know as well as I do. If there are nuclear warheads in those birds, the guys on the surface are gone. If the weapons are even small tactical nuclear warheads, we don't stand a chance at 350 feet."

"Sonar, do you have the goddamn sub yet?"

At the White House

"Missiles now less than a minute from impact. Mr. President, I have the captain of the *Eisenhower* on the line. The missiles are now at fifty thousand feet. There are no detonations we can detect. *Ike* reports no detonations and no detaching warheads. We have missile impact in the water! The second one is down, too!"

"What's the damage?"

"Sir, as far as we can tell, there isn't any. Looks like the missiles were just test birds, sir."

"General Stoneman, did we just get all worked up over somebody just testing a missile?"

"I think we did, sir. But we had to in case our people were endangered. Shouldn't we respond? Either way, they shot at our ships."

"You're right, general. I'll handle it." The president threw down the phone and grabbed another one. "Get Blaine Graham for me, right now." The call immediately went to the secretary of State's office.

"Yeah, Blaine? The Iraqis just shot some missiles at our ships in the Persian Gulf. No, nobody got hurt. But that's not the issue. I want you to protest immediately and call a meeting of the U.N. Security Council for tomorrow. Let's let these guys know they can't get away with that crap any more."

Two Hours Later
At the Iraqi Presidential Palace

"Mr. President, we have received a message from the Americans protesting the missile attack on their ships."

"Yes, yes. But what else? What has their carrier done? Have they fired on our ships? Has their submarine sunk ours?"

"No, Excellency. Nothing. Not a shot has been fired, and our ships came within three miles of their carrier. All they did was have two fighters fly over our ships, but they did not shoot."

"But why, Hassan? That may be a question we have to answer ourselves."

CHAPTER 11

AT THE ALT+F5 KEY

In the old days, he thought, reporters would type #30# at the bottom of a page to show where their stories ended. Nowadays, there were no pages, only images on a computer screen. No more shouting for a copy boy like they did in the old movies. Just spell-check it and blink it over to the editors. They would do their job and probably hose up the best sentences he had written, but most of it ended up on the front page anyway. He filed this story by hitting the Alt and F5 keys on his computer at the same time. He was due to write one more today, and that could be done pretty quickly. If he got the interview.

All the public ever saw of the White House press room was the big blue backdrop with the White House seal up on the wall, maybe the podium where the president or one of his people was making a statement or explaining away the scandal *du jour*. Behind the cameras were row upon row of cheap folding chairs and a corridor that led to a dozen or so small cubicle offices and the most fought-over bank of pay telephones anywhere in the world. It was pretty much standard pressroom tacky decor, and he loved every inch of it.

He came to work every day loving his job, too. His newspaper, the *Washington Herald*, was unpopular with the rest of the media elite covering the White House. The *Herald* seemed to pick on the president more than the other papers, and certainly more than the TV and radio people, who acted like they were on the White House payroll. He came to work in a leather jacket, white shirt and tie, and hiking boots every day, except in the summer, when it was too hot for the jacket. He traveled on Air Force One in that getup. Hell, he looked better than most of the TV people. The TV gals would dress pretty well, but the guys were funny. Coat and tie from the waist up. Jeans and jogging shoes below. Only the part that got on the air mattered.

His charter, as the top White House reporter for the *Herald*, was to keep on top of breaking stories and to be in a position to get information from the right people quickly. Sometimes he could, and his paper was first on the street with something, or he waited and got there last. He had a nasty streak of integrity, which made him check facts before they were printed, much to the dismay of White House Press Secretary Art Henry.

As the time for the press conference approached, Art looked at his watch about every thirty seconds. He turned to one of his minions.

"Jerry, stick your head out and tell me who's there." A young college intern jumped at his command, and quickly surveyed the room.

"Mr. Henry, there's a crowd. I see all the networks are here, and the major print people. And, oh, your favorite guy is here, sitting right in the middle in the second row."

"Ah, shit. I thought Mussilli was out of town." Henry reached into his pocket and popped a couple of Tums in his mouth.

"No such luck, boss. Why is the *Herald* so rough on the president all the time?"

"Because they sell to a market nobody else does. There's a radical right-wing fringe that they cater to. Remember, that Guido Mussilli can't be trusted, so don't you talk to him." Henry remembered the last intern who had tried to help by befriending Mussilli. The girl had let him in on the president's plan to appoint a former college friend of Mrs. Brandon to a federal judgeship. Mussilli had enough lead time to research the woman's background and ran a story about the woman's links to casino gambling and the Mob. It was outrageous. It was unfair. Unfortunately, it also was entirely true. Henry remembered the dressing down he had received from the first lady when the nomination was withdrawn.

"Just stay clear of this guy. Remember when the president went to Martha's Vineyard last year for a summer vacation? Everybody knows how much he admires President Kennedy. Remember what this bastard wrote? We'd been pushing the idea that Brandon was the second coming of Kennedy. By the time we got to Cape Cod, everybody in the whole world was writing about the similarities between the president and Jack Kennedy."

Henry's staff was standing, listening to their boss get louder and louder. "The goddamn next day, this asshole writes that the Kennedy family should get a good laugh out of 'the copycat president.' Do you fucking believe it? The 'copycat president.'"

By now, the staff was hushing Henry. He started to calm down, and reached for more Tums. He turned from the intern to one of his assistants. "Make sure that the cameras are positioned to keep Mussilli off-screen. If there's any damage, at least it won't make the networks. Okay, is Touchman here yet? Let's get this over with." He waved to the secretary of defense to follow him out the stage door.

"Ladies and gentlemen, before I turn the podium over to Dr. Touchman, I wanted to share with you the president's excitement about the new defense budget. The president has set our nation's priorities straight. No more spoon-feeding the military. No more support for forces or weapons we don't need. We are turning the power of the defense establishment to the good of our nation and the world. Mr. Secretary?"

"Thank you very much, Art. As you said, the president has set some very new priorities for the Defense Department, and all of us are very proud to be in the vanguard of change. In the budget which we have just sent to Congress, there are several new policy directions for the military that I want to point out.

"First, there will be no more research or development of missile defenses. We have wasted enough money on that to feed all the children in America and put them through college, and that's where that money will go now. Into our new Defense College Fund, which will be spent entirely in minority neighborhoods and colleges. Second, there will be no more discrimination against women in the combat services. Women will be in every part of the army, navy, and air force. Third, we are also taking money out of a few useless programs to fund school lunches, breast cancer research, and peacekeeping training for our fighting men. For too long, we have only trained them to kill. Now we will teach them to build societies.

"Most importantly, we have now received the report of the President's Blue Ribbon Commission on Environmental Defense. You may remember the special initiative begun by the first lady to study the role of the Pentagon in saving the environment. That report is being copied now and will be distributed to each of you at the end of this session. When you get the report, you'll see the source of some of the most important changes President Brandon is making.

"Starting tomorrow, a special team of ambassadors from the United States will leave for conferences with the leaders of many of our Central and South American allies. The purpose of those talks will be to begin planning for the implementation of the Environmental Commission's most important recommendation. The commission recommended that at least twenty percent of our army and marine troops be redeployed to guard the Central and South American rain forests. The president and first lady are wholeheartedly supporting this recommendation. The president will be taking it up with Congressional leaders this week."

The dodger stepped forward again, and Guido flipped open his notebook. "Thank you, Mr. Secretary. Dr. Touchman will now take your questions."

The softballs flew. Yes, there will be money for schools in every big city in America. No, the threats to our security have shrunk so far that we really don't need any more submarines. Yes, the small war scenarios are much more realistic than the strategic conflicts we planned for in the Cold War, so we really don't need strategic missiles any more. No, none of our interests in European security will be threatened by the rain forests redeployment. Guido raised his hand. Art reached for his Tums.

"Ah, Mr. Secretary, *Jane's Defence Weekly* reports that the Khazaks have organized a bunch of former Russian special forces troops into a sort of freelance terrorist force. My sources say they're hiring these groups out to anyone who can pay. You're cutting the SEALs and the Army Special Forces down to almost nothing. How can they counter the Khazaks?"

"Guido, I think the entire U.S. Army can take care of any small band of Cossacks that try to invade, don't you? Heck, the Park Service Police could outmatch 'em." There were chuckles from the broadcast guys. They couldn't believe Mussilli. He asked the stupidest questions.

And so it went. Guido closed his notebook and started to leave. He didn't have the heart to question them about the report just released by the Democratic National Committee's "defense policy group." It was entitled "The Growing Threat of Unconventional Warfare." It wasn't about the threat of bad guys overseas. It was about the threat to America from its own armed forces.

It literally said that America's freedom was in danger from the very people who had preserved it for over two centuries. It took on the Marine Corps, labeling it "extremist" and "disconnected from society." It said the air force was too elitist in selecting pilots, and that people with poorer eyesight should be allowed to fly high-performance fighters as a matter of equal opportunity. According to the paper, America was in danger of a military coup if it didn't take steps to make the services, particularly the Marine Corps, more like society at large. "Building, not killing" should be their new creed.

Guido sighed. He would go back to the newspaper and write about the men and women in uniform he knew. There were a lot of them, from all walks of life. They were very different from civilians, in ways the civilians no longer understood.

On the surface, the differences were easy to spot. The academy grads, with their air of superiority. The fighter pilots with their usually well-founded arrogance. The mud Marines with their fatalistic view, saying, "When your number is up, that's it, and nothing you do before that moment can hurt you."

All of them had one thing in common, and that was the real difference between them and the civilians they were sworn to defend. Each had made the decision to risk his life, and maybe lose it, in defense of the system of values, beliefs, and principles they thought of as America.

Any one of them would risk his life for his country at the drop of a president's hat. All they wanted to know was that it wasn't a useless exercise. They all said it, one way or another. "Don't waste my life. Spend it if you have to, but don't throw it away."

In any event, it would be a good week. Tomorrow he would get the front page with his story about the first lady's latest denial that she had ordered the purchase of $600,000 worth of computers to track campaign donations illegally. Right under that headline, he'd print some quotes from the memo she had written ordering the creation of the database for tracking large donations. Damn. This was just too easy.

CHAPTER 12

AT THE CITY OF NORTHERN CHARM AND SOUTHERN EFFICIENCY

14 March
0555 Hours

Jonathan Forsythe woke slowly. Stretching, he ran his hand up and down the soft body beside him. Jennifer Lundgren looked like an advertisement for the Swedish womens' ski team. She was nearly six feet tall, and when she walked her long blond hair flowed behind her like a cape. She didn't walk, she floated. He remembered the first time he met her. He was sitting in his Dirksen Senate Office Building cubicle, still staffing education and funding issues for the senator. The secretary had buzzed him to see a lobbyist for the American Professional Educators' Society, a teachers' group that always donated a large chunk of money to Senator Manfredi. Manfredi had a near-perfect score on their legislative scoring system and had made it clear to his staff that APES was to be listened to and taken care of.

That first meeting was nothing but surprises for him. After talking briefly with her, he accepted her invitation to lunch, where she asked him all sorts of personal things. He didn't mind telling her so he could keep her next to him. He couldn't place her perfume, but it was the sexiest smell he had ever run into. She drove him crazy with desire. Lunches became a ritual for them, soon turning into dinners, and the quick trip to his apartment, or hers. He made sure the APES legislation was attached to other bills passing through the Senate on unanimous consent, keeping it hidden in the middle of other bills. Forsythe made it his practice to be able to tell his boss that there was no problem with an APES project.

He heard the rumors about other staffers having slept with her. He had to get the Senator to fire one man who he thought was competition for her. The gossips said she was well known as a round-heeled act. Forsythe didn't care. So long as she came to his bed, he was willing to ignore the rest.

Forsythe rolled over toward her. She was unbelievable in bed, doing anything he wanted. She even understood the problems he had and always was ready with a solution. He wanted one of those solutions right now. There was plenty of time before he had to be in the office. Maybe today he should skip his workout.

She rolled over at his touch. He started stroking her breasts with his palm, feeling the nipples get harder. She moaned softly and turned over on to him, licking his lips, his neck, and then his chest. He pinched each nipple softly and she moaned again, looking down at him. She knew what he needed, and grasped him, trying again to get him up for the task at hand. She sighed to herself, knowing how hopeless it was. Her boss had made it clear that she was to keep Forsythe happy. For the extra $10,000 a month, it was almost worth it.

14 March
0900 Hours
Little Creek, Virginia

Cully knocked on Schaeffer's door. "You sent for me, sir?"

"Yeah, Cully. That little exercise with the Senate staffers a couple of days ago isn't over. Apparently, they're writing some committee report on us, and the DCNO wants us to have someone on top of it. You're the spear-catcher on this one because you're the guy they know."

"When do I leave?"

"Now. Pack a bag and be at the airfield at 1000. Turn the training schedule over to your exec. You'll probably be up there for a couple of days. Maybe more."

"Any ideas about how I should approach them, sir?"

"No. The L&L guys will try to help with that, but just give 'em straight answers and try not to piss on any Senator's rug."

14 March
1405 Hours

The flight from Little Creek landed late, as did everything else at Washington's Reagan National Airport. Cully caught a cab from the terminal. "Russell Senate Office Building, driver. It's on—"

"I know where it is, son." The old black man in the front seat glanced back in the mirror. "Your first time up here?"

"No. Just a little nervous about where I'm going. Gotta meet with some Congressional staffers."

"Watch yisself wit those people. I been told too many times that nobody but the big boys leaves that place a winner."

"Thanks, man. I'm not that worried. All I have to do is talk about what I do for a living."

"Yeah, man. That's what everybody says on the trip up there. They sing another song on the trip back to the airport."

The captain from L&L was waiting for him at the Russell Building's southeast entrance, which faces the Capitol across Constitution Avenue. Captain Joe Morton was, as usual, peeved at the world. "Mr. O'Bannon, you were due here at noon. Great start. We missed a lunch with the committee chief counsel and an introductory meeting with the minority staff."

"Sorry, sir. Where do we go from here?"

"You're going to spend the next two days with the Armed Services and Appropriations Committee staffs. I've arranged a couple of meetings with members, and we may get more requests for you after word gets out about you being here. We're at the White House tomorrow for a meeting with the national security advisor himself. SecDef will probably be there, too. Don't plan on resting much. And whatever you do, *don't* get into an argument with them again. Several of them really didn't like what you said when they visited Little Creek. My job is hard enough. Don't make it harder. Now, follow me. Senator Barrett wants to meet you. He's our best ally on the special ops issue, so don't piss on his rug, understand?"

Morton lead him down the hall to a reception area in the senator's office. Two very attractive girls sat at word processors, greeting visitors and answering the phone. Cully was eyeing a perfectly dazzling redhead at the desk nearest him. She was behind a reception counter that hid her legs, but everything from the waist up looked positively edible. She didn't look a day over twenty, either. "What's that badge you have over your left shirt pocket, sir?" she asked. He gave her his best Big Combat Hero smile.

"It's a SEAL badge, Laurie," said a voice behind him. Cully turned. Those dark blue eyes froze him in his tracks for the second time. "It's also called a 'trident' and the guys who wear it call it a 'budweiser' because they say it looks like the beer trademark. Kate Reilly, Mr. O'Bannon. Come this way. The senator is waiting."

Cully and Morton fell in behind her. Cully saw Morton nodding toward Reilly's body and grinning. Then and there, Cully decided the guy was a real jerk. All pleasure, no business.

Nate Barrett sat behind a desk so large it could serve as a conference table. He was chewing on a very large unlit cigar and finishing a phone call. He gestured them into three chairs arranged in front of the desk.

"Give me the three best reasons your unit shouldn't be defunded, young man. As Katie probably told you, I'm on your side, but I need help on explaining why."

Cully decided to start at the beginning, which was a big mistake. "Sir, the SEALs are an outgrowth of the old Underwater Demolition Teams of World War II—"

"Cut the ancient history, son." Barrett's normal voice sounded like the growl of a very large bear. This was louder. Cully mistook it for a danger signal. "I know the background of the SEALs. What I don't know is why they sent you here to help us, rather than one of those savvy old admirals that Captain Morton here reports to."

"Sir, I'm sorry—"

"Come on, boss. Give him a break." Katie was smiling at both of them. "Or I'll tell them what an old softie you really are."

It was Barrett's turn to smile. "Young man, don't ever put yourself in the power of one of these modern women. They'll turn you inside out every day before breakfast. Okay, Katie, I'll be good. Mr. O'Bannon, what you don't understand is that every year, everything we've done before is fair game to be taken apart and redone all over again. It's not like it used to be when a deal was a deal. Every day is a new day up here. I know, and I guess most of the Senate knows, that the SEALs have served with great distinction. But the only question anyone wants answered is what have you done for us lately. Admiral Pierson said you could explain that to me."

The whole room relaxed. Morton contented himself with staring at Kate's ample bosom while Cully recounted a top-secret description of SEAL operations over the entire history of the force. Long before O'Bannon was there, the SEALs were training Afghan guerrillas to fight Russian helicopters and armored columns. "They were using stuff only one step above muskets when we got there. But those guys are pretty smart. We taught them that a stinger can kill a $30 million fighter plane, and they took to it like ducks to water."

Cully and Senator Barrett went back and forth for almost an hour about the SEALs' accomplishments. Grenada: landing almost a week before the invasion, sizing up targets, freeing hostages, and attacking key targets hours before the marines arrived. Panama: where half of a SEAL platoon was killed by dropping the men into the very center of a heavily armed airport garrison.

"The intel guys failed us big time, senator. If we stay in business, I'd like to talk to you some more about that problem." The abortive attempt to rescue Italian Premier Aldo Moro when he was captured by terrorists. Raids into Palestinian camps, which the Israelis were too squeamish to do themselves.

When he finished, Barrett questioned him for another hour, going over operational strategies, weapon systems, and what the teams needed over the next few years. Cully had been before examination boards before, but it had never been this tough. The senator knew his stuff. He felt just like he did after finishing his senior electrical engineering exam at Annapolis. Suddenly, the senator stood up.

"Mr. O'Bannon, thank you very much. I think we've made a good start, but I want you to stay around for a day or two to help Ms. Reilly write up our part of the committee report. Can you do it?"

"As long as my boss okays it, sir. I'd be glad to help."

"His boss will okay it, senator. I'll call him right now. We'll both be glad to help." Morton was practically licking his lips looking at Reilly.

As they walked out of the office, Reilly stopped them. "If you can do it, Mr. O'Bannon, please meet me back here at about 6:30 this evening. We'll start working on the report."

The next stop was Senator Berkely's office. They were met by the short blond who had toured Little Creek. "Good to see you again," she said through clenched teeth. "Let's talk with the senator."

Like Barrett, Berkely sat behind a big desk, but hers sat facing a wall full of testimonials to herself. In the military this was known as an "I love me" wall. Every admiral had one, but almost nobody of lesser rank did. Berkely turned her chair to face them. The blonde stayed in the outer office gathering papers.

"I'm Barbara Berkely. I'm glad to meet you, Lieutenant. So you're to be our expert on the SEALs for the next few days."

"Yes ma'am. I'll be glad to answer any questions you have."

Johnson entered. "Before we start, let me introduce my legislative assistant for military matters, Ms. Johnson."

Cully turned to the blonde. "We've met before. Tonya came to the presentation we made a few weeks ago at Little Creek. I never forget a pretty face."

Morton's face blanched. Senator Berkely looked as if someone had shoved an icicle up her rectum. The meeting went south fast. Both Berkely and Johnson were committed to disbanding the SEALs before the meeting started. By the time it ended, they wanted to destroy the whole navy. Cully and Morton beat a hasty retreat.

"Nice goin', O'Bannon." Morton, as always, was ready to apportion blame. "I've never seen anyone less in tune with what they're doing, and I intend to tell that to Captain Schaeffer."

"Sir, I'm sorry. I was just trying to break the ice."

"Well, you broke the ice and your own head in the process. Let's get on to the next session."

When Cully looked at his watch again, it was 6:35. Already late to meet Reilly, he said good-night to Morton and ran back to the Russell Building. She was waiting.

"Where do we start, Ms. Reilly?"

"We start by you calling me Kate. Have you ever seen a Senate committee report, Lieutenant?"

"No, and please call me Cully. What do I do in this mess?"

"What you do is go over again all of the stuff you spoke about with Senator Barrett. I'll ask questions and type. You talk, and look over my shoulder to make sure I get it right."

"Sounds simple enough. Got anything to eat around here?"

"No, we'll have to get something later. I need to get the first half of this done tonight, so we can get it edited tomorrow. We'll do the second half tomorrow night, and it'll be printed the following day." Kate sat down at her desk, a small desk in a large cubicle shared with another staffer and desk. They worked for hours in front of the glowing screen. At 11:15, she called a halt.

"Enough for me for one day." She looked at Cully. He seemed to have just awakened and was pretty wound up. " Aren't you even a little tired?"

"Nah. We stay up most of the night about three times a week. We train at night, and most of our real work is done at night. I'm just getting started."

"Well, I'm beat. Let's skip dinner." The disappointment must have shown on his face.

"Walk me home? The boss says this is a lousy neighborhood at night. We've had a couple of staffers assaulted in the past year or so. He worries about me."

"He should. You're certainly an attractive target."

"Cut the blarney, Irish. Just walk me home." *Am I imagining things*, she thought, *or is this guy the real thing? Or is he just coming on to me like every other guy the Navy or Air Force ever sent up here? He's so confident, he doesn't have to brag about what he is like the fighter jocks. He's real all right. It's obvious from everything about him.*

Cully smiled for the first time since he got off the plane. "Okay. Can't blame a guy for trying."

"No, Cully. But neither one of us has time for this stuff now. No, I'm not involved with anyone now, and no, I'm not going to be for a while. So can we keep this just professional?"

She smiled, and his knees went wobbly again. "Well, at least for now. You are kinda cute."

They walked the few blocks to her apartment, in a townhouse behind Union Station and all too close to the Hart Building. He found himself just wishing some punk with a knife would try to come at them. He wanted to show her what he did for real, but that was crazy. What he did was so far from her world. He hoped she would never really have to see it up close.

But he wanted to prove something to her. Be her hero, not just another soldier. But she was out of his league. She probably has some asshole lawyer boyfriend with a Ferrari and a summer house in Cape Cod.

Katie, too, was thinking as she walked. *This guy is really something. After all the jerks I meet every day, it's nice to meet a real human for once. There's nothing phony about him. But he's part of the political equation. I have to use him. I have to drain him of every drop of information that will help Barrett. After that, what?*

When they reached the door to the apartment house, she pulled her keys out and swung the door open. He followed behind her. She stopped and put her briefcase down.

"Thanks, Cully. I usually enjoy my job, but not as much as I did tonight."

"Me, too, Katie. I love what I do, and I don't really know what you do, but you're working hard to save something that means a lot to me. I know it's your job, but I want you to know I'm grateful."

"I'll let you in on a deep dark secret. Yes, I do it because it's my job. But I'm a really lucky girl. I have a job that lets me do what I think is the right thing to do, and I'll bust my butt to get it done. Not that I'll need to, but I'll make sure my boss does the same. And when he talks, there are a whole bunch of these guys who listen."

Cully leaned back and cocked his head to one side. "You're serious. You aren't just pulling my chain."

"Damned right I'm not. You were in the Gulf War, Cully. You know how well it went and with so few of our boys killed. What you don't know is that one of those few was my brother. I'm doing it for him." Her dark blue eyes warmed him with their light.

"And I'm doing it for you, too."

"Maybe we could continue this over breakfast?"

"Not tomorrow morning. Maybe the day after. You never know where you'll wake up, Lieutenant."

As she trotted to the elevator she yelled over her shoulder. "And be at my office again tomorrow at 6:30. Just like today." And then she was gone.

"Dammit," he thought, "she knows what she's doing to me. Patience, lad, whatever the hell that means."

Now what the hell was that about? he wondered as he walked out the door. *She's something. There had to be one good person in this garden of bozos. She's really going to fight for us. She's gorgeous. She's smart as hell, and she has more balls than most guys I've ever met. She and her boss sure know how this game is played. Maybe we have a chance to beat this after all. But she's a real handful. Too bad. Maybe I can get to know her. Naw. Why the hell does every woman I like make my mind short-circuit?* He was thinking so hard he had almost reached the Marine barracks before he realized where he was.

The following day was another blur. They started off with three meetings on the Senate side, and walked across to the House side, passing in front of the marble front of the Supreme Court. It said "Equal Justice Under Law" over the doors. "That's what this is all about," thought Cully. He started to say something to Morton, but the captain was too busy talking into his cellular phone and looking at every skirt that passed by.

At 1 P.M. they caught a car that took them to the White House West Gate. They were looked over by the Secret Service, their passes checked, and they were led through a metal detector to the West Wing reception area. As they walked in, a tall thin man with an Abe Lincoln beard was coming out. Morton, ever anxious to brown-nose, stepped to one side and said, “Good morning, Dr. Krueger.”

The man stopped in his tracks and sneered, “I don’t talk to you military thugs. Now let me pass, dammit.”

Cully was too surprised to say anything. Morton looked grim. “That’s Steve Krueger. And if you don’t know, he’s chief of staff to the first lady.”

“Is everybody like that in here?” Cully whispered. “No. Just most of them,” was the reply. “He was a big wheel in the campaign and they had to keep him somewhere. He was an academic with some Institute for Modern Peace or something like that.”

The meetings with Dr. Anthony and Touchman went as well as they could. Hunter wasn’t there, so Cully failed to meet the man who Morton had told him was the only ally he had in the White House. On the way out, they were practically run over by a short, chubby guy charging down the hall. The vice president literally bounced off Morton. Cully caught him before he could fall. “Thanks, young fella. Who the hell are you?”

Morton stepped forward. “Mr. Vice President, let me introduce you to Lieutenant Cullum O’Bannon, a platoon commander from SEAL Team 4.”

“Pleased to meetcha. Come on into my office for a minute, if you got the time.” La Guardia had a smile in his eyes. Cully couldn’t make up his mind who it was meant for, or if this was just another jolly empty suit. They trooped up the stairs to the VP’s office. The clock said 5:50 P.M. Cully started wondering how long this would take. Kate expected him soon, and he was looking forward to another evening with her.

La Guardia went to the far end of the room and opened a liquor cabinet. “I can’t deal with these bozos any more today without a little bracer. Get you anything, Mr. O’Bannon?”

“Just some ice water, sir. Thanks.”

“For you, Captain?”

“A bit of that Maker’s Mark bourbon would slide down nicely, sir.”

La Guardia stepped up to the little bar and poured the drinks. “Okay, you two. I need you to level with me. I know that you’ve spent two days on the Hill by now, and that Pete Manfredi and Barbara Berkely are ready to do you in. Even though Mike Porter is saying he’s still undecided, he’ll back their play. I also know that the first lady’s chief of staff is pissed at you, and I can’t figure why. I want you guys to stay in business, but Jesus, you gotta do better for yourselves.” Cully was surprised that he knew so many details of what had been going on. His face must have showed it.

"Shocked, Mr. O'Bannon? Washington's a pretty small town, and I have a lot of friends. You don't. Good gossip travels faster than light around here."

"Sir, I really don't know how to do this. I swim and jump out of airplanes for a living. This is a new thing for me. What am I doing wrong?"

"Lieutenant, you're not doin' anything wrong. You don't speak the same language as these clowns. I'm gonna give you a list of people to see tomorrow. You, Captain, make sure he gets there." La Guardia went into a list of House and Senate members and committee staffers who were involved in the Armed Services Committees' business. Cully didn't recognize any of the names. "And this is what you need to say to each of them." Cully took notes furiously, and when they finished it was almost 7 P.M.

"I'll see he gets to each of these people, Mr. Vice President," said Morton.

La Guardia stood and shook hands with each of them. "You're lucky Nate Barrett is on your side. He's the best of a good bunch, and his staff is pretty damned good, too."

Morton couldn't resist. "Mr. O'Bannon is very lucky. He's working *very* closely with one of Senator Barrett's people."

Cully bristled at Morton's none-too-subtle shot at him and Kate. La Guardia noticed.

"Just remember one thing, O'Bannon. Good men are hard to find. You'd be surprised how clear that is, especially to people who work on the Hill, where there's a serious shortage of real people. Nate Barrett is good people, and so are his staff. Good luck, son. I'll do what I can from this end."

They went out the West Gate far more quickly than they came in. Morton held out the cell phone. "Want to call her to say you're on the way? Wouldn't do to keep a piece of ass like that waiting too long."

Cully bit his tongue. "Thank you, sir. I will." He called Kate's office, and only managed to leave a message on her voice mail that he was on his way. They were there in ten minutes. "Good night, Lieutenant O'Bannon. I don't think you'll need it, but here's the number for the motor pool. They'll pick you up and get you back to the Navy Yard. For a change of clothes in the morning if nothing sooner." Morton was still smirking when Cully ran up the steps to the building entrance.

Kate was waiting, immersed in the draft report. She waved him to a chair in the corner while she finished typing a paragraph. She clicked the "save" button on the word processor and looked up.

"I hear you've had quite a day. Got to the veep, pissed off the president's wife, and generally made a nuisance of yourself at House Approps."

"Jesus, does everybody in this town get an hourly report on how bad I'm doing? Was it on the goddamn network news? Yeah, I probably stepped in it a couple of times, and I'm damned if I know what Krueger's problem was. For God's sake, all we did was say good morning to the asshole."

"Hey, Cully. Calm down. I'm not criticizing you. You're a fish out of water here. You made a big hit with the veep, which is mucho important. As for Krueger, anybody who was a senior fellow at the World Institute for a Modern Peaceful Society is a really hard sell for what you're peddling."

He sighed a very long sigh. "Sorry, Kate. It's been a long couple of days."

"Look, I just finished the classified annex to the report. Or at least our side of it. Why don't I load the unclassified stuff into my briefcase and we can do the rest over Chinese take-out at my place. I want to get out of these business clothes and into my sweats. This is going to be at least three or four more hours of work tonight."

"Are you sure you don't want me to wait here while you go home to change?"

"In the time it would take for me to go home, change, and get back, we can order dinner and eat and get back to work. Come on." She punched a button on her speed dial, and a garbled voice said "Hunan City."

"Yo, Cully. You like hot and spicy or moderate?"

"The hotter the better." She ordered three or four things and he grabbed the phone out of her hand to give the restaurant his American Express card number. "You didn't have to do that," she said.

"I know, but it's about the only thing I've done right since I got to this screwy town."

She threw a stack of papers and several reference books into a very large briefcase, which she consented to Cully carrying, and practically ran out of the office. As they went out one end of the hall, Jonathan Forsythe was coming up the other. He recognized Kate's figure, and knew the navy uniform next to her was Cully. Feeling anger rise, he nodded recognition to their backs.

When they got to her apartment, she led him in and turned on the big computer on the desk in one corner of the living room. The place was a shambles, but had feminine touches like curtains that didn't clash violently with the carpet. Papers and books were stacked everywhere around a large table across from the computer desk. "Listen for the guy with the food, will ya?" She ran back into the bedroom and came out five minutes later, just as Cully was turning from the front door with the big bag of hot food. She was even more beautiful than before, despite being clad only in shorts and a purple sweatshirt that said, "Moody's Diner, Waldoboro, Maine". Her hair was tied back and her face scrubbed. Cully thought she was far more delicious than the food could possibly be. He smiled at her, and she returned the favor.

"What's a Waldoboro?" he asked.

"It's simply the best place for pie in the whole world. We were up there visiting the Bath shipyard, and the Navy L&L guys took us to Moody's for lunch. I had a piece of the blueberry stuff and thought I'd died and gone to heaven. You like pie?"

"Who doesn't? Take me there some time?"

She smiled again. "You betcha, sailor. We'll celebrate the preservation of the SEALs. Now let's eat. I'm starved."

But with Kate, starting to eat did not mean stopping the work. "Okay, Cully. So we're done explaining the SEAL mission, and why it's different from the other Special Ops groups. Now what's the biggest obstacle between you and doing the job the way you want to do it?"

"Easy, Katie—retention and training. Right now, all my guys are learning is how to string telephone cables across freezing rivers in Bosnia. When you're stringing wires, you're not practicing insertion techniques or close-quarters combat. I'll trade twenty hours of wire-stringing for two hours of honest-to-god CQB practice."

"You sound a lot like the fighter jock the air force sent to talk to me a few weeks ago. He was complaining that all his guys were doing is flying circles in the sky over Iraq. He said they were losing more of their combat skills every day because their training was all wasted on crap like that."

"Right on the nose, oh Wise One. You really do understand us. Jesus. After the past few days, I didn't think anybody in this stupid town understood."

"Well, I understand a bit of it, and I want to learn more. Okay, we have to put some recommendations in this report. How about these. First, we say the committee should require that at least two-thirds of the training budget be spent on field combat exercises. Second, we prohibit the combat arms folks—you clowns who sit at the pointy end of the spear—from being used for these 'nation-building' exercises. Third, we set up a 'War Fighters Caucus'—and this'll have to be outside the committee report—to make sure that the defense bucks are spent on people, bullets, and bombs. That'll be right unpopular with the White House, but that's what it's gonna take."

Cully raised an eyebrow. "Katie, if you could make those things happen, you'd solve ninety percent of the problems. But we still have too many people serving too long away from their families. The military life is a hard one, but the people who sign up for it understand that. What we have to do is make it so that a family dosn't have to be without its father or mother for six months out of every year."

"Cully, that may be more than we can handle. What you're talking about is the president's power to send troops anywhere any time. We can't interfere with that. But maybe we can redirect his foreign policy focus."

"You're right on the money. But when we have nearly fifty percent of the SEAL officers resign in one year, it's a problem we damned well better fix."

"I know. Let me think on that one, pal."

At one in the morning, she finished running the spell-check program. They were both exhausted. He stood behind her, rubbing her neck and shoulders.

"I'll give you two hours to quit that, buster." She was almost purring, feeling her tight neck and shoulders loosen up.

"It's the least I can do for someone working so hard to save my job."

"I'm doing it for more than you, Cully. But I'm glad it'll help you." His hands worked their way across her shoulders and down her arms. He reached up again and started massaging her head, his thumbs pressing at the base of her skull and his fingers rubbing her temples.

"Where did you learn all that? Some part of your past love life?"

"No, I'm just making this up as I go along."

"I can think of a few other places you could rub." She took his left hand and placed it on her left breast. He squeezed it gently.

"Mmm. Keep going." She purred and reached down, rubbing him erect through his pants.

He lifted her out of the chair and kissed her, hugging her whole body. His hands searched under her shirt, back and forth, finally grabbing the button to her shorts. Her bare skin was too cool, too smooth. His mind flashed back over the past two years. There had been Mary Jane, Annie, and before them, Beth. They all started too easily. He had ended them, none too soon.

"Kate, I'm not ready for another one-nighter. I have to leave for Europe at the end of next week. I won't be back for two weeks after that, maybe longer."

"I don't do one-nighters. But neither of us is ready to make any heavier decisions tonight. Let's just be happy. I think we can be happy together for a long time."

"I'm already happier than I've ever been." He slid his hands under the sweatshirt again. Her nipples were already hard. He stroked them lightly, teasing her into a moan. She reached down and grabbed his pants, opening the zipper and grabbing his erection with both hands.

He slipped her sweatshirt off and began kissing her breasts, reaching for the button on the front of her shorts. The shorts dropped off, and he reached inside her, feeling the hot wetness. They walked sideways to the bed, hands and mouths exploring. Their exhaustion made way for an adrenaline rush, and they took turns going at each other for almost two hours.

He awoke at 5:15. She was wide awake, grinning at him, nestled in his left elbow, her nose crinkled in a goofy look. "I can't believe we did that. I can't believe you're here."

"Are you sorry we did, Kate?"

"No. Are you?"

As an answer, he pulled her closer. They made love again, this time more hurriedly.

At ten after eight, they were dressed and ready to return to her office. As they walked out of the lobby of the building, Jonathan Forsythe smiled. He wasn't sure the pictures he had taken of them kissing at her door would come out. It didn't matter. All he had to do was describe what he'd seen to his boss.

• • •

Cully decided to take a few days of vacation before the team left for their two-week stint at the SAS School near Hereford in Britain. They and the SAS took turns visiting each other's schools. Every other year, it was the SAS's turn to host the SEALs, and Team 4 was the next to go. A few days in Washington, seeing Katie in her environment, would be more than just a fun diversion. He had gone through so many women since graduating from the academy that he was leery of anyone who seemed interested in a longer relationship, but she was unlike all of the others. There was a brain there, and someone who stood for something. He was coming to the conclusion that she was his kind of people.

He called in his leave request, which was granted by Captain Schaeffer. He wandered around the Capitol, seeing how things worked. His surprise was at the seeming formality of everything the Senate did. Beneath the formality was a staff-driven agenda. Most of the senators had stopped kidding themselves about it. Their legislation was thought up, drafted, and carried through the process quickly by a staff that controlled the senators' access to most of the information they needed to make a decision. This enormous power over national affairs was normally respected by the unelected staff. There were some notorious exceptions. Like the staffer whose business card said he was simply "deputy." In his own mind, he was deputy senator, and made that clear to all who crossed his path.

Katie would meet Cully for lunch in one of the cafeterias found in the Senate office buildings, or if he insisted, in one of the expense account restaurants that still dotted the Hill. After restrictions on what lobbyists could spend to entertain staffers and senators, many of these hundred-dollar lunch counters were having a tough time.

One day found them at the Monocle, a long-time Senate landmark, known for crab cakes and good whiskey. The very tall, dark-eyed Greek host eyed Katie with a smile that made Cully uncomfortable. Her return smile made it worse. She seemed very much at home. And she noticed her man heating up to a slow boil.

"Easy, Cully. Nick and I have been buds for years. He takes care of me. But he is kinda cute." She looked at Cully with an impish grin. He looked into those dark blue eyes and promptly forgot what he was mad about.

"So what's on the agenda for this afternoon, gorgeous? You gonna take me into the Senate inner sanctum and ravish my body on a pile of *Congressional Records*?"

She smiled again. It seemed that she did that a lot when he was around. "Sounds like a great idea, Irish, but we have a big committee powwow this afternoon. Seems like the prez wants to make sure we have girls on the SEAL teams."

"Say, what?"

"Yup. They have an amendment that would fully integrate all the combat forces with women. You can start worrying any time. I think it will pass."

"What the hell are these guys thinking about, Katie? Women can do most anything, but combat just doesn't fit the NCAA definition of a co-ed sport."

"Well, I had a hunch you would agree with my boss on that. The trouble is, by his head count, we're gonna lose this one big time. Logic and reason don't matter in this, Cully. This is politics, pure and unsimple."

"Wow. I can't believe this crap. These guys will ask me and my men to risk our lives, and they want to make it harder for us? Do they really want more of us to get killed when we go in for a fight? Because that's what they're aiming for. Jesus, Katie, I thought people up here cared about more than the next day's headline."

"Cully, I hear you. But some care, and some don't."

They ate their crab cakes in silence. When they left together, they kissed briefly, and Cully headed out for a long walk.

CHAPTER 13

AT THE RUSHIN' FRONT

The Senate Armed Services Committee, unlike some of the other committees, holds its executive sessions in true privacy. No lobbyists, no reporters, no outsiders at all are permitted in the room. One of the functions of these meetings were the annual "mark-ups" where the committee worked out the final version of the Defense Authorization bill to be reported to the full Senate for a vote. In those mark-up sessions—which went on for days or even weeks—everything from the next year's purchases of ships, planes, and tanks to retirement pay for the military was decided.

It is the usual practice for the legislative policy issues—those not dealing with spending money—to be debated and voted on last. This year, there had been quite a number of these, including the one most desired by the president, the mandate for full gender equalization of the combat arms. Rumors had it that the president had a bet with the U.N. secretary general that he could send the next U.N. expeditionary force under the command of an American woman.

As usual, there were those, including the secretary of Defense, who were lobbying hard for the president's ideas. But there was resistance as well, from the senior senator from Missouri, among others. Nate Barrett was old-fashioned enough to believe that there were moral not just political questions here, and he intended to raise them. Barbara Berkely wanted no part of Barrett's issues. In Manfredi's absence, she held the gavel.

"The chair will introduce the chairman's amendment as its own, and will ask that reading be dispensed with. Without objection, so ordered. This, ladies and gentlemen, is the president's amendment, not just mine or Pete Manfredi's. It comes from the man who has done more than anyone else to correct the years of sexual discrimination and oppression of women in the military, our president. He has asked us to take this final step, which will mandate the sexual integration of all combat forces in the U.S. military by the end of next year.

"To recap this measure, it will require that 25 percent of all pilot trainees, 10 percent of all special forces trainees, and 35 percent of all officer candidates be women. More than that, it will prohibit by law the selection of a man over a woman for any combat assignment, hazardous duty, or any situation in which there is a risk of injury or death. Every time a job like that comes up, I want to see a woman get the job."

"Madam Chairwoman, I understand the chair's enthusiasm for this measure." Barrett had not stirred, but the junior senator from Texas, who after only one year in the Senate had become one of its most respected debaters, was sliding in front of Berkely. Senator Joey Diggers was a roly-poly guy with a Texas accent as thick as an enchilada. He was the junior senator from his state, but junior only in service in the Senate.

An old air force pilot, his service record wasn't something he told everyone about. Not that they would have understood anyway. There were precious few members of the Senate who knew the kind of risks you take in combat, far less the ones you take on your way to winning an Air Medal. Joey had thirty-one of them. Fewer still knew how you won the Distinguished Flying Cross. Joey had seven of those, one from Korea, and the rest going all the way up to Vietnam.

"Well, Madam Chairwoman, I'm just trying to figure out just how far this amendment would take all this sechshuwal integration stuff. The way I read it, my old buddies in the marines better look out. Their jobs are in danger. I guess this amendment would put women in the infantry, wouldn't it?"

"Yes, it would. And it's high time they were there. A woman marine who doesn't serve as a combat infantry officer has virtually no chance of rising above the rank of major."

"Well, couldn't we just leave the combat arms alone and maybe authorize some more senior officer slots for the ladies?"

"That's just the kind of thinking that the president wants to end."

Barrett stirred. "Madam chairwoman, I would like to raise another issue. I think there are some very distinct moral issues we should consider before we vote." Berkely tensed. She knew what was coming.

"In the Gulf War, an army helicopter pilot, I believe she was a major, was captured by the Iraqis. They beat her and raped her repeatedly. She survived, luckily. I think America has always fought to protect its women from that sort of treatment. If you put women in the combat arms, you're saying America values them less for the other things they do."

Berkely jumped on him. "What other things? Raising babies? Baking cookies? It's high time that the full opportunity offered by a military career was really opened to women. The only way to do that is to make them truly equal."

"Now, senator, don't get angry with an old man. I may have some funny ideas, but I think that the role of women in our society is different from the role of men. Women civilize us. They teach us to love and honor our families. I think sometimes that if it weren't for women, us men would still be running around in the woods wearing bear skins and howling at the moon." There were a few snickers from the staff.

"There's nothing dishonorable about raising babies, and it isn't me that designed the way our species works. It is the women who have the babies, who nurture them and raise them into the people we are proud to call our friends and neighbors. Men can't do what women can."

Berkely was warming to the debate. "Well, senator, I won't dispute that point, but I don't see where it leads. We want to integrate women into all the combat arms. We know that the women of America deserve it and want it. You say you have a moral point, but I think it smacks of male chauvinism and outright prejudice."

Diggers was unable to sit still. Most of the cowboy drawl disappeared. "Senator, that's the silliest damned speech I've ever heard. You think there's no moral point here? You think that our society will not be changed forever if we subject the people who raise our children to the horrors of war? Don't you think we should take a little care in doing that?"

"That's just another excuse to perpetuate discrimination, senator. These days, children are raised in a cooperative environment. Parents play a lesser role. The real work is done by the day care centers and the schools."

"You think so?" Barrett was rising out of his chair, and pacing around the table. "If that's true, then we have really failed as a nation. Look through history. Those nations that left child rearing to the society at large turned out like the former Soviet Union. Less free. More oppressive because they lacked the moral roots to judge their own actions. More prone to violence against their neighbors. Think about it. It doesn't take a village to raise a child, it takes a family."

"What the hell are we talking about here? Some damned social experiment?" Diggers was out of his chair as well. "There are seventeen of us on the committee. Of the seventeen, only Nate Barrett and I have worn the uniform. Barbara, I know you'll say that doesn't make us the only ones who are qualified to determine this issue, and you're right about that. But this isn't about discrimination. It isn't about social policy. It's about whether we want our armed forces to be able to beat the hell out of whoever we tangle with.

"We all know the facts. We can kid ourselves about it, but the facts are there. There are physical differences between men and women. There are differences between how men and women look at life and death. And these differences should be preserved, because they're part of what makes us Americans.

"There is a culture in the military which many of the members of this Committee condemn every day. I know what most of you think about the macho man image the combat services thrive on. Even for most men, the image is something they can't live up to.

"But ask yourself this: how many of our wars have been won by men who fought beyond their abilities because they believed they could? How many of our battles were won by men fighting for the safety of the women and children they had at home? And ask yourselves this: Why is no other large nation placing women in combat? Why have the Israelis taken women out of combat roles? We all know the answer, but no one wants to say it. Women are not in Israeli combat forces because they tried it, and it doesn't work. And there aren't too many women who are NFL linebackers, either.

"What are we doing to our nation when we toy with something that has to succeed, first time, and every time? Make no bones about it, my friends. We are tinkering with something we can't afford to mess up. Most of the government initiatives we talk about are fairly harmless. We spend the taxpayers' money, and if some housing project gets fouled up, we can fix it by spending more money. We regulate an industry, and maybe they have a bit more difficulty competing in the world markets. But this is different. This isn't something that we can afford to screw up. If we break this one, we may not get a chance to fix it again.

"America is what it is because of the jobs our people do. Doctors, teachers, mothers, and fathers. Each performs a function that makes us what we are, and without them, we wouldn't be the strong, generous, and kind people the world knows us to be.

"But this is a very different job. This is a job that has to be done right, first time and every time. If this job isn't done right, just once, all the other jobs don't matter because no one gets a chance to do them. That one special job is to defend our country. We can't risk not doing it right. Anything that reduces our chances of doing it right isn't worth the risk of doing it wrong. I say vote no on the amendment. Because we vote for it at our peril, and the peril of our homes, and our children.

"And what are we doing to these women? We've all read the report about that navy pilot who put her F-14 into the side of the carrier. And we all know the report was a whitewash of what happened. Plain and simple, it was pilot error by a pilot who shouldn't have been flying that bird. Did we do her a real favor? Both she and her back seater are dead because she couldn't cut it and the navy kept her flying."

Berkely had been waiting for this. She had spent the whole morning with Major General Gensler in her office preparing for this moment. Her staff had prepared the talking points and copied the papers Gensler had leaked to her. She smiled.

"Senator, I think you are right. We aren't doing these women a favor when they are treated like that pilot. I have here her flight school records. My staff will hand them out to you now. What you see is a perfect record, with favorable comments from all of her instructors."

Diggers looked the papers over quickly. "Senator, these records are incomplete. You're saying she had a perfect record, but these papers only show undergraduate pilot training. What about her combat training and checkouts in the fighters? I understand from some of the top people in Naval Aviation that she had three down checks and continued flying. Senator, a down check is a failing grade. Any man with two down checks on his record fails and won't even get his wings. Why was this lady given her wings and allowed to fly with three? I think we ought to investigate why she was still flying, not vote to make more victims out of women trying to do a job they aren't cut out for."

Berkely cringed. "Senator, I don't know where you got those ideas. I have hard facts here, and you are trying to confuse things with rumors and innuendo. We all know that women pilots are expected to meet the same standards as men."

"Senator, that's what people always say, but what we all really know is that it isn't true. All of the service academies have lowered their physical fitness standards so women could pass them. Women get waivers of all sorts of standards. That is wrong. It sends the message to the world that we are less concerned with winning wars than we are with winning votes. That's wrong, and it will cost this nation a very high price if we let it continue."

The debate continued for another ninety minutes. When the vote came, the amendment passed by a vote of fifteen to two.

CHAPTER 14

AT THE MOUTH OF THE BEAST

30 March
0745 Hours

"Good morning, gentlemen," said the man with the slight Scottish burr. "I trust we're all ready for the next stage of our little exercise together."

Cully just barely had the strength to open his eyelids. Even after the ten-kilometer run, his head felt like someone had hit him with a hammer. He forced his eyes open and saw what he feared he would: a very large captain in British battle fatigues with an incomprehensibly healthy look about him. He also wore a distinctive sand-colored beret, which had a small flash on it reading, "Who Dares, Wins." On the right arm of his jacket, just where the sleeve met the shoulder, there was a small pair of light-blue upturned wings, the shoulder patch of the the Special Air Service. He was British Army all the way, right down to the David Niven moustache.

All six feet, six inches of Captain Ian MacPherson seemed to have survived the previous night's exercise, which had started innocently enough. After they had all changed to civilian clothes, Mac had invited his students to join him and the SAS faculty at a local pub. When they had had a few drinks, some of the locals started shouting insults at the SEALs. It seemed that a group of college-age punks objected to having Americans in their pub and wanted to draw a line at Wilson, who they called a "Yank nigger." They had been at a soccer match and obviously were feeling their booze.

At that point one of them took a swing at Wilson, who, as Cully looked on in amusement, quickly had the man down on his knees, three fingers of his left hand bent back, and screaming in pain. The other four grabbed bottles and came out of their chairs, but Wilson held up a hand.

"Not, yet, fellas." They stopped, glaring at him. "Now, just let me tell you that you have this all wrong. There are five of you and one of me, right? Well, I think you got the math wrong."

One of the hoods broke a bottle on the edge of a table. "We'll cut you up and send you 'ome in a box, nigger. I'm first. I'm gonna cut your nose off. Then my mates are gonna throw you out the window."

"Ah, I don't think so." Wilson waved his free hand across the tables nearby. "Would all my swim buddies please stand up?"

With a scraping of chairs, the four standing punks were suddenly looking at fourteen SEALs, all of whom—with the exception of Wilson—were moving very slowly, some forward, and some sliding around behind the locals. For good measure, the eight SAS faculty members slowly rose from their seats when MacPherson said, "Is this a private party or can we play, too?" The punks looked around, and were suddenly sober. Crashing over each other, they ran through the door. Wilson let go of the one he was holding, and assisted him out the door with a very hard kick in the tail.

After that, the evening was all downhill. MacPherson introduced Cully and his team to an unholy game called "pint or point." As far as Cully could remember, his SEALs and the SAS faculty had more or less destroyed the pub by trying to see who was the most accurate knife thrower. If you missed the target, you drank a pint of the local brew. Cully recalled missing a half dozen or so throws, and very little else.

MacPherson sounded perversely chipper. "This is the fun part, if you lads are still up to it. Mr. O'Bannon and the other two of you who have been here before know what's coming." He grinned even more widely. Cully thought, *Oh, God. Not today. Not . . .* and groaned aloud.

"Righto, Cully. As the final stage of your training with us, we're going rope riding this morning, and we'll make a few forced entries to our practice building before lunch." MacPherson smiled, and all fourteen SEALs all looked at him with the same expression. Master Chief Wilson muttered. "If he means what I think he means, this guy is nuts."

For the SEALs, helicopters were something that you were usually flying in or jumping out of. Fast-roping out of helos was standard fare in attacking almost any ship or inserting from the roof of a building. Actually, fast-roping was kind of fun, unless you were the first guy out. He usually fell and made a soft landing pad for the guys who followed.

For the SAS, helos were also something you hung out of on ropes at high speed, and were then flung into targets. It was a dangerous, cold way to travel, but for putting people on or into a building where hostages were held, it proved highly effective. The SEALs had done it all before, but each new training stint with the SAS brought some dangerous new variation on the theme.

Cully's team drew their equipment and followed MacPherson out to the flight line. The platoon had been at the SAS school outside Hereford for ten days. They were scheduled to rotate back to the States in two more days.

"Mac, have you people figured out what happens if the helo jock misses the assigned height by just a couple of feet?"

"It's perfectly simple, really. Whoever is at the end of the rope goes into a wall at about thirty knots. Not a good way to start the day."

"Great," said Cully. He looked around and saw a welcome sight. "TA, have you figured this shit out yet?"

Atkins smiled. "No way, Cully. But I've figured out enough to know that I'm a lot smarter than you fellas, 'cause I get to stay in the chopper. I'm just learning to fly you clowns around while you dangle below. I've been here before. Believe me, it's a piece of cake."

"Tommy, I think you're going native on me." He turned to the platoon. "Okay, everyone into the first two helos. Wilson and me with pairs three and four in Mr. Atkins's ship. The other four pairs in the other bird with Forbes as lead. Standard split, guys. Make it good."

Cully turned to see his favorite SAS man jump in the bird ahead of him. "You going along for the ride, Captain?"

The young, slim man they all called "the Rajah" smiled back at him. "Yes, Mr. O'Bannon, I always like to see the best of our students go through their paces. I like to watch your bunch as well."

The Rajah was Captain Rajiv Singh, SAS. His Oxford background showed in his speech, and all his wealthy parents could do politically wasn't enough to keep him out of Her Majesty's Special Air Service. Their son the doctor had turned out much to their disappointment, his skills with a knife having nothing to do with those of a surgeon. Nevertheless, he still had all his uniforms, even his BDUs, tailored on Savile Row.

The Rajah was the fastest man Cully had ever seen. He was also the chief unarmed combat instructor at the SAS school. And he could do things with a knife that could only be described as artwork, unless you were on the receiving end. Cully grinned.

"Raj, can you spend another hour with me before we leave? I need some more help with that sliding move you were showing me."

"Not to fear, Cully. I'll drop the inscrutable Oriental act long enough to teach you properly. By the time you leave here, you'll all be moving like the Rajah."

All four helos lifted off the pad together and formed a circle, twenty meters apart and fifty meters up. As the crew chief on each chopper started unwinding the wire-cored rope on the electric winch, a SEAL or SAS man put his foot in a stirrup-like loop and was lowered until four men were dangling from each side of each chopper.

Cully looked up at Wilson's boot soles. "You ready, Chief?"

Wilson shouted down. "Boss, I've been in this business for twenty years, and I've stayed alive by avoiding shit like this. Yeah, I'm ready."

Going slowly over the moor, they went over a low hill and saw the practice building coming up at eleven o'clock. They had all practiced in this and other shooting rooms in the United Kingdom. It was just like the SEALs' shooting rooms back in Little Creek and San Diego, but much bigger. Instead of just one room, it was made to look like a small house, with two rooms downstairs and three on the second floor. The difference between it and a typical suburban house was that it was made of used automobile tires filled with sand. The tire-and-sand walls made a very effective trap for small arms bullets, which were frequently flying around within them.

As with any hostage rescue practice, the rooms had an assortment of life-sized paper targets. Some were hostages, the rest were hostage takers. The point of the drill was to shoot all the bad guys without shooting the good guys or others taking part in the rescue. The only shots that counted were the ones in an eight-inch circle on the heads and chests of the bad guys. A shot anywhere on a hostage target counted.

As they came up to the target, Cully pulled back the slide of his MK-5 9mm submachine gun, a short, ugly gun built by Heckler & Koch specially for the SEALs and the SAS. Quite simply it was the best light machine gun in the world. It locked open with a click, and he looked out to see the target.

As they got still closer to the target, the helicopter seemed to rock back, causing Cully to swing back like the pendulum of a clock. As he swung forward again, the helicopter was practically on top of the building. He swung through the opening where a window should have been, grabbing the wire-cored rope with his right hand and shooting two of the terrorist targets with the machine pistol in his left hand. He held the rope tightly while Wilson slid in the window and leveled his gun at the targets as well. From there on it was standard stuff. Kicking doors in and shooting bad guy targets. The other parts of the team came in through other windows and doors and it seemed like the whole exercise was over as soon as it started. As soon as they finished, MacPherson loaded them all back into the helos for another run, and then went back to the armorers to set up for a third.

"Hey, Cully. Can I give the fellas a coupla new toys for their next run?" Cully and MacPherson turned to see a short, husky man with close-cropped blond hair walking toward them. Cully turned to MacPherson. "Mac, have you met Steve Lemoyne of H&K?"

"If you mean the kind gent that makes all our best small arms, yes I have. Where do you think he gets all his good ideas? Very pleased to see you again, sir."

"Please call me Steve. I was just in the neighborhood. Thought you'd like to try out a small experiment of mine." He reached into a small case and brought out a very large handgun.

"Watch and learn, guys. This is our experimental model of the new special ops offensive pistol. As you can see, we've gone back to the old .45 ACP, with a few extras, like the laser sight and the big trigger guard so you can shoot with heavy gloves."

"Like diving gloves," Cully said as he hefted the new gun. "How many, Steve?"

"Twelve in the magazine, and one up the pipe. If you mean how many of these do we have, precisely fifteen right now. We're waiting for the big guys to give us the go-ahead for more."

"I guess it's a coincidence that there're fourteen men in a SEAL platoon and that leaves one for you."

"Would I do something like that?"

"I think you'd take a twenty-foot dive into a glass of water if you thought it would help us. Okay, guys, everybody stack the Berettas here. We'll try it again with the new shooter." And they did. This time, all the holes in the paper targets were much bigger. And closer together.

They came back to Lemoyne. "Steve, can we hang on to these for a while?"

"Sure. By mere coincidence, I have a few cases of ammo for you in the truck. Don't worry, it's the good subsonic stuff. You might also find a new holster rig for each of you, and a couple extra mags. I'll see the armorer gets 'em." He smiled, almost to himself, and walked away whistling tunelessly.

"Last shoot of the day, Cully?"

"Lead on, Mac."

After the last shoot, Cully and the team met MacPherson outside. They were feeling pretty cocky, but MacPherson was having none of it. "Seventy-two seconds, Mr. O'Bannon, and one hostage killed by our own men. Pretty good, but not quite up to SAS standards." Cully gave MacPherson his best shitty grin. "Mac, it's a lot easier to do when there's real people involved. You want to try it again?"

MacPherson grinned and slapped Cully on the back. "No, lad," he said, "let's head for the barn. We need some sandwiches and a little talk with the armorers before we try this again. I want you to try it again later without the flash-bangs. You have to be a bit quicker without them."

"We'll try it however you'd like. You ever try that with a pump shotgun?"

"Me lad, we've tried it with everything including brass knuckles. Let's get a beer. I know another game I'd like to show you. No, really. It's very different from pint or point."

They walked together back to the choppers and in a few minutes were back at the base.

30 March
0930 Hours
Portpatrick, Scotland

"Welcome, Madame Prime Minister. We're very honored that you and Mr. Tournier have chosen this site for your meeting."

Peter Bruckner was at his best. His small country hotel in the remote corner of Scotland had been chosen for a meeting of two of the most powerful leaders of the world. Sheltered from the mainland by three surrounding cliffs and facing out to the Irish Sea, Portpatrick Lodge was the smallest and most exclusive resort in all the United Kingdom. It had quite a history of its own. Its secluded, beautiful setting made it a favorite secret meeting place for Churchill during the Battle of Britain. Now, a small wealthy clientele usually filled its ten guest rooms and dined in the five-star dining salon.

"Thank you, Peter. It is a pleasure to be back. I hope the crowd we might attract does not damage the image of your private little resort."

"No danger of that, I'm sure, madam. There have been more than enough secret state meetings here. It is a relief not to have that concern. Your talks with Mr. Tournier about the economic union will, I hope, be productive."

"I hope so, too, Peter. Mr. Tournier and I seem to get on quite well. We'll be at it for two days. That's about as long as I can stand meeting with anyone."

"The rest of your party will be accommodated in the third story. You and Mr. Tournier have the second floor to yourselves," said Bruckner.

"Thank you very much, Peter, I'm sure it will be excellent as usual." She gave him her best TV smile. "It's not often we seek such a level of privacy, but I'm sure you understand what we are doing."

"Indeed I do, ma'am, and we will make every effort to accommodate any needs you may have. After your meetings perhaps you and the prime minister would like to sample a couple of our single malts. I think my collection is comparable to any in the world."

"Thanks, we just might do it."

Bruckner nodded and excused himself, thinking, *What a tough job she has for herself. But then she's not known as Old Iron Pants for nothing.*

Both Britain and France had enormous stakes in the outcome of these discussions, as did most of the rest of Europe and their trading partners. The newly reunited Germany had as much at stake, but the British distrusted Germany after the Bundesbank's 1992 attack on the British banks. That incident had cost John Major the prime ministership. His successor was a woman much like his predecessor, Margaret Thatcher. Evelyn Broughton was tougher and smarter than anyone expected her to be behind her innocent, schoolmarm looks. Over six feet tall, even her friends called her "Big Ev." Her enemies called her "Son of Thatcher." One tough lady, indeed.

Broughton's security chief, Charles Digby, was walking the grounds for the umpteenth time. Bruckner saw him and crossed the broad lawn to catch him.

"Mr. Digby, I trust my staff is making things easier for you?"

"Oh, no problems, Mr. Bruckner."

"Then why the troubled look?"

"No special reason, sir. It's my business to be worried. I can't help thinking that across that twenty miles of water is Belfast."

"But the prime minister should not be a target, should she?"

"Mr. Brueckner, you may not have been following the news, but Mrs. Broughton has thrown the IRA out of the peace process. She gave them an ultimatum to lay down their arms before we would talk to them."

"So you expect them to make an attempt on her here?"

"Hardly. But there are so many others who could as well. I'm telling you more than you should know, but as you've asked, there are more terrorists now than there ever have been. And we now have a new kind of terrorist."

"How is that?"

"We have been told by our own intelligence people and even the Americans have picked this up. Many of the most highly trained of the Soviet soldiery are now turning mercenary. And that includes freelancing as terrorists for hire. They really are very good, and make a very formidable adversary for us."

"Mr. Digby, if you mean to frighten me, you have succeeded. I assure you, if Mrs. Broughton were not here already, I would ask her to not come."

Digby chuckled. "It's not as bad as that, Mr. Bruckner. We can handle anything that might come along. And I can tell you truthfully that we have absolutely no indication that this meeting is threatened in any way. Our intelligence people are very good. We almost always know of a threat before it comes to pass."

Five Miles Away
Portpatrick Village
1105 Hours

Moving from the elegance of Portpatrick Lodge to the rustic Portpatrick Hotel in the village was no treat, but the new guest didn't mind. He was quiet and did not wish to impose or be imposed upon. He had arrived a few days before, having walked the countryside from the lodge with his two bags slung over his shoulders. He had made many harder marches over the years. He looked comfortable and almost could pass as a British tourist, with the Barbour jacket and the turtleneck.

His broad face, high cheek bones, and slightly swarthy complexion bespoke an Asian heritage, but no one inquired. He mused that the Scots were the perfect hosts. If you wished to talk, they would talk from sunup to sundown and only pause for a dram of whiskey. If a man wanted to be left alone, they would leave him alone and take no offense. The new guest had said he was seeking a refuge from the stress of daily life, and wished to be in the quietest corner of the hotel. The manager had obliged him, and word passed quickly throughout the staff that the new guest was a quiet one who should be left alone.

The new guest registered as "Mr. Adjani," a businessman from Crete. He went to his room as soon as he had checked in, closed the door, and only came out to take a meal or walk along the cliffs.

Adjani was the name on the Greek passport in his pocket. In one of the hidden pockets of his big bag, there were four other passports: one French, one Spanish, one Turkish, and one Russian. The Russian passport was the only one with his real name. Yuri Ivanovich Petrov. It showed many ports of entry around the world. It did not show his former military rank of major or his former Spetznaz unit flash. The latter had been tattooed on his left shoulder, and erased crudely after the fall of 1989.

Also hidden in the bag were three cell phones, each usable anywhere in the United Kingdom or on the continent. And the Makarov automatic, with several extra magazines. And one Spetznaz-issue ballistic knife. This was a particularly nasty item, designed to throw a knife blade with bullet-like speed. It had a range of only twenty feet, but was exceedingly lethal in the right hands. Few people in the world could recognize it, and fewer still knew how to use it.

Six days later, Petrov was still roaming the cliffs, using his cell phones to make arrangements to put his plan in motion. He put the phone back into his pocket and looked down at Portpatrick lodge from his perch on the northern cliff side. His near-perfect sketch of the lodge, made in his room during the casual afternoons at the lodge, was spread on a rock by his left hand. He leaned against it, anchoring it from the wind. All three floors of the lodge were shown in meticulous detail, especially the windows and doors.

His planning of the operation was as slow and meticulous as his sketching of the hotel had been. He had made the walk from the village several times. It relaxed him, and gave him a chance to think his plan through. The French and English security forces were professionals, but there were only a handful, and they were totally unequipped to handle what he was about to throw at them.

His team was all well equipped, in place, and on time. That was nothing new for any of them. Former KGB or Spetznaz, like himself, they had all gone freelance when the Soviets had been bankrupted out of the evil empire business.

After walking about a half mile along the cliff, Petrov saw the landmark of the castle ruins ahead. The rest of his team was waiting there for him. About two hundred feet above the beach, the three stone walls of what once had been Dunskey Castle rose alongside the path used by hundreds of summer tourists. March was too early for tourists, so it became a perfect meeting place for Petrov's men.

There were twenty-three of them. Some had been with him in the West before. Their specialties were all in "wet work," as their KGB bosses had called it. Wet work was the kind that left blood on the walls. Others had been with him in Afghanistan, where the wet work was called combat, but it involved a lot of things other than fighting soldiers. Such as wiping out whole villages suspected of helping the Mujaheddin guerrillas who were resisting the Soviets.

The rain was light, and the cold was not cold by his standards. Dunskey Castle lacked both a fourth wall and a roof, but it would do. As Petrov turned from the main path to the castle, he saw his "client" walking out to meet him.

The client looked a bit like Petrov himself. Short, stocky, but florid-faced, the man looked quite at home in the Scottish drizzle. It was so much like his native Ireland that the difference was not worth mentioning. The man's face was partly concealed by the hood of his Barbour jacket, but Petrov knew Bobby Craighan by his walk. He limped from a wound suffered in the British ambush that had captured his two brothers. "Petrov, is everything set?"

"Of course it is Mr. Craighan. Our group will go in at about 3 A.M., and we should have the whole place under control three minutes later."

"But they will be prepared. They may know that you're coming. They expect assassins."

"Yes, but we are not assassins. And they do not know unless you told them." Petrov looked into Craighan's eyes. It was always possible. Was Craighan sending them into a trap?

"They may be prepared for a fanatic with a gun or a car bomb. Their security people have never faced an assault by a force like mine."

"Yes, yes, Petrov. I have heard your speech about the nobility of the Spetznaz soldier. But the truth is that you're just a bunch of starving, out-of-luck boyos like the IRA."

"No, Craighan. You have no idea. I was Spetznaz. For twenty years I wore the uniform of the proudest soldiers in the world. In Afghanistan, in Cuba, in Argentina. But when the Berlin Wall fell, they cast us out."

"Cast you out as the Brits cast us out from the homes we own, from our churches, and from our birthright."

"No again, Craighan. This was no outsider, no colonialists like the English. It was our own govenment who did this to us. They did not simply take away our homes. We were left to starve. We had no pay, no supplies, no food. At first we stole from the local people. Then there was no more left to steal. But we had seen the wealth of the West almost everywhere we went in the world. And then a man came, Craighan. A man like you who said he would pay us to do the jobs we had been so proud to do for our country.

"Now we work for you, and others like you. But we are not you. You will die for your cause with a smile on your face. We will fight because you pay us."

Craighan looked at Petrov again. His face was twisted into a wolfish grin. Craighan blinked.

"Good, good. Remember, do not pull your people out until you get my message that my brothers are free. In the meantime, you must hold them. Even if a rescue is mounted, you must hold them. If they die before my brothers are free, you will fail and the Provisional Wing will not pay the rest of your fee."

Petrov smiled. "You do your part and leave ours to us, Craighan. If we succeed and you do not pay, I will kill you and your brothers."

At Portpatrick Lodge

Charles Digby was not a happy man. He could and did put up with the whims of the PM, her family, or even of the queen herself. Being chief of security for Britain's leaders was often frustrating, but nothing compared with this. For two weeks, British and French security commanders had been meeting and deciding the arrangements for this meeting. But, as usual, when the French actually showed up, they wanted to change everything. Digby wanted a stomach powder. What he got was Jacques Milert, his French counterpart.

"My friend, you look ill. Please be assured that all is safe here. As you said yourself, this must be the most defensible position in all of the United Kingdom"

"Jacques, it's not whether we are defensible that bothers me. We are on short details here. Now your man wants everyone withdrawn to the back house where the staff lives. I'm sorry, but two of our people will be near the PM at all times."

"Very well, my friend, but you should know—Monsieur Tournier will insist that everyone be pulled back at the time of the meetings. He is very concerned that the results of these meetings not get into the press too soon."

"All right, Jacques, let's go back inside and look at what we have." Digby put his arm around the other man's shoulder, and the two walked down the drive, turning right to enter the main door of the lodge.

What they saw would please any visitor. The long main hall was flanked on the left by a dining room, a sitting room, and the front desk, behind which was the kitchen and the door to the driveway. On the right were two sitting rooms, in one of which was an ornate bar, and the stair to the second floor. All the sitting rooms had fireplaces burning warmly.

On the second floor, the front suites looking out to sea had been reserved for the two prime ministers. Their immediate staffs were quartered on the floor above, with two rooms at the back of the second floor occupied by communications and security teams. The other staff had taken over two more rooms, and the rest of the security details housed in the owner's house behind the main lodge. There were only the front, side, and rear entrances. The long, wide lawn sloped down nearly one hundred meters to the narrow, rocky beach.

Petrov looked over the cliff from the castle ruin to see the boats and equipment his men had assembled. As midnight approached, they would start off. Ten would head over land by van, coming down the narrow gravel road behind the lodge. Another dozen would come in by sea, swimming up to the beach. Petrov would retrace his steps along the cliffs to the path above the lodge. They would, of course, all attack at once. The meager security details posted by the French and British would be overwhelmed in seconds.

As darkness fell, they spent their time preparing the equipment. The swimmers, clad in dry suits and full scuba gear, would go at midnight. The overland party with Petrov would go at 1:30 A.M., and the van would leave last, at about 2 A.M.

The afternoon turned into evening, and the evening wore on quickly. For the security men outside, the sunset into the mist over the Irish Sea was a sight to warm the coldest of hearts. At 11 P.M., Digby took a final turn around the lodge. Big Ev and Tournier were safely ensconced in the right-hand sitting room off the bar, having finished a meal Michèle had been preparing for days. Shellfish lightly sautéed and served in a sauce made from their shells. Salmon poached in bouillon. In all, seven courses found their way in front of the two PMs, who finished off a bottle of champagne and a bottle of fine Bordeaux before retiring for coffee in the sitting room.

Bruckner stopped in for a final check on his famous visitors. "May I offer either of you a nightcap?"

Broughton turned to him, and gave a small polite smile. "I suppose you have something in mind."

"I do indeed, Madam Prime Minister. There were a great many fine single malts laid down in the 1960s, but two were very special indeed. May I suggest a wee dram of the '64 Black Bowmore or the Glen Rothes '68?"

"Well, trot them out and we'll have a look."

Bruckner brought out a tray with two crystal snifters, and two bottles of what appeared to be dark rum. "The Black Bowmore is my favorite. May I pour?'

"When in Rome, I suppose. Go ahead, Peter, you choose for us," said the French PM.

Bruckner poured two drams from the dark bottle. He picked one up and held it up to the light. It sparkled like a gemstone, seeming to generate its own heat and light. "I'm sure this will not disappoint you. Please accept my thanks again for choosing our lodge for your meeting." He bowed out of the room, and the two leaders continued to talk into the night, the warmth of the whiskey combining with the firelight to make each seem more reasonable to the other.

"A remarkable whiskey, Madam Prime Minister."

"Thank you, Monsieur. The wine you brought for our dinner was equally remarkable. We will continue this in the morning session?"

"Yes, madame. I think we are so close now that we can perhaps finish early enough for some golf in the afternoon."

"It will be a pleasure." Big Ev turned to the stairs and went to her suite, confident only that she could beat him at golf. But could she get a real agreement, or would it be just another agreement to talk further?

By 2:15 A.M. Petrov had managed to conceal himself atop the hill directly behind the lodge. The others would be in place soon, and if all was ready, they would go in early. He was satisfied. The last lights were out in the lodge, and only two spotlights lit the grounds outside. He could see clearly the three French and one British security men strolling around the front and two sides of the lodge. No one patrolled the back, which was covered from the staff house. He kept his night vision goggles connected to the binoculars and scanned the sea. He knew he could never see them coming, but then again the British and French security men couldn't, either. Five minutes and they would be ready.

Digby awoke instantly when his radio beeped once. "Who the bloody hell could be coming in this late?" he thought. He threw on his pants and a jacket and walked out of the staff house in time to see a large van come down the gravel road toward the lodge and stop at the security checkpoint.

The Frenchman manning the post lit a cigarette slowly and sauntered up to the van. He saw a dark bearded face of a very large man. As he raised his flashlight to the driver's face, the man inside rolled his window down. The face looking out from the van looked nothing like the local populace. It was a huge face with many scars. The man grinned as he swung the sawed-off shotgun up from his lap and fired both barrels into the Frenchman's face.

"Attack on PM, attack on PM. This is Cheshire One. We have an emergency." Digby screamed into his handset as he ran through the back door into the lodge. The other security men, all five of them, were already clustered around the two heads of state. Digby charged in. "Out the front with them. Take cover in the rocks by the beach."

They all ran down the stairs, three men leading with guns drawn. At the same time, the van screeched to a halt behind the lodge, and the first ten of Petrov's group split up, five going into the staff house and five into the main lodge.

The first two into the lodge were killed by the third French security man, who in turn fell to a burst from a Russian who had thrown himself atop the two bodies ahead of him.

Digby had Big Ev by the arm and was running out the back door, half dragging her, half blocking her from whatever stray fire he could imagine. "Mayday, mayday, mayday. All security, this is Cheshire One. We have an attack on PM. Where is everyone?"

Petrov smiled from his post atop the hill. The small radio jammer he had brought worked well, he thought, and Digby's cries for help would never be heard beyond the house. He saw the group with the two prime ministers in tow run out of the back of the house just as the swimmers finished dropping their fins and charged toward the lodge. In another moment, Digby and two others were dead. The lone security man had raised his pistol to fire when Evelyn Broughton brought her hand down on it. "Not now, son," she said. "We'll live to fight another day."

One of the divers came up to her, looking her up and down like a bidder examining a calf at a cattle auction. He said nothing to her, just casually swung his weapon up, shooting the young man between the eyes. "You will, he won't."

Petrov smiled and turned back up the path toward Portpatrick. He would hike back there and be safe in bed before any of the hotel staff noted his absence. After breakfast, there would be more for the tourists to see. One of the divers, an Afghani called Abdul, spoke to the two leaders, still staring at the body on the grass at their feet. "It is a privilege to meet you both. I must ask you to go back to the house immediately. I expect we shall have company shortly."

Broughton and Tournier turned and walked slowly back to the lodge.

There was a security backup team in Portpatrick, and despite Petrov's jammers, they had heard Digby's cry for help and put out an alert before launching their group's small helicopter to race to the lodge. The chopper slowed to a hover as it rounded the curve made by the north cliff. The pilot keyed his radio to what had been Digby's frequency.

"Cheshire 1, this is Forward. What is your situation?"

The pilot inched around the face of the cliff as daylight started coming up over the lodge in front of him. As he moved forward, trying the query signal, he was suddenly silhouetted by the spotlight Petrov's men had moved to the base of the cliff. As he pulled back to climb out of the light, his ship was hit square in the center by a shoulder-fired missile. A second later, it was a small burning pile on the beach.

The captives were herded into the sitting room near the main stair. Broughton and Tournier were still in their nightclothes, and wet from the dash to the beach. Broughton turned to the man nearest her. He was at least six feet, six inches, and had to weigh 300 pounds. But it was his face that was so unusual. His head, even for so large a man, seemed outsized. His face was an enormous oval. It was a caricature of the man in the moon.

"You, there," said the prime minister. "I have no intention of staying here in my dressing gown all night. I will wash and get some clothes on. You may follow if you wish."

"I don't wish, but he will," said the giant. He gestured with the machine pistol which hung around his neck. "Abdul, take the lady upstairs. Search her luggage carefully and allow her to dress. Bring any papers you find to me. Hazak, you do the same with Monsieur Tournier."

"So, you are spies as well as thugs. You'll find little of value in these papers."

"All the same, madame, we will take them."

Abdul, a scruffy-looking thin man, made an exaggerated bow to Broughton and pointed her up the stairs. She walked slowly, thinking as hard and fast as she could. All of the training she had had now had to be used.

She entered her room, one of two on the second floor facing out on the Irish Sea. "If you wish, go ahead and search my clothes. You won't find any weapons."

The thin man tossed her clothes on the floor, slit open the linings of the suitcases, and stalked back out, carrying her briefcase and wallet. Broughton huffily closed the door behind him.

For a sixtyish schoolmarm, the lady could move. As soon as the door closed, the water went on in the sink and Broughton dumped her cosmetics on the counter. She grabbed a pair of blue sweat pants and a sweatshirt that said "Oxford" on the front. There were three lipsticks among the makeup, a large number for a woman who seldom wore it. She slipped one into her right pants pocket, and another into a pocket in the sweatshirt. She reached for a pair of athletic shoes and lifted the inner sole over the heel of one. Under it she found the switch she was looking for. It turned 180 degrees clockwise. She returned the inner sole to its original position and put the shoe on. It would give her an edge, for at least twenty-four hours.

When the alert helo had taken off and not reported back at the required three-minute intervals, an alert had been sounded throughout the United Kingdom. The forces converging on Portpatrick were coming from every direction and distance. The rescue helo from Portpatrick was missing, Digby was off the air, and everyone assumed the worst. One aircraft commander had the advantage of some extremely sensitive electronic sensors. The RAF Canberra ECM aircraft was old and slow, but its equipment wasn't. The flight to Portpatrick had taken only thirty-five minutes. It orbited at less than 20,000 feet above the lodge, unseen and unheard. Its pilot was busy mapping the precise coordinates of the lodge, the beach, and the rear staff house with the airborne GPS. The map was so detailed, it was accurate to within one meter. His work was being transmitted back to several RAF bases in real time. The chief engineer smiled as he picked up the signal.

"Good girl, Ev," he whispered to himself. He turned on his intercom to relay to the pilot. "Sir, we have the PM's rescue beacon. It's strong, coming from the front of the building, probably the second floor. We can pinpoint her pretty easily when the time comes." The aircraft stayed in a loose orbit around the lodge, looking and listening, undetected.

By 8 A.M., the captives and the captors had made themselves comfortable in the dining room. Having nothing else to do, Michèle Botetort produced a breakfast of kippered herring, porridge, fried eggs, and fresh biscuits. It was a cardiologist's nightmare, but seemed to restore Broughton and the other captives. Even more the Man in the Moon seemed to be enjoying himself.

"Now we can begin the game." He pushed the table back and gestured for the telephone. He dialed quickly, having memorized the number of the CNN bureau in London. He soon found himself talking to a very confused night editor who was just about to end her shift.

"You heard me right. We are the Afghani Liberation Army, and we have both Madame Broughton and Mr. Tournier hostage. If our demands are not met by noon tomorrow, we will kill them both."

"Of course, sir. And I'm Mahatma Gandhi."

The huge man shoved the phone into Broughton's face. "Speak to them, and make them believe you or, or—" He looked around the room. His eye fell on one of the serving girls. He pointed his machine pistol at her head. "Or I will shoot her now."

Broughton took the phone. "Whom am I speaking to, please? Well, Miss Carstairs, I am Evelyn Broughton. You must recognize my voice. . . . I know someone could imitate me, but you call 10 Downing Street right now. The number is Whitehall 06275. Yes, that's my private office. It will be answered. You ask the duty officer where I am, and tell him I asked you to verify it. Yes, I'll hold."

Big Ev was already growing tired of the game. When the call came back, it was a three-way call, and her military aide, Admiral Charles, was on the line. "Admiral, we have a bit of an emergency."

"That's enough," said the huge man, grabbing the phone back. "Now you know what I say is true. By noon tomorrow, the following demands shall be met.

"First, all British troops will withdraw from Northern Ireland. Second, all political prisoners, including all members of the Abu Nidal group captured last month, will be released from French jails. Third, all members of the Provisional IRA held in British jails will be released. That is final. We will not negotiate." He hung up the phone and turned back to another helping of kippers and fried eggs.

30 March
0822 Hours

Cully reached for another huge scone. The pastries were supposed to be saved for tea at 4 P.M., but they never lasted that long. "Mac, the grub you guys serve is better every time we come here."

"It's all a put-on for you Yanks," MacPherson smiled. "We plan to raise the rent, so we may as well give you good eats."

Cully started to respond, but MacPherson's beeper went off, and his face changed to all business. "Excuse me for a minute, old boy." He got up and ran for the telephone.

Ten minutes later, the entire SAS group and the SEALs were in a briefing room. They could hardly believe their ears. The British naval captain was talking fast, and making all too much sense.

"All we know is that the PM and the French PM, Tournier, have been taken by a group that has already killed about a dozen people. Some of them came in by this van." The overhead projector showed the blurred image of the white van.

"Apparently, some came in another way. They are very heavily armed, with automatic weapons and probably at least one heavy machine gun, or some other antiaircraft weapon. These fellows aren't doing this on the cheap. They shot down the helo carrying a relief team shortly after the initial assault. At this time, there has been no decision on action, but as a precaution this unit will be moved by helo to RAF Prestwick in five minutes. They have demanded the release of political prisoners—meaning the Abu Nidal terrorists the French just bagged—and an agreement keeping Britain and France out of the EEC treaty, which is quite strange because the French are already in. Recon flights are on the scene, and more are being launched now. We have architectural plans of the lodge coming in from Edinburgh by fax in the next few minutes. Questions?"

Cully couldn't stay still. "Sir, have you received any orders for us?"

"No, Mr. O'Bannon. Your team may accompany our SAS team to Prestwick if you desire, but if there's a go, it's something you'll have to watch. The helos to carry you to Prestwick will lift off in three minutes. Your armorers and intelligence team will meet you there. Right, gentlemen."

Cully froze Wilson with a look. "Chief, I'm gonna get on the secure radio and get through to SOCOM. You get everybody in the choppers with a full load-out, and get ahold of Atkins. Tell him we need him, and we need him *now*. This ain't practice any more."

With an over-the-shoulder "Aye, aye, boss," Wilson ran off. Cully looked at the short man's broad back. He had been carried on it once, after a Bosnian Serb sharpshooter had hit him square in the chest. The kevlar vest had saved his life, but the shock of the blow left him unable to walk out of the line of fire, so Wilson had carried him. Wilson was always there.

Wilson was already with the platoon when Cully joined it. He had his twenty in the Navy, and maybe a few more. Wilson's story came out in bits and pieces over coffee, on long flights all around the world. He had grown up poor, fatherless, black and uneducated in the Bronx, a tough part of New York by anybody's measure. He was on the fast track to nowhere when his mother insisted he get a part-time job. The local hardware store was a place where several kids from his high school worked from time to time. It was family-run, and the boss was a gruff old bastard who carried a gun every day.

Wilson grew to trust the grumpy old man, as many had before him. By the time he had worked there a month, the old man knew Wilson's troubles and how badly he needed something to break him out of the mold closing around him. He came in one day after spending a night without sleep, helping his mother sober up one more time. His little sister had moved to his aunt's apartment long before. But Wilson was at the end of his rope. Usually talkative, he changed. His enthusiasm for work turned to a sullen, hostile attitude. After a few days of this, the old man stood in front of Wilson and pointed him to the one chair that stood behind the counter. Wilson sat.

"What say, Rome? How you doin' today?" Wilson's name was Romeo, but he insisted on being called Rome.

"Dunno, Mr. R. I can't do this no more. Looks like I gotta quit."

"What are you sayin', man? You quittin' school, too?"

"I guess so. I gotta stay home an take care of my momma. She in bad shape."

"How you gonna do that? No job, no nothin'."

"I guess we'll go on welfare and I'll stay home wit' her."

"Bad choice, Rome. Your momma won't get better just because you're there. What if I tol' you about another choice?"

"There ain't no other choice, Mr. R. My grandma is at home takin' care of momma every day as it is. My aunt Jan comes over about every other day to help out. But I just gotta be there."

"No, Rome, you don't. You're about to quit here and join that gang I heard you talking about, right?"

"Yeah, but wit' them I can do somethin' for my momma. Make some money an' pay da rent, man."

"Wrong again. We're goin down the street. Come with me, son. We're gonna get you straightened out right now."

The office two blocks down was small, and the gunnery sergeant sitting behind the desk looked at them with amusement. "Got another one for us, Mr. R?"

"Yeah, gunny. This one's navy if I read him right."

The big man with the short hair had more stripes on his arm than Wilson had ever seen in the movies. "Awright, son. How do you want to deal with your problems? Just what do you want to do with your life?" he asked in a low rumbling voice. Wilson thought it sounded like a subway train coming down the tunnel.

"I don't got no problems, man. I can do alright without you or Mr. R."

"When you speak to me you say, 'yes, sergeant' or 'no, sergeant,' and give me a straight answer, son." The train was rumbling right into him.

"Easy, Tony. Rome here needs to break away from a bad situation. I think you can help."

"If you mean I should join up, you're both crazy. I gotta stay home an' help wit' my momma."

"An' join a gang an' get in trouble an' wind up in jail. No way, Rome." The old man was fired up. "What you need is a good job, which will teach you self-respect, give you a way out of the mess you're in, and maybe pay your way through college."

As Wilson later told Cully, "I sat there figuring that there were two ways out of the ghetto, and I couldn't play basketball worth a shit. So I joined, and I still send half of my paycheck home every time. My momma died two years later, but I helped my sister get through college. There was no way I was goin' back into that shitty mess. Mr. R. saved me from that. I owe him and the navy everything I have."

Rome Wilson had "raised" several young SEAL platoon commanders. He thought of Cully as he had thought of the others—a little brother to be taught and protected. That same thought occurred to Wilson again as he gathered the SEALs and their gear. He found Atkins, too. TA was already preflighting the helo he had flown earlier in the day in exercises. Now he was checking weapons, not just the comm gear.

RAF Prestwick
0840 Hours

RAF Prestwick may be the most beautiful base the RAF has anywhere, located just off the coastal highway north of Portpatrick. Normally, the sea birds and the wind are the only sounds when air operations aren't going on, and they hadn't happened often in recent days. But by the time the first Viscount transport landed with the SAS equipment and two more came into the control pattern, the sleepy base was covered with people rushing in and organizing command centers, munitions, a seemingly endless variety of aircraft from the Viscounts to fighters, and two ungainly looking aircraft, which looked like bombers, but had just landed after hovering motionless over the taxiway. Wherever it went, the Sea Harrier looked out of place.

But the men climbing out of the Harriers looked very much at home. Both were test pilots, and both had service in the Falklands. Their real specialty was wrestling the Harrier into a low, fast run to put ordnance in places where the laws of physics say it shouldn't be able to go. They, and their Royal Navy flight suits were a familiar sight to the SAS team, who knew them well from endless hours of training together. The two pilots tossed their helmets to the waiting crew and ran into the briefing room.

Overhead, the choppers from the SAS school were closing on Prestwick. Cully had a large backpack in front of him, with a satellite phone sending coded microwaves through a navy satellite back to Little Creek. On the other end of the line was Captain Schaeffer.

"No way, Cully. No authorization from the boss. It's the Brits' show, and the French are already rasing hell about waiting for their group to deploy."

"But sir, the French can't get here for another day at least. The SAS wants to go in this afternoon or midnight at the latest. They need us. Can't we ask again?"

"Mr. O'Bannon, you have your answer. Foxtrot platoon is to observe only. If we get a special request from the British, CINCLANT will take it up to the president. But for now, stay out of the operation and do not, I say again, do not intervene."

"Aye, aye, sir. Foxtrot out."

Cully took off his headset and threw it down in disgust. "How do you like that, master chief? We're gonna watch. We got a front-row seat, but the orders are to stay out of it. They're gonna let this thing go down without us."

Wilson shrugged. "Boss, I think sitting this out is probably a good idea. Too many cooks stirring the pot. If the SAS gets to go in, I'm bettin' the Frenchies will be right in the middle. It'll be a real goat rope."

The helos touched down. Cully and Wilson saw to the off-loading of the team and their equipment. "Chief, go to the armorers and get everything Lemoyne gave us, and our regular stuff, too. Then have everybody join us in the briefing room. Maybe they'll change their minds." He turned and trotted to the briefing room where the intelligence team had set up aerial photos of the lodge, as well as a blow-up of the interior and floor plans.

A British Army colonel was briefing the SAS team, which was gathered around MacPherson in a tight half circle. "We expect to go ahead in six hours, but we may have to move it up if they start knocking the hostages around. Efforts to open negotiation with the terrorists have failed so far. Their leader, who has spoken to reporters by phone, has a Middle Eastern accent, probably Afghani. We understand that they are demanding air transport out of the country, but that's not their biggest demand.

"These blokes want the UK to pull everyone out of Northern Ireland. We don't know if they're connected to the IRA, but they sound like they are. They also demand release of all 'political prisoners,' which they say are all of the IRA killers and terrorist bombers we now hold. He mentioned two specifically—the Craighan brothers, who are truly murderous scum. There's no chance we'll let those two out. Or any of the others for that matter.

"They want the French to release even more. So far the French are holding, but the foreign minister says they will agree to that demand if they have to, to get Tournier back alive. We aren't going to wait.

"Your orders, gentlemen, are to attack in six hours, at approximately 0500 tomorrow. As you'll see from the weather briefing, sunrise is at 0512, and the usual morning fog is expected." Another officer put a chart on the overhead projector and turned off the lights. "Now you see the plan of attack. Your team will be split into two groups, as usual. Mr. MacPherson will be the lead, with half the team in one helo. Mr. Singh will be the other lead in the second helo.

"All of you will helo from Prestwick, about ten air minutes at regular speed. We lift off at 0450. MacPherson's group will stop and deploy to rope ride just before you attack. There will be perfect concealment for you behind the cliffs.

"Mr. Singh will take the first group to the landward side. You will come in fast over the hill behind the lodge, pop up, and then drop down between the buildings. The staff house will be behind you and the main lodge in front. There is about fifty or sixty meters between the buildings. Also, there is a thin line of trees blocking the staff house from the view of the main house. You will land on the staff house side, penetrate the tree line, and enter the main house through the rear door that leads to the kitchen.

"Your job is to force entry into the staff building as well as the main house. Neutralize whomever you find there. We know of about fifteen people on staff at the lodge, but how many are in the staff house or the main, or how many have already been killed is unknown. We're hoping the rear team's fire will draw the terrorists away from the seaward side. We know that the two PMs were staying in the front rooms on the second floor. Mr. MacPherson and his group will attack from the seaward side, and go right into the windows of the rooms where we believe the PM is being held. MacPherson, your call sign is Red 1. Singh, you are Red 2.

"Once you're on the ground, Mr. Singh, Mr. MacPherson's helo will come in from the seaward side. That group will enter the front windows, and get the PM out. Her rescue beacon is working. You should pick it up on 430 megacycles.

"The Harriers will be on station orbiting at 20,000 feet, about four or five miles offshore. Their call signs are Blue 1 and 2. They can strafe the hill behind the lodge and the lawn on the seaward side in one pass. They will each have 30mm cannon, and a pair of those new Hydra 70 rocket clusters." Even the SAS raised an eyebrow at the mention of the Hydras, a particularly nasty weapon. Each rocket contained about 1,200 flechettes, the 60-gram size, each about the size of a ballpoint pen. When fired, the flechettes were launched at close range at Mach 2, and would literally tear a man to pieces.

"We think that the Harriers should be enough to provide cover in any situation which you may encounter."

"MacPherson's helo will be coming in rather slowly. You'll be going in at about thirty knots, gentlemen. First, you'll stop at one edge of the horseshoe cliffs to deploy your ropes and hear the signal that Singh is engaged. Right. That's all."

They stood up to leave. Cully had to try one last time. "Sir, we're holding a full team with a complete assault package right here. If you ask, maybe we can get authorization to help."

"Thank you, Mr. O'Bannon. We'll take it from here. Your team can observe from the fourth helo, which will approach from the seaward side at about 5,000 feet."

Portpatrick Lodge
2245 Hours

"You people have kept me awake since three o'clock this morning. I am going to my room." Evelyn Broughton stood up, her chin thrust forward at the man in the moon. The giant looked at her, and sighed.

"Go sleep if you wish." He snapped his finger at one of his men. "Go with her. Search her room again, and stay awake. Watch her."

"I will not have anyone sleep in my room. A British lady without her husband sleeps alone."

The giant laughed. "At home you sleep alone. Here you will not. You. Go with her and do not fall asleep. If you do, I will see that you never wake up."

The lady walked out of the room and up the stairs, her companion close behind. At the top of the stairs, she turned left, back around the staircase to her room. The man following her had a machine gun slung across his chest. He walked to a chair in the corner of the room and slumped into it. After a minute, another came through the door. He sat down facing the first man.

Methodically, as she had done all her life, Evelyn Broughton brushed her hair one hundred strokes. After brushing her hair, she went into the small bathroom, closing the door behind her. The two lipsticks were still in her pockets. She thought briefly about the head of MI-6 who had given them to her, and the SAS colonel who had explained their non-cosmetic use. She took off her shoes and walked out to the bed. Without a word, she snapped off the light and snugged into the goose down comforter.

0330 Hours

The Man in the Moon relaxed. If they hadn't launched a rescue attempt by now, it would probably not even come until the next night. Every one of these Special Operations groups trained the same way. They always wanted to attack at about 0300 when people were sleeping soundly, just as Petrov had done in the attack on the lodge. He drifted off to sleep thinking of the escape boat he had stashed on the beach, and the one million American dollars he had earned that day.

0450 Hours

Cully and the team helped MacPherson's group and then Singh's get loaded properly. They launched precisely on schedule and disappeared into the fog. The SEALs scrambled into the last helo, which already held their gear. Cully found Atkins in the co-pilot seat. Next to him was a very young flight officer named Prim.

"What do you have on this mission, Prim?"

"We are to follow about a thousand yards behind the rear helo, Mr. O'Bannon. My orders are to let you have a look and stay out of the fight."

Cully frowned. "Okay, let's go."

Not everyone at the lodge slept. The terrorists were still, for the most part, professionals. The fifteen of them who were former Spetznaz didn't need an officer to tell them to post a watch. There were two with each of the PMs, one awake at all times. Two others were awake on the front lawn, looking up into the fog and listening. Nine more were around them, waiting for an assault they were hoping would not come.

0458 Hours

Although the helo was the quietest in the British Army, MacPherson still had to shout to make himself heard. He and five others readied themselves to deploy on the ropes. They were keyed up for action and ready to fast rope into the lodge that instant. The helo came down the coast, hugging tight to the cliffs. It slowed short of the turn into the horseshoe where the lodge sat. They held there, waiting for the signal that Singh's group was on the ground. They played out the ropes, slid down into position, and waited.

Singh's helo, taking a different route, came up over the cliff at the rear of the lodge with a roar. Quickly, it dropped between the buildings; Singh's team hit the ground and split, half running toward the main lodge, half toward the staff house. At the same instant, the guards on the beach heard Singh's helo. One picked up his radio and shouted a warning. Another picked up a green metal tube and swung it up onto his shoulder.

Over his radio, the pilot of MacPherson's helo heard Singh's call that they were landing. MacPherson and his team cocked their weapons as the helo leaped forward.

MacPherson's helo was just beginning to pick up speed as it rounded the corner. Cully couldn't see it clearly through the fog. Prim had closed the thousand yards to about three hundred when MacPherson's slowed to make the turn. Around the corner, there was a pocket in the fog, and the image of

MacPherson's helo was suddenly clear. Then there was a burst of light and flame as the shoulder-fired missile hit the helo. The SEALs' helo was rocked back by the explosion. Prim fought it and steadied back to a hover. Below, where MacPherson's helo had been, burning wreckage marked its end. Prim turned the helo out to sea, and pushed the cyclic forward. The radio came alive. Both Cully and Atkins had headsets and could hear everything.

"Red 2, Red 1. We are under heavy fire. Say again, we are under fire from the lodge and the staff house. We are pinned down."

"Red 2, Red 1. This is Singh. Where are you, over?"

Cully turned to Atkins, who was already pushing the talk button.

"Ah, Red 2, this is Atkins. Red 1 is down, no survivors. Can you extract?"

"Negative. We can't go anywhere. They have heavy fire on the helo. It's out of action. We need help."

Cully pushed the intercom button. "Tommy, I'm dealing us in right now."

"No way, Cully. We have orders to stay out of this. We can't do this without orders."

Singh's voice interrupted. "Tommy, Cully, anybody, please!"

"Tommy, we gotta do this. If we wait one more minute, the Raj and his whole team will be dead."

Cully looked at Atkins, who reached forward and put his feet on the rudder pedals.

Prim looked surprised. "Mr. Atkins, I still have the aircraft. What are you doing?" Cully grabbed the radio headset off Prim's head. "Mr. Atkins has the aircraft."

"Mr. O'Bannon, you can't do this. I'm in command. You have orders to stay out of the action."

"Sorry, kid. Mr. Atkins has the aircraft." Prim gulped. Cully had drawn the H&K .45 and was waving it close to Prim's nose. The muzzle gaped at him.

"I suppose he does."

Cully dove back through the hatch to where the team sat. He shouted, "Mac is dead and the Raj is pinned down. We're going in hot, everybody on the second floor. Get your fast rope gear on now. Once we start moving, dangle the ropes. We'll fast rope onto the roof, and then swing down through the top-floor windows. I want pairs one, two, and three to head for the back of the second floor of the lodge and clear it. Pairs six and seven, clear the stairs, and relieve the SAS at the back door. Wilson and me and pair five will grab the two hostages and make for the front or side door. Ready?"

Atkins was shouting back to Cully. "If we're gonna do this, we're gonna do it our way."

Cully moved back up front to hear. Atkins was on the radio issuing commands in rapid-fire sequence. "Raj, hang on. We're comin'. Blue 1 and Blue 2, make your run on the beach and lawn from south to north with cannon and Hydras now, now, now. All other units, Red 1 is down. Watcher 1 going in for him."

As Atkins held the helo, the SEALs played out the four ropes, and Cully, Wilson, and six others went out the door. As they did, they heard the high-pitched whine of the Harriers coming in from seaward, turning parallel to the coast to make their run. A second later, the whole beach and lawn erupted as the Harriers let loose their Hydras and 30mm cannon, earth spouting up where the rounds hit, killing the eleven Spetznaz who had dug in along the water line and on the lawn back to the lodge. Nothing survived the first run, but the Harriers made another pass quickly to make sure. Atkins slipped the helo forward toward the lodge.

In Evelyn Broughton's Room

The sound of MacPherson's helo exploding was like a sharp clap of thunder. The prime minister awoke, listening carefully. Her right hand inched to the pants pocket for one of the special lipsticks. "Rescue. Have to stay calm," she thought.

She scrambled off the bed, grabbing her shoes. In a corner of the room, behind a big chair, she lay flat on her back and struggled to put her shoes on. When the Harriers made their strafing runs, another man ran into the room, and then all three thugs were looking out the window toward the beach. Then she heard the other helo approach. She pulled the cap of one of the lipsticks up halfway, twisted it a half turn, and pushed it back down. She lobbed it at the wall, aiming for a spot between two of the thugs. She turned her face away and put her hands to her ears.

The miniature "flash-bang" grenade hit the wall and exploded with a tremendous boom and a blinding flash. As quickly as she had turned away, she leaped to the other side of the room, turned back with the other grenade, and lobbed it at the three men, who were firing blindly at the walls where she had been. She lay flat on the floor.

Atkins was hovering as the SEALs slid down their ropes onto the sloped roof, then swung themselves backward and slid down into the windows. Cully saw the flash-bangs go off, and thought for a second that the SAS team had broken through. He and Scott hit two window openings, crashing through into different rooms. Cully's eyes flashed around the room and saw two dazed men to his right and another to his left. He swung the H&K MP-5 machine gun, firing two quick bursts, killing the two terrorists to his right. Wilson, behind him, shot through the door at the third who was leaping toward the stairs. Wilson ran to the door and fired the shotgun three more times down the stairs. Other shooting pairs poured through the window, and there was fierce fighting throughout the top two floors as the SEALs moved to the building's rear to relieve Singh.

Cully saw Broughton, flat on the floor behind a chair. "U.S. Navy, ma'am. We'll get you out. Stay right at my back. Chief, let's get the hell outta here."

Sandwiched between Cully and Wilson, Broughton inched toward the door with the men. Cully flicked his head into the hall and back in, drawing a burst of fire from below. He snapped his head around the corner again, and saw two SEALs lying at the foot of the stairs, dead or wounded, but no targets coming up the stairs.

The hallway ran right and ahead, the stairs two steps to the left. Farther to the right, Scott and his low man came forward, with the French PM across one of the SEALs' backs in a fireman's carry. Cully and Wilson came out, scanning below and ahead. The other pair came out behind them.

"Put him down. If he can walk, we need to cover him." Immediately, Tournier was back on his feet. "You two, go to the rear windows and help relieve the Raj." Cully had barely finished his sentence when the two men disappeared at a run.

"Chief, me, the lady, the Frenchman, and then you. Keep his head down, and cover the rear."

"Aye, aye, boss." Wilson was shoving more double-ought buckshot shells into the pump gun. "Let's go."

They crept along the hall in lockstep, Cully scanning the front, Broughton crouching behind him, Tournier behind her, Wilson's strong left arm across his back, holding him down while the SEAL kept his eyes at their six o'clock.

They reached the stairs leading down to the front door. Fifteen steps down and ten yards through the door to the safety of Atkins's chopper. Cully went down slowly, the muzzle of his MP-5 sweeping from side to side. The firing at the rear of the lodge was intense for a moment, then suddenly stopped. Cully and Wilson came six more steps down. Just a few more steps. Check six, two more steps, listen to the lady panting behind him. She seemed out of breath, gasping for air. The other pair were close, almost on top of them.

Near the bottom of the staircase, the left wall ended at the archway leading to the study. Cully stopped the group and leaned across for a look. At the top of the stairs, a man appeared, swinging a weapon toward them. Wilson fired, reaching for the pump slide on the shotgun, letting Tournier slip out of his grip, Cully saw two more men appear at the bottom of the stairs, both raising their weapons. Tournier fell into the burst of fire from the first man below, Cully shooting the thug and hearing the MP-5 click on an empty chamber. The huge man, bleeding from several wounds, was raising his own weapon, grinning as he saw Cully reach for the pistol on his leg. Then the giant was coughing and falling as the handle of a throwing knife suddenly was sticking out of his throat, the blade having gone all the way through.

The Raj leaped to Broughton's side before the big man hit the ground. Ten more steps, the four of them running, bursting out the door. Twenty more steps, Atkins's helo on the lawn waiting, Cully threw Broughton into the helo, Wilson and the Raj jumping in behind, covering the rear. Cully shouted to Tommy, "Go, go, go." The big chopper lifted immediately. Seconds later they were out to sea, minutes from Prestwick.

"Thanks, Raj." Singh was bleeding freely from a nasty scalp wound, and seemed to be favoring his left leg. "You're a mess. Can you make it?"

"It's nothing my tailor can't fix. Thanks for coming for us. MacPherson's group . . . Did anyone make it?"

"I don't know about Mac. I think they're all dead, Raj. And you're welcome. I know you'd have done the same for us."

"You can count on that."

"I know."

They fell silent. For some reason, the three men were all looking at Broughton. The look on her face was one of shock. She had never seen men die before. For an instant, she thought it was her fault. *Nonsense. Get a hold of yourself. You did nothing to endanger anyone. You are prime minister. Act like it.*

Broughton had seen the dead French PM. She knew at once that the blame for Tournier's death would not be borne by the terrorists. She turned to Cully who, with Wilson, had practically carried her out of the house. She shouted over the chopper's rotors. "Young man, you saved my life. God bless you."

Cully looked back to the door of the lodge. *One out of two isn't good enough*, he thought.

RAF Prestwick
1115 Hours

Coded reports of the action went out almost immediately. The orbiting surveillance aircraft transmitted the visible outdoor action live to the admiralty in London. Moments after the helicopter carrying Broughton lifted off, reports of Tournier's death had reached London and Paris. More and more coded messages went back and forth, now with Washington in the loop. The bureaucracy began to take hold where the warfighters had loosened their grip.

In the usual sequence, intelligence officers would debrief the fighters, mainly to learn as much as possible about the enemy and their tactics. But this was something different. The operation took place as no one had foreseen, and there was blame to assign. The word quickly went out. After the intel guys were finished, the investigators would take over. Soon there were lawyers swarming over everyone who had seen the action at Portpatrick Lodge.

The investigators already were figuring out who to blame for the incident and the death of the French PM by the time the helos had returned to RAF Prestwick. The intel team separated Cully, Singh and Atkins to get their individual statements. The investigators arrived soon enough. Now there would be no conversation between any members of the rescue team. After another hour, people started recording their answers to questions like, "Who told you to go in?" and "Why did you let the French PM get killed?"

0545 Hours
Washington, D.C.

The basement of the Hart Senate Office Building has many features unknown to the visiting public. One of the nicest is the private health club and spa, open to senators twenty-four hours a day. Staff members could use it, too, but only in off hours. Off hours meant that Jonathan Forsythe had to work out, take his time in the steam room, and be out by 6:30 A.M. He didn't mind. The mornings when he didn't wake up next to Jennifer Lundgren were good mornings for a workout. Standing on the treadmill, he jogged a few miles, watching CNN replay the Senate proceedings of the day or recap world news. The first reports trickling in from the action at Portpatrick Lodge just ticked him off.

"Incredible," he muttered to himself, in grudging admiration of the daring of the SEALs and the SAS. By the time the steam bath was over, rumors had started that the SEALs had acted without orders. He took the elevator up to the fifth floor and opened his office. He picked up the phone and called the navy legislative liaison, the Defense Department Public Affairs office, and a continuous string of his allies in the Pentagon.

An hour later he was still on the phone. "What do you mean Captain Larson isn't available? Get him on his beeper and have him call me *now*. I don't care where he is, my senator is ripshit about this. We need to know how and why Navy SEALs were involved without orders. This may be a violation of the War Powers Act." He smiled as he slammed the phone down, hoping to scare the young ensign on the other end of the line. Time to make a few more calls and get a cappuccino before the boss came in from his morning run.

0705 Hours

Tom Pierson looked at the briefing sheet. He could hardly believe his eyes. He looked tiredly over his glasses at the captain and admiral from intelligence who had caught up to him in the Pentagon Officers' Athletic Club. Many a time Pierson thanked the Lord for the PO-AC as the gnomes of the Pentagon called it. It was the source of energy that kept him going. That and too much coffee.

"Okay, here's what we have to do. I want CINCLANT over there right now to take command of the investigation. Put a tight lid on this until I get to the CNO and SecDef. Nobody talks to the press."

"Yes, sir," said the admiral, who looked all too young for the star on his shoulder boards. "But if I may, sir, the press already has this. We should go out with something about how our guys participated in the action and rescued Broughton."

"No, way, Mort. Not until we get more facts. I agree that we'll have to open the kimono pretty quick, but I don't want to put out one story only to have to change it later. Now you two get over to the public affairs guys and get them clear on it."

0740 Hours

Senator Manfredi felt really good. After another long-distance argument with his wife, he had walked out of his apartment the night before and spent the rest of it with his current girlfriend, a twenty-something receptionist at the Armed Services Committee. By the time he got to the office, he had heard bits and pieces of the news from Scotland. Forsythe was waiting for him with hands full of papers. Manfredi smiled knowingly.

"Jonathan, I see you have the news for me. What happened over there? I assume our boys in blue covered themselves in glory again."

"It's a bit more complicated than that, Senator. I think we may want to dust off that amendment disbanding the SEALs."

"Jonathan, I know we've talked about that. I know we'd both like to do it, and Barbara Berkely will fall on her sword for it. But we both know that Nate Barrett will oppose it, and he controls enough votes to tie it up, if not defeat it outright."

"Senator, what if I told you that Senator Barrett will take a walk on this one?"

"What the hell have you been smoking? If you've got something, tell me and quit this fucking around."

"The SEALs went in against the orders they had at the time. They caused the death of the French premier, and we have the ugliest situation with France since they told off Churchill in 1939. I've talked to their military attaché just a few minutes ago. The French parliament will pass a resolution today demanding the prosecution of the SEALs responsible for Tournier's death. And what's more, I have some information about Senator Barrett's staff that will prevent him from working against us. Let me tell you how we can do this."

Twenty minutes later, Forsythe left Manfredi's office, and headed for his own back at the Armed Services Committee. He had a lot to do. But first, another stop at the cappuccino bar. The girl there was cute.

0810 Hours
Washington, D.C.

Forsythe couldn't call many of his allies at this hour. The reliables at the *Washington Post* didn't show up until at least 9:30 or 10 A.M., depending on how rough the previous night had been. But the Pentagon and some of the think tanks were awake. The "tankers" as the senate staff called them were often just auxiliary staffs to the committees, paid by grants from foundations pursuing their own political agendas.

But some of the bureaucrats were even better. The "whistleblower" community was small, but consistently liberal and entirely activist. They were interspersed throughout the senior bureaucracy, in virtually every part of the Pentagon. Most of them were regular civil servants, which meant that they were almost impossible to fire. Some, like Dr. Richard Petulant, were granted that status by the courts. When two successive defense secretaries tried to fire him, his lawyers got the courts to agree not only that he couldn't be fired but that he couldn't even be removed from the job he had or denied sensitive information. Most of his time at work was spent gathering dirt for Congressman John Dingell's famous inquisition of industry and Pentagon executives in the House Committee on Energy and Commerce. A Dingell subpoena often threw the entire Pentagon into a panic.

Forsythe reached him early. Petulant, ensconced in his job as deputy assistant secretary of the Navy for Management, affected importance by refusing to answer his own phone. Blanche, his long-suffering secretary, put Forsythe right through.

"Richard, glad to find you in. What's your take on the rescue of Broughton and the death of the French PM?"

"Looks to me like a botched job, Jonathan. And just at the time when Pierson thought he had everybody on the Hill lined up to leave the Special Forces types alone."

"What makes you think he believed that?"

"Well, he's been having the legislative guys over for most of the weekly staff sessions. He mentioned a couple of weeks ago that he thought they'd be okay because Senator Barrett was on their side."

"Did he mention anything about having people come up to work specially with Barrett's people?"

"Come to think of it, he did mention that one of the SEAL team officers would be on the Hill. I think he mentioned Barrett's people as one of their assignments."

"Would you be surprised to learn that the SEAL team leader was having an affair with Kate Reilly on Barrett's staff? And how about the fact that it's the same guy who was involved in the death of the French PM?"

"No, nothing these guys do surprises me any more. They're entirely without morals. I'm sure it's no accident that they sent a big stud up there with the objective of seducing Barrett's staffer."

"Just what do you remember Pierson saying about all this?"

"Just that he was bringing this guy up to work with Barrett's staff, among others."

"Are you sure he didn't say he wanted this guy to come up to get Barrett's vote by romancing this staffer?"

"I really couldn't say that. It's too much of a stretch." Petulant didn't need another hint. "But I could say that when he mentioned it, everybody understood him to mean that the guy was supposed to seduce her. These guys do that kind of stuff all the time."

"And you'd swear to that in testimony before the committee?"

"If you subpoena me, I'll be glad to. Just so long as I can say I'm not volunteering to do this."

"Thanks, Richard. You're a great help."

"Always happy to oblige."

Forsythe's next call was to Steve Krueger in the first lady's office. "Steve, I need your advice. What do the president and the first lady think of this business in Scotland?"

"Well, Jonathan, I haven't been able to speak to either of them yet this morning, but I'm certain Mrs. Brandon will be very upset at the death of the French PM."

"I know she will, as will every thinking person. But this goes farther than that. What do we do about these military types running amok?"

"As a Ph.D., I can tell you how these people fail to fit in our society. When I was a senior fellow at the World Institute, we studied the dangers of maintaining these so-called special forces. You may have read my paper on it, which was published last year. It was entitled, 'A Study of the Dangers to Society Posed by Our Own Elite Troops.'"

"Yes, I read it. But is there anyone still at the World Institute who could testify about the findings at a Senate hearing on the issue, if there is one? Giving your work appropriate credit, of course."

Krueger began again. "From a Ph.D.'s perspective . . . I think I should be presenting the work, but of course that wouldn't be proper from my new position. My former associate, Frank Metzger, could do it. He's a Ph.D., too, you know."

"Thanks. Would you call him to let him know I'll be calling him later?"

"Of course. Anything else?"

"Well, I was wondering what I should tell the senator about how the first lady is reacting."

"You can tell him that the first lady is shocked at the violation of orders and of all sorts of laws. I'm sure she will insist on punishment of everyone responsible."

"Thanks very much. You've been a great help."

"Of course. Thank you for the call."

1000 Hours
The Capitol

Room H-615 in the Capitol Building is a small garret tucked away several floors above the House chambers. Few people know of it, and even fewer go there. It is the only SCIF—Sensitive Compartmented Information Facility—in the Capitol. It is a room as secure as technology can make it, and its security procedures mirror those for the Pentagon's "tank." Everyone who goes in has a top-secret clearance, and each meeting's attendance is recorded. No one takes papers or tape recorders in, and none come out.

The corridor outside H-615 was uncrowded as Senators Porter, Manfredi, and Berkely and the rest of the Armed Services Committee members filed in for their classified briefing about the incident at Portpatrick Lodge. The CIA briefer was, unusually, the director of Central Intelligence, Harvey Miters. Like virtually all other high-ranking Brandon appointees, he was a lawyer. His distinction was having been counsel to the House Permanent Select Committee on Intelligence.

Miters turned on the overhead projector. Like the Pentagon, the CIA's culture required viewgraphs. If a speaker didn't have them, the speaker wasn't properly prepared. Instead of the usual factoids and statistics, these viewgraphs were of Portpatrick Lodge, some from satellite photos taken during the SEALs' assault.

"As you can see, senators, the fire in the upper right-hand corner is the wreckage of the helicopter carrying half of the SAS assault team. We understand that they were killed immediately, either from the missile's explosion or the crash. Most of the fighting went on inside, but you can see the British helo that delivered the SEAL team close to the front of the building." The questions began before Miters explained what happened to Tournier. Berkely, as usual, interrupted the briefer.

"Okay, Harvey. You said that the SEALs went in against orders, correct?"

"Yes, senator."

"Well, had they requested orders, or contacted their commander to get the orders changed before acting?"

"The information we have from interviews of the SEALs indicates that they tried to obtain authorization, but were refused."

"So they were acting directly against orders, and Tournier would be alive right now if they hadn't jumped the gun."

Barrett had heard enough. "Barbara, we don't know that. The terrorists would probably have killed both Broughton and Tournier before the battle was half over, anyway."

"Nate, I know these boys can do no wrong in your eyes, but what we have here is a damned mutiny. These guys went against orders, and the French PM is dead as a result. That's not an argument. It's a damned fact."

Miters tried to interject. "What Senator Barrett says is probably right—" Berkely cut him off again.

"Well, I can't speak for the rest of you, but I've seen enough to convince me. Who was the senior officer there?"

"The SEAL platoon commander was a Lieutenant O'Bannon, but the senior man was a Commander Atkins. He flew the helicopter they used."

"Well, Atkins should be court-martialed for allowing this to happen, and the rest of those guys have no business being in our navy." She stormed out of the room, all righteous indignation.

Barrett wanted one more question answered. "Did the SEALs know the SAS men who were killed? Were they friends?"

"Yes, senator. They all knew each other and had trained together both here and in the U.K." The meeting ended, and the senators began filing out of the room. Manfredi took Barrett aside.

"Nate, I'm going to move the amendment to the authorization bill that will disband the SEALs."

"Fair enough, Peter. I appreciate your telling me, but you know I'll have to oppose you."

"Do you really? I think you ought to consider the careers of your staffers. They could be totally destroyed by certain disclosures. So could some senior navy people."

"What the hell are you saying? Out with it. If you're trying to blackmail me out of opposing your amendment, well, you damned well ought to know better."

"Really? Maybe you should ask Ms. Reilly how long she's been sleeping with a certain SEAL officer. Maybe you should know that Richard Petulant will testify, under oath, that he heard Admiral Pierson give orders sending that boy up to the Hill for the sole purpose of getting into her bed. "

"You know and I know it's not true."

"Maybe and maybe not. But it rings true. Enough to be on the front page of the *Post* for a day or two. Maybe Admiral Pierson would like to follow Petulant's testimony with his own."

"Peter, I—" The man from Missouri suddenly felt very old. "I've been in politics all my adult life. I've been in the Senate for almost thirty years. I've never seen or even heard of anyone doing what you just did."

"I'm sorry, Nate, but if you force my hand, this will all come out." He turned and walked out behind the others. At the bottom of the stairs, the hallway led to the stairs down out of the Capitol and the way back to the Senate office buildings across Constitution Avenue. The TV cameras were clustered around the bottom of the stairs. Berkely, Porter, and Manfredi were already giving interviews by the time Barrett came out. The reporters were sharks in a feeding frenzy.

"Senator Manfredi, do you agree with Senator Berkely that this was a mutiny?"

"Senator Porter, are you going to disband the SEALs?"

"Senator Berkely, are you going to demand that these people be court-martialed? What has the navy said they will do to punish these guys?"

"Why was the French premier killed? Did the SEALs have orders to only save Mrs. Broughton?"

"Did the president know that the SEALs were going into action?"

"Was the Pentagon in on this? Why didn't somebody there alert the president?"

Barrett heard most of this as he pushed his way through the crowd. "Senator Barrett, do you agree that the SEALs' actions were illegal?" The reporter pushed a microphone into Barrett's face. "Cindy, I need to get more facts before I comment on something as serious as that." Deep in thought, Barrett walked slowly back to his office.

CHAPTER 15

AT THE HOME OF THE BRAVE

1005 Hours

The Cabinet used to meet in the Roosevelt Room, across the hall from the Oval Office. But the government had grown so large that by the time the Brandon administration came in, the cabinet had to meet down the hall in a much larger conference room. Cabinet members sat at the table. Their staffs, who numbered from none to five, sat in chairs that lined the walls behind their bosses. Like H-615, it was a SCIF, but the random comings and goings of the various cabinet big shots precluded security measures like those Hunter was used to.

The Brandon administration had changed more than just where the Cabinet met. In every prior administration, the Cabinet members sat around the long oval table with the president at the center of one long side. Nearest him to his right was always the secretary of Defense. On his left, the secretary of State. Other Cabinet members were arrayed around the table in order of the rank of their department. The vice president sat across from the president, near the center of action.

The Brandon gang, however, rearranged the seating chart. On the president's left was the secretary of Labor. To his right was the secretary of Health and Human Services. Across, in the vice president's usual place, was the first lady. Her voice was heard at these meetings as much, if not more, than those of most of the Cabinet members. To her left sat Vice President La Guardia. He didn't seem to mind. The secretary of defense was down at one end; the secretary of state sat next to the vice president.

Hunter had been called about the special meeting to discuss the Portpatrick Lodge incident, as the press was now calling it. He had ten minutes before the meeting, just enough time to get the straight story on what happened. He reached for the STU-3 scrambled signal phone behind his desk, thankful for the legendary skill of the White House operators. Since the start of World War II, when a "former naval person" named Churchill was speaking to another former naval person named Roosevelt, these operators had prided themselves on being able to reach anyone on earth. And they could, too. Their jobs were too important to be turned over as patronage. When the Brandons started to replace them, Hunter had practically begged to keep at least one of the experienced people on, in eight-hour shifts, around the clock. He picked up the STU-3.

"Mabel, this is Hunter. I need to reach Admiral Charles in Prime Minister Broughton's office in London right away. Find him for me, schweetheart," he said. His Bogart imitation was none too good, but he saved it for the brief words he had with Mabel and her companions at the switchboard. "Anything you say, you devil," came from the seventy-plus Mabel.

Two minutes later, his phone rang. "General Hunter, I have Admiral Charles for you."

Admiral Sir Percival Charles was airborne in the prime minister's private jet carrying her back to London from the RAF Prestwick recovery area. He took Hunter's call partly because he knew the man, and partly because the White House operator indicated it was important. Hunter and Charles had served together during the Falklands crisis, with Hunter on a secret loan to the admiralty. He was a full colonel then. Charles was already an admiral, but the two had become friends in need. Rank didn't stand in the way of friendships being created. Now Charles guessed who his friend reported to when the White House switchboard placed the call.

"Perce, how is your lady after all she's been through?"

"Fine, James. A bit shaken, but recovering to the point that she wants to declare war on somebody. She sends her heartfelt thanks for your boys rescuing her. I think it's safe to say that she would be quite dead now but for your people jumping in the way they did."

"I need the straight skinny on this. Congress is in an uproar over the fact that our boys went in contrary to orders. They want heads to roll, and my guess is that the president is inclined to agree. I have a meeting with him in two minutes."

"The way it went, as I understand it, was that your people were there to observe. The team leader had the foresight to take all his people and their equipment on the exercise. When our chaps bought it, he took charge and literally saved Mrs. Broughton's life, at least twice."

"What about the Frenchman getting killed? Our boys may have blown it. "

"James, you and I both know we'll never be sure. But the PM was literally crouched behind Lieutenant O'Bannon's back when it happened. She says that there were so many people shooting in so many directions, she's not even sure who shot whom. The poor lady has nothing to measure it by. At the risk of stating the obvious, she's not familiar with that kind of action."

"Okay. I'm sorry to press you, but I have to know. What did she say, exactly?"

"She said that your team chief went first down the stairs, then her, then Tournier, with another of your chaps covering the rear. They were going for the front door. When they got halfway down the stairs, she thinks terrorists appeared at the top and bottom of the stairs. Your SEALs started shooting. She thinks Tournier either fell or intentionally dived forward. She saw Tournier fall forward into about ten rounds of nine millimeter. Your chaps got out with one of the surviving SAS people, and your helo driver made good the escape. By the way, he landed so close to the action that he took quite a few rounds into the aircraft. Should charge you for a broken windscreen, actually. Seriously, it sounds like they did everything right. Tournier's death can be laid at the feet of the terrorists, no one else."

"Perce, how about I buy you dinner next time I'm there or you're here?"

"As you Yanks say, it's a deal, pal." Hunter hung up the phone, logged the call, and grabbed his notes as he ran to the meeting.

Hunter's boss, Dr. Anthony, actually showed up for this cabinet meeting, contrary to his usual practice. Hunter sat behind him, trying to convey what he had just learned. The room buzzed with current wisdom.

"I say we should convey these people to France for trial. How dare they violate their orders?"

"I just spoke to the French ambassador. They may even sever diplomatic relations if we don't punish these men."

"I think we should run them out of the navy, and make sure no more units like these SEAL teams get started ever again. We should have some direct civilian control over these people."

La Guardia said, "I thought that was what we had Touchman for. What do you think, Freddy?"

"I don't know how many times I've warned the first lady about how dangerous these people were, and how little control we have over them." Dr. Steve Krueger looked around to see who was paying attention. As a self-appointed expert, and a Ph.D., he thought he should make the decisions today. He looked across the table into Hunter's stare. If looks could burn, Krueger was toast. Bella Brandon glared back at Hunter.

"I think we're about ready to start, don't you, Ike?" The First Lady was first on the agenda on many days, and this was obviously going to be one of those days.

Hunter looked around the room. *Jesus wept*, he thought. *I'm the only asshole in the room that isn't a lawyer. And the only guy who ever wore the uniform.*

The president looked at his wife with a bored smile. She was on the rampage again. Might as well let her run with it. "Yes, I think Bella has a point. Let's get started."

Bella was rolling on. "I think if we can get a quick summary from Fred Touchman on what happened for those who didn't get this morning's CIA briefing, we can proceed. Freddy?"

Touchman gave a ten-minute summary of the incident, emphasizing that the SEALs had gone in against orders, that "clearly" the French premier died as a result of their precipitous act, and that the civilian control over special forces in general and the SEALs in particular was in bad need of repair. "And I suggest we appoint a presidential blue-ribbon commission to study that matter."

"Freddy, who the hell sold you on that?" the first lady demanded. "We need to take some drastic steps now to control the damage to this presidency, and to fix the problem once and for all. That idiot idea must have come from someone who wants to bury the problem, not fix it. This could be a major political disaster for us in the core constituencies. We have to be the bosses of the military, not the other way around.

"I've been listening all morning to the briefings by the CIA, the navy, the British military advisors here, and a dozen other people. The facts are plain. These people acted in violation of orders, they caused the death of Tournier, and nobody's voice was enough to stop them. We need to put these guys out of business."

"Easy does it, Bella. We need to find out what happened from the people there, don't we?" La Guardia said. Going gingerly with the great lady herself wasn't easy for him, but she had more than the president's ear. "I don't see this as a political issue. The French are pissed, but they're always pissed at us. It's just a matter of degree. Tournier's death is a tragedy, but not an apocalypse."

"If I may, Mr. President." Every face turned toward Anthony Daniels. No one could remember if he had ever spoken before at one of these meetings.

"My deputy, General Hunter, has just spoken to Admiral Charles, Mrs. Broughton's military aide. Perhaps we should let him tell us what he has learned."

"Thank you, sir. If I may—" Hunter looked around the room. Those who were listening were sneering. Those who weren't listening were talking to someone else.

"We have a situation that is way out of the ordinary. We have some of our people who were observing a military operation which they were themselves uniquely suited to perform. At a critical point in the assault on the hotel where the hostages were being held, they saw half of the British force killed in an instant. We train these people very well, to react quickly—" The bored faces were now all speaking at once.

"Hunter, are you an impartial witness? Didn't you command a unit like the SEALs at one time?" from the attorney general.

"Hunter, did you speak to Mrs. Broughton or just her aide? How useful is his information? Was he there?" from the secretary of Labor.

"General, how do you know we don't have better information from our own sources?" from CIA.

"Hunter, you know Admiral Charles, don't you? Did you two cook up a story to sell to the civilians?" from the secretary of Transportation.

It went on like that for five minutes. Finally, the president said, "Thanks anyway, general. I think we can move this along." He turned back to the attorney general. Known as "Will Do Wanda," Wanda Harrold looked a lot like Broughton. She once had a reputation as a tough prosecutor, but Washington changed her as it had so many before her. Her version of the Justice Department was at the president's political disposal, as many courts found to their dismay—particularly those hosting investigations of the president or the first lady, of which there were many.

"Wanda, what are our options here?" asked the president.

"Mr. President, I suggest you order Mr. Touchman to have the chief of Naval Operations convene a board of inquiry under Article 32 of the Uniform Code of Military Justice. That is the military equivalent of a grand jury. They can make proper recommendations for the disposition of the cases, if any are brought. That's our first, and best, option."

"Freddy, make it so," said the president, quoting his favorite *Star Trek* character.

1424 Hours
Capitol Hill

When Forsythe looked at the clock, it was nearly 2:30 P.M. He had been on the phone most of the day, arranging testimony, gathering votes for the measure to disband the SEALs, and getting the press and others ready for the push. Time to report back to the senator. It took only a few minutes to brief him.

"Okay, Jonathan. Get legislative counsel to draft language eliminating the SEALs permanently. Throw in Army Special Forces, Marine Force Recon, and any others you can think of. I'm sure Nate Barrett will cave today or tomorrow. By then, we should have everything arranged. Get Admiral Pierson on the phone and tell him we want him and the SEAL team commander for a closed hearing on Thursday. Get as many of the others who were there as you can. Everybody will be under oath."

1305 Hours
RAF Prestwick

By the time the first round of interrogations had been completed, Cully was looking for a shower and a clean uniform. The place was swarming with lawyers, military lawyers, civilian lawyers, and investigators of all stripes and sizes. By noon, he had told the story three times. He had been checked by the medics and gotten the briefing from them about casualties. Aside from the French premier, three SEALs were dead, two wounded. None of those aboard MacPherson's helo survived. Counting the men on the beach, twenty-three terrorists were dead. None survived to be questioned. Six of the staff of the lodge had been killed, and the owner wounded slightly. Singh was not seriously hurt, but five of his men were dead, and most of the rest had suffered serious wounds.

One of the lawyer/investigators was a military prosecutor, a lieutenant commander named Snyder. He had rushed over from the big sub base at Holy Loch, eager to take charge. He looked at Cully with a cocky grin.

"O'Bannon, I think you'd be wise to give us the straight scoop. You and your boys all tell pretty much the same story, but the differences will kill you later. Why not give it to me right now?"

Cully was beginning to dislike this guy. He needed rest, not more goddamn questions. He wanted to call his mom to tell her he was okay. He desperately wanted to call Kate. No calls were allowed.

"Mr. Snyder, I've given you the truth, as best I can remember it. You should know that things move quickly in combat. Not everybody sees the same things. Of course there will be differences. If you would let us get together, we'd be able to piece together a good after-action report for you."

"O'Bannon, you shouldn't be worried about after-action reports. You should be thinking about getting a lawyer for yourself. Don't try to protect people like Atkins. We know the violation of orders was his idea. He's the senior guy. He should take the fall."

"What the hell do you mean, I need a lawyer? What the hell for? And what do you mean Tommy should 'take the fall'? Fall for what?"

"The last time I checked, willful violation of lawful orders was a court-martial offense."

CHAPTER 16

SO HELP YOU GOD

2 April
1030 Hours

The Armed Services Committee hearings usually attract about half the members unless there are votes scheduled. At this hearing, despite the fact that no TV cameras were present, the house was full.

Tom Pierson didn't like what he saw. Barbara Berkely, Manfredi, and Porter were leaning back, obviously talking strategy. Of the Republicans, only the old man from Texas looked interested, and Nate Barrett hadn't shown up yet. His people, ranging from Chief Wilson all the way up to CINCLANT, Admiral Ted Schiller, were being held in various side rooms. They were all under subpoena, allowed to speak only to their own lawyers and unable to hear other witnesses' testimony.

Porter called the hearing to order. "Today we will hear testimony from the naval officers involved in the unfortunate events at Portpatrick Lodge in Scotland last week. This is a closed hearing, and the transcript will be classified at least secret or at a higher level if committee counsel so recommends. We will hear from the officers and men involved in the incident, their superiors, and various experts on military law and the constitutionally established civilian control over the military.

"I spoke earlier with Defense Secretary Touchman. He assured me that this hearing will not interfere with the Defense Department's own criminal investigation of this incident.

"Our first witness is Captain Stanley Schaeffer, USN. Captain Schaeffer, I see that you are not accompanied by counsel. You have been subpoenaed to testify before this committee under oath. Have you been advised of your right to counsel?"

Schaeffer stood uncomfortably behind the witness chair. He had never felt so alone. "Yes, sir. I don't think I need a lawyer."

"The reporter will swear the witness, and we will begin." Schaeffer was sworn and sat down behind one of the microphones. Pierson was not going to be a witness, so he was allowed to stay. He looked at Manfredi, thinking, *What is that little bastard smiling about? There aren't any cameras to pose for.*

Porter finished the introductory remarks. "Captain Schaeffer, do you have an opening statement?"

"No, sir."

"The chair recognizes the senator from California, Mr. Manfredi." Nate Barrett entered the room, Kate in tow. He sat heavily and looked down at his papers.

"I thank the chair. Mr. Chairman, I know my time is limited, but I would like to have my introductory statement considered as read and included in the record."

"So ordered."

"Captain Schaeffer, you are commander of all of the SEAL teams assigned to the Atlantic Command. They are based in Little Creek, Virginia. A platoon from one of those teams, your Team 4, is the bunch that was involved in the incident last week in which the French prime minister, Mr. Tournier, was killed."

"Yes, sir."

"Captain, you had a conversation with the platoon commander, Lieutenant O'Bannon, just before the incident in which you confirmed to him that his orders were to stay out of the fighting, isn't that correct?"

"Yes, sir, on the scrambled radio frequency we use for such matters."

"And did Mr. O'Bannon ask you to get those orders changed so that they could join the fighting?"

"Yes, sir, but—"

"But me no buts, Captain, did he make that request?"

"Yes, sir."

"And did you do so?"

"No, sir. I informed Mr. O'Bannon that it would not be possible to do so unless the British requested our intervention and the orders were changed by SOCOM or CINCLANT."

"You mean Admiral Schiller?"

"Yes, sir."

"And did the British request intervention? Did you ask Admiral Schiller for a change in the platoon's orders?"

"No, sir, there wasn't time, because—"

"Thank you, Captain. That is sufficient." And so it went for another half hour.

Porter called the next witness. Chief Wilson looked twice as uncomfortable as Schaeffer had.

Porter, Berkely, and Manfredi took turns kicking him around.

"Chief Wilson, before the SAS and the SEALs left the RAF base, what did Mr. O'Bannon tell you your orders were?"

"We were supposed to observe. The SAS guys wanted to handle it themselves."

"Did Mr. O'Bannon tell you he wanted to join the fighting?"

"No, sir."

"Why, then did you order the SEALs to take all of their weapons? You said in your deposition to committee counsel that O'Bannon ordered a 'full load out.' What is that?"

"Sir, we always like to be prepared for every situation. I don't want our guys going into a hot landing zone without the means of protecting themselves."

"But the answer to my question is that a 'full load-out' is to carry all your weapons loaded, and make all preparations for a fight, isn't it?"

"Yes, sir."

"And O'Bannon asked you to get Commander Atkins to fly the helicopter, didn't he?"

"Yes, sir. He told me to get Mr. Atkins."

"And did he say anything else at that moment?"

"I think he might have, sir, but I was already moving out."

"What exactly did he say, master chief? And let me remind you, you are under oath, and we have perjury laws for people who have convenient lapses of memory."

Wilson swallowed hard. "Senator, he said something like, 'this ain't no drill.'"

"Let's get to the point where Mr. Tournier was killed. You said in your deposition that you had your left arm resting across his shoulder, keeping his head down. When the terrorist appeared at the top of the stair, you fired your shotgun at him and let go of Tournier. Why?"

"Sir, you can't pump a shotgun with one hand. After I fired, I had to reload."

"Chief, I have a statement here from the chief engineer at the Mossberg company, which made the shotgun you were using. This sworn statement says you could pump the gun with one hand. Now, why are you saying you can't?"

"Sir, all I can say is that in the movies, guys do that. Not in combat, when if you take too long to pump it, the next bad guy can shoot you before you can shoot him."

When Barrett's turn came, he lifted his head and looked straight at Wilson.

"Chief, did you know the SAS men who died in the helicopter shootdown?" From the other end of the room, Manfredi glared at Barrett. "What the hell is that all about?" thought Pierson.

"Yes, sir. Me and most of the team, including Mr. O'Bannon, had trained with them a lot over the past couple of years."

"Had you been in combat with them before?"

"Ah, sir, that's something I can't answer now."

"And why not?" Porter practically came over the top of his desk with the interruption. "We're cleared for anything you have to say."

"Ah, sir, can I talk to Captain Schaeffer before I answer?"

"No, you may not."

"Ah, Sir, respectfully, I can't answer that question."

Porter shouted again. "Chief, you are excused. We will take up a contempt citation with the Majority Leader's office as soon as possible. The committee will recess for fifteen minutes."

The senators and staffers filed into a conference room behind the hearing room. Manfredi grabbed Barrett by the arm. "Remember what I told you, Nate."

"I remember all too well."

Manfredi stalked off. Kate gave her boss a puzzled look. "What was that all about, senator?"

"Nothing, Katie." Barrett looked very tired again.

Kate was not just puzzled but worried. She had never seen Barrett like this before, no fight, no spirit. She had been trying to reach Cully since it happened. He had left a short message on her answering machine at home the day after the action to let her know he was unhurt. His voice sounded enormously stressed. She still hadn't been able to talk to him. The Navy was holding him incommunicado. The committee had taken his deposition in a secret session in the Pentagon. Kate had asked for the transcript and was turned down by Forsythe. When she asked Barrett to intervene, he shrugged it off. Now Cully was next on the witness list.

The members filed back in, the staff trailing. Cully was already sitting at the witness table. Sitting beside him was another officer, who looked very intense. Cully was sworn in and told Porter that he had no opening statement.

"Lieutenant O'Bannon, who is the gentleman sitting at the witness table with you?"

"Sir, this is Commander Hiltz from the navy general counsel's office."

"Is he appearing as your personal attorney here today?"

"No, sir, but I was told by my superiors that Commander Hiltz should be here with me."

"Do you want a personal lawyer here to counsel you during your testimony?"

"No, sir. I don't think so."

"Then Commander Hiltz, you are excused. Please leave the witness table."

Hiltz rose from his chair, looking more annoyed than anything else. Kate caught Cully's eye. He seemed to be asking, "Why aren't you helping me?"

across the room. For the first time, Kate became very scared. She looked at the front row of visitors. She recognized three people from the Justice Department, all of whom were taking notes furiously. "Jesus," she thought. "They're going to get him either way. Either perjury or violation of orders."

The questioning began. "Lieutenant O'Bannon, you called Captain Schaeffer before you left the RAF base to see if you could get orders to join in the fight. Why?"

"Sir, I knew the capability of our platoon. It seemed that without the reinforcement we could give, the SAS would have only a marginal advantage."

"But you loaded up your whole team, with all of their weapons, even after you had been told you wouldn't be permitted to intervene. In effect, you had foreseen some way you might intervene, correct?"

"Sir, I never intended to join in the fighting—"

"Come off it, Lieutenant. You told Chief Wilson this was no drill before you even left Prestwick. You intended to intervene from that moment, regardless of orders, isn't that correct?"

"No, sir. I just wanted to be prepared for any emergency."

"An emergency that you planned to invent as an excuse to join in the fighting. You planned it when you loaded your men into the helicopters, correct?"

"Sir, I wanted to be prepared, but I never thought we'd see our friends killed and have the whole situation go south."

"Lieutenant, when you saw fit to join in the fighting, you went in through the seaward second-floor windows, directly into the room where Mrs. Broughton was. You immediately sent most of your team to the opposite side of the lodge. Now, you have to admit that if you had properly kept those people with you, you could have saved Mr. Tournier during the shooting on the staircase."

"Sir, I had to send those people forward. We couldn't risk moving out of that room without the rear and the staircase being cleared."

"But you kept only one man with you, and two others who came out with Mr. Tournier were also sent back to the opposite side of the building. Every tactician we've spoken to says your action was criminally negligent and that Tournier would almost certainly have been saved if you had kept that pair of men with you." Cully looked over at Kate and Barrett. He seemed asleep, head sunk on his chest. She wouldn't look at him. "Why aren't they helping me?" he thought with growing desperation.

"I don't know who those experts are, but they weren't there trying to rescue friends under fire. Sir, all I can say is that I regret Mr. Tournier's death as much as anyone. If it had come to my giving my life to save his, you know I would have done it."

"Spare us the Horatio at the bridge routine, Mr. O'Bannon. Do you realize the actions you took were an act of war against France?"

"Sir, how can that be? Three of my men were killed trying to rescue Tournier."

"They weren't your men, Mr. O'Bannon, they were the navy's men. But it was *you* who put Tournier in danger. It was you who neglected to keep enough of your team together to save him. It was you who split your force to save the SAS men. They're pretty tough. The experts we've spoken to say they were perfectly capable of handling the situation themselves."

"Sir, those experts should have been there. I'm sure the SAS would have gladly traded places with them. Those people were our friends. We thought they would be killed if we didn't help. In combat, you have a higher loyalty to the men you fight with."

"What higher loyalty? Higher than the oath you took to defend the United States? Who are you loyal to, Lieutenant? Just whose navy do you think you're in?"

Cully swallowed hard. "Sir, I am and will always be loyal to the United States. I have always followed orders to the best of my ability. But those orders didn't count when the SAS chopper went down."

"So you think you had the authority to act on your own and change your orders just like that?"

"Sir, the situation had changed so drastically the old orders didn't make sense. My only thought was to get the hostages out and save the surviving SAS team members. They'd have done the same for me. We're taught to improvise, to change our tactics as often as the action demands. In my eyes, we had to change our role from watching to fighting if we were going to save those guys."

"So you admit that you weren't really interested in rescuing Tournier. Why did you bother rescuing Mrs. Broughton? Why not just help your buddies?" Cully was looking at Kate and Barrett again. Why didn't they help?

"Sir, we put ourselves in the place of our friends who had been killed. Their mission was to rescue both Mr. Tournier and Mrs. Broughton. That was our plan, too, when I made the decision to go in."

"Mr. O'Bannon, let's tie this up neatly. I understand from committee counsel that you have been advised of your Miranda rights against self-incrimination. Do you understand those rights?"

"Yes, sir."

"Do you desire a lawyer before we proceed with this questioning further?"

"No, sir. The facts are the facts."

"Okay, so when you left RAF Prestwick, you had lawful orders, clearly communicated by Captain Schaeffer, to stay out of the fight. Correct?"

"Yes, sir."

"And when you saw the SAS chopper blow up, you made the decision to violate those orders and commit your entire SEAL team to the battle. Correct?

"Yes, sir. And let me add that it was my decision, not Commander Atkins's."

"You won't save yourself by pretending to sacrifice yourself for a friend. When you got inside Portpatrick Lodge, you made the decision to commit almost all of your men to the fight at the back of the lodge, and keep only yourself and Chief Wilson to get the two prime ministers out. Correct?"

"Yes, sir."

"And as a result of your actions, the prime minister of France was killed. Correct?"

"Sir, you make it sound like we killed him. We didn't. The terrorists did."

"Thank you, Mr. O'Bannon. That will be all."

"The committee calls Commander Thomas Atkins."

Cully stood and walked unsteadily our of the room. Before Barrett could stop her, Kate ran out to catch him. Manfredi looked directly at Barrett and smirked so broadly the whole room saw it. "So that's how it is," thought Pierson.

Cully was practically running down the hall. Kate did run to catch him.

"Cully, wait. You don't understand—"

"Understand what? Understand that you and your boss let them crucify me? Understand that those guys think I killed Tournier? Understand that I'm about to be court-martialed for doing what was right? Don't those pricks know that I had to visit the families of the three SEALs who were killed and try to explain why their sons and husbands were dead? And why I let that happen?"

"Cully, I'm sorry. I don't know what's with Senator Barrett. He hasn't been himself for two days. I know you did right."

"Yeah, well. It's just out of my league, Kate. Goodbye. When I get out of jail, I'll call ya."

"Cully, wait—" He stalked off down the hall. There wasn't anything else to say.

Porter called his last military witness. "Commander Thomas Atkins will take the stand."

"Sir, my name is Tommy, not Thomas."

"Okay, Commander Atkins, you were the senior naval officer at the scene at Portpatrick Lodge. You outranked Lieutenant O'Bannon, right?"

"Yes, that's correct."

"And when the decision was made to commit the SEAL platoon to the fight, it was Mr. O'Bannon's decision, right?"

"No, sir. It was my decision. I'll take full responsibility. It happened with me in command, so it's my responsibility."

"Whatever you say, but Mr. O'Bannon already said it was his decision. You called in the Harriers to clear the beach and lawn area. By what right did you issue orders to British naval aircraft?"

"Sir, it was my right as the on-scene commander."

"So, in fact, you had previously arranged with the British pilots that they would respond to your orders. Correct?"

"Ah, no sir. I knew who they were, and they knew who I was. I knew I could count on them, just like they knew they could count on us."

"So they knew you would join in the fight if they needed you?"

"Sir, that's not what I meant—" Fifteen minutes later, Atkins was excused.

Porter said, "Our last witness is Dr. Frank Metzger from the World Institute for a Modern Peaceful Society. Welcome, Dr. Metzger. We understand that you are here to present the work of your former colleague, Dr. Steven Krueger, who is now chief of staff to the first lady. You have given us your prepared remarks, and Dr. Krueger's study, all of which will be included in the record. Mr. Manfredi will begin the examination of Dr. Metzger."

CHAPTER 17

AT THE END OF THE WORLD

Same Day

The rest of the day went past Katie in a dull haze. The hearing was followed by a long press conference with Porter, Manfredi, and Berkely all trying to outdo each other in their fever to take apart the SEALs. "We cannot tolerate military violating the principles of civilian control," they said. "We must prevent such irresponsible actions," they said. "Legislation is being drafted to disband the SEALs and all other uncontrollable military units, like the Army Special Forces," they said.

She sat through the press conference, even though Barrett didn't stay for it. She figured that he would want to know what they said. She was wrong again.

By 11:30 P.M., Kate was just depressed. Her apartment seemed empty without Cully. She had gone to Barrett's office right after the press conference and forbidden anyone to disturb them. He told her about Manfredi's threat, and how he couldn't ruin her, Cully, and Pierson. He said it reminded him of the Vietnam days. He was old and sick at heart. She called his wife, and when Mrs. Barrett came, Kate had walked out. She, too, felt tired and old. She left, not taking any work home for the first time in three years.

She walked a long loop around Washington. Down Capitol Hill to the White House, back around and up Independence Avenue, across the Hill to the Senate office buildings, and finally to her apartment. She hated the town, Congress, and her whole existence. For a sleaze like Manfredi to be able to blackmail Barrett like that wasn't right. She had picked up the phone to call her friends at the *Washington Herald* to tell them about it, but doing that would give Manfredi the scalps that Barrett had saved. She tried to call Cully at the Navy Yard BOQ, at the Pentagon, even at the Officers' Club at the War College. No one knew where he was.

She had drunk a whole bottle of wine, but she wasn't drunk. She realized that her career really meant very little to her. She wasn't suicidal. She just wanted to kill her profession. "What a lousy place this town is," she thought. A little after midnight, the phone rang.

"Katie, I just wanted to say I'm sorry. If you can see your way clear, maybe we can get back together in a couple of weeks."

"Cully, where are you? I've been sitting here all night worrying and trying to find you. You don't need to apologize. I should have protected you in there. I have to tell you what happened. Senator Barrett was blackmailed, and they were threatening you, me, and even Admiral Pierson."

"It doesn't matter. No one could have protected me, Tommy, or any of our guys. The whole point of it was that I had to take my medicine. I can stand it."

"I know how much being a SEAL means to you. I know what this is going to do to you."

"No, you really don't. I've trained for this job all my life. I worked hard to earn it. Now that part of my life is over. I have to go on. It hurts bad, but I've got something they can't take away. I know I did what was right. I also know we saved only one out of two. In baseball, you get into the Hall of Fame for batting .500. In my business, you fail the test."

"Cully, I need you here with me. I want you so badly. I can't do anything but plan revenge on those bastards. You come to my office tomorrow morning. I've got it all worked out. We'll get ahold of the *Herald* and the guys at—"

"No, Katie. We won't. The one way for me to stay sane is not to play their game. My grandpa always said you can't please everyone, so you gotta please yourself. I'll go quietly. But I don't want to lose you, Katie. It may take me a day or a week or a month, but I'll be back. And I need you, too. Don't lose me."

"No way, bud. Will I see you tomorrow?"

"Not tomorrow, but not later than Sunday. Deal?"

"Deal. Take care of yourself, my love."

Washington, D.C.
0400 Hours

Cully had walked a long time. From the Capitol to the Marine Barracks in Southwest Washington was not a very long walk, so he went the far way around. Sitting on the steps outside the Jefferson Memorial, he watched the sun rise. Another day in the Capitol. Nothing had changed for the powers that be. But his whole world had collapsed around him. It took a long time to get up the courage to call his grandfather and tell him of the coming court-martial.

The old man was understanding and told Cully to come home as soon as he could. When he hung up the phone, he walked back to the Marine Barracks. The look on his face was enough to keep people away. He sat on the edge of the bed in his room at the BOQ, looking down at his shoes. There didn't seem to be any answer for it.

He called his mother and talked very briefly. There was a phone message waiting for him from his brother. He was staring at it when the phone rang. He let it ring. After ten rings it stopped. A few minutes later, it started again.

"Is this Cully O'Bannon?"

"Yeah. Who'm I speaking to?"

"You don't know me. My name is Howard MacMahon. I'm a lawyer in Portland, Maine. I heard that you were in some trouble."

"Mister, I don't know who you are, or how you found out about what's going on. But the last thing I need is some headline-hungry lawyer butting in."

"Whoa. I said you don't know me, but I know you. I served with your dad in Vietnam. We were in college together. If you don't believe me, check with your grandfather. Bart knows me from when he had to break up the beer parties your dad and I were having in his house. I don't want any publicity. I just called to say that if you need a defense lawyer, I owe your dad. I've been doing criminal trials for twenty-five years, and if I say so myself, I'm damn good at it. It won't cost you anything, and I'll be there any time you need me. Whatever it is, if they decide to do an Article 32 or if it goes ahead to a general court, you won't have to go through it alone."

"Thanks, Mr. MacMahon. Give me your number. If it gets that bad, I'll call you."

The Next Morning

The Pentagon Early Bird was full of the hearing. The "closed" nature of the hearing meant nothing to those who wanted to leak the story. More than a little bit had gotten out. Many of the papers had a transcript of the whole thing.

The clipping from the *New York Times* said it had proved the dangers of having elite forces "so far removed from society that they endanger the people they are supposed to protect." The one from the *Washington Post* said, "The eloquence of the testimony of Dr. Frank Metzger was an understated counterpoint to the emotional statements of the Navy officers. Dr. Metzger got it precisely right. No military unit should be permitted to exist if it refuses to subordinate itself to civilian command. Senator Manfredi should be congratulated for his efforts to rein in these rogue soldiers."

Pierson threw his copy down. It hit his coffee mug, nearly turning it over. He picked up the phone and growled into it. "Get me General Rubia at Fort Meade."

The young lieutenant at the other end of the growl turned to the STU-3 on his desk and logged a call to the National Security Agency's commander, Air Force Lieutenant General Dan Rubia. The connection through the NSA's own switchboard was always fast and clear.

"Danny, how's it hangin' today?"

"Not bad for an old fart, Tom. How's by you?"

"Got a bit of a problem, and I need a favor."

"I owe you so many, I lost count. What can an obscure old intel guy do for the DCNO?"

"I have a young officer who got hit pretty hard by a Congressional committee. You probably got the briefing on the action at Portpatrick Lodge in Scotland where the British PM was rescued and the French PM died. This boy is the SEAL platoon commander who led that raid?"

"And you want me to keep him under wraps for a while till things cool off."

"I never could keep a secret from you spy guys. Seriously, Dan, he's a fine officer from a long line of fine officers. I need to keep him alive and motivated and out of the public eye for a while."

"Send him over. I'll be glad to keep him busy for a while. What skills does he have that would be useful to me?"

"Well, he was first in his Annapolis computer science class. He was a math major for a time. Look, he was a senior lieutenant on the list for lieutenant commander when this shit hit the fan. He has to face a board of inquiry and maybe an Article 32 investigation in the next couple of days. If all of that goes well, I'll have him frocked with the promotion and get him to you in a week or ten days, Okay?"

"You bet. Glad to be able to help."

CHAPTER 18

WITH THEIR BACKS TO THE WALL

22 April
0900 Hours

The entire team was waiting for him. They all stood silent in their summer whites. Cully nodded to them and knocked on the office door. Someone said "enter," and he pushed the door open. The team filed in behind him. They all stood at attention.

In the room were Admiral Pierson, Captain Schaeffer, and four other officers Cully recognized. One was a captain named Nix who had served as commander of the board of inquiry. Sitting next to him was their JAG advisor, a particularly slimy lieutenant commander named Snyder. Cully walked up to the conference table and waited for the team to file in behind him. "Lieutenant O'Bannon and Foxtrot platoon, sir, reporting to the board."

"O'Bannon, we'll make it short and sweet," Snyder sneered out his words. "The Article 32 proceeding has concluded. We've heard a lot from a lot of people. Seems like everybody we talked to wants a piece of you guys." Pierson gave Snyder a look that froze the words in his mouth.

Nix immediately took over. "That's enough, Mr. Snyder. I think these people know how much trouble they have caused. And how much they're in." He paused for what seemed like an hour. He studied the papers in his hand as if they were in some strange code.

"Mr. O'Bannon, the Article 32 investigation finds that you intentionally disobeyed your instructions from Captain Schaeffer, which were lawful orders. You subordinated your command to a British officer without proper authorization. You hijacked a Royal Navy helicopter after threatening the pilot with a handgun. And you conducted an unauthorized operation that led to the death of the Prime Minister of France.

"The board finds that these violations of your duty, and of the Uniform Code of Military Justice were willful and premeditated. Admiral Pierson has received our recommendation that you and Commander Atkins be charged in general courts-martial. I will let him explain what action is being taken. Sir?"

Pierson felt as tired as he looked. He had aged a great deal over the past few weeks.

"Mr. O'Bannon, the only reason we are not going to court-martial you and run you out of this navy is that one Evelyn Broughton, prime minister of Great Britain, yesterday called the president and personally asked that you be given a pardon for your actions. The president agreed. None of Foxtrot platoon will be charged with any offense under the Uniform Code of Military Justice. Mr. Atkins has voluntarily requested retirement from the navy effective immediately. His request was granted.

"But you have no idea what you've done, young man. At this moment, the Senate Armed Services Committee is bringing a bill to the Senate floor to deauthorize the SEALs as a unit. The bill also does away with Marine Force Recon and the Army Delta Force. In a nutshell, your actions have given those pricks just what they needed to do us in altogether." Pierson gave Cully a very hard look.

"Sir, I'll take the blame. I'll resign from the navy. Can't you tell them that it's not right?" His voice cracked. "Sir, they can't do that. It's crazy. How in the hell can they do that? Sir, these people can't be serious. What kind of people are they, anyway? Is that little bastard Forsythe behind this? I'll drive to Washington tonight and strangle him in his bed."

"Now you listen to me, boy. If you want out of the navy, fine. Submit your papers. But for now, you'll stay here and keep your mouth shut. When it's good and ready, the navy will tell you what it has decided to do with your skinny white ass. Right now, I have to go and try to pick up the pieces.

"In a better world, I'd be decorating you for the action, instead of telling you that you're lucky not to be in jail. I think everybody in this room understands why you did it. Those men in the SAS chopper were your friends. Other friends were under fire, and probably wouldn't have made it if you hadn't jumped in. I know that.

"I know your family history. The O'Bannon name goes a long way back in the marines, all the way back to the beginning. It's a good name, a navy name. You might be interested in the fact that I talked to General Hunter this morning. He knew your dad. He knew your grandfather. He wanted to take this up personally with the president, but I talked him out of it.

"I'm DCNO, so I have to deal with a lot of peoples' opinions. I don't need anybody to tell me that what the White House and Congress are doing is stupid. I never thought the president would go along with doing away with the SEALs or the other Special Forces. Guess I was wrong.

"But we're the professionals. We have to be ready to do the job, with whatever tools the politicians let us have. Right now, we've lost a good one.

You guys are good. You were the best we had, but now you're something we can't keep. All by yourselves, you've done the impossible. In one day, you proved why we need you and made sure we can't have you. I guess if you'd all been killed in action, we'd be talking about a memorial, instead of disbanding you.

"I have to figure out how to fix what's broken and make sure we can still do the job. It's gonna be hard as hell, if we can do it at all. Go home and wait for the phone to ring, mister. It may be a long wait.

"Foxtrot platoon, you are disbanded as of now. You are no longer authorized to wear the SEAL insignia. You will all return to your duty stations to await reassignment. Dismissed." Each of them stood motionless for a second, then slowly undid the top two buttons of their shirts, reached inside and unpinned their SEAL badges. They walked up to the table, one by one, and laid them down in a neat row. Cully saluted, turned, and led them out of the room.

Cully was ashen-faced. He tried to face the team, but instead ordered them all into civvies and over to the beach house where the Old Man lived. "You all head over there. Wilson and I will get the beer. We need to talk."

The team knew Cully's grandfather as the Old Man. They hung out at his house, ate his steaks, and drank his whiskey. Almost eighty now, the Old Man always welcomed them with a growl and a smile. He never asked questions, and the platoon had grown to think of his place as their own private club.

Bart O'Bannon knew what these kids did for a living. Crouching beside Colonel "Red Mike" Edson on Guadalcanal, he learned all he needed to know about what the job was, and how you did it when your country needed you. His outfit was one of the predecessors to Marine Recon, and his nightly crawls into Japanese camps to steal maps and code books earned him the code name Black Bart. In a drawer, covered by socks and skivvies, he still had his Marine Corps K-Bar Bowie knife. The bloodstains on the blade were indelible, as were his memories of how they got there.

The world was a fairly simple place for the Old Man. There were Americans, and there was everybody else. He didn't believe in starting fights, just finishing them. He couldn't fight any more, but he could listen and throw a few words in where they did the most good. When he talked, they listened. His advice had saved more than a few lives.

Wilson jumped into Cully's Jeep Cherokee without saying a word. Cully sped off the base and headed down Ocean Avenue to the beach house, some ten miles away. His mind churned with fear, not knowing what he should do or where he should go. Up to now, everything had been in place. The navy was his whole life.

His thoughts were racing in all directions. *Maybe the French still operate the Foreign Legion. Naw. Can't speak the lingo. Mac is dead. Maybe if I became a Brit I could get into the SAS.*

Without thinking, he pulled into a 7-Eleven parking lot and jumped out, Wilson following. "Chief, you get the chips, I'll get the beer." They both charged through the door and made a beeline for the snacks. Cully grabbed two cases of Miller Lite and turned around into the muzzle of a 9mm automatic. The beer crashed to the floor, and he raised his hands to shoulder level.

The punk shouted, "Gimme your wallet, now." Cully saw the gun shaking in the man's hand, only inches from his face. A wild gleam came into his eyes, and a death's-head grin onto his face. Tears started to stream down his cheeks. His words came from somewhere else, choked out by a man who was crying.

"Hey man, you really don't want to do this. I've had a really bad day. You don't want to do this. Just get the gun out of my face and walk away." His eyes started to blur. He blinked hard.

"Shut up, motherfucker. You scared of guns, sailor boy? Shut up and gimme your wallet now or I'm gonna put a big fucking hole in your head."

Cully glanced left, and saw Wilson, hands in the air, facing another punk with a sawed-off shotgun. Glancing quickly to the right, he saw a third one holding a gun on the old man behind the counter. He started to reach behind him as if going for his wallet. It was as if he were back at the SAS unarmed combat class. He heard the Raj saying, "To take a pistol away from a man, grab the muzzle and push it up with one hand while slapping down on the wrist with the other."

As Cully moved, the gun went off, putting a shot into the ceiling. He controlled the gun and kicked the man in the groin, pushing him down prone on the floor. The shotgun went off over where Wilson was. Turning, Cully aimed a high kick at the head of the thug near the counter, neatly knocking him unconscious. He pivoted back to see Wilson holding the shotgun on the other attacker, who was lying there screaming. The shotgun blast he'd heard had taken out one of the front windows.

Wilson stood up as Cully said, "You okay, Chief?"

"I'm okay, boss." The old Korean man behind the counter was crying and shouting something neither SEAL understood. Cully and Wilson looked at each other and grinned just as the first cop car roared up.

Two hours later, the team sat around the Old Man's den, all sober despite their best efforts to drink away what Cully had told them. "That's it, guys. No more teams. I'm gonna have to resign just like Tommy did. All of you should think about going back to real jobs or trying to get into flight school or something."

The Old Man had sat silently through the Cully's explanation of the incident at the 7-Eleven and Cully's speech about the end of the SEALs. He looked down and closed his eyes. It was all there, just like it had been almost every day for the last fifty years. The jungle. The muddy foxholes, filled knee-

stinking water. The bare patches where the naval gunfire had blown clearings in the jungle. The young face inching over the edge of his foxhole.

"Mr. O'Bannon. Colonel Mike wants you, right now."

He slid over the back edge of the hole, and down the line. After twenty yards, he could get up to his knees behind the mud bank and crawl the rest of the way. The colonel was there, just as muddy as he was. A smoldering Lucky Strike dangled from his mouth.

"Bart, the plain dope is that the Japs have come down the Slot. No reinforcements. No resupply. But we're gonna take this goddamn island if we have to spend the next ten years doing it."

"Got any more smokes, Colonel?"

"Sure. Help yourself. But none on the line tonight. Keep your boys awake. And tell 'em no rifle fire until the main attack comes. If they hear something, throw a grenade at it. I don't want our positions spotted from muzzle flashes. Got it?"

"Aye, aye, sir." He turned and began crawling back. There was sadness then for the men he knew would die that night, and sadness in his grandson's voice now. It had only been this bad once before.

Bright sunshine, in the southern California way. The child, not quite five years old, throwing the ball overhand for the first time. The grandfather, a man of sixty, moved like he was twenty years younger, catching the ball and throwing it back so the boy could feel it hit his glove, but not hard enough to sting.

1972 was a tough year in the world. A president was reelected, but the country was divided. The war was ending, and the whole world knew it was to end in defeat. The whole world, except for the men fighting it, who couldn't admit it was going that way.

They played catch until the car stopped at the end of the driveway. Two men got out. The short, broad-shouldered man wore two stars and the uniform of a marine. The other man was a priest. Cully saw them and yelled, "Grandpa, look at me. Look or I can't throw the ball." Bart looked General Michaels in the eye, and spoke very slowly.

"Sir, is it about Patrick?"

"Yes, Bart. I had to come myself. He's MIA, but there was a really hot ambush. Intel doesn't think anybody made it. I wanted to be the one to tell Shelly."

"No, sir. I'll tell her. Just give me a minute before the two of you come in." He looked at Cully. The boy saw the tears in his grandfather's eyes and dropped his baseball glove. He started to cry and the priest stepped forward to him, but he clutched at the khaki pants nearest him. When he was smaller, he had thought every man wearing those khakis was his father. They were an anchor for him.

He looked up and saw tears in the general's eyes. Bart held out his hand. "Come with me, Cully. We have to talk to your mom."

Bart's eyes opened. He was back, and the sadness had taken him. But he was determined that the sadness wouldn't take them all. There wasn't much to say after all Cully had laid on them, just one thought.

"I wonder what those cops said when the old Korean guy told them what you did."

Wilson chuckled. "He said we were something he'd never seen before. He said we could do things even Jackie Chan couldn't do."

"But what did the cops say?"

"They said something like, 'Thank God you're on our side.'"

"Doesn't that tell you something?" asked the Old Man. "What do you think about that, Cully?"

"Hell, Grandpa, I don't know. I don't know much of anything any more."

"I'll tell you what it means," said the Old Man. Standing up slowly, he grabbed his cane and took a short step forward. "It means that you guys can do things that no one else can do. It means that whatever the bureaucrats and assholes in Congress say, you do something that our country can't do without. It means that you need to stop all this self-pitying crap and get back on the job."

"But Grandpa, there isn't a job to do. They took it away from us."

"So what are you going to do? Give up? Crawl back from the fight and go coach high school swim teams? I'll tell you what you're gonna do. You're gonna take any assignment the navy gives you. You're gonna stay in shape, and you're gonna stay in touch with each other. Because someday, maybe soon and maybe ten years from now, they're gonna need you. And God help this country if you're not there when she calls."

CHAPTER 19

IN THE WILDERNESS

When the Senate passed the resolution doing away with the SEALs, both Katie and Barrrett wanted to quit. They both knew why he hadn't fought against it. She had gone to him the day before the vote, pleading for him to act regardless of the consequences for her or Cully. He had refused. *It's like the guy said in that novel*, she thought. *Politics is a whore's game. It broke Nate Barrett. I have to get out of it before it breaks me.*

After a few days, Cully came back. They talked of his new job at the NSA. She pretended to be excited until he said he was going to mark time until he could find a good civilian job. He was getting out of the navy, he said, and wanted her to agree with him. Katie couldn't do it, at least not yet. Her blessing was reserved for his future, she told him. That future was far from defined, at least in her mind. For him, his life was all in the past.

They settled into a routine. He took an apartment near Fort Meade, just about a half hour's drive from Capitol Hill. Sometimes they would stay at his place for a few days, and she would commute. Some times, when she was busy with Senate work, they might not see each other for a few days. Other times were spent at her place on the Hill. The routine was comfortable, but pointless. Neither of them spoke about the future after a little while.

Cully had seemed serious about his job search, but soon Katie saw he was only going through the motions. He had about 500 copies of his résumé printed, after hiring someone to help him write it. He had kidded her about the short result. "Hell, Katie. If I put in what I've really done, the whole damned thing will be classified." He had dutifully mailed them out, made follow-up calls, and even gone for a few interviews. But he always came back saying it just wasn't right for him. She knew he had lost the only job that would he would ever want.

Weeks turned into months, and then almost a year. The days were all the same to him. Nothing changed, nothing seemed worth worrying about. He spent his time at the NSA, dutifully analyzing the raw data from the satellites. His application to go into field work stopped at Rubia's desk. Rubia had called Pierson, and they both thought it wouldn't be right.

"Tom, I think he would be dangerous to himself out there."

"Right again, Danny. Let's keep him busy, but keep him in-house. I'll take him off your hands in another month or two."

"No rush. We'll keep him out of trouble as long as you need us to."

Cully's life was as interesting as anyone could hope for. He sometimes thought about it driving to or from Fort Meade. He had a job analyzing the hottest classified intelligence data that the country had, and much of his work ended up in the president's daily intelligence briefing. His quickness was appreciated by everyone there, from Rubia on down. But instead of being satisfying, it was just one more thing he couldn't get excited about.

Life was a chore for him, except for his time with Kate. She was the only thing in his life that he really cared about. She kept him as busy as she could. She made him eat when he wouldn't have, sleep when he couldn't have alone, and she always loved him. They never talked of marriage and the future any more. He was always wondering how soon he'd lose her. She was never going to stay with a loser like him. Such a lady. Such a body. Such a brain. She could do better any day of the week.

Katie saw all this. She worked hard during the day, and even harder when they were together. Most nights they would stay at her place, and most weekends at his. Sometimes they went to Norfolk to visit the Old Man. Between Kate and Bart, Cully almost came alive. But most of the time, he'd just walk down the road, looking off at the horizon. Sometimes he would walk down the beach so far, he lost track of distance and time. She would be waiting up for him, even if he came back near dawn.

The seasons changed, but Cully's routine always stayed the same. He'd be up at 5:15 and out the door at 5:30 for a run of at least three miles. When he could, he went to the officers' club at the Navy Yard and swam. The morning run was his favorite, because it gave him time to think.

The run from Katie's apartment was the best for him. Seeing the sights of Washington still made him feel proud. Leaving the Hill, he'd go across to the House side, down Independence Avenue past the Air and Space Museum. If he went down the Mall side of the museum, he'd see the World War II bombers hung from the ceiling. Grandpa's war.

He'd sometimes go left, down to the Tidal Basin, and look in at the Jefferson Memorial. He circled back past the Lincoln Memorial, back to the White House and the Constitution Avenue hill back up to the Capitol. He often thought how he'd run the White House if he were inside looking out. It was depressing to think how it was being run by those who were inside looking out.

Life had little meaning for him now. The job he had been bred for was no longer his, and would never be again. Making money for its own sake didn't interest him. Beside Katie, nothing seemed to matter. She was the light of his life, but he knew he was a drag on hers. She loved him, he was certain of that.

He thought he loved her as well. But beyond that, he couldn't accept the idea of a family.

His father and his grandfather had raised families. Their wives had sat home while they went to war. His mother had stayed home when his father went to Vietnam, and he never came back. Their lives had meaning, and now his didn't. He couldn't see a future, and Katie didn't know how to help him find it.

For Katie, the days flew by, but the nights dragged. Her job was still exciting, Senator Barrett still at the lead of the Republican charge to save the military and foreign policies of the country from the Brandon crowd's repeated cuts and changes in direction. Every month, they seemed to come up with some new way to do in the military. First there was the disbanding of the special operations capability. Then they went deeper, cutting the military retirement pay. Nothing was out of range of the budget cutters.

She heard stories that were so ridiculous they had to be true. Like army tank units that didn't have enough money to buy diesel fuel to drive their tanks more than a few hours a week. Like the marine major who couldn't get money to take his two companies out in the field, so he made them pretend to be in the field and pitch their tents on the lawn in front of the barracks. The more bizzare the tale, the more likely it was to be true.

She still went to the office every morning fired up. Her respect for Barrett was restored after a while. He had to do what he did to save not only her but Cully, Admiral Pierson, and a whole host of other people. She couldn't understand how people like Manfredi could exist. Forsythe was a mystery. But her people, Barrett, Cully, and the others, could weather the storm. Or could they?

When the day ended, she always went home thinking Cully would be his old self again. But his confidence was gone, his manhood stolen. He was loving, attentive, and sometimes funny—everything her mother had told her she should look for in the man she should marry. But the spark had gone out of him. What she had seen on that first day at Little Creek was what she had loved. That man was confident, capable, and knew what he could do in the world. When he stood up, his presence had filled the room. But no more.

This man, the man she was virtually living with, was different. He was still strong. He was still very good at his job, very smart and capable. But his vision of himself had been destroyed. She wondered if he could ever rebuild what had been there. She was trying everything she could think of to help him.

After a while, Katie began to doubt he would ever come out of it. Her mother said to keep trying, but the friends she worked out with in the Senate gym had other opinions. The worst was her college roommate, Claudia. Claudia was as smart as anyone Katie had ever met, but she was also impatient. She was talking more now than she had in a long while. Every time they talked, she said the same thing: If he doesn't shape up soon, stop wasting your time. After six months had passed, Katie began believing Claudia was right. She found herself snapping at Cully for no reason. They went through evenings hardly speaking. When this had gone on for a while, he started going out alone some nights, and she really started to worry. Finally, she shipped him off to a long weekend with his grandfather.

As soon as Cully got on the train to Norfolk, Katie called the Old Man. They talked for a long time. She poured it all out for him, and he listened, carefully. His words of encouragement cheered her more than she intended them to. When Cully came back, he seemed better, but he still wasn't himself.

Christmas came, and with it the inevitable trip home. Cully went to San Diego for a few days with his mother, then flew to St. Louis to join Katie's family for the rest of the ten days they had taken off. When he got there, the whole family was gathered: three aunts, one uncle, a dozen cousins, and the grandparents from both sides. Some of the cousins had married and had kids of their own. Only the kids seemed to draw Cully out of his shell. He was tireless, running and playing with them. Any game they wanted, he joined in, as long as no one tried to get him into an adult conversation.

Katie's parents were warm to him, and even her Uncle Pete tried to make him feel at home. After the first two days, Cully went back into his shell. It happened when Pete asked an innocent question. "Cully, so what was the deal in Scotland? You have some bet with the Brits about keeping you out of the fight?"

"No, it wasn't anything like that." Kate saw the look on Cully's face. The light in his eyes went out as he started talking.

"What it was, was murder. We went out with a bunch of friends. People we'd known for years. People we ran with, swam with, ate with, and damn near died with every time we jumped out of a helo into a hot LZ. We sat there, and watched them get blown up. It was so fast, and so final, that it took me a minute to realize what had happened. In one second, the missile hit the helo, it blew apart, and one of my best friends and nine of his men died."

"But so what, man? Cully, we all know you could have just backed off." Pete was clueless, and Kate started to jump up when Cully's glazed look turned to the rawest, fiercest emotion she had ever seen on anyone's face.

Cully stood up, beer in hand. "Yeah, Pete, we could have just gone home, and left our other friends to die. We could have radioed a very detailed report without doing a goddamn thing. But my kinda people don't watch their friends die when they can do something about it. My kinda people won't make excuses for what we do wrong, but my kinda people will do what we think is right, and when it's right to do it.

"I was a SEAL. You may not know or care what that means, but it means that duty to my country, and to the people who fight with me, means everything. There is no doubt in my mind that if the positions were reversed, the SAS would have come in for us. I saw some of my friends die. Others were going to die if I didn't help them. I helped them because I couldn't let them die.

"You know, what really gets me? It's that nobody, not in the White House, in Congress, in the press, or anywhere, *nobody* has said we did the right thing. Nobody has said that we did what we were trained to do. Everybody seems to think this was some goddamn classroom exercise. Well, Pete, I'll tell you one more thing. What I did was right. It cost me my job and my future in the navy. But I'd do the same thing again if I had the chance."

Pete muttered an apology and walked off to find another beer. Cully went out the door for another long walk. He did that a lot since the disbanding of the teams. He couldn't talk about the future without the teams. Whenever Katie tried to, he would just change the subject. She wanted to help, but all she could do was wait.

Kate sat down at the kitchen table with her mother. Mary Reilly looked worried. Her daughter was the pride of the family. Kate was always the best at whatever she tried. First in her high school class, first in her class at Georgetown Law, Kate always was one step ahead of the crowd, but not now. Mary saw her daughter facing the first problem she couldn't solve by the sheer force of her personality.

"Kate, has he spoken to his grandfather about this? Has he seen a priest or a psychiatrist? He seems so far gone, how can you reach him?"

"Ma, he talks to his grandpa all the time and so do I. Bart says that the only thing that will bring him out of this is to feel needed again. I do what I can. Sometimes I try to make him think I need him to solve some stupid problem at work, or with one of my friends. He helps, but nothing changes. He knows what I'm doing."

"But why does this mean so much to him? Any normal man would just put this behind him and get his life back together."

"He's not a normal man, and that's why I love him. His whole life means nothing to him if he can't do the job of fighting for our country."

"That's crazy. What makes a smart beautiful man like Cully go off the deep end that way? I just don't understand."

"Neither do I. But he told me a story about when he was in high school, and he thought his mother was dying. Cully was a senior, doing real well in school, and suddenly his whole world was falling apart."

CHAPTER 20

AT THE FAMILY TREE

14 November 1984
0855 Hours

At eighteen years of age, Cullum O'Bannon had a lot on his mind. Being a high school senior was enough trouble for someone who was only eighteen years old. College loomed ahead, but where should he go? Clemson? Virginia Tech? His grades were good enough, but there wasn't enough money for places like Duke or Villanova. Not that it mattered anymore.

He rushed down the hall, dreading the session with the guidance counselors. He knew it would be just like all the others. The school had a big deal policy about having the seniors meet with the guidance counselors in groups. His group had a rather dim view of his ambitions. He slipped in and headed to the back of the room, taking his usual seat near the aisle in the middle.

For the first thirty minutes, all was well. The guidance counselor, Mrs. Davis, went around to most of the other students first. It was only a matter of time until she got to him.

"Okay, who's next? Cully. Why don't you tell us about your thoughts since our last session." In the last session, his ambition to serve in the military was the butt of endless jokes. Or were they jokes?

"Well, I really haven't thought much about it, Mrs. Davis."

"Let's talk about it. You have good SAT scores. You could probably get into a very good school. In our last meeting, you said you wanted to go into the navy or something like that. You have a lot of talents. What else would you like to do?"

A girl in the front row piped up. "You lost your father in Vietnam. I think your mother has suffered enough. You should have more consideration for her than to go get yourself killed."

"That's not quite fair, Sara," said Davis. "More people come home safely. But you have to admit, Cully, it is dangerous."

"Yeah, unless you get one of those jobs like my father had. If you want to go into the army, why not be a journalist?"

Another boy said, "Yeah, that sounds pretty cool. My dad had a friend who was a lawyer in the military. The worst wound he ever had was a paper cut."

"I don't know," said Cully. He always said that when people spoke of his father. He was four years old when his father disappeared in Vietnam. He hardly remembered him. The bell rang. He jumped up and headed back into the hall.

Another hour, and he'd head home for lunch. Seniors had the privilege of leaving the building at lunch if their parents had given written permission. His mother had signed the form right away, smiling at him as she always did. He wondered how much longer he'd be able to see her smile.

His mother had leukemia, and Grandpa and the doctors all said she might die. Shelly O'Bannon was a strong woman, raising two boys without their father's help. The bubbly, slightly chubby mom he knew was gone. In her place was a thin woman, who hardly had the strength to speak above a whisper.

His father was lost, long ago in a war far from home. His grandfather had worked hard at being a father to him. Grandpa had always been there, as far as the boy could remember. The boy vaguely remembered the day when the men came to tell his mother that his father had disappeared. After that day, it seemed that his grandfather was always around.

The doctors said that his mother needed whole blood, and months ago everyone in the church had gone down to the Red Cross and donated some in her name. But that had run out, and the chemotherapy and the radiation treatments kept her in need. Relatives ran out first, and his grandpa was angry his own blood wasn't good enough for the hospitals to accept. He had come back from World War II with malaria, and his blood was permanently tainted. He couldn't even donate it to save his daughter-in-law's life.

They were running out of friends to hit up for donations. He went home for lunch, and wasn't surprised to see his grandfather's car in the driveway. He leaped up the four stairs, and pushed the door open with the flat of his foot. Gently, not kicking it in, but thinking it was the same motion.

"Hey, Grandpa. What's goin' on?"

"Hi, Cully. Just came over to do some things for your ma." The old man's face was worn by too many days in the sun, but his face showed more worry than age. He looked at the younger of his two grandsons with pride. A good kid, he was turning into a fine young man. About five foot ten, maybe 160 pounds, and all muscle and hormones. No drugs, no car wrecks, no pregnant girls claiming him as somebody's daddy. He could talk math with the best of them at the high school. If he could only get focused.

"Cully, the docs called when she went up for a nap a couple of minutes ago. She's in tough shape, son. We've run through all the whole blood we can find. We have to get more, and the Red Cross says they can't let us have any more unless we can replenish their supply. It isn't a question of money. We gotta get more blood, or she's gonna die."

"I've started going around the school again. Maybe we can get the church to go to other churches for help."

"Good ideas, but we've done that already. Twice. Go ahead and try, son. I have another idea. There's only one more card I can play."

From Norfolk, Virginia, where they lived, to California was a long-distance call, and the old man knew the number by heart.

The sign in front of the building said, "Headquarters, Second Battalion, First Marine Division." The duty sergeant answered the phone. "Second Battalion, Sergeant Brown, sir."

"Sergeant, this is Bart O'Bannon. Put me through to the XO." The young sergeant's eyes went wide, and he immediately pressed a button buzzing the major in his office.

"Sir, a guy who says he's Bart O'Bannon is on line two." The major looked up at the wall of his office which had pictures of all of the battalion commanders back to Guadalcanal. The biggest picture there was labeled "Col. Bart O'Bannon. Black Bart."

When the major picked up the phone, a gravelly voice said, "Major, I need a big favor. I brought home a souvenir, and I can't donate my own blood to save my son's wife." A few moments later Bart hung up the phone, and so did the major. The major thought for a minute, and picked up the phone again.

15 November
0615 Hours

His parking space was labeled "Chief of Surgery," and Major Abe Davidson, M.D., loved his job. He loved it so much he never even turned down the regular sick call duty. Whenever one of the other doctors wanted out of it, he always volunteered. He had graduated with honors from DePaul, and then applied to medical schools all over the country. His parents were thrilled, but couldn't afford the tuition for med school. He found a solution. When Johns Hopkins accepted him, so did the Corps. He was going to stay in only for the couple of years he was obligated for, but they passed quickly and the thought of getting out of the service just didn't come to mind much any more.

At sick call, it wasn't the usual crowd of goof-offs you'd expect to find. There were some who weren't really cut out to be marines. The few genuinely sick troops who showed up usually wanted a pill so they could get back to their platoon. These guys were so motivated that he sometimes had to give them a written order to stay in for a day.

But today was different. There must be a whole company, almost 200 men, lined up around the clinic. There were more arriving every minute, lining up, standing, and talking with each other in low tones. Davidson walked through the crowd to the admissions desk. The duty nurse was a cute redhead named McKinney. "What's the epidemic, McKinney?"

"Doctor, there's no epidemic. Didn't you hear? Black Bart's daughter-in-law needs blood donations. Someone put notices up in the bars at the NCO Club and the Officers' Club last night. These guys are all volunteers."

"Okay, I'll bite. Who the hell is Black Bart? I thought he was some Wild West train robber."

At the ripe old age of twenty-four, McKinney was already "old Corps." She had to train every new doc in the ways of this small, closed society called the First Marine Division. Davidson was the hottest hot shot surgeon in the Corps, and this was his first tour with the First Division. "You're new here. You don't know the history of the battalion. Colonel 'Black Bart' O'Bannon practically invented the Second of the First. Even a new guy like you knows who Chesty Puller was, right?"

"Yeah, so?"

"So rumor has it that Chesty Puller said Black Bart was the toughest goddamn marine he ever saw."

He had heard how the marines take care of their own. Now it was time to really do it.

"McKinney, call City General, the Red Cross, and St. Mary's Hospital. Beg, steal, borrow and buy every blood bag you can find. And call in the off-duty nurses. We have a long morning ahead."

1145 Hours
Same Day

Cully was home for lunch again, and saw his grandfather, who told him about the turnout at the clinic at Camp Pendleton. When he repeated it to his friends at school, some of them shrugged, and a few even thought he was kidding. The one kid who called him a liar went home with a swollen ear and a big headache.

16 January 1985
1620 Hours

His mother was better. The leukemia was in remission, and he was back to his own problems. After the blood donations he had applied for a nomination to go to Annapolis, and the Air Force Academy as well. He did it out of curiosity and to please his grandpa. Home from school, studying was far from his mind. Looking out the window of his bedroom, Cully saw the dark green car drive up and went down to get the door.

A not very tall man with two stars on each shoulder rang the door bell. Cully looked through the peephole and opened the door.

"Are you Cullum O'Bannon?"

"Yes, sir. Won't you come in?"

The not-very-tall man looked around. Cully led him through the house toward the kitchen. They sat down across the kitchen table. "I asked your grandpa to be out when I came by today. My name is Tom Dunham. I knew your dad in Vietnam. I knew your grandpa when he commanded the Second Battalion of the First. And now I want to know you. I want some straight answers from you, young man. What do you want to do with your life?"

"Well, sir, I don't know for sure. I plan to go ROTC in college and be in the navy or air force for a while. But I don't know if I want to go career. I kinda like computers and math. I guess designing aircraft or something like that would be where I'll end up."

"Good answer. Nobody your age really knows what they want to do forever. What you need to do is put yourself in a position where you're making the decisions for yourself, not having someone make them for you."

"That sounds a lot like what my grandpa says, sir. I don't plan on working for someone else all my life. I want to be the very best at whatever I do so I can be my own boss. Sometimes I'm not too good at taking orders."

"Cullum, I've talked to your grandpa, and your mother. They told me it was okay to talk to your priest, and he sent me to the computer guy you worked for last summer. They all tell the same story. You're a fine young man.

"I want you to know something. This visit is something I promised your dad a lot of years ago. I promised him I'd see how you grew up and make my own decision on what came next.

"You're at a real crossroads in life. The choices you make now really matter, and you're damned fortunate to be able to make them for yourself. There are two worlds around you. You can be a civilian and be very successful in life. If you make the decision to go that way, I'll wish you the best.

"But there's another choice. I'm here to tell you that if you want to, you're going to Annapolis. And if you go there, I want you in *my* Marine Corps." He pulled out a business card and handed it to Cully. "If you want it, you call me. But don't take too long in making up your mind."

Cully took the card, and looked at it hard. "Sir, can I just accept now? If I can, I'd like to. But I have to make it on one condition."

Dunham frowned severely. "And what might that be?"

"Well, sir, I think I might want to just be a fighter pilot or a submariner."

Dunham's frown disappeared. An amused smile replaced it. "You drive a hard bargain, son. Okay, but remember. Your ass is mine for at least one summer before you graduate. A few weeks with the First and we'll bring you around."

Back in Mary Reilly's Kitchen

"Katie, that's a hell of a yarn. If he grew up that way, I guess I can understand why he can't take being kicked out of that life. But what about you? How long can you hold onto a man who isn't there?"

"Ma, I don't know what's gonna happen. All I know is that I love him, and he's worth saving. Maybe Bart is right. Something will happen to shock him back to life."

"I hope so, dear. I hope it happens soon, because I think he's fading away. He may come back to the world. But if he stays away too much longer, you have to think about yourself. You can't devote your life to an emotional cripple."

"I know. Let's keep going for now. He's worth it, I just know he is."

Mary looked at her daughter. Right or wrong, she would stick with her man. Mary respected her daughter's judgment. They would both try to help, and watch, and wait.

CHAPTER 21

NATURE ABHORS A VACUUM

Others were doing more than just watching and waiting. Halfway around the world, in Moscow, business was good. Petrov was used to the new entrepreneurial attitude that his former Spetznaz comrades had taken. They were in Spetznaz for their pride. Now they were in business for the money. A few had questioned him about the loss of the whole team at the Portpatrick Lodge incident, but the younger ones, the ones he wanted to recruit, didn't seem to care.

Business was good for his customers, too. Mr. Craighan was satisfied with the Portpatrick Lodge results, even though Broughton was left alive. Tournier was dead, and only a few of the terrorists had been released by France. Craighan's brothers were still serving life sentences for murder. Petrov had received his full fee, and the rest of the pay the dead team members would have gotten as a token of Craighan's regard for him. Or fear of him.

Petrov's operations grew. Craighan had taken his success in Scotland as a sign of things to come. Soon Petrov was receiving business from a whole rogues' gallery of Third World nations. For Qaddafi, he blew up an Air France jet coming out of DeGaulle Airport near Paris. An anerometer bomb took the left wing off when the plane reached 20,000 feet. The bomb, built according to Petrov's own specifications, was hidden in the galley by a French-speaking former Spetznaz sergeant, who was paid £1 million for the job.

After the airliner, business grew so fast Petrov thought he couldn't keep up with the need for his own security. Too many people, too much to know. He grew a staff, which he had promised himself he never would do. There were only two of them. Irina, his mistress, doubled as a cutout for customers asking questions or asking prices. She was trustworthy, as long as he paid her and watched her like a hawk.

His operations officer, true to form, was an Afghani. Like the huge man at Portpatrick, Salim was someone he had found in Afghanistan. When Petrov was there, his job had been to kill Afghani resistance fighters and their families. Salim was a boy when Petrov found him. Ten years later, the youth was a man.

Petrov had been careful raising him. Salim was a fighter in his own right now. He had learned everything Petrov knew how to teach—which was a great deal—about hand-to-hand combat, explosives, and guerrilla fighting. Salim thought his family had been killed by the Mujaheddin rebels, not by Petrov's people. Salim hated the West and would do anything Petrov told him to.

Salim made a good cutout between Petrov and the teams he sent to do the wet work. The Spetznaz veterans wouldn't take orders from Salim, but Petrov soon taught Salim how to stand in his shoes. The men they brought in from the Moscow underworld soon followed Salim faithfully, as long as the money kept coming.

Petrov's clientele had grown large, and his profits larger. An assassination here, a bombing there. Even Libya's Qaddafi wanted to hire him. For Qaddafi, Petrov charged special rates, because he always wanted the hardest jobs. For him, Petrov sent teams to the United States to assassinate Libyan expatriates speaking against the repression of the colonel's regime. The printing plant for the Paris newspaper *Le Monde* was burned to the ground after a critical editorial appeared. Qaddafi wanted the editor dead as well, and the man was found floating face down in the Seine. Another team was caught and killed trying to assassinate the Israeli prime minister. Qaddafi shrugged and paid anyway.

As the pay increased, so did the risk, but Petrov had worked out his own way by now. The job didn't matter, nor did the risk to the team. His people were expendable so long as the job was done. The risk came only in his own identification. But no one was really looking, so his minimal security worked. His banker, an old Cayman Islands lawyer, knew Petrov only as a man who arranged multimillion-dollar wire transfers from all over into the Islands, and then back out again to numbered Swiss accounts. All perfectly legal in the Caymans, if not anywhere else.

But the money was not all Petrov wanted. He made sure of his people by giving them huge sums as bonuses. A year after Portpatrick Lodge, Irina and Salim were each getting part of the profits on every job. Irina wanted him to quit, retire with her to Corsica, and live a quiet life on their millions. But Petrov wanted more, so he solicited the contracts and the confidence of the world's most successful criminals, those like Castro, Kim, and Qaddafi, who had taken whole countries for their own.

After a while, Petrov realized what he wanted. It was pride. Pride like he once had as a Spetznaz soldier. Money, yes, but not for its own sake. Power? No, that can be bought. But the pride. It came only from achievement in his own eyes. Once he sustained his pride by killing Afghan resistance fighters better than anyone else. Now he earned it from the skill and danger of the operations his teams performed. He still thought of these acts as military operations, not terrorism. Terrorists kill for religion, some fanatical nationalism, or some other vague cause. Petrov and his teams killed for money, just like the soldiers of any nation. But his soldiers were only loyal to the highest bidder.

Aside from Qadafi and his Middle Eastern cohorts, Petrov's favorite customer was still Mr. Kim, as he called himself. Petrov never really was sure of the name of the chief of the North Korean Secret Police, but Mr. Kim was always asking him to plan and execute tasks for which he could charge the most fantastic prices.

Mr. Kim was not an ideologue, like so many other of Petrov's clients. He acted purely in the interests of his country's security—which covered a great many subjects, as the North Korean government had almost cornered the market on government-sponsored paranoia. He also acted in matters of the economy, which complemented the security issue to cover every imaginable subject.

As he had told Petrov so many times, "My country is poor, but we have a huge army. Our allies, the Chinese, also help secure our borders. We have taken American ships hostage, and can threaten the South with nuclear weapons bought from the Russians. The only thing we cannot do is compete economically. Thus the little jobs you do for me have one purpose or the other: to weaken our military enemies' economies, or to strengthen ours. We have no other need for these games you play, Petrov. If you do them for me, you do them for money."

Petrov could understand someone like that. Mr. Kim paid him handsomely, and he performed. After the 1993 bombing of the South Korean Cabinet meeting, their government had proofed itself against such attacks, but it had not proofed its economy. Petrov's groups had brought South Korea to a state of crisis. Their stock market had been bombed out of action. Several shipyards had suffered massive, mysterious fires. The booming electronic industry, growing to rival those of China and Japan, had ground to a halt when a dozen of its key executives were found shot to death the same week. Mr. Kim was very happy with Petrov, and Petrov grew very rich on the commissions he received.

With South Korea falling apart, the North grew militarily adventurous. There were weekly patrols of the demilitarized zone by ever-growing ground and air forces. When South Korea protested to the United Nations, it ended up being the one condemned for "military interventionism." When South Korea pleaded with the United States, the Brandon administration defaulted to the United Nations for guidance. And Boolah-Boolah Gemali was always ready to make decisions that cost him nothing. Spending other people's lives and treasure was easy, and he was very good at it.

CHAPTER 22

AT THE MIDDLE KINGDOM

0850 Hours
The White House

The second floor of the West Wing of the White House contains some of the most prized offices in the nation. Small, crowded though they are, they are closer to the power of the president simply by being closer to the Oval Office. Hunter sat behind his desk in the cubbyhole-sized office he had been given. After the first lady and her staff and the vice president and his staff got theirs, the NSA and his deputy were left with the dregs. But the dregs were still pretty good. He looked out the window down into the Rose Garden. It was empty. The Cabinet was meeting downstairs in a typical hurricane of activity, staffers hurtling through doors to carry important messages like, "The president plans to go out for lunch."

The traffic past his door never bothered him. Unless he was having a conversation on classified matters, the door was always open. He looked up from the telephone to see an army brigadier with a worried look.

"Jim? I'm Theo Baxter, I think we met at charm school." Hunter vaguely remembered one of his classmates from the "generals' school" where all generals and admirals-to-be go just before their promotion to one-star. Charm school supposedly teaches officers how to remember not to belch publicly and choose a necktie good enough to wear in high society. Hunter thought it was one week of work crammed into four weeks.

"Yeah, Theo. How be ye?"

"Not bad. I'm the trash man for General Stoneman now. He sent me up here and asked that you join him in the Cabinet meeting immediately."

Hunter grabbed his uniform jacket, notepad, and pocket computer and hurried down the hall with Baxter in tow. A summons from the chairman of the Joint Chiefs of Staff was unusual enough, but this had never happened before. Hunter stopped outside the room and turned back to Baxter.

"Before I jump in, what's going on?"

"You'll have to hear it to believe it. You know the big fiftieth-anniversary celebration of the founding of the United Nations is coming up, right? They're talking about letting every member country send a military delegation."

Hunter pushed the door open, thinking *What's so bad about that?* He found the discussion under way with a lively fight going on between the secretary of state and the vice president.

"Do you guys think I'm crazy just because I don't want every Third World schmuck parking his navy in New York Harbor?"

"No, Mr. Vice President." The secretary of state was a dour lawyer with a deathly pale face named Blaine Graham. Whenever something went wrong on his watch—which was often—the joke was always, "This wouldn't be happening if Blaine Graham were alive." He was so thin and frail-looking, he often seemed to be sitting up only by virtue of the excessive amount of starch in his shirt.

"We have to accommodate the wishes of the secretary general. He invited every nation to send a military delegation. Some want to come with their navies to have a parade up the East River. You know they're not coming to make war on us."

"Blaine, I don't know any such thing. How do we ensure that they're not gonna do something underhanded? These guys include people like the Libyans and the North Koreans, for God's sake. Are you telling me you trust those bastards to send their navies into New York without some way of keeping track of what they're doin?" La Guardia was building up a good head of steam.

"Easy, Vinny." The president looked across the table at La Guardia. "We have a responsibility here. We're the host nation, and we can't let petty squabbles with some of these countries stand in the way of the celebration."

"Mr. President, if I may." All eyes turned to Stoneman. He sat with Defense Secretary Touchman a long way down the table. "I think the vice president has a point. There is a list of nations which we have labeled terrorist nations by law. I don't think that we should take the risk of inviting them to send their military forces through our front door. Isn't there any way to satisfy them short of that?"

The first lady shut down Stoneman with her icy glare. "General, this is a matter of state. Thank you for your opinion. It will be noted."

Oh, hell, thought Hunter. *Here we go again. Another chance to win friends and influence people.* He looked around for any possible allies. There were none, as usual.

"Ah, Mr. President, Dr. Daniels was called away for a presentation at the Kennedy School of Government. May I throw in a thought or two?"

"Sure thing, Jim. Whaddya think? Shouldn't we just post a few guards around these guys? After all, how much harm can they do to New York?" A few of the Cabinet laughed, and the president winked at one of them. Now the first lady was glaring at both Hunter and her husband.

"I'm sure General Hunter can repeat what General Stoneman has said quite well." She looked at Hunter, challenging him to open his mouth.

"Mr. President, I think your wife is right about me repeating what the chairman has just said, so I'll just skip all that." He gave them his best cowboy grin. "When I was growing up, out West, we didn't have much to worry about somebody stealing stuff from us. There wasn't much we had worth stealing. But I always remember my mom saying, 'never give a thief the key to your front door.' I think General Stoneman is right to be concerned about some of these guys. What's to prevent them from putting some poison gas canisters on a ship and letting them go right in Manhattan?"

"I think we've heard enough alarmism," said the president. "We have to do this for world peace. I don't think for a minute that if one of these people came in to open fire on Rockefeller Center that you fellas couldn't handle it in a New York minute." The president was very pleased with his own joke. Everyone around the table laughed politely, except the first lady, who was still glaring at Hunter.

"So that's that. Okay, everybody. See you day after tomorrow." The president was grinning at everyone as he swept out of the room, staffers scurrying behind.

Hunter picked up his things and walked out of the room. Only three steps beyond the door, he heard his name and turned.

"Mr. Vice President, what can I do for you?"

"Come inta my office for a minute, Jim. I need your advice."

Hunter walked in behind the smaller man. He was always surprised by the speed at which the chubby little guy moved. La Guardia waived him into an easy chair next to a small table and dropped into another one. "Sophie, get us some coffee, I'm dyin."

"So, you really think one of these assholes is gonna blow up New York?"

"Mr. Vice President, I don't think they will. But I'm worried. There will be maybe a hundred presidents and heads of state at the celebration. It's a mighty tempting target for one of those guys to sneak a shot at somebody."

"Yeah, but we'll have security. I don't think there will be too many assassinations. At least not more than the usual number of casualties in New York."

"Sir, you're probably right. But what if somebody tries something different? Like a chemical or biological weapon? Unless the intelligence people warn us, there's no way to stop an attack like that, and no way to keep a lot of people from dying."

"But we've got the CIA, the FBI, all those fancy satellites workin' around. Won't we have good enough intelligence to find them before they hit us?"

"Sir, I'm not the resident expert on that. All I am is a beat-up old marine. But let me tell you, I don't think we've got enough intelligence-gathering talent to have a clue what's coming. Ever since the 1970s we've hamstrung our intelligence operations to such a degree that they just don't work very well. When those bombings happened in Beirut, we lost a lot of marines because we didn't know it was coming. None of those bombings—in Oklahoma City, the Lockerbie Pan Am airliner, the World Trade Center in New York—none of those bombings were predicted. If one of these guys wants to, and can get a ship of any size into that harbor, he can hurt us. Bad."

"Okay, so let's you and me plan to minimize the risk. I'll talk to Ike. He'll go along with moving some troops around. He loves parades. You get with Stoneman and tell me what you need."

"Sir, we have to go through Dr. Touchman. Chain of command and all."

"Yeah, Okay. You do that. But keep me posted." La Guardia reached for his cigars. Hunter beat a hasty retreat. It had taken him five years to quit smoking for real. Now was no time to start it all over again. There was much to do, and another black tie dinner to go to. Marvelous.

1940 Hours
Same Day

Hunter looked at himself in the mirror. Being a bit over fifty years old was no excuse for the growing slackness of his waistline. He still fit into the marine dress uniform, an elaborate business with short coat, striped trousers, and everything except a sword. Hunter was a lot more comfortable in fatigues, but when the president of Burkina Faso was being honored—or for that matter, anyone else in the world who happened to rate a state dinner—the president wanted all of his military officers in their best.

His wife of twenty-six years was ready just when he was. Maddie was as slim as the day he married her, and he was still crazy about her. She was ready when he was because she knew her man. He was ready to go when he was ready, not when the rest of the world was. They climbed into their Crown Victoria and left the Marine Barracks in southeast Washington for the ten-minute drive back to the White House.

His White House job gave him special parking privileges, so the big car was left on the ellipse near the West Gate and the general and his lady were quickly ushered inside. It was a relatively short walk through the West Wing to the East Room, where most of the big dinners were held.

As they entered, the president and first lady had not yet arrived, so the secretary of state was heading up the reception line. They passed through, muttering pleasantries, and headed for the bar. Three steps along the way, they ran into a navy lieutenant Hunter knew. He was holding a tray of canapés in his left hand and a stack of napkins in his right. Hunter looked at him and froze.

"What the hell are you doing, mister?"

"Uh, we were all asked to help serve the hors d'oeuvres, general. The staff was short-handed, so Dr. Krueger asked us to pitch in."

"And you agreed?" Hunter was so shocked that he couldn't even growl. "Don't you think that your dignity as an officer should compel you to refuse?"

"Uh, general, Dr. Krueger made it clear that this wasn't an option."

"Okay. Let me make myself clear, and so I don't have to do it twice, get every single officer serving anything together in that corner double-quick. Now move." Hunter didn't have to raise his voice. Everyone in the room heard him.

In less than a minute, fourteen army, air force, navy, and marine junior-grade officers were lined up in a corner of the East Room.

"Now, we don't want a scene, any more than we've already created. You will all retire quietly from this room and resume your other duties immediately. Is that clear?"

"Yes, sir," they said in unison, and started for the door. Then a whiny voice said, "Where are you all going? There's work to be done here." Hunter turned to see Dr. Steven Krueger placing himself between the young officers and the door.

"Dr. Krueger, I have taken it on my own authority to dismiss these officers from serving as waiters. They are now under my order to return to their other duties."

"Hunter, you have no right," Krueger hissed. "These people will stay and serve as directed. Do you want to embarrass the president?"

"Dr. Krueger, these people are dismissed. If you have a problem with that, let's talk to the president."

Krueger turned red and stalked away. Hunter glanced back at the young officers still milling around the room. An air force captain came up to him. "Sir, shouldn't we stay? I really don't see any harm in what they asked us to do."

Hunter sighed. "Captain, you don't have to see the harm. I do. Now what part of the word *dismissed* don't you understand?" The young man saluted, turned, and practically ran out of the room, the others three steps ahead of him. By then, Krueger was back, this time with the secretary of state in tow.

"Mr. Secretary, let me introduce you to the man who just sent half of our serving staff to the showers."

Blaine Graham looked over his half glasses into Hunter's eyes. "So what have you done, Hunter? Apparently you think you should run our state dinners for us?"

"Mr. Secretary, I don't think anything like that. But the military tradition of our nation precludes officers from acting as servants."

"I don't know what you were thinking. Those men and women are employees of the federal government, just like Dr. Krueger here. They need to do the work they are assigned to. Is that too complicated for you to absorb?"

The sour-faced lawyer was building up a considerable rage. "So you think the military tradition, as you put it, is more important than this state dinner? You must be out of your mind, general. I'll tell you the result of this. You're out of this White House, right now. Pack your office and get out tonight."

Hunter stood his ground and smiled. "Mr. Secretary, I will be pleased beyond anything you can imagine to leave this assignment. You still don't see it, do you? That officers of the military are due a certain respect? And that respect is one of the things that makes our military work? Think about one thing, Mr. Secretary. Under the Geneva Convention, prisoner of war officers are exempted from manual labor. Those officers would be treated with more respect in an enemy prison camp than they have been in our president's house." Hunter turned, squared his shoulders, and marched out of the room, Maddie on his arm.

CHAPTER 23

IN THE MIND OF THE ADDER

Petrov looked out over the western Mediterranean. The villa he had chosen was beautiful, like so many on the French coast. He had thought of retiring there, but the calls continued to come from his customers, and the people had to be chosen and dispatched to do their deeds. None of the so-called international police agencies had even begun to trace his organization. There were some worries voiced by his soldiers, but Petrov's usual assurances were enough to calm their nerves. The millions of dollars kept rolling in.

Salim was there with the morning newspapers. The *London Times*, Paris's *Le Monde* (after the attack by Petrov's men the great Paris newspaper had recovered nicely) the *New York Times*, one Moscow paper and the Tokyo morning papers were delivered every day. Irina read the Japanese papers for him. Some of the other papers he took from his online service. The reports of the day were of only minor interest to him. His thoughts were on gathering intelligence about targets and how he would be making the news. If they only knew about him.

He sighed. The planning for three new operations was well under way. When the messenger arrived with a summons from Qaddafi, he was not surprised. The surprise came from the message—not to take some assignment, but to come to Libya, to Tripoli, to see the great man himself.

Petrov and Salim had flown there many times in his private jet, without an international flight plan. No one could know who they were or where they went. Flying in and out of Libya had its advantages. The small jet picked them up from the airport on the coast and flew them directly to Libya. One short stop for fuel, and the limousine waiting for them in Tripoli whisked them away to the desert encampment.

The colonel moved the camp every day. After the 1981 raid by the American air force, he never slept in the same place two nights in a row. The limousine's blacked-out windows and air conditioning kept them comfortably isolated from the desert's heat. Driving two hours, they stopped for a short break, then went on for another hour. The roads wound on, until they came abruptly to a halt.

The colonel walked quickly out of the tent to greet them. They sat, drank tea, and talked.

"Petrov, I have a vision about how the Great Satan will finally be brought to its knees," said the great man.

"I am all ears, Excellency." Petrov rocked back in his chair. *What insanity is he devising now?*

"You have heard of the anniversary of the United Nations, Petrov? They are inviting all of the heads of the great nations to New York for the festival at the United Nations. They have already published the schedule for all of the events. There will be a great dinner at the U.N. itself. A parade of naval ships from all over the world directly into New York Harbor. And many banquets and receptions. And all the world press will be there to watch.

"My plan is very complicated, but each part breaks down into a very simple element or two. Two major strikes are to be made inside the United States, with forces you shall conceal in among the workers and servants who will put on the great celebration they are planning for the anniversary of the United Nations. The two strikes must be completed within a few minutes of each other. That will be the simple part."

Petrov's appetite for pride was growing. What if he could pull this off?

"Why all of this now, Excellency? Why try to crash the biggest party in the world, where very heavy security will make the matter very expensive? If you wish to end the lives of many of these heads of state, perhaps they can be approached individually?"

"Petrov, you are good at what you do. But I am a leader, a shaper of history. Around this effort, I will unite my Arab brothers in a way they have never been united before. We will achieve greatness here, even as you do our bidding there."

As the day wore on, Qaddafi explained his plan: the commencement of a major war at the same moment Petrov's strike paralyzed the West. All Petrov required for this plan were a few ships and some good men. The chemical weapons were ready. When Iraq wanted to hide some of its stockpile during the Gulf War, he had obliged. They never asked for them back, so here they were.

The ships were easy. Iran, Iraq, and Libya had been buying new Russian ships for years. There would be no problem just buying a few almost-new ones on the open market. Commercial hulls were easier to come by. The Danish shipping lines sold their ships after only a few years' service. Buying one of them was like buying a new ship. The missiles were equally simple. The Chinese and the North Koreans sold them on a spot market to Third World countries. Even if he had trouble buying them initially, Mr. Kim would come through with whatever he needed.

Petrov knew better than to question the Great Man, but there were too many vague answers.

"Excellency, once we have taken the hostages, after the chemical bombs have been detonated, how long will this keep America in chains? What about other nations, like Britain and France? What of Germany or Japan?

"Petrov, you know much, but you must leave the politics to me. Once our objective is clear, that we only wish an end to Israel, none of them will fight. America holds itself hostage even now. The others will never threaten their oil supply."

Petrov knew this would be his last job and said so. Qaddafi was an old horse trader. He said, "How much?"

"One billion dollars, Excellency."

"Done. If you succeed. If you don't, you will die."

"I know."

25 July
0710 Hours

They had been at sea for over a week, which wasn't really a long time by other nations' standards. At the Russian submarine school, he had learned how to cruise submerged for up to eight months. On his graduation cruise, they had taken him under the Arctic ice cap for a month, where they sat motionless listening for traffic around them.

The Victor-1 class nuclear submarine was crude by the standards of the 1990s. It had a poor propulsion system, and the screws were prone to cavitation even at low speeds. But for the new navy, it was the finest ship they had. The mullahs named it *The Hand of God*. They had big plans for this boat.

When the mullahs chose him to take command, he thought he had achieved his life's ambition. Captain Ali bin Muhadi was a proud man. With this boat, with the crew he had trained himself, he could succeed in any mission they gave him. They had given him a mission, all right. One beneath the dignity of his fine boat. Ferrying a bunch of fighters into a celebration in America. He was capable of more. Much more. He turned back to the crew chief standing beside him.

"Fool. I said we would remain on this course and reload the aft torpedo tubes. We will have to do this again and again. Can you not keep this boat on the course I order?" The man looked at him with fear. He knew failure meant removal from the submarine, and probably worse. Several of the crew had disappeared, and the rumor of their executions was probably true.

"Captain, we will hold this course and depth as long as the captain orders."

"See that we do, or you shall suffer as you never have before."

25 July
0711 Hours
Five Thousand Yards Away

"Captain to the bridge."

He swung his legs off the bunk. The letter home to his wife and daughter could wait for a few hours. It would be days before he could mail it anyway. They always waited too long while he was at sea. The days of long cruises seemed to be over. COMSUBLANT had told him the money wasn't there for the operational tempo they had maintained for all those years. The cutbacks that had started in the late 1980s were really coming home to roost. Most of his crew were top notch, but there were signs of slippage.

The 688 boats were old, but they were still the best we had, if you didn't count the two Seawolf-class boats built in the early '90s. *We can still chase anything the bad guys put in the water*, he thought, *and they still don't know we're there when we do it.*

The cruise in the eastern Mediterranean was a cake cruise. Few, if any, Soviet (yeah, yeah, they ain't Soviet any more) boats came out of port for any time at all. The new challenge was the boats they sold to others, like that old Victor-1 piece of crap they were following now. It was no challenge to find her, and it would be no challenge to sink her if the order came. But there were precious few times U.S.S. *Bayonne* got to track anybody these days, and they had to make the most of the opportunity. Training was hard to come by. Commander Alan Ahearn stepped up the ladder into the bridge. He saw what he always saw, the bosun's mate on the wheel, the young kid on the sonar, and his exec watching them both.

"Whattya got, Steve?"

"Sir, we have that Iranian Victor-1 boat at 5,000 yards. He's running some sort of new drill. Thought you'd like to listen."

Ahearn put the gain on the passive sonar up to maximum. As usual, the Victor's power plant was making enough noise to drown out almost everything else. He heard what sounded like a torpedo reloading drill, but there was something else, faint, in the background. It almost sounded like fingers scraping across a blackboard.

"What the hell is that, Eddie?"

The sonar man shrugged. "Beats me, Skipper. Keep listening. It comes and goes."

They stood in silence, leaning into the electronics. It came and went, over and over. A dozen times he thought he knew what it was, but couldn't believe it. After fifteen minutes, the youngster in the sonar seat gave voice to his boss's thoughts.

"Jesus, Captain. Are they beating their people or something? It sounds like two men screaming."

30 July
1140 Hours

"Petrov, you say that your plan will work. It is good. The colonel will be pleased."

The Paris sidewalk cafe was an ideal place for Petrov to meet his contact. He had taken a table away from the street, and away from the door to the cafe. As always, he sat with his back to the wall.

"It will work, but only if the colonel can bring unity to the meeting, and get them all to agree. It will fail even if they agree, if someone tells the Americans of the plan."

The contact motioned to the third man at the table. "He knows. Who else from your organization knows? Can they be trusted?"

"Monsieur, I trust this man far more than I trust you. Salim has been with me since he was a boy. I rescued him from the mujaheddin in Afghanistan. He is like a son to me."

Petrov looked at his Afghan "son." He smiled inwardly, remembering how he had saved the boy from his own men, and how he had ordered the deaths of the boy's sister and parents. But that had been his duty. A Spetznaz officer like himself never thought to question orders like that.

"There will be a meeting, in two weeks in Tripoli," said the contact. "The colonel has invited all of the parties, and all have said they will come. You will be there, too, to explain and help in the planning."

"Yes, but I only meet with you or the colonel. No one else will see my face."

14 August
2100 Hours
Tripoli

There was no press coverage. Where there is no freedom of the press, there is a convenient veil of secrecy that governments easily draw around their affairs. This would be no different from many oil cartel meetings or some meetings to discuss ways to finance construction of cities on the desert. One of the hundreds of meetings that bigger or smaller groups of them held every year. The foreign press would notice the lack of other nations attending, but that was not so unusual as to excite speculation about other motives for the meetings.

Qaddafi was pleased with the plan, and as he explained it, it seemed only to stir the discussion, and the discussion was not favorable to his plan. That was as it should be. They would come around to agreement, but only when it seemed that they had thought of it before he had.

The meeting had been going all day, and they had decided nothing. As usual, they were arguing among themselves.

"The whole idea is preposterous," said Syria. "The Americans may seem weak, but no one, not even this president of theirs, could keep them out of such a war."

Iran was also skeptical. "How can you smuggle a whole navy into New York harbor undetected? There will be leaks in the security for this whole scheme, and it will fail just as all the others like it have failed."

Immediately, Iraq and Syria were shouting at him. "There will be no traitors to this plan unless they are Iranian traitors."

"You say that to me, here? I say we may wish to put off this fight with the Israelis. We may need time to dispose of the unbelievers in this room."

Qaddafi sat back. There would be agreement later. They would fight perhaps one day longer. And then they would agree.

15 August
1000 Hours
Tripoli

"There are three key parts to this plan. First, it is the surprise we will achieve by using the chemical and biological weapons we have amassed in the past three years. With our Rodong missiles, we can hit Haifa, Tel Aviv, and every other major Israeli city in the first day of the war."

"You say you can, but why use them?" asked Syria. "We have two small nuclear weapons we bought from the Russians. Why not use them?"

"Simply because you have no means to deliver them."

"We have never been failed by our suicide bombers. They can do this as well."

"That is foolish. The missiles will work. The second part of the plan involves some new pilots."

"About time," said Lebanon. "Every time Arab pilots have faced the Israelis, they have failed."

"This time they will not be facing our pilots." Qaddafi smiled so widely they all fell silent, for the moment.

"None of you study warfare as I do. There is one man who has revolutionized air combat. His name is Victor Pougachev, and he is Russian. For the past five years, he has been the star performer at every air show around the world. His squadron of Russian Su-27s is probably the best squadron of fighters in the world."

"So what? We have used Russians to train our men before. Nothing changes the result."

"But the result changes if Pougachev flies for us, not just trains our pilots. I have arranged with the Russians to hire Pougachev, his squadron, and all of their support equipment and personnel. Add to them five other squadrons the Russians will send, and you have almost 100 aircraft that will fly against the Israelis without any of our pilots leaving the ground.

"The Russians will fly here secretly, paint our markings on their planes, and when the Israeli Air Force rises to challenge us, they will be defeated."

There were murmurings around the table. It would take a short time for them to digest this, and speak to their air commanders at home. There was just one more thing to lay out.

"The United Nations' fiftieth anniversary will give us the opportunity. For this to be done, we will require a very large assault force, more than 100 men. But even such a force could never hold the U.N. building itself; it is far too big. We will have to move the hostages to a better place. Fortunately, there is a perfect place right inside New York Harbor."

"This gets worse and worse at every turn," said Iran. "Hiding navies in New York. Russian pilots. Now what have you to say? Shall we hold the hostages on the floor of the New York Stock Exchange?"

Qaddafi looked coldly at the man. The other man shivered at his smile and looked down at the floor. Qaddafi spoke very softly.

"No, not the stock exchange. But there is a place in New York which is perfect. It is a monument, built like a fortress, with yard-thick stone walls twenty feet high all around it. Only a few doors. A forty-foot-wide walkway on top of those walls, with clear fields of fire almost all around. The whole thing sits on a tiny island, maybe 500 meters long and half as wide. It would be a perfect place to defend for just a few days. It is called Liberty Island, and the American Statue of Liberty sits on the fortress. Look."

He flashed slides of the statue and the island on a screen at one end of the room. No one spoke. They had all seen pictures of the statue, and some of them had walked through it on tours of New York. Every one of them had hated it because of what it stood for—America.

Now they looked at it differently. It was a fortress. No one could approach it unseen. A small, determined group could hold it against assault almost indefinitely. There were many murmurs around the room. And the beginnings of an agreement.

Every one of them was a member of the United Nations. Every one of them wanted to be the force that led to victory, but only Libya and Iran had any ships larger than small patrol boats. No problem. There were surplus naval ships for sale everywhere, not just Russia and China. The French had a whole group of fast frigates that could be bought. Crews for those ships need not be numerous or skillful. It didn't take very much to light off the gas turbines and drive the ships along in a column. A few merchant seamen could be paid to navigate and supervise the crews. The freedom fighters only had to ride along and be ready when they reached their destination.

The meeting went on into the night, and then began again the next morning. By then the staffs had agreed, and the process of buying the ships had begun. No one thought about the consequences of failure, least of all Petrov's employer.

On the third day, they talked about the air war. There were other plans for the Israeli air force. The Arab nations had learned their lessons in the 1967 and 1972 wars. The experience of the Beka's Valley in the 1980s was burned into their minds. In the earlier wars, their air forces had been caught on the ground and wiped out by the aggressive strikes Israel made in the first hours of those wars. Now, they would not be caught again. Their pilots were better trained after years with the Russians, the Chinese and the North Koreans. They still lacked experience, but they knew enough to obey orders. And Pougachev was their ace in the hole.

Pougachev would lead the force of Su-27s and Mig-29s which were to be staged for an ambush of the Israelis. The Russians would be renting out the equivalent of two wings—almost a hundred aircraft—for the battle. The air battle would not be one-sided, at least not in favor of the Israelis. This new alliance would pay the hundreds of millions of dollars the Russians wanted for their planes and best pilots.

The meeting ended, and each of those attending slipped off to his own capital. The talks continued, and soon the reports of the meetings and some new trouble brewing were filtering into every intelligence agency in the West. The intelligence men went about the business of tracking it down. It might take months, but they were convinced they would crack the puzzle. And so they told their superiors, who said the same to their heads of state.

CHAPTER 24

AT THE MUSICAL CABINET CHAIRS

0755 Hours
12 August

Dr. Steven Krueger was having a very good day. After the firing of the deputy national security advisor the night before, he had spent hours picking over the résumés of several dozen candidates sent over by presidential personnel. The open secret around town was that the first lady had veto power over most presidential appointments, but what was not widely known was that she—and her staff (which meant Krueger)—were more and more taking over the job of vetting candidates for the top White House jobs. Sure, the president made the final selections, but only from the lists that Krueger and the first lady put together.

One of the résumés had caught his eye. Dr. Maria Sanchez was a full professor at Harvard's Kennedy School of Government and had written several books on national defense policy and America's diminishing role in the world. She had served as a deputy to the U.S. permanent representative to the United Nations and many years earlier had led demonstrations against the Vietnam War. He had the presidential personnel shop call her to come in for an interview with the first lady. Dr. Anthony was not consulted about the selection of his new deputy.

The president's meeting with his national security staff would be short that day. The plans for the United Nations' anniversary were proceeding, but because they were the prerogative of the State Department, there was nothing for Defense or the NSA to do. There had been discussions of the parade on naval units, the state dinners, and the speeches. All of those events were to be handled by the State Department and the foreign service officers who made up the United Nations staff for the U.S. ambassador. Dr. Sanchez was put on the list of invitees for the future meetings. As soon as she was confirmed by the Senate, she would be included in the deliberations.

0810 Hours
12 August

There were good days in this business, and there were bad ones. Hunter had called the commandant the minute he left the White House the night before. All the boss had said was to come in at 0830 the following morning. Hunter parked his car in a visitor's spot near the Mall entrance to the Pentagon and walked briskly up the stairs to the office of the commandant of the Marine Corps.

General Tom Dunham was the senior general in the marines, and carried four stars on each shoulder. His career spanned almost four decades and was a legend in the Corps. Caught trying to enlist at the ripe old age of fifteen, Dunham had his nose twisted nearly off his face by the recruiting sergeant. Failing that attempt, he won a scholarship to the Virginia Military Institute and managed to graduate first in his class with a commission in the marines. After that, there was no fight the Corps was in that Dunham wasn't. Guantanamo Bay during the Cuban missile crisis. Vietnam saw him return for a second and a third tour.

The Middle East saw him come and go so often he learned fluent Farsi (which served him well in dealing with Washington cab drivers). From there he was sent to Grenada. The Falklands, on secret loan to the British to help plan their landings. Lebanon. When the Iraqis invaded Kuwait, he reached for the phone to request orders to go there. He commanded the First Marine Division there, and was on the way to Baghdad at high speed and low altitude when President Bush ordered a halt. Just like Hunter, at the age of sixty-two, Dunham could still take a man down.

Hunter stopped outside Dunham's office. This wasn't going to be pleasant, but he knew how to take his medicine. He took a deep breath and walked through the door. The master sergeant manning the front desk motioned him to a chair and walked to the coffee urn to get Hunter a cup, but Hunter waved him off. He wasn't so old that he needed them to pour. He filled a mug and turned to see Dunham walking out of the inner office.

"Jim, come on in." The two went in and the boss closed the door behind them. "Siddown."

"I gather you had a bit of an argument with Sec State last night."

"Yes, sir. I plan to call him to apologize. If you think it's advisable, I'll put in my papers."

"Wait one goddamn minute. First tell me if it's true that they had officers serving cocktails like waiters."

"Sir, they sure did. When I walked in, there were about a dozen junior officers serving drinks and hors d'oeuvres from silver goddamn trays. I did give them a direct order to quit serving. That's when Dr. Krueger came after me, and I had some words with Sec State."

"Okay. You're not retiring, not on my watch. And don't let me catch you apologizing for doing what was right. What the hell are our junior officers being taught? Didn't any of them think to object?"

"I guess not, sir. They were kinda caught up in the culture they're working in over at the White House. They didn't see anything wrong in it."

"Here's what you're gonna do. I want you to report to the commandant of cadets at Annapolis today. As of now, you're on detail to him to develop and teach a course on how officers should behave in the civilian government environment."

"Sir, I can take it. If I should retire, I'll do it now. Please don't put me out to pasture."

"Jim, for an honest-to-God scientist, you're pretty dumb sometimes. Cool your heels in Annapolis for a while, while I figure out how to get you back in something we both know you're good at doing."

"You mean another political job, sir?"

"Jesus, you're dumber than I thought. No, goddamn it. I want you to take my old job. In about two months, you're gonna get the Big Red One to command. Now get outta here, and keep your mouth shut for at least a coupla weeks."

Hunter smiled. "Thanks, boss. I won't let you down." He saluted, turned, and walked out with the feeling that he'd just been welcomed home.

1018 Hours
12 March

There was not going to be a war. Blaine Graham had promised himself that much. He had been flying back and forth from Washington to Bagdad, from London to Teheran, from Teheran to Tel Aviv. He liked the shuttle diplomacy made famous by Henry Kissinger. Hell, Kissinger had gotten a Nobel Prize for it. Maybe Graham would get one, too. He thought he should.

The meetings were short and often unproductive. But Churchill said that "jaw-jaw" was better than "war-war." He knew in his heart that he would go down as one of the great peacemakers, regardless of what the generals in the Pentagon thought.

The last two weeks had been rough on him and his staff. They had spoken often with the Israelis, urging caution and restraint. He had said the same to the Syrian president once by telephone, and had been invited to the Presidential Palace. He had gone the following day, at the appointed time, but the president could not see him, even though he had waited for an hour and a half. He stayed, and returned to the palace the next morning for another appointment his staff had confirmed. He waited three hours this time, and President Assad would not see him. This precipitated an ugly conversation with the American president and vice president.

"Mr. President, I believe I should stay and continue to try to see Mr. Assad."

"Well, if you think it will help, Blaine, you go right ahead." Brandon's mind seemed elsewhere.

"Wait a minute, Blaine. I think this guy is playing you for a real sap. Why play around? If he wants ta meet with ya, why doesn't he show up when you're suppose ta meet him?"

"Mr. Vice President, I don't think you fully appreciate the delicacy of this situation."

"Blaine, I don't think you understand a goddamn thing about this guy. Here you are the representative of the only superpower in the world, and he's treating you like dirt. Why put up with it?"

"Because, sir, this is the only way we can preserve the peace process."

"Blaine, peace is about winners and losers. The losers agree to the peace because they have no choice. This peace process you seem so anxious to fall on your sword for—and take all of us with you—is nothing more than an exercise in public relations."

"Mr. President, I submit this to you. I think the vice president, coming from the background he does, is not, ah, properly experienced to deal with matters of diplomacy such as this."

"Goddamn it." La Guardia was up out of his chair. If Blaine Graham had been in the room instead of the speaker phone, La Guardia would have been right in his face. "You pompous asshole, you really think that because I didn't go to Harvard like you that I can't see what's going on? Doesn't your shit stink?"

"Vinny, calm down. We govern by consensus, not confrontation. I just know if the two of you keep talking, we'll reach the right decision." His big smile was back, aimed at La Guardia.

"Let Blaine finish. I think Vinny might have a point, too, though, Blaine. Don't you?"

"Of course he does, Mr. President, but the point isn't applicable here. The point of Mr. Assad's actions is not to snub the United States. He knows how we must be reckoned with in matters of diplomacy."

La Guardia sat back down. He sighed heavily and looked at the ceiling.

"Blaine, you go ahead and wait another day or two if you want to. But I want you to visit with Ben David again in a day or so, 'cause they're getting really antsy." The president smiled. Another tough call made.

1445 Hours
12 March

Haffez Assad smiled. The Americans seemed completely pliable. Whenever he wanted the secretary of state to come, the man came at a run. When Assad refused to see him, it was Graham who apologized and went back to his hotel. Today would be the same. He was enjoying this game.

But there were bigger stakes. Qaddafi had bet his country on this ambitious war. Syria had agreed, but it was Syria that would risk most if not all of its army and its billions of dollars worth of equipment. What if the Americans did not hold back? This game with Graham was a test. Were they all so spineless that they would be treated this way without complaint? He could not believe it would be this easy, but Graham was proving him wrong. Maybe Qaddafi was right. Maybe America had lost its manhood.

He had heard all the tales from Washington. The president who snuck out of the White House to sleep with young Hollywood starlets with his wife at home. The other scandals which seemed to follow him everywhere. How could a man with such things on his mind concentrate on anything else? It was clear that the American president had no will to fight. When he allowed a few Haitian thugs to turn away a U.S. Navy ship by waving a few pistols around, Assad shook his head in wonder. There had to be a deeper game he was playing.

But now, after Haiti, after Somalia, after sinking thousands of men into a Bosnian swamp, it was all clear to Assad. There was no deeper game. There was no game at all. The American president acted on reflex. And his subordinates did as well. *If Allah gives us luck, we shall hold their president hostage, and with him, what little is left of their national will. The plan may just work.* He turned to pick up the telephone. He would have his most junior minister call Mr. Graham and invite him for lunch. The junior man would have orders to stand Graham up as well. *How long can we play this game?*

CHAPTER 25

AT THE BOTTOM OF THE FOOD CHAIN

0310 Hours
13 March

The young lieutenant smiled. He knew the job was dangerous, far more dangerous than anything he was told he would have to do, but the thrill of the stalk was more than enough reward. It was a stalking, after all. He sat quietly, in a draw behind the Syrian position near the Golan Heights. Ever since the 1972 war, the Golan had been Israel's. There were endless talks about how it should be surrendered, but the talks never amounted to more than just words. The defense of the nation could depend on what went on at the top of the hills.

The Syrian tank units were always on alert, but their maneuvers were different this time. He couldn't put a finger on the difference, but their thrusts toward the border seemed to have a purpose this time. Their logistic support, in the form of fuel bowsers and ammunition trucks, seemed closer at hand than before. He never could get confirmation, but there was a feeling about this that he hadn't had before. It was worth a talk with the colonel.

The colonel had been warned by intelligence months before. The satellite photos from the Americans had been coming in steadily for weeks now. There was not much doubt—the Syrians meant to make war. What was most disquieting about it, the Jordanians, the Iranians, the Iraqis, the Libyans, and even the Egyptians seemed to be joining in. The general had been curt with him. "Zvi, I don't have time to explain. You worry about digging your brigade in to defend the Golan. Our air force and army will strike first if we have to, just like in '72. Now get out of here. We have much to do."

The colonel had not attended the long string of meetings between the general staff and the prime minister, which had been going on almost nonstop for a week now. The PM wanted to go slowly at first, but when he had heard the plans and saw what had been done in the first hours of the 1972 war, he realized he had no choice. But there were other things now, missiles and gas.

That was why the colonel was brought into this particular meeting. One of the few missile experts in the Israeli Army, he was needed to tell the prime minister how real the threat was. And how little the defenses could really do.

The Israeli Arrow antimissile system, like the American Patriot system, did work, but not all the time, and it wasn't very effective against short- and medium-range ballistic missiles. It also shared another serious problem with the Patriot.

"Sir, we have confirmation that the Syrians and the Libyans have both chemical and biological warheads for the Rodong and other missiles. We have Arrow and Patriot sites in place around Tel Aviv and Jerusalem, but there aren't enough missiles in our inventory to hold off more than one or two salvos."

"But how many missiles do *they* have? Surely they can't have that many."

"Sir, they do. They have hundreds of missiles. We have precisely seventy-six warshots for the Arrow batteries, and only eighteen for the Patriot batteries the Americans sold us."

"So do we just let our people die?"

"Of course not, prime minister. But we do have to launch the air attack before they launch their missiles. Or we can sue for peace and hope their missiles are not launched before we can react."

"I see. There is truly no other way. We will not go down without a fight. Let us move before they do. When do we expect the attack?"

"Of course we can't be certain, but it will most likely be in the next three to five days."

"Very well. Then our air strike must be in two days."

"Yes, prime minister. We will not fail."

CHAPTER 26

AT THE EDGE OF THE CLIFF

0705 Hours
March 13

Like the American president, Israeli Prime Minister Shimon Ben David was a man of peace, with little trust of the military. He was a Sabra, born at a collective farm in the 1950s when Israel had to fight for its life every day. Now, with the advent of the Pax Americana, Israel slept a little more easily. The Russians still sold the Arabs their best weapons, but there was little for them to do with their new toys.

Also like Brandon, Ben David had steered his government away from expensive military buildups. Yes, the IAF was still a potent force, with a wing of F-15s and two of F-16s. But the pilots didn't fly much anymore, and their training had grown lax. When the chief of staff asked the prime minister for more training money, Ben David shrugged. "Things are tough all over, Avram" was the answer the air force chief had heard. After him, the army chief heard the same when he asked for more men and more tanks to replace the aging M-1As. When they both showed up to ask for a missile defense, they both received a shrug. Ben David got two for the price of one.

But the Israelis always had the confidence of their intelligence services. The legendary Mossad was still there, but the military intelligence people were so good, they never called Mossad unless there was "wet work" to do. Assasinating terrorists wasn't a job you could pass on to the military. Their ethics allowed them to kill without mercy, but not people who sat at their desk or slept in their beds, not in cold blood. The Mossad had no such limitations.

The next day, Ben David would leave for New York for the U.N. anniversary celebration. He wasn't sure if he should leave when a war was about to break out. His orders had been given, and the air war would begin the day he landed in New York. There would be more than enough communications between him and his government. He could return in only a few hours. His advisors were unanimous. He could do more in New York than in Tel Aviv. The force of world opinion would be brought to bear immediately. His job would be to let the fighters do their job, and to do his well. He could not let the world turn against Israel. He was confident he could bring America in on his side, and immediately.

There was a lot of movement of aircraft in Syria and Libya. The Iraqi air force was on alert, and there were fresh reports of Russian pilots manning the Iraqi planes. Those reports came in every time there was a crisis, but this time the intelligence was that the Russians had brought their own ground crews. That was a new wrinkle. He would have the IAF fly a double reconnaissance run in the morning. They would have the results before he left.

There were hourly conversations with the American president and secretary of State. They seemed in a state of terminal indecision. One moment they assured him that American forces would deploy immediately in support of Israel. The next moment they said only humanitarian aid would come.

The most urgent need was for the twelve more Patriot batteries Israel wanted. He begged, pleaded, threatened, and cajoled. But President Brandon was still thinking it over. Ben David tried explaining, slowly, why the Patriot batteries, if they were going to be of any use, had to be in place within no more than a day. If the air war started, and the missiles flew, there would be no preventing a mass slaughter of civilians.

Brandon first would not believe a war was coming. Then he offered to begin a negotiation with the other nations. Ben David begged him not to reveal what he knew, at least not until the Patriot batteries were in place. Brandon had relented, but still failed to see how he could strip the Patriot batteries from their stations in Germany and England to put them in Israel. He would not act without conferring with the German and English governments, but there was no time. So the Arrow batteries waited alone, for an attack that might quickly overwhelm them.

The Israeli air force was under no such constraints. The American navy and air force seemed to want to flood them with more intelligence data than they could absorb. General Stoneman was on the phone every few hours with his Israeli counterpart. The satellite photos were not wonderful, so Stoneman had rerouted two of the KH-12 secret reconnaissance satellites.

13 March
0810 Hours

He walked up and down the flight line in complete frustration. Even his own ground crews couldn't straighten out this mess in time. He had two wings of fighters, a mix of Mig-29s and Su-27s, which they had flown in from Russia only hours before. The aircraft were secure, and they could be launched on fifteen minutes' notice. All of the pilots were billeted safely and on alert. They could go a few days without hot food.

But the rest was a nightmare. The armaments were all in disarray. The avionics test equipment, including the carload of gear he had ordered set up first was still in its boxes. No one admitted to being in charge, and when he screamed at his Iraqi host, he just got smiles in return. Victor Pougachev was a very unhappy man. He had been walking up and down the flight line for almost twenty-four hours, and the strain was beginning to show. His temper was always short, but now he was a walking exposed nerve. No one could deal with him when he was like this.

Now, finally, things seemed to be heading the right way. His own people, having run their Iraqi helpers out of the area, had settled in to a long day's work. By tonight everything would be up and running. He could take his squadrons up today with the confidence that someone who knew more than how to inflate the tires would be waiting for them when they returned. He shook his head and turned back toward the ready room he had set up in the rec room of the pilots' barracks. They would be airborne within the hour. His orders said that they must be ready to spring their trap by the fifteenth. They would be.

13 March
0820 Hours

The Great One was satisfied. He would not go to the United Nations meeting, but so many who had scorned him over the years would be there. Inevitably, some of them would die. The rest would be humiliated, like the Americans. The Libyan forces had advanced to their attack staging points. Within forty-eight hours, the greatest war since World War II would begin, and the Americans would be powerless to stop it.

There was so much confusion in America. He had seen it first hand when he had been on state visits in the old days. When he visited the United Nations, years ago, he had been amazed at the crowds, the noise, and above all the disorder. There was no rule of law, no rule of man. Just the rule of whim and greed. But that would all be shown for what it was.

Two days until it would start, and three more until the war would be over. The Israelis couldn't possibly hold out for more than that. Their Air Force would meet the great Pougachev and his fighters, and would be defeated. The fact that the Russian pilots would have the victory would not be known. The Libyan, Syrian, and Iraqi markings on the sides of the aircraft would be what they remembered.

And all was ready, including the messages to all believers around the world. The call had gone out to his friends and paid agents around the world. In every major country, wherever their was an economy worth mentioning, there would be demonstrations and maybe an assasination or bombing. The whole world would be off balance. In that time, no one would come to the aid of the Israelis. He would spend this night in Tripoli, in his palace, near the communications room. The details were too important to leave to the staff.

13 March
0755 Hours

The vice president sat back in his chair smoking an enormous cigar. Both the President and his wife frowned at him, but his mind was concentrated on the intelligence briefing they were receiving.

"In short, Mr. President, and Mr. Vice President, we have a scenario which in all likelihood points to a war in the Middle East within a few days unless something changes radically. We have the Syrian and Libyan tank force deployments close to the Israeli borders, we even have the mobilization of the Egyptian army, and last but not least, what looks like a sizable force of Russian fighters on alert in Iraq. The most unbelievable part of this whole situation is that the Arabs seem unified over it. They usually find some excuse to shoot each other instead of the Israelis, but not this time.

"What's even crazier, we don't know who the unifying force is among them. In the past, whoever has been the lead dog was clearly identified. Now all we know is that they all seem intent on getting together in some huge wargasm to wipe out the Izzies."

La Guardia drew in a big puff, and let it out in a gush. "So what we have is a war about to break out two days before the U.N. anniversary? What do we have that can stop this from happening?"

"Sir, as you may recall, we have only two carrier battle groups left in the Atlantic Fleet. One is in home port in Norfolk, and the other is in port in the U.K. They can be ordered to sea tonight, but they wouldn't be able to get there for three or four days."

"So what you're telling us is that we can't do anything to put the cork back in the bottle."

The president stirred. "What he's saying, Vinny, is that we have to wait a bit to do anything. That's okay with me."

"But Mr. President, I thought the whole idea was to act now to prevent a war, not intervene after it breaks out."

"All I can do is wait. We don't have any way to offset what the Libyans, Syrians, and Iraqis are doing."

La Guardia walked out of the room just after the president. Head down, he walked back to his own office quickly, slammed the door behind him, and picked up the phone.

"Sophie, get me Admiral Pierson or General Stoneman, whoever you reach first."

"Hullo, general? I don't know what the hell is going on between you, the Izzies and the president. I just sat in a room with the best intelligence people we have, and I still can't understand what the hell we're doing to head off a war. And why the hell are we so sure that a war is gonna start, anyway? All I've heard from you guys for the past three years is that the Arabs can't cooperate long enough to organize a three-car funeral. Was that all bullshit? Why aren't they just shooting each other as usual?"

Stoneman smiled to himself. He had been there when the veep had blown off steam before. Within a minute, he always calmed down and listened seriously to his military advisors. More than he could say for the president.

"Mr. Vice President, perhaps I can help you a bit. I can't tell why they're getting along with each other. It's certainly not something that has happened before. But we are clear that the forces are moving in a way that can only mean war. You just don't do this for show.

"On your other question, the only way to stop a war like the one that's about to break out is to have enough force in the area to enforce a peace. We just don't have what it takes to do that, not now."

"What do you need, general?"

"Sir, I would have to move two carrier battle groups and get them there in a day or so. We have one in Norfolk, which is five sailing days away even if they left this second. The only other one in the Atlantic is in port in England. I just checked. It couldn't be at sea for at least two days. Sir, the only way to get those mothers' attention is to put a couple of army and marine divisions on the ground in Israel before the shooting starts, and have them all ready to go, with armor, air cover, and the whole shebang. Something like the Army's 18th Airborne Corps. When we had them and the way to deliver them, it was just the ticket for a situation like this. But now we don't have 'em. We couldn't mount an operation like that for at least a couple of months, and the Izzies won't last that long. Sir, we've been stripped down past bare."

"General, are we gonna lose this one?"

"Right now, it sure as hell looks like it, sir. If the Syrians and Libyans fire those chemical warhead missiles at civilians, there will probably be hundreds of thousands of dead. But, Mr. Vice President, if we can get our guys there, if the Israelis can hang on for a while, and if they get lucky in the first day of battle, maybe, just maybe, we can get this one back."

"General, let me not put this too bluntly. I think the president is not taking this matter as seriously as he should. What can you do without his orders?"

"Mr. Vice President, I have to wait for the president. That's how it works." Stoneman sat back. He thought of the still-classified pictures he had seen of the mass killings in Bosnia, Laos, and Cambodia. Mass slaughter was something he had never seen first hand. But he thought it his personal moral duty to stop it if he could.

"Ah, Mr. Vice President, there are some things we can do. Move some people on routine training maneuvers, exercise a few of our submarine guys along with them. And ya know, those air force types always want more flying hours. I guess I could get into a lot of hot water using up all our training budget and fuel stocks for the next year, but that's something I'll worry about later."

"General, I may not fully understand what you guys do for a living, but I do understand the Hill. You burn all the gasoline you want. I'll see to it you get more later."

"Sir, it's a pleasure doing business with you."

The Pentagon
Ten Minutes Later

"Admiral Pierson, I have General Stoneman on the line."

"Good morning, Tom. I have a big favor to ask."

"No problem, boss. What's new from the White House? Are we getting a go signal on deploying to the Middle East?"

"No, nothing like that. The president is sure he can wait this one out. But another, ah, highly placed administration person told me to start getting some things in order, and that's where you come in."

"What do you need, sir?"

"Remember that other asset the air force has? Well, we are going to be doing some, ah, test flights over the Iran-Iraq area, over Syria and Israel. Now, we don't want any problems if they have to make a detour over France. They won't cooperate, at least publicly. I thought a call from you to that guy you were telling me about, what the hell was his name?"

"You mean my old friend who was recently promoted?"

"Yeah, him."

"General, let me try to give him a call. I'll get back to you in a little while."

Pierson hung up. *Well. This may put a whole different light on this mess.* He buzzed his secretary. "Donna, get me General Gagnier in Paris ASAP. Find him for me. He's either at his office or the, ah, apartment he keeps on the West Bank. You have both numbers."

He didn't have long to wait, but what time he had was spent re-reading the morning intelligence briefing. This stuff was big-time bad news. Then the call came through.

"Good day, Tom. And how is life treating you in the Puzzle Palace, as you used to call it?"

"Good day to you, too, Jean-Claude. And I am well. Congratulations on your recent promotion. Being chief of staff of the French air force is no small honor."

"Thank you. I only wish my father were alive to see it. For the son of an old peasant Resistance fighter, I think I have done well."

"I wish I were only calling to congratulate you, but I assume you have as good a reading on the Middle East as we do. We are in a position where some of our friends who should be helping either cannot or will not."

"I know how difficult it must be for you. We, too, have a lot at stake there. But we cannot just jump on the bandwagon until we know where it is going. Tell me, is your president going to do more than just threaten Iraq and Iran?"

"I don't know. Candidly, he has not made up his mind, and he may just wait too long to decide. Which puts us in a real spot."

"And us, too. It is reminiscent of the conversation you and I had in 1981. We were so much younger. And maybe wiser."

"You have the memory of an historian. I think we may have just the same situation now. If you could arrange the same solution for four or five days—"

"My friend, four or five days is too much, and you know that. Maybe two or three."

"I assume that the same price will be exacted?"

"Exactly the same, *mon ami*. I will call you back within the hour. When should the time begin?"

"Either tomorrow or the day after."

Pierson looked at the telephone he had just hung up, remembering the conversation in 1981 just before the American air raid on Libya. The problem was that the aircraft making the attack were based in England. If you wanted to go to Libya from there, you either had to fly over France, or take a long, dangerous, westward detour. For the American pilots, it involved too many added hours in the air. The French didn't want to be seen supporting the United States in what they thought was a mere gesture, so they forbade American warplanes to fly over France. When one aircraft was lost, there was a brief burst of indignation from the American public, and the French just shrugged.

What the public did not know was the French government's decision to do in secret what they disavowed publicly. American warplanes couldn't fly over France without being spotted. But then-colonel Jean-Claude Gagnier suggested—after a huge dinner at a Washington, D.C., restaurant with his friend Tom Pierson—that if France declared a general aviation holiday, the skies would be so full that no one would notice a few aircraft at 75,000 feet and close to Mach 1. So the F-111s flew across France for two days unnoticed in the crowded skies.

The price Tom Pierson had paid for this breakthrough was a steak dinner for four at the Palm Restaurant in Washington. Jean-Claude Gagnier would never admit publicly his love for thick American steaks. But Pierson knew his secret. A thousand-buck dinner—with Gagnier in charge of the wine list, all sorts of expensive things happened—was well worth it. Too bad naval officers don't have expense accounts.

Pierson smiled again. People. Now the air force's "other asset" would be able to cruise over France, far above the crowd of small planes which would contain an enormous crowd of Frenchmen in small private airplanes celebrating a respite from their government's regulation of the skies. Sure don't want to fly in that wine-soaked sky. He picked up the phone and called Stoneman.

14 March
0740 Hours

The pictures they had taken, and the transmissions they had recorded, had already been digitized and transmitted in real time to Langley and Fort Meade. They had loitered around Iraq, Syria, and Libya as long as their fuel permitted, and it was time to go home. One spin around Baghdad was enough for the day. The air over the Mediterranean was clear, that azure-blue color that was different from any other sky in the world.

He had seen every sky in the world, or almost every one. From home at RAF Upper Heyford in the United Kingdom, they had the speed and range to cover any spot on earth, and they weren't alone in doing the job. There was another very small squadron of them in Hawaii at Hickam AFB.

Even though their height and speed made them almost invulnerable, they still were air force, and they still had to fly by the book. Mostly. The book said that they couldn't fly over French air space on undeclared missions, and they never flew any other kind.

"Low fuel pressure on Number 2 engine,"said the co-pilot.

"Yup," muttered Lieutenant Colonel Hank Moody. The plane he flew was so secret few beside the president, the director of Central Intelligence, and a few guys at Lockheed-Martin even knew it had been built. It was called the SR-72 in the top secret–special access plans for its operations. It was the only air breather that had ever flown faster and higher than the old SR-71 Blackbird. Its pilots called it the Dream Machine. Its builders called it Aurora.

Moody drastically cut his altitude and speed to 50,000 feet and Mach 1.1. He knew his bird could cruise at that speed forever. If things held together. Having passed over Tripoli three times that morning without drawing a single missile shot, he knew his luck would carry him only so far.

Moody went on the intercom. "Chip, plot me a course straight home. No detours, nothing fancy."

Captain Chip Mason, the back seater, started punching numbers into his computer. "Come to 310, Hank. But we have a problem."

He steadied on 310. "You mean beside the fact that his goddamn thing may fall apart around us?"

"Yeah. If we go straight home, we'll pass over a big chunk of France. You know we can't go there without clearance. What was that stuff they gave us in preflight about the French letting us go through?"

"Ah, we apparently can go over France today. Wonder of wonders, there's a general aviation holiday in France, and the skies are crowded. Three minutes to the French border. When we get there, take a peek."

They cruised for the three minutes, nervously watching the gauges. A problem with one engine they can handle. If the other one goes, they walk. As they crossed the border, Mason took one sweep with the look-down camera. From 3,000 feet up to almost 20,000, all along their flight path the sky was crowded with bobbing and weaving small aircraft. Whoever was flying those things couldn't be fully sober.

"Looks like they couldn't see us if they tried, through all that traffic."

"Okay, just keep me on top of the traffic and let's get home."

Even at Mach 1.1, the Aurora ate up the sky. Her only reason for being was to be faster than anything ever built. The Lockheed Skunk Works built her from plans they didn't know they had. The team that designed the U2, the SR-71, the F-117, and the F-22 had all drifted apart or retired. The last of their great original leaders, Ben Rich, died of throat cancer. Ben had driven his people like he drove himself, without a break. As the great Kelly Johnson had taught him, innovations are intuition-driven, but only hard work and more hard work can bring them to life. Around the plant, they called him "FBR," and the "F" wasn't for "friendly." Ben's successor, Pete Sellers, was a brilliant engineer in his own right, but didn't inspire people the way Ben had. At least until he opened a file in the back of a safe that had been Ben's.

In that file were drawings for the Aurora. Compared to anything short of a strategic bomber, she was an enormous aircraft, the size of a medium-sized airliner. Five engines. Two to get the aircraft almost to Mach 5. A mechanism to reform the aircraft's skin over those engines and open three others, ram jets to push the craft to Mach 8—about 6,000 miles per hour. And the metallurgy to hold it together at temperatures that would melt a gun barrel. The CIA bought the design in a New York minute, funded the development, and started buying more computer power to handle all the data they were expecting to get. The air force pilots all were astronaut-qualified and hot stick men. They were the best in the business, flying the best reconnaissance system ever designed.

They crossed the French border at 55,000 feet and Mach 0.9. The regular engines were open, the ram jets hidden by the movable skin.

"Hank, they're sending someone up to look us over."

"Shit. This wasn't part of the deal. Nobody lays eyes on us without permission. Where are they?" He nudged the throttles forward.

"Two hundred seventy miles at eight o'clock, closing fast."

"What are they?"

"I read 'em to be Mirage 3s or Super Etendards. They must have full burners going, 'cause they're closing on us at about 300 knots."

"How soon will they have a clear visual?"

"Dunno. If their long-range TV is as good as ours, they'll have us in less than two minutes, and by then they'll have a good shot for their scrapbooks."

"Well, I'm not going to enjoy explaining how we gave up the first look, even if it is to an ally. We'll have to limit their view. Somehow."

He dropped more altitude and speed. The Mirages, a pair, closed on his six and nine o'clock. The pilot of the 9-o'clock ship was signaling "follow me" and pointing down.

"He wants us to drop our gear and follow him in, Hank."

"I know. Signal him we're complying and then hold on to your ass. Low pressure or not, here we go."

Mason spoke rapidly over the guard channel. "Ah, French Air Force, this is U.S. Air Force flight Alpha. Request you move away from us by another fifty yards, we have stability problems." The French pilots chattered with their ground control and flew closer.

Michaels reached to his left and pushed the throttles forward to full military power. The big ship shot ahead, accelerating rapidly. Mach 1.2, and the French Mirages were still with them. Mach 1.5, then 2.0, then 2.5 and the Mirages were sliding backward fast. The French pilots had long since kicked in their afterburners, going to full power trying futilely to keep up. Mach 3. The French had tried to lock on with their missile radars, but the big ship shot ahead and out of targeting range.

The specs said they weren't supposed to move the skin and open both sets of engines at this speed, but his squadron leader had done it and lived to tell the tale. Now there was no choice. He hit the skin switch when the meter said Mach 3.5. Too soon. Too slow? The Aurora seemed to pause in mid-air. To the French pilots watching their TV screens, it appeared to be shrugging its titanium shoulders as the air intakes for the ram jets opened. Then they found themselves flying alone without even an image on their 200-mile-range TVs, chasing a cloud of smoke while the Aurora accelerated past Mach 5.

"Home in twenty-three minutes, Hank."

"Yeah, I get the same numbers. What the hell did you say to them? Why were they drawing in so tight?"

"Well, they were in so tight, I took off my mask, and grinned at them. I swear the lead smiled back and the sonofabitch saluted me. Go figure."

CHAPTER 27

AT THE HEAD OF THE PARADE

15 March
0820

Raw power, that's what she was before they had changed her. A proud, fast woman with the power to turn the world. He thought of her, and how his head throbbed at the thought of climbing on. She had been the fastest, most powerful tug in the harbor before she was converted to a fire boat. The huge "M" on her stack, which stood for her former owners, the Moran Tugboat Company, had been painted over with the seal of the City of New York. She had been the *Tillie Moran*, but in her new harness she was the *Brooklyn*. The city had five fireboats, one named for each of the boroughs.

They cruised past the U.N. Building, going downriver toward the parade of ships, which had formed up outside the harbor. One of the fun jobs that the fireboatmen had was leading the nautical parades. Whenever a new oceanliner came in, when a head of state came in by ship, when the mayor just wanted to throw a bash on the river, the fireboats would lead the way, cruising along with their hoses pointed skyward, sort of a moving fountain creating arcs of water high in the air, rainbows on clear days, seeming to touch the decks of the boats.

Frank Clooney had been on the fireboats for a long time. Just back from 'Nam in '67, he was on a boat when the S.S. *France* first came in. Then the Italian liner *Michelangelo*. Those beautiful ships. Sculpture was never something he understood, but these ships were art. No one could look at *Michelangelo* for the first time and not feel something stir in him. Those beautiful ships helped him forget the months on the river in the delta. Forget how he lost both his boat and his friends one night to an ambush. Clooney had escaped the world through drugs, booze, and then drugs again. But he always came back to the fireboats. He had been sober for almost twenty years. The boats kept him that way.

Clooney took the binoculars off the rack in the wheelhouse and scanned ahead. He could see the parade forming up. They would all sail into the harbor in about an hour or so. As captain of the *Brooklyn*, he would lead them in. Two other boats, *Bronx* and *Staten Island*, would flank him and three of them would provide quite a show. Their water cannons would create huge arcing rainbows above the ships. Every time they did it, Clooney felt like a kid again.

Forty minutes later, he was in line, and the ships lined up behind him seemed to be in order. What a motley mess they were. The French, Canadians, Spanish, Brits, and Germans looked pretty good. But there were flags he hadn't seen before. Iran. Iraq. India. South Africa. There seemed to be an endless string of them, and there were about 100 ships in all.

They were all fitted out in their Sunday best. The crews were "at quarters," lined up as for a parade on the decks of their ships. Some had bands tuning up to play. He kept the binoculars up, enjoying the show. There were all kinds of ships. The French had sent their only carrier, the Germans a pair of destroyers. The British frigates looked sharp, with the Scottish pipers on the foredeck. The Turkish cruiser was all spit and polish, and the captain had a mustache that looked a yard wide. Clooney grinned and waved as they passed.

There were a few submarines, which looked sullen, slipping through the water slowly. The Iranian boat, an old Russian Victor-class, was followed by a small frigate from Libya. Both of them rode low in the water. Only a few sailors were visible on decks. "Probably can't stand on those decks," thought Clooney. He looked again. There was something wrong with those two boats. Were they ballasted wrong? They wallowed around like walruses even in the calm waters of the harbor. Hmph. Those guys probably did screw up the ballast.

CHAPTER 28

PETTING THE COILED SNAKE

15 March
1145 Hours

When you cover the president, you go where he goes. Guido Mussilli sat back in his chair on Air Force One. He, along with a few of the other White House regulars, were the "pool" for the event. They would see, hear, interview, and write the stories to be shared with the news organizations which didn't have someone on the trip.

He usually enjoyed this kind of work. It had taken him to a lot of the plusher, more interesting parts of the world. When Bush was president, the summer White House was in Kennebunkport, Maine. A couple of weeks eating lobster and walking the coast was a welcome sort-of vacation. His wife and daughter usually went with him. The best trips were with President Brandon, though. He liked to imitate his hero, John Kennedy. So the president with his family, and Mussilli with his, went off to Cape Cod some years. There was always some new reporter who hadn't seen the infamous bridge at Chappaquiddick. There were helicopter rides over that bridge almost every day.

On real vacations, the president went west, to places like Jackson Hole. The work there wasn't hard. Go to the morning briefing, write a bit, and hit the streams for a few hours of fly fishing. The trout were huge, and catching them was only half the fun. Releasing the ones you caught was the other half.

This trip was going to be too short, so the girls planned to stay home. He was going to drown his sorrows in pasta and red wine. There were too many places in Little Italy that he hadn't tried yet. Just a quick early look at the meeting and dinner, and off to the East Side for his own late dinner. It wouldn't take more than a few minutes to file this story.

15 March
2010 Hours

The state dinner planned by the secretary general was to be the highlight of the celebration. All of the heads of state from the member nations of the

Security Council would attend, as would most of the others. The entire great hall had been cleared after the sessions that afternoon. Stages had been built, chairs and benches replaced by dinner tables, and a huge dais at which the secretary general would host some of the more powerful heads of state. He had planned the seating himself, trying to mix the powerful with the not-so-powerful. His staff had rebelled, particularly his new Jordanian chief of staff. Reluctantly, he agreed, but only to an extent. The Arab nations would sit with each other. All of the others would be seated at random.

At 8:30 P.M. the dinner would begin. The secretary general would give his welcoming speech, after which some entertainment would begin and last through dinner. The New York Philharmonic Orchestra would play, opera stars would sing arias, and a play honoring the U.N. written especially for this night would be performed. It would be memorable.

15 March
2135 Hours

The parade was over, the ships tied up, and the fireboats long docked at their home piers. The many security forces of the nations attending were all arrayed around the U.N. building and everywhere inside. There were so many of them that the New York City cops had given up trying to tell them apart. Each security detail had a city permit, and supposedly only a few had guns, but the cops knew there was no way to keep track of them.

NYPD Captain Aaron Weinstein knew damned well that the only thing he could count on was that these clowns were so suspicious of each other, there was no way they'd spot an assassin trying to get in. They were fussing over the hundreds of reporters from all over the world here to cover the event. There were too many people pushing and shoving, trying to get a better angle on the dignitaries, large and small, going in and out of the big U.N. Headquarters. He, along with the 200 uniformed cops under his command, would have to keep the lid on.

It was always a good feeling to get back into the dark blue heavy wool uniform he wore today. After almost thirty years on the force, and too many donuts, it was a bit of a squeeze.

He looked around. His people were there, in noticeable force. He had about a hundred and fifty officers all around the building and another fifty inside. They were all keeping their eyes open, trying to look out for any of the waiters or staff who seemed unusually nervous. Weinstein knew people would usually be nervous when so many bigshots were around. The trick was to spot the one who was too nervous.

He walked down toward the river side of the building. It wasn't his choice, but if he could have told them not to moor other countries' ships so close he would have. But threats wouldn't come from those ships. They were part of the show, nothing more.

15 March
0415 Local

The Israeli chief of air staff had been flying around for almost twelve hours, trying to plan for a strike the prime minister might cancel. He knew enough alert aircraft could be kept in the air to save them if an attack came. If they let him keep the birds up. But there were too few pilots and too little fuel to keep up the pace for very long. The prime minister's order canceling the planned attack on the Syrian and Libyan air bases had come only minutes before the planes were to launch. He had gone to the prime minister's office just as darkness fell. The conversation had been ugly.

"But Mr. Prime Minister, what good are the words of the American president? Has he the power to stop what is coming?"

"Avram, you have your orders. If you don't like them, I suggest you call a meeting of the general staff and get them to change my mind. I have promised President Brandon that we would not strike, that we would wait for his efforts to negotiate with the Arabs. We cannot tell America we will not cooperate."

"But prime minister, if we cooperate now, and he fails, there is no second chance for us. The Americans will not be able to help in time. There will be thousands of dead if those missiles hit our cities."

"Avram, I know. I know what you say may be right. But the time for war is not come. We will wait."

Only a few hours later, the attack had come without warning, and now, in the predawn light, the damage he had seen was frightening. But the attack had come and gone, and many of his aircraft had been saved through the initial assault. All of the Arrow batteries had been exhausted, but only one missile had hit the port city of Haifa. There were thousands of dead. Intelligence reported that the Arabs were trying to fire more of their missiles, but for some reason they had not. After the first salvo, the Israeli pilots flying combat patrols wanted to kill the missiles with their own air-to-air missiles, but the ballistic missiles being fired at their country were too high and too fast. More were sure to come.

The Israelis had mounted a counterattack planned to hit the remaining missiles and the Arab air forces, but that attack had gone very badly. There was a new sort of Arab flying the top-line Russian fighter. The rumors of Russian pilots flying their ships must be true. After a running battle lasting more than twenty minutes, the Israelis withdrew. They had suffered over forty percent casualties among their pilots, and the lost aircraft amounted to half of those that flew. The pilots, whoever they were, were taking their jobs very seriously. And doing them all too well.

15 March
2030 Hours

The ballroom was dressed up in elegance well-suited to the gathering of most of the world's leaders. The dinner itself, with the endless speeches, would start in just a while. The cocktail chatter was not the usual, even for New York. Politicians of all shapes and sizes worked the room, sniffing at each other like dogs.

President Brandon was working the room with skill and ease. The president of Venezuela spotted him and rushed over.

"Señor Brandon, I was so pleased with your announcement of the plan to protect the rain forest. I have today addressed our parliament and received their approval. We shall be glad to accept the presence of American troops to guard the rain forest, so long as they are under U.N. command."

"Señor Gonzalez, our Congress is also very excited by the plan, but there are many people who want to see this plan fail. You must help me get the funding legislation through Congress. I know you have many friends there."

"Yes, we do. And I promise you, we will deliver. Thank you." The man moved off, replaced immediately by the premier of Ecuador, then Brazil, Italy, and South Africa. Brandon glanced up to see a very tall bald man with a huge moustache.

"President Brandon, it is so good to see you. We have not spoken since the global warming conference in Sweden last year."

"Ah, yes, it is so good to see you. I was just saying to my wife last evening how good it would be if you were here tonight," Brandon's mouth ran on while his brain thought, "Who the hell is this guy?"

Then he saw a target of opportunity. The president of Honduras, and his wife.

"Señor Fuente and Mrs. Fuente. What a pleasure. Señor, I have always heard of your wife's beauty, but these reports have not done her justice."

The first lady of Honduras gave him a smile that lit up the room. "Señor Brandon, you are too kind to a small lady from a very poor country." Her smile was still bright as Brandon put his arm around her.

"Señor Fuente, your wife is your best ambassador. May I speak with her about your country?"

"Of course, Mr. President. I think I need to find a bar."

Brandon's gaze flashed back and forth from Señora Fuentes's breasts to her smile. He guided her to a corner of the room.

Suleiman Semret spotted Brandon as soon as he came through the door. He toasted his wife and nodded to her. She knew what that meant. Back to business. Before Semret could move, two men came up to him.

"Greetings, prime minister. It is always a pleasure to be able to speak with you."

"The pleasure is mine, general. The president of Egypt is not often enough a guest in my house." He looked to the third man.

"I have not seen my Libyan friends, either. You, prime minister, should visit Istanbul. We have much to discuss. What good can come from this new war?"

"Ah, you do not see it? We do, we do. But what else shall we discuss? I have heard that the European Union has rejected your petition to join their little Christian club. Will you stay at their side in war when they reject you even in peace?"

"Those discussions were only preliminary. They—"

"They will never give you the privileges you want. Why do you still remain loyal to them? We should speak more of your joining your brothers before God."

Semret frowned. "I am a man of God, just as you are, my brother. But I will not bow down to the mullahs. Remember, you remain free only while we stand in the path of the bear."

"Cling to your memories, Semret. Soon they will fade away like all false dreams. And think, Semret. Soon you may be forced to choose. Will you stand with your true brothers, or die with your European kings?"

As the men walked away, smiling their hatred of him, Semret again looked for Brandon. He spotted the president heading for one of the champagne bars. Just as Brandon grabbed at a glass, a hand weighed down on his shoulder. He looked up and smiled at the ridiculous face staring at him. The man's eyes seemed to be resting on the enormous moustache.

"Mr. President, I am Suleiman Semret of Turkey. We have not met before."

"Yes, yes, Mr. Semret. It's a pleasure. Now, if you'll excuse me—"

"Mr. President Brandon, I apologize for the interruption, but we must talk, and not here. There will be war in the Middle East in hours or days. Turkey will stand by its NATO partners, but we must know how you will respond. I have been talking to your staff every day for a week, and I do not get any answers to my questions. What will you do?"

"Mr. Semret, as I know we have told you before, America will act in concert with our allies. You may rest assured that you will be consulted."

"Mr. President, we know of the Iraqi and Iranian troop movements. The Kurdish population in northern Iraq will flee into Turkey to avoid another slaughter by the Iraqis. We are not a rich country. We cannot absorb these refugees. We will not tolerate another Iraqi assault on these people. What will America do if this happens?"

"Yes, I know you will not tolerate that. And I fully understand the need for Arab solidarity. I have said many times, and I say again, America is not willing to fight alone. Now if you'll excuse me, I really must talk to this lady privately."

Brandon shrugged, smiled, and turned away. Sulieman Semret's eyes raged at Brandon's back. He watched them walk away, Brandon's left hand drifting down from the lady's back to her waist, to her oscillating hips. He glanced back to Semret and smiled again.

15 March
2138 Hours

Petrov was right on schedule. The crew of the Libyan submarine and the Iraqi frigate had performed admirably, although concealing his strike force while the ships paraded in was not a very great task. They simply had to remain below decks and silent.

They could afford a little noise now. They had stowed their sea gear, and all 132 of his men, a few on the submarine, most on the frigate, were only waiting for his signal. One hundred of them were dressed in ceremonial uniforms, and some even carried musical instrument cases. They looked colorful with plumed hats and shined boots. The instrument cases, of course, held the heavy machine guns and grenade launchers. Every one of his men had a machine gun, two grenades, and a fighting knife.

Petrov was once again banking on the fact that the security people would be prepared for a lone gunman or even a small group of fanatics wired with bombs all around them. But like at Portpatrick Lodge, they would be totally unprepared for an assault by a large force of trained men. This group was the equal of four reinforced platoons of troops. As he had been before, Petrov was right again.

And the men were good. Again, he had picked them well. He and Salim had gone over each of the prospects. They were all mercenaries, not the unreliables his sponsor wanted him to use. Some were North Korean, some Russian ex-Spetznaz. Some were former East German Staatspolizei. Each was very good in his own right. They knew the weapons, the objectives, their orders, and their escape routes. They were as professional a group as he could muster, which was very professional indeed. Having an unlimited budget helped. Each man had already received a $1 million deposit into a Swiss numbered account. Those who completed the mission had been promised another $2 million. It was enough, more than enough, to get these men to take foolish risks.

And the risks were not all that foolish. If things went wrong, they could disappear into America's largest city. Every language was spoken in some neighborhood here. Many of the men had diplomatic passports. They could get to Canada in no more than a few days and from there, anywhere. Others planned to sail home on the ships they came on, with hostages to keep them safe all the way back.

He climbed up through the hatch into the clear night. It was cold and crisp, the New York skyline all around him. The U.N. Building itself was lit up from top to bottom. He signaled below, and the men began climbing up and forming

followed suit. He looked calmly at the objective, and started walking toward the river entrance of the United Nations. First one group fell in behind him, then the other. They looked like a large military band.

Weinstein spotted them almost immediately, and stuck his hand in his jacket to pull out the master schedule he had been given. According to that, no more military bands were due. But the schedule had been changed so many times that this might be just one more screw-up. The diplomats didn't think it was important to keep the cops advised of their plans. He slipped the schedule back into his jacket and grabbed his radio from the outside coat pocket.

"Aaron to Stan. What's this band coming up from the pier?" Weinstein looked at the man leading them. He was not in any uniform. Just a guy in jeans and a leather jacket.

In a command post van a half block away, the police sergeant scanned a computer screen. "Dunno, boss. Nobody else is due, but you know how these mutts are. They probably changed the schedule again without telling us."

Petrov reached the lower stairs, and started up. Halfway up, he was challenged by a city cop, who asked for ID. "Sure, officer." Petrov pulled a silenced Makarov from his pocket and shot the man between the eyes. He began running up the stairs, and his men followed.

Weinstein, only thirty yards away, saw the officer go down. He pulled his service automatic and his radio at the same time. "10-13. 10-13. Officer down, shots fired, river side of the U.N. This is Weinstein, everybody up." All around the United Nations, security people were drawing guns, most of the uniformed cops running to Weinstein's position on the river side, responding to the 10-13 call.

But Petrov's people had planned well, and their first group assaulted the thin blue line with automatic weapons fire. The cops were dying by the dozen. Weinstein had a bead on Petrov, and thumbed the safety off on his big Beretta automatic. Weinstein kneeled, taking aim. "Not in my city, you cocksucker." Just as Weinstein fired, Petrov stepped aside for two of his men, who shot Weinstein three times. Weinstein lay on his back, breathing in gasps, gazing up when they jogged past. Two more shot him again, and the captain died with his eyes open.

By that time all of the security details were rushing around. Hundreds of them were shouting into handheld radios, some grabbing their prime ministers or presidents, pushing them toward the doors, colliding with others doing the same thing. By then, Petrov's people had sealed off all the doors. There were dead security people everywhere. Some of them fought with pistols, hands, and feet. But Petrov's men were patient. They had all of the security troops massively outgunned, and had the added advantage of not caring who they killed. The Spetznaz leading the assault advanced quickly under the cover of others' fire. The assault was quick, and overwhelming. More than seventy

others' fire. The assault was quick, and overwhelming. More than seventy ambassadors and other diplomats were killed in the rush to get to the Security Council members.

Armed only with a tape recorder and his personal camera, Guido Mussilli could only hug the ground and pray. He had been standing in the anteroom outside the dinner hall when the attackers burst in. A few reporters had been shot, in the line of fire between security people and the attackers. An AP guy he knew was lying on the ground next to him and didn't seem to be breathing. There were a lot of people running back and forth. He turned his head a bit, trying to see what was going on.

Rashid, Petrov's third in command, was walking quickly past Massilli and saw him move. The muzzle of his machine gun was brushing against Mussilli's head.

"Get up."

"Who, me?"

"Yes, you, fool. Are you a reporter? Who do you work for?"

"Yeah, I'm a reporter for the *Washington Herald*."

"You report this. We have these people hostage. Every leader of every nation in the world is now dead or our hostage. We will kill them all if our demands are not met."

"What do you demand?"

"You will find out. When we call you in two hours, you will come to see how we have kept them safe. You must tell the world that they are safe, and that we will kill them all if the West interferes in our war."

"What war?"

"Back on your belly. If you move again, my men will kill you, and I will get another reporter." Mussilli dropped to the ground thinking, *Just what the hell is all this?*

Four minutes into the fight, many of the heads of state were already kneeling, hands behind their heads, under the cover of Petrov's guns. A few, including the American president and his Secret Service detail, were hiding in stairwells and bathrooms, hoping that the help that inevitably would come would arrive in time.

Salim and ten of the men were searching the stairwell on the 34th Street side of the ninth floor, four floors up from the banquet hall. They moved with the quiet they had been taught, and they moved well. They heard someone whispering above them. Salim hand-signaled for a halt.

"Mister President, just hold on. Our guys will be here in a minute or less. Just keep your head down and we'll get you out of here." Special Agent Tony Liguorio had just been promoted the hard way. When the head of the Presidential Protection detail had been killed a minute ago, Liguorio had taken charge. But his man wasn't having any of it.

"No," whispered the leader of the free world. "I can talk to these men. They won't hurt any of you if I talk to them."

"Mr. President, that's nuts. I won't let you move until help comes. If they try to get up this stair, they'll have to kill me and all three of the guys I have left. We gotta stay in front of you."

"No. I'm the boss here. You fellas stay here." Brandon stood up, and started down the stair. Liguorio stood, and blocked his way.

"Mr. President, you can't do this. It's nuts." As the last word left him, Salim shot the back of Liguorio's head off and smiled at the president.

"Please come this way, Mr. President. We will be glad to talk to you."

Brandon didn't look back. "What government are you acting for?"

15 March
2231 Hours

The phones in the vice president's study were enshrouded in smoke. There was the normal phone and the secured STU-3 which he knew was to be used only for classified conversations. He had lived in the big house in northwest Washington for three years, and he had not used that phone yet. La Guardia sat in his favorite chair, re-reading a novel he had read years ago.

No matter how many times he read them, the history, the humor, and the style of George MacDonald Fraser made the *Flashman* books his constant companion. Flashman, the faux-heroic Victorian soldier, Flashman the coward, the classic rotten s.o.b., made the books a very good read. The term *womanizer* had been invented with Flashy in mind. Flashy was the last person in the world you'd want your daughter (or wife) to meet. Reading these books, La Guardia escaped the pressures of the real world. The STU-3 secure phone rang just as La Guardia reached the passage where Flashy was recounting how his best efforts to stay out of danger in the Crimea put him in the front rank of the Charge of the Light Brigade.

"Yeah?"

"Mr. Vice President, I have Mr. Forbes for you." Forbes was the acting chief of the Secret Service. Had Brandon been shot?

"Mr. Vice President, if you would please get dressed immediately, and ask your wife to do the same, we have a heavy convoy on the way to bring you to the White House. There has been an incident in New York. As far as we know, President Brandon is now the hostage of an unknown number of terrorists. They have taken him, along with about 100 other people, out of the building and put them on a ship in the harbor. Right now, that's all I know."

"You gotta be kiddin'! This is some kinda drill. This shit doesn't happen, and I'm too old to play practice games with you guys at this hour."

"Forgive me, Mr. Vice President, but this is no joke, and we need to get you to the White House ASAP to keep you safe. You may have to run things for a while."

"We'll be down in two minutes."

From the Naval Observatory to the White House is a ten-minute trip if you have the Secret Service war wagons clearing the way for you. Thirteen minutes after the phone call, La Guardia was in the Oval Office. Now all the phones began to light up. His secretary, Sophie, had somehow gotten word and was already there, brewing coffee. She knew it would be a long night.

"Sophie, get me General Stoneman at the Pentagon. Tell him I want a meeting as soon as he can get here. And find Jim Hunter for me. Where the hell did they send him when those putzes fired him?"

There was the beginnings of news coverage, but only the sketchiest of reports coming from the horde of reporters who actually had been near the United Nations when the assault had been made. Nothing was clear, except that there had been enormous loss of life. Further reports dribbled in. A few minutes later, General Stoneman knocked on the door. With him was the CNO, Admiral Freeman, and the vice CNO for Surface Warfare. Pierson was in California visiting his daughter and had been ordered back. He would be in D.C. by 0300 the next morning. Bringing up the rear was a marine general with four stars on each shoulder. Tom Dunham had met with the president many times, but had never really spoken to the vice president. They looked each other up and down. In stature, they could have been twins.

"What's the scoop on this mess, general?"

"Mr. Vice President, all we can piece together so far is that the president was taken prisoner, along with the heads of government of most of the world. Of the people in the banquet room, the only ones we know weren't taken were the Iranian, North Korean, and Iraqi prime ministers. Pretty much everybody else was taken or killed. Whoever did this has already slaughtered about 200 people, security men, diplomats, servants, and others.

Freeman spoke up. "Sir, there's worse news than that. The Arabs are attacking Israel as we speak. We know of heavy missile salvos from Libya and Iraq. The Israelis have launched a counterattack, but from what we can tell, it hasn't gone well. They didn't kill all the missiles, and they didn't catch the Arab air forces on the ground."

"Okay, but what the hell does all this add up to? What can we do to help the Israelis, and how do we get our President back? I don't want to pussyfoot around, guys. I want to get Brandon back, and fast."

La Guardia was sitting at a side table. The big desk was not his. His office was down the hall.

Bella Brandon stormed into the room. Immediately, she walked around the president's desk, pulled out the chair and sat down. "What's really going on here, general? What do these people want? How quickly can we get him back?" Freeman looked at Stoneman, who looked at his shoes.

La Guardia said, "Ah, Bella, we are very concerned about Ike's safety, and we're talking about the best steps to take to restore order to the situation."

"That's a bunch of bullshit, and you know it." The first lady had already worked herself up into an acute panic. "You're not going to order anything until we figure out who these people are, and what we can do to get Ike back without bloodshed."

La Guardia stood up. "We're all as worried as you are about Ike. We'll get him back safely. But you have to let us do these things without interfering. Please let us do what we're doing, and we'll keep you up to speed."

"You listen to me. You wouldn't be on the ticket if it weren't for me. You wouldn't be here unless I said so, and when Ike gets back, you may not be here at all."

"Maybe that's so, and maybe not. But we're going to do what needs to be done, and until Ike is back, I have to make these decisions."

"No way. No way you're going to do this without my permission. Who the hell made you the boss?"

"Something called the Constitution. Now, are you going to leave the room, or do I have to call the Secret Service to have you thrown out?"

Bella Brandon glared back at him. "Goddamn you, Vinny. I'm not going anywhere. What have you told him, General?"

Mrs. Goldberg pushed the door open. "Mr. La Guardia, there's an emergency call from the Pentagon for General Stoneman. They want us to put on CNN."

15 March
2342 hours

"This is CNN live from behind the U.N. Building in New York. The top story of the hour is that the leaders of the free world have been taken hostage in the submarine you see behind me. As of a minute ago, the submarine and the other ship have been blowing air horns, apparently as a signal. Look. Let's get a shot of this. The sub is moving and the Coast Guard cutters *Mannerly* and *Proudfoot* are trying to get in front of it.

"Jim, there are shots, we have shots fired from the Libyan sub! You can hear it in the background, and we can see someone on the deck of the sub shooting what appears to be a heavy machine gun at the two Coast Guard boats. They are not returning fire, Jim, I guess for fear of hurting the hostages on board. They are moving back, out of the way of the sub. The other ship is moving up next to the sub, and they're both going down river. The Coast Guard boats are swinging in line behind them.

"The two hostage ships are picking up speed and moving out, down the river. We'll switch to the feed from the CNN helicopter over the scene now. New York police and state troopers have sealed off the area around the pier near the East Forty-Third Street side of the U.N. building."

Petrov was pleased at how the operation had gone. He had seized half the leaders of the free world, and now he could make his plan work. Most of the high-ranking hostages had been loaded on the sub, with a dozen or so going on the frigate. His team of mercenaries had suffered only a few casualties during the assault. Six dead and five wounded. That still left more than 100 to carry out the rest of the plan.

All of his men had been briefed on the plan, and they herded the hostages onto the ships immediately. While the shots were still ringing in the air and the hysteria of the moment was at its height, Petrov moved away, calmly walking down the street. Just another guy in a long leather jacket.

Petrov picked a digital phone out of one pocket and dialed a number. The call went through immediately. His second in command, his Afghan son, Salim, was on the other end of the call, standing on the bridge of the frigate.

"Now you must begin the calls we discussed. The first should be to the CNN station here. Then to all the local television stations, then the three networks. You will have several press conferences, as we planned. They will be spaced unevenly, at least two hours apart. Tomorrow morning, you will invite them to send negotiators at noon. In the afternoon, a very small group of press will be invited in to see that the captives are well. I will call you again to tell you how to go from there."

"Yes, my father. Is there word on our holy war?"

"Not yet, my son. Be patient. In Allah's name."

"Yes. *Inshallah.*"

15 March
2346 Hours

General Dan Rubia scratched his head as he read the transcript. The NSA had intercepted reports of the incident as soon as it had happened, and every asset had been turned to focus on it. Some satellites were easier to reposition than others. But soon, Rubia knew, no mouse would squeak in New York without being recorded.

Listening into cellular calls was no big deal. They could listen in on any one, at any time. The trick was listening to the right ones, especially in a busy place like New York City, where there were tens of thousands of those calls every minute of the day. This sounded like the real thing.

Rubia's dark, penetrating eyes showed his every emotion. He had never been a field operative. In this job, he didn't need to hide what he felt. His network of satellites and other sources allowed him to listen to almost anything going on in the world. Many people could listen, but Rubia's gift was the intuition and intelligence to interpret what he heard and read. He picked up the phone and called Pierson.

15 March
2347 Hours

Petrov tossed the phone in a trash can as he passed. He had three others with which to direct the operation. No need for him to risk his own safety any longer. He waved at a passing Yellow Cab, and ordered the driver to Penn Station. He could still make the 12:30 A.M. Metroliner to Washington. The train would leave before every way out of New York was clogged with panicked people fleeing the nuclear bomb. The first-class ticket in his pocket would ensure a comfortable rest for about three hours. After that, another ticket would get him from Washington to Zurich and his money.

The second phase of the attacks would come in a few hours. The teams Petrov had sent to London, Paris, Bonn, and The Hague would detonate explosives right in the middle of crowds of people on their way to work. Then Salim would announce that those explosions were from bombs planted by more of his men. There would be no chance of the Western nations dealing with these combined incidents. And more attention would be drawn from helping the Israelis.

Petrov had ordered the sub to fire a few shots at the coast guard cutters from the machine gun mounted on the bridge. It was enough to make them hesitate, and in the moment they did, both the sub and the frigate made speed down river. Their objective was only a few miles away.

The two ships' captains had their orders. They turned down river at flank speed, heading south, and then east. Almost immediately, they were at the tip of Manhattan and saw Liberty Island ahead. Covered almost entirely by the statue itself, the island was a perfect fortress for their small group. The coast guard cutters, joined by a New York City fireboat, motored alongside the whole way.

Frank Clooney couldn't believe it. His boat was right on their beam, the whole way to Liberty Island. He wanted to close on the sub and ram it, but the coast guard guys kept signaling for him to clear off. No way.

The closer they got to Liberty Island, the more Clooney wanted to bump them around. Sure, they could sink a fireboat, but they would have to move fast. With any luck, a ram into that frigate would heel her over so badly, she'd never get upright again. Maybe they could get the hostages off.

The sub and frigate had it all worked out. Liberty Island has two piers, one on each side of the statue. The sub went to the east pier, the frigate to the west. As soon as they docked, the hostages were rushed off, into the statue itself.

Through his naval binoculars, Clooney counted 105 hostages marched into the base of the statue. He saw dozens of soldiers running all around the island, bursting into the buildings at the north end, which housed the National Park Service people who ran the island park.

Liberty Island itself is only about twenty-five acres. The island holds the statue facing out to sea. Behind it is a brick-paved avenue running about 150 meters from the base of the statue to a tall flagpole that sits in a large bricked circle. The avenue is tree-lined, and the administration buildings and the gift shop are all out of sight for someone standing on the bricked path to the flag.

The base of the statue is as Gustav Eiffel designed it over a century ago: an oddly shaped star with eleven points. The statue sits atop the star on a three-level stone rectangle. Inside the statue itself is the single circular staircase going up twenty-two stories to the crown. The stair, made of iron, is wide enough for two people to pass, one on the way up, the other going down. About two-thirds of the way up, a branch leads off to the statue's raised arm, which holds a torch to light the harbor. Inside the base, there is one large room covering the expanse of the statue's base.

Inside Liberty's head is an observatory, her crown a semicircle of windows looking out to sea. There is one large set of doors leading into the front of the base and one more going out the back. For rescuers, getting in would be no problem. Getting in without being spotted would be impossible.

For most of the statue's 120 years, the stair to the arm was judged too rickety to be safe, but Petrov had his own ideas. In 1986, as part of the statue's centennial, French metalsmiths had strengthened the arm, which as it turned out, had been incorrectly installed. As soon as the hostages were inside, six men wheeled a cart off the sub and into the base of the statue. On it was a nuclear warhead bought from the Russians a year ago. Qaddafi wasn't sure it would work, but Petrov knew it was his ace in the hole. No rescue mission could succeed without first dismantling the bomb. The six men began the slow process of manhandling the 200-pound device up the stairs and into Liberty's arm.

CHAPTER 29

AT THE GRANDFATHER'S KNEE

15 March
0015 Hours

La Guardia sprang out of his chair and flipped on the television. Rashid, one of Petrov's men, was on the screen. He looked directly at the camera. His masked face was calm, his eyes alert, searching around him. "I will say this one more time, and then you will not be warned again. The enslaved peoples of Palestine have taken this action. We demand that you do nothing while we fight a just and fair war with the enemies of God in Israel. If you do anything to help the Israelis, if you send one ship, if you fire one shot, all of your presidents will die. You will do nothing to interfere.

"If you interfere in our holy war, we will explode the nuclear bomb placed in your harbor. Yes, I have one. Check with your Russian friends on their weapon stocks. We will not explode this unless you help Israel. Now go, and pray that we will be more merciful to you than you have been to us."

Stoneman hung up the phone. "Mr. Vice President, we have confirmation from the Russians that they're missing a warhead with the same serial number as the one these guys claim to have, but the Russians say they don't know where it is. They claim it was stolen. They say it's a big one, about 200 kilotons. Enough to incinerate the whole city." La Guardia, Stoneman, and Dunham sat in silence as the image faded. Again, Freeman spoke up. "What a pile of shit we've landed in now."

The secretary's head appeared again in the doorway. "Mr. La Guardia, there's a phone call from the Israelis. It's Mr. Levy, their deputy prime minister."

"Mr. Levy, this is Vincent La Guardia."

"Mr. Vice President, I have very little time to speak. There have been two missile attacks against us. They have dropped poison gas on Haifa and Tel Aviv. There are thousands of dead. What can you do?"

"I don't know yet, we—"

"This is no time for delicacy! We have lost half of our air forces. If there is another missile attack, there may be nothing left."

"Will you use nuclear weapons? Promise me that you will not, at least without warning us first."

"I will not make a promise I may not be able to keep."

"Very well. Give me a few moments with my people. I will call you back."

La Guardia turned away from the phone and spoke slowly. "General, what are the immediate questions, and what are our options?"

"Mr. Vice President, there are three big issues, and we don't have any good options. First, we need to decide whether we negotiate with the terrorists, and if so what do we offer. If we don't negotiate, we can just sit and wait or mount some sort of strike on them and free as many hostages as we can. In any operation like that, at least some of the hostages will be killed.

"The second problem is their nuke. If we try a rescue, or try to help the Israelis, we need to find that weapon and destroy it before they kill about three million people with it.

"The third problem is how and when we help the Israelis. We need to move fast if we're going to do anything at all. They have sustained enormous losses in the past day. What Mr. Levy said is consistent with what our own people have estimated. Half of their air force is gone and most of their tanks. If we move, we need to do so in less than forty-eight hours.

"Sir, we have the aircraft and heavy stuff to make one strike, but no more. If we go, we have to go all the way, or we'll just lose a bunch of our people and not help them much. We don't have enough ground forces that can get there in time. We can put maybe one or two divisions over there in a couple of days, but it would take us at least three to four weeks to mount a ground offensive. By then, the Izzies will be finished.

"Our options are pretty poor on the New York City situation, too. First, there will be complete panic now that this scumbag has said on worldwide TV that he has a nuke. There will be nothing moving on the roads, the trains, or anywhere else. People will be killing each other to get out of there. We have to restore order, but that's not something we're gonna be able to do right away.

"To hit the terrorists, we need a special ops group, something of considerable size and mobility. We don't have the SEALs, Marine Recon, or Army Delta Force any more. We can't mount an effective rescue operation without those forces, and they were disbanded about a year ago. Second, the British and French may be able to provide the troops to pull off a rescue.

"Sir, we have to find a way for the Israelis to get help. From the experience with some of the Arab armies over the years, we have a pretty good guess about what they will do if they win. Saddam killed thousands of Kurds when he put down their rebellion. He used poison gas on the Iranians several times in that war in the 1980s.

"Sir, this is not our kind of war. But we have seen it before, and not that long ago. Remember Cambodia? We're talking about a mass slaughter. Women, kids, everybody. We can't just sit by and let this happen."

"Even at the cost of Ike Brandon's life, general?"

"Sir, that's the choice you have to make. I don't like it either, but that's all the choices we have."

Bella started up, but La Guardia cut her off. "Gentlemen, wait here. I'll return in fifteen minutes with my decisions."

La Guardia didn't hear the rest of what they said. His mind was elsewhere. His career had started in Staten Island, New York. He was a guy who knew how to deal with the Department of Sanitation when the garbage hadn't been picked up. His constituents called him when the potholes in front of their houses weren't filled on time. He had never seen battle. He had never sent men into battle to die. He had never made a decision that could cost anyone's life, far less thousands of lives, including that of the president of the United States.

He walked slowly down the hall and up the stairs to his own office. He had served as vice president for more than three years. He had served his president well, even when they hadn't agreed. He had faced several decisions that had caused him to think of resigning. That wasn't an option now. He had been a Congressman for almost twenty years, and the closest he had come to making a military decision was voting on some appropriations bills. That seemed a long time ago and a long way away.

He swung the door closed and sat down heavily in the chair. He looked around and knew the answers weren't all written down for him in the piles of papers his aides had left. Absentmindedly, he flipped on the television and tuned in to CNN. Background noise sometimes helped.

He looked around the room. There were all sorts of testimonials to him and awards he had received. There were pictures of his wife and children, of his parents, and of his grandfather, the mayor. His eyes wandered to the bookshelves and he saw a row of leather-bound volumes. They were the private diaries his grandfather had kept throughout his political career. He reached out for one.

He flipped through it. Some entries were short, and others went on for pages and pages. It seemed the mayor had simply written about whatever interested him whenever it happened. He stopped at one July Fourth. The mayor had a custom of seeing veterans in his offices for a couple of hours every Fourth. He helped them when he could. There were so many who had returned from the Great War with wounds the doctors couldn't heal. Even two decades after World War I, they still flocked to the mayor's office on the Fourth. He started to read:

> *July 4, 1941. We had a great day with a concert in Central Park and fireworks. I made a short speech about how we were blessed by being Americans. Even those of us who weren't born here. I said it*

because I believe it, and the crowd seemed to agree. There were the usual outbursts from the German Bundists, but they were shouted down pretty quickly. But everybody is worried about the war, and I just don't know how much longer we can stay out of it.

Later in the afternoon, I had a few veterans in and they asked the usual favors. I sent one fellow to a doctor I knew at Manhattan General. Even if the army doctors can't fix that leg, Pete Petrucci can. He's the best surgeon in the city, and I told the guy the city would pay for it. When he left, another old fellow came in. I thought he wanted some sort of favor, but he said he just wanted me to help him figure something out.

He told me he had been a medical orderly in a hospital in France. He had to run errands for the doctors, clean up after the amputations and feed and bandage the casualties. He told me about a marine private who was brought in with about six bullets in him. Seems like he had charged a German machine gun nest in Belleau Wood single-handed and paid the price. The marine was from New York City, somewhere in the Bronx, and wanted this fellow to carry a message back to his family. After the war, he came to New York and started looking for the family. He found them, after a while. I thanked him for his service to the country and started to get up, but then I remembered the puzzle he wanted to solve. I asked him what it was.

The man got pretty choked up. He said, "This guy was going to die, and we both knew it. He couldn't have been more than eighteen years old. I sat down with him and offered to give him a pain killer, but he didn't want it, so I just kinda held his hand. He started talking about how his rifle squad was pinned down, and how only he had an angle for a shot at where the Germans were. He knew his buddies would die if he didn't do something, and he only had his rifle and a couple of grenades.

"He said he stood up and ran at the Germans, firing his rifle and tossing the grenades. When he was hit, he kept going, because he couldn't let his friends die. He asked me to find his parents and tell them how it happened. He also told me to tell them it was worth it. I sat with him for about ten minutes, feeling his hand grow cold. He bled to death. I said 'God bless you' to him just before he died. I think he smiled at me for that simple blessing.

"It took me a few years to find his family. I lost his address, but I knew the names of his mother and father. When I finally found them, I went to give them their son's message, that it was worth it. They said that the message was all they ever wanted to hear. Mr. Mayor, I don't know why that was all they wanted. Do you?"

said, "Mr. Mayor, I don't know either. But I think it was because that message proved to them that their boy's death meant something, that it was worthwhile because the boy himself thought so.

I asked the old timer if I could do something for him, and he said no. He said that my speech was all he needed to remind him of how good America really is. He said that as long as we have such fine men, who are willing to lay down their lives for their brothers, we will never have to fear anything. I shook his hand and he left. I'll never forget that man.

The CNN coverage was back to the Statue of Liberty. It abruptly went dark. The reporter, suddenly solemn, said, "There have been shots fired from around the statue. I think the terrorists have shot at some of the news helicopters that have been circling around the island. I can't tell if they hit anything, but it's forcing the helicopters to orbit farther out. It seems like Liberty herself is one of the hostages."

La Guardia stood up and whispered back at the reporter. "No, not today, goddamn it. And not ever if I can help it. It is worth it. " He looked down at the book. "Thanks, Grandpa." He threw open the door and ran back to the Oval Office. Stoneman, Freeman, and Bella Brandon heard his decisions. She stayed to argue. They left to carry out orders. He reached for the phone and told the operator to get Mr. Levy from Israel on the line right now.

The calls on the secure phones started immediately. Stoneman to Pierson. Pierson to CINCLANT. Five minutes later, the captain of the U.S.S. *Iwo Jima* was sitting up in his Norfolk, Virginia, bed, talking to his executive officer, who was aboard the ship. The whole crew was under emergency recall orders, and the standing watch was making preparations to sail.

Iwo Jima and her sister ships, the landing helicopter assault ships, are the backbone of the Fleet Marine Force. A small carrier, she could launch helicopters, Harrier fighter bombers, and landing craft in coordinated assaults anywhere in the world. Below decks, there was room for a brigade of marines, landing craft, and all their other tools of war. In less than two hours, *Iwo* would be under way, headed north. Along the way, her empty decks would quickly be filled. In less than a day, she would be circling outside New York harbor, loaded for bear and looking for trouble.

16 March
0300 Hours
Camp Pendleton

The sign on the lawn in front of the building said, "Headquarters—First Marine Division," and the one on the office door said, "Commander." It wasn't unusual to see all of the lights on in the office at that hour, but the entire staff

unusual to see all of the lights on in the office at that hour, but the entire staff had been called in, and the few not already there were on the way. The coffee had been made, and was being consumed at a pace that was heavy even for these men, who seldom went through a day without a potful or two. There was a huge bowl of fresh fruit in the middle of the table, and it was being refilled regularly from a supply the general's lady had appeared with a few minutes before. Coffee and raw energy was what they needed.

The man with two stars on each shoulder looked like everyone else in the room, except for the rank. Hunter was in his BDUs and well-worn combat boots. An M-16 that had been issued to him was leaning against the wall. His helmet was upside down on his desk.

All of the operations team was there, and most of the logistics guys. Enough to get started. He pointed to the conference table on which two sergeants had stacked every available map of the New York City area and of Israel. There were neat piles of reconnaissance photos of both areas. New ones came in almost continuously.

"Okay, here's the dope. The president, along with a bunch of foreign bigshots, has been taken hostage at a U.N. dinner. They are being held somewhere in New York City. We don't have the SEALs or Recon any more to deal with that. What's just as bad, the Israelis are about to be overrun by a big Syrian-Iraqi-Iranian tank attack. They have lost most of their air forces and tanks. They could go under at any time.

"It's joint operations time again, fellas. As in we're gonna take the lead, but if this is gonna work, we need navy subs and surface support. Army Rangers will back us up in both theaters. You know the drill. If all the parts don't work together, we lose. This is a big job and it has to be done in as short a time as anything the Corps has ever done.

"I don't know what we're going to have to deal with, but General Dunham wants plans for the following options.

"One, we need an assault operation organized to take the terrorists down and get the president back. Find any former SEALs or Marine Recon troops we have and get a group together. We need a four-company-sized force, split into amphibious landing and air assault teams. They have to be in New York by 0900. See if the army can give us a half dozen of the stealthy helos that they had when Task Force 160 was still in business, and some Rangers to ride 'em. Use the army helo drivers. We can also add a few Harriers for close air support, or maybe some F-18s. Maybe the air force has a C-130 gunship they can lend us. See what you can scare up. Connect with the navy through COMSUBLANT. They will support our landing, if we make one. We don't know where we may have to land to rescue the president, or the threat we face when we get there.

"Two, the Boss wants a plan for a regiment to land in Israel by regular air transport by 1800 local tomorrow. He wants the entire division there by D plus

2. The army is moving the 101st and 82nd Airborne divisions as well, but they may not get there for a few days after we land. We need to secure the area around Haifa and move east from there, engaging whatever we come across. There will be heavy fighting around there, but that beachhead and the area inland is all ours. We'll have as much air power as we want. The boss says we can have it all, F-15s, F-22s, B-1s, and B-52s. Figure what we need and get it there.

"Call the air force and line up the C-17s, C-5s, and CRAF if we need them. We gotta give the Pentagon these options, and nobody but us can do it. Questions? Okay, let's do it. I'll be here until we deploy. If we go to Israel, I will make the landing with the Third Battalion. If we go in New York, Colonel Harrigan will take his battalion in and run the show there. Now let's get busy and make it happen. Dismissed."

A gunnery sergeant walked over to Hunter, holding out a pistol belt. "Sir, I thought you'd want a sidearm. I pulled this Beretta 92 for you."

Hunter slid the weapon out, grunted, and tossed it back to the sergeant. "No thanks, Franklin." He reached into a drawer and pulled out a well-worn web holster. He threw back the flap and pulled out an equally worn Colt .45 automatic. The gun's grip slid into its old home in his palm. Ejecting the magazine and tossing it on the desk, he racked the slide back and let it slam forward. "That one's for show. This one's for go."

16 March
0515

For Cully, the morning run was always good; he could think. Nothing made much difference to him any more. Kate's patience and love were really all he had. The portable radio on his belt was tuned to CNN news but sometimes, like this morning, he didn't turn it on. He was lost in his own thoughts, trying to remember what his father had said before he left that last time to go to Vietnam. Cully had been so small then, the memory wasn't clear. After a while, he turned on the Walkman. The CNN coverage was frantic. The 5:30 report was screamed in his ear.

"This is CNN continuing coverage of our top story: All the world waits for an answer to the question, what can be done? As war broke out in the Middle East, a large group of heavily armed men took the president and most of the United Nations Security Council prisoner late last night in a raid which left dozens of dignitaries and security people dead.

"We have confirmation now that at least ninety people were killed or injured during the assault. Among the dead are several heads of state, including the prime ministers of Norway, Italy, and Pakistan. The terrorists are making only one thing clear: They demand that the West do nothing to help Israel, and reports from Jerusalem indicate the war is not going well for the Israelis. There are reports of poison gas attacks being launched by missile. Here is Marla Jenkins with a live report from New York."

"What you see here is a picture of the Libyan submarine in which we believe the president and the other world leaders were imprisoned last night. The other ship near to it is an Iranian ship, which we believe contains some of the captives who were not taken to the sub. These two ships moved, a few hours ago, from the east side of Manhattan Island to Liberty Island, and have apparently discharged some of their hostage passengers. We don't have a clear view of Liberty Island from here, Jim, but reports which we believe to be accurate are that the president and the other U.N. leaders have been taken inside the base of the Statue of Liberty itself.

"The biggest worry officials have is whether the announcement the terrorist leader has just made is true. In a live call to this reporter, the man claiming to be the leader of the terrorists claimed to have a nuclear bomb somewhere in New York Harbor. New York is panicking over the threat of the bomb. Roads are jammed, and the airports are so clogged with people that no aircraft are making it out of the terminals. It's chaos here, and there seems to be no way for the police to set things right.

"We have no confirmation, Jim, but it appears that there were about ninety members of the Security Council and their staffs taken prisoner. Confirmed among them are President Brandon, British Prime Minister Evelyn Broughton, and Canadian Prime Minister Pierre Chandron. Back to you, Jim."

Cully had heard enough. He turned back to Kate's place. By the time he was halfway up Capitol Hill, he was sprinting.

The duty officer at Fort Meade took calls from all sorts of people in all sorts of places. The OD logged the call from Lieutenant Commander O'Bannon at 0547, along with the routine approval of a week's leave for emergency family business. He wished O'Bannon a speedy recovery for his grandmother and hung up.

16 March
0810

Donna Kramer was a ranking Pentagon "moat dragon." Her job, to put it politely, was to block anyone from seeing Admiral Pierson whom Pierson hadn't invited. She was very good at her job, all the more so because she did it without fuss, and those turned away seldom had their feelings hurt. This young lieutenant commander just wouldn't go away. He sat there, his sea bag beside the couch, wating for Pierson. He had been there almost since she opened the office at 0700.

"Mr. O'Bannon, the admiral probably won't be back for hours. The SecDef has him in the tank with General Stoneman." Cully knew the "tank" was a closely guarded conference room in a vault, used only for highly classified discussions.

"That's okay, ma'am. I'll wait. I took a week's leave."

Pierson flew in the door. "Donna, get me Admiral Charles in London, and get General Hunter in on the call. He should be at Camp Lejeune and—" He saw Cully standing near the couch, looking at him anxiously. "Don't just stand there, O'Bannon. Get your ass in here. You should hear this." He ran into his inner office. Cully followed, closing the door a bit too hard.

"Well, what do you think I should say to you? What do you think you can do now? It's been almost a year since the politicos put you out of business."

Donna Kramer's voice came over the intercom. "General Hunter and Admiral Charles on one, Admiral."

"Perce? Jim? All I've been able to do so far is precautionary. If we need to make an assault on Liberty Island, we need a platform to jump from. *Iwo Jima* is on the way. I have a squadron of Harriers going to her, as well as a few other assets. What do we have that we can get into play in the next few hours?"

"A few things from here, Admiral," said Hunter. "I'd like to put a couple of companies of my men on *Iwo*, and have you give me a couple of Army Ranger companies to put there as well. We're scrambling to put together a scratch team of ex-SEALs and Recon boys, but that will take another twelve to twenty-four hours. I have my staff planning an assault on Liberty Island and a deployment to Israel. We can go either way or both ways, just give us the word."

"Okay for starters. But we need another option that can go sooner if we need it. How about you, Perce?"

"We have a bit better report. We have one SAS team and one SBS team enroute. They should be on the ground in New York in about two hours. If you want, we can also provide air cover."

"That's a pretty good start. Let's confer again in two hours. I should have more for you then." He hung up the phone and turned back to O'Bannon.

"Okay, O'Bannon. What do you have to say?"

"Sir, I think if I could get my people together, we might have a chance, especially if we can hook up with SAS."

"Great idea, sport. You seem to forget that your team is scattered all over the navy and all over the country now. I doubt the personnel weenies could even find them in time, far less get them here."

"Sir, maybe personnel can't find them, but I can. At least my grandfather can. He's kept up with everybody. Sort of a project he took on for himself."

"As I recall, your granddad was a marine and so was your father. Right?"

"Yes, sir. Grandpa retired about twenty-five years ago, when I was about four years old."

Pierson suddenly cracked a fiendish grin. “What’s his phone number, son?”

0812 Hours
Sandbridge, VA

The Old Man sat dozing in his easy chair, a breakfast of half-eaten toast and half-drunk tea sat on the end table beside him. The morning papers were strewn across his lap as he sat dozing. The newspapers had been carefully arranged by his housekeeper, Mrs. Woods, but as usual he had thrown them around. The headlines were all about the hostages in New York, and the war in the Middle East. There was a frenzy of inaction described in each front page.

He seemed to dream a lot more these days. He dreamed of his war experiences, the friends he’d seen die. He dreamed of his marriage, so long and happy, and his ultimate sadness when Fiona died. His daydreams were sometimes frightening. He imagined himself on a horse, charging up a hill with men firing at him from all along the ridgeline. That daydream kept coming back. He awoke with a start.

For no reason at all, he thought of the time, so many years ago when he and Fiona had gone to see the Gettysburg battlefield and the museum there. He had signed them up for a helicopter tour of the battlefield in one of those noisy old Sikorsky’s with the bubble face. The helo driver had earphones on them, playing guide for the tourists who had never been there before.

At one point on the tour, the pilot pointed down to a place in the treeline at the edge of the field, saying it was the site of Lee’s headquarters. For no reason, Bart had suddenly pointed to another site, a few hundred yards away, and told the pilot he was wrong. When they got back to the museum, they checked it out. Bart had been right, and it had spooked him badly. He knew where Lee’s headquarters had been, but he had never been there. That thought came back to him as he dozed. It still scared the hell out of him, and he didn’t know why.

Mrs. Woods had taken care of him for the past year, doing his check writing, buying his food and clothes, cleaning the house. He hardly went out any more. She worried about him just falling asleep and not waking up again. The telephone rang, and she answered it.

“Just a moment. Mr. Bart, there’s somebody on the phone for you. Some admiral who has Mr. Cullum in his office. Sounds like trouble to me.”

The Old Man grunted and took the phone from her. “Bart O’Bannon here.”

“O’Bannon, this is Admiral Pierson, the DCNO. Do you know who I am?”

“Yes, sir. Linda said you had my grandson there. Is Cully in some trouble?”

“Yeah, we all are. And I need both you and Cully to help us out of it. Cully says you were a colonel in the marines, and you retired a while back. Guess you had a regular commission, didn’t you?”

“Yes, sir, I did and so does Cully.”

"Cully says you know where all the members of what used to be his SEAL platoon are. Is that correct?"

"Yes, Admiral. I've kept in touch with all the boys."

Pierson's grin grew shittier and wider. "Turn your TV to CNN for a few minutes. We have the worst terrorist incident here in our whole recorded fucking history. We need that SEAL bunch and we need them now. Colonel, as of this minute you're back on active duty. A car will pick you up in fifteen minutes. Get to Little Creek and get those boys gathered up and to New York by tonight. That's an order."

"Aye, aye, sir." Bart hung up the phone. He rose slowly from the chair and didn't pick up his cane. He started to walk, slowly but purposefully, toward his bedroom. "Linda, come on in here." She almost jumped at the sound of his voice. He sounded louder and clearer than she had ever heard him. She ran into the den. He was standing a lot straighter. The Old Man was gone. Someone she didn't know was here instead. He looked like one of the pictures on the wall. Colonel Bart O'Bannon, United States Marine Corps. Older, thinner, frailer, but back on the job.

"Linda, I've got fifteen minutes to shit, shave, shower, and shine. Get me a clean suit and tie and some shoes that look like they've seen a shine in the past ten years. After I get picked up, you take my credit card. Call the base exchange and order me a couple of uniforms. Find my eagles, and get a proper uniform to me this morning. I'll call and let you know where to have it sent."

She didn't know whether to cry or salute. She did neither, running to carry out his orders. A lot of other people would be doing that before the end of the day.

• • •

Pierson looked at Cully again. "Hadn't you better get youself to Andrews, Commander?"

"Yes, sir. I'll be in New York in an hour or so." Cully grabbed his seabag, saluted and started for the door.

"Just a minute, O'Bannon. You're out of uniform."

Cully looked back, puzzled. "Sir?"

Pierson had a cabinet in the wall open and was picking through a small box. He put it down and walked over to Cully, holding out his right hand. "Put this on, Commander. That's an order." He pressed an object into Cully's hand. Cully looked down and smiled a big shitty grin, even bigger than the admiral's. In his hand was a bright gold SEAL badge.

16 March
0910 Hours
FBI Academy, Quantico, Virginia

The phone rang in the office, and kept ringing for some time before the duty agent put down the newspaper he was reading and answered it. He swung his legs off the desk and walked out to the pool area.

Rome Wilson calmly let a few bubbles of air out. He sat in the deep end of the pool, his right arm around the throat of his attacker, who should have gotten the message by now. The man had come in quickly, forgetting that attacking someone, even in the water, was something you did smoothly and quietly. Rome had the man blocked and locked before he could bring his rubber knife to bear. The man was really struggling now, for air rather than to attack. Rome let him go and they both kicked for the surface as the duty agent stepped up.

"Rome, there's a call for you in the office. Says it's navy business and very urgent. You can take it there or up in the office.

"Thanks, Frank. I'll take it here.

"Rome, this is Bart O'Bannon. There's a car on the way to pick you up, and a plane waiting for you. There's a job in New York, and Cully is already on the way."

"What's the dope, Colonel?"

"All I can say is grab a newspaper on your way out the door. I'm calling everybody to get all of you fourteen sorry bastards in the same place by tonight. I suggest that you shag ass out of there right now, master chief."

"Aye, aye, Colonel." Wilson ran for the locker room.

Calls went out across the country from the small office in Little Creek. There were a gunnery sergeant and a chief petty officer fielding calls, placing calls, and faxing orders all over the place.

"This is WTOP traffic Eye in the Sky. The New York Avenue accident is still there, with the D.C. police still milling around it, but nobody's picking up the pieces, folks. As usual, we have three police cars there, with everybody eating donuts, and nobody directing traffic around the accident. Don't they buy these guys whistles any more?

"If you want to get inta town before your lunch break, better divert to Kenilworth Avenue or stay on the Beltway to Georgia Avenue. I'll be back in a few with the bad news from the Beltway." Tommy Atkins flew his chopper with a casualness that his peers thought eerie. His on-air comments about the way things went on the roads around the nation's capital were the source of much glee among commuters, so much so that even the mayor couldn't get him fired, as often as he tried. The flying was fun, and he actually went home to see his wife at the end of the day. She was beginning to get used to him again. After twenty-two years of flying for the navy, her husband was back in her life.

His radio carried news to him, as well as directions to the next traffic jam or story to be covered from above. The news director was on the horn, and she sounded miffed. "WTOP-1, this is Carol. We have an emergency call for you, Tommy. We'll patch it in."

"What's up? Everybody okay at home? Hello?"

The radio crackled and a new voice came on. "Tommy? This is Bart O'Bannon. Can you still fly worth a damn?"

"Yeah, Colonel. And it's great to hear from you, but what the hell is the emergency?"

"Tommy, you're their personal driver. They need you. Now."

"Colonel, do I read you right?"

"You sure as hell do. You're back on active duty as of now. Make your best speed to Reagan Airport. You'll be met there."

"Message received and understood. Atkins out."

Atkins turned tightly and pushed the cyclic all the way forward. This little Bell 407 could really haul ass. Five minutes later, he was climbing out of the bird, rotors still spinning. He ran for the hangar office, but stopped a short before he reached the door.

"Captain Atkins?" asked a short, stocky man in Navy Class As.

"Yeah, I'm Tommy Atkins. But if I'm a captain, it's news to me. Who're you?"

"Sir, I have an Air Force G-IV waiting for you in the next hangar. The DCNO wants you in New York ASAP."

As an answer, Atkins sprinted toward the waiting aircraft. Seeing him approach, the pilot started winding up his engines, and got a priority take-off clearance from the tower. They thought of everything. His flight boots and BDUs were there waiting for him. Someone had sewn eagles on the collar. This mess in New York must be worse than he thought. As he changed, a steward wearing three stripes on his shirtsleeve came up to him.

"Sir, there will be a meal service in about ten minutes. And what would the captain's preference? A 9mm Beretta in a shoulder holster or a .45 Colt on the belt?"

Atkins looked around at the plush cabin. No shit. There were curtains on the windows. "You air force pukes sure live right. I'll take the Beretta *and* the .45. And a cold beer if you got one."

The captain of an oil rig in the Gulf of Mexico was rudely awakened. He had drunk the better part of a bottle of bourbon the night before, and was in no shape to understand why his two best divers were being picked up by a coast guard helicopter in ten minutes. Not that anyone gave a good goddamn whether he understood or not. No one would tell him, anyway. The two men had been borrowed from the navy as part of some project developing new underwater tools, and the navy wanted them back, right *now*. Tommy Thompson, a very blond, very big man from Nebraska, looked at his roommate, who had taken the call. "What the hell is it?"

Mike Scott was shoving gear into his seabag as fast as he could, and pulled a long black knife out of his personal belongings safe. "It was Bart O'Bannon. There's a job in New York, and they want us back together. We gotta reform the platoon by tonight." Out of the safe came another personal item. Scott put his navy blue baseball cap on. On the front was the SEAL emblem embroidered in gold.

"Get the lead out, Tommy. We be back in bidness."

16 March
1010 Hours

Salim and Rashid had set up their headquarters inside the statue as Petrov had planned. No detail was spared. There were satellite uplinks for radio and television, as well as telephone links both by cell phone and by the Park Service switchboard, which they had taken over. The hostages had all been gathered in the room at the top of the pedestal, near the stairs leading to Liberty's crown. It was about seventy-five feet square, with a single glass door on the north and south sides. Two stairways came up from the floor below, one on the east side, one on the west.

Their calls to the press and the short broadcast to CNN were all the international press needed. There were helicopters circling constantly with reporters shouting down through bull horns and radios, all asking for interviews. The shouters were waved off. The ones on the radio were invited to land on the brick avenue behind the statue where the flagpole had been cut down. They were told to wait. Salim promised to talk to them at 11:30 A.M.

Guido Mussilli was one of the first ones on the ground. He had spoken with his editors, rented a helicopter and a pilot, and had been circling the scene since shortly after the hostages had been herded into the statue. Only three other helos landed, and a crowd of about one hundred reporters, cameramen, and sound technicians sat motionless around them under the guns of about a dozen terrorists. Petrov's men kept good discipline. There was no chatting with the reporters. Their nervous questions went unanswered.

At precisely 11:30, Salim and Rashid both came out of the statue's back door and walked up to the reporters, who were allowed to stand and start their broadcast. Salim and Rashid each wore a sort of ski mask made of thick black material. The reporters were asking questions faster than Salim could understand what they were saying.

"Enough. Silence. You ask who we are. We are Palestinians, and you need know nothing more. We have taken your leaders hostage to prevent America and Israel's other allies from intervening in our holy war against the Zionists. If America helps Israel, all your presidents and prime ministers will die.

"What are your other demands?"

"You must wait. We will explain this in time. We have much time here. We will talk with a delegation from your United Nations. If they come here at three o'clock this afternoon we will meet with them. You must negotiate, or your American president and all the others will die."

"Were any of the hostages hurt during the battle? Will you permit medical help to reach them now?"

"They are unharmed so far. Some cuts and scratches, but for now they are well."

"Can we see them and talk to them?"

Rashid smiled through his mask. He looked at Mussilli. "I have seen you before. Where?"

"At the U.N. During the battle. I thought you were going to kill me."

Rashid laughed. "No, no, no. I will save my bullets for those worth shooting. You want to see them? You, and two others, come with me."

Mussilli turned around. A reporter and cameraman from the BBC were standing behind him, taking it all in. He motioned them to follow. They looked at each other and followed.

Rashid led them back up the brick avenue and into the statue. Through the first room, where the original torch stood, back to the two small elevators, and then to the top of the pedestal. The BBC cameraman was muttering that the signal wasn't getting out through the statue's metal skin. The elevator doors opened, and they saw the hostages sitting on the ground. Twenty or thirty terrorists were in the room, waving their machine pistols around. Salim stood there, pointing at the hostages.

"See? We have treated them well. We have not beaten them. It will amuse me to shame them when the time comes."

Mussilli stepped forward. "Can we speak with them?"

In answer, Salim smiled. He walked over to President Brandon and kicked him. "Get up. Speak with them. Tell them that you have been well treated."

Brandon rose slowly and looked at the BBC camera. "We all are unharmed. We have spoken to the leader of the band that has taken us prisoner. They have assured me that no harm will come to us if no action is taken against them. I think I speak for everyone here when I say that we all want this to be resolved without violence, no matter how long that may take."

Salim shouted. "Enough. You there." He pointed at the BBC reporter. "Which one is yours?"

The BBC man said he was British. Salim looked around, as Broughton stood.

"Prime Minister, are you all right?"

"Yes, so far. And I want to join President Brandon in wishing a peaceful resolution to this situation. This is the second time I have been a victim of this kind of violence. I do not want to see more lives wasted here. Please tell that to all of the people working to bring the world back to peace. Tell it to our generals and admirals. Tell it to all the armies and navies. We need no bloodshed here." Her face took on a harder look. "And as the Americans say, tell it to the marines."

• • •

The tape went out by satellite link around the world. Bella Brandon saw it and called her newspaper contacts to tell them that the prime minister of Britain had joined her husband in a call for a peaceful solution.

Stoneman, Pierson, and Charles saw it. Dunham saw it and called Hunter.

The helicopters lifted back off Liberty Island, and made a dash to Newark or Manhattan. When they got back, military intelligence and CIA people met them, bombarding them with questions about what they had seen. Some of the reporters cooperated. A few insisted that they couldn't talk to the intelligence men, because it was contrary to their reporters' code of ethics, or so they said. They could only observe, not participate.

By then, Mussilli had slipped away to another part of the hotel and spent the next half hour typing and e-mailing his lead story back to the paper in Washington. The *Washington Herald* had a small New York bureau, but none of those guys could get anywhere even close to the story. And they also didn't have a helo of their own.

Now the pilot of the chartered bird was demanding $100,000 for another flight to Liberty Island. Mussilli agreed. Hell, the paper could pay for the biggest story since World War II. They had landed at the heliport on the roof of what had been the Pan Am Airlines building. Mussilli didn't know who owned it now, only that it was the only place they could refuel and launch again for the afternoon conference at the statue. The thought of not going never entered his mind. He went back to the roof to talk to the pilot again. He saw the man leaning against the bird, another, larger helo now parked across from it.

Climbing out of the other helo, a thirtyish man in fatigues walked up to him. "Sir, could I speak to you a minute?" Mussilli looked behind the man. A Navy Sea King, its engines turning at idle, sat waiting.

"Who're you?"

"Ah, sir, I'm with the navy, and we're trying to talk to everyone who has seen what's going on."

Mussilli's mind had just calmed down from the session at the statue. Now it was racing again. This guy's face was familiar.

"Okay, I'll tell ya what I know. But first you tell me. I've seen you somewhere before, right? In Washington, right?"

"I don't think so. I haven't been there for a while."

"Not so fast, pal. I do know you. You're not just with the navy. You're the SEAL guy from the deal in Scotland a year or two ago, right? You're O'Bannon."

"I'm Cully O'Bannon, and I was the guy at Portpatrick Lodge who almost got thrown in jail for it, and I'm still with the navy. And all I wanna do is get a line on how to help these people get out of there without getting them all killed. You gonna help me or not?"

This was just too good to be true. He pointed his thumb back at the small helo and the rent-a-pilot leaning against it. "You got somebody who can fly that thing?"

"Maybe. Why?"

"Well, I got an invite to go back there at three. You ever run a big TV camera?"

Twenty minutes later, on another rooftop, Guido looked back out through the glass walls of the rooftop ballroom to the roof of the Battery Park Hotel, where he saw his little rented helo sitting, and another, bigger one right behind it. A crew was painting a big helo, which looked vaguely military. It was white, rather than dark green. Large red letters were going on each side which said, "CNN-TV" and "*Washington Herald*." He gulped when he read it. It was his idea to smuggle these navy guys in to have a look. Now they were talking about going back a second time, and not just for a look-see. Jesus. Momma Mussilli did raise some damned fools.

Cully looked through his binoculars across the harbor. Ellis Island had been the point where his mother's grandparents had entered the United States for the first time. When Lee Iacocca turned it into a museum, it had become a celebration of the immigrants who had made America strong. O'Bannon stared out the window at the museum. From his vantage point atop the hotel, he could see the statue perfectly, with Ellis Island behind it to his right. How many thousands of the children and grandchildren and great-grandchildren of those immigrants had served their country well?

The Battery Park Hotel and its rooftop ballroom had been commandeered by Admiral Pierson for the SEALs. It was swarming with communications people, the intel guys running in and out. Best of all, it had a rooftop helo pad large enough and strong enough to hold two Sea Kings and one smaller chopper. One part of the rooftop had been turned into a briefing room for the SEALs and their support teams.

Alan Ahearn was "sitting" in the briefing room waiting for the intelligence update. He wasn't really there, of course. The digital secure satellite phone allowed him to see and hear as if he were there, but *Bayonne* had just picked up a few special passengers at the Naval Air Station at Patuxent River, Maryland,

and was racing to reach her designated position. It would be just a few hours before she got there, but her commander needed information now.

Others really were there, and some of them had similar thoughts. Rome Wilson was the first of the SEALs there after Cully and immediately went about his old job, assembling the equipment they would need for the whole team. After half an hour, he seemed to have found everything, and was glad to see his old Mossberg twelve-gauge really was waiting for him.

"Hey, boss man. You really okay now? Your grandpa told me you kinda had a rough time for the past few months."

"Yeah, it was rough, Rome. But I had a great lady to help me out. Is anybody else here?"

"Nobody but you an' me and Mr. Atkins. Sure is good to see both of you."

"Let's get busy, master chief. Tommy and I have just got an invitation to a party this afternoon. We need to get ready."

Singly and in pairs or threes, they came in. By 1300 every member of the platoon was there and more. The Raj was there, with one full SAS team, and the SBS folks were already out swimming around the target, unseen. Their reports would form the basis for the operational plan.

The reports were confusing at first, but as usual, passage of time and some daring maneuvers by the SBS boat team on the scene gave them enough to go on. The reporters were as helpful as they could be, but Mussilli and the BBC team didn't have an eye for the details the SEALs needed. There were over 100 hostages, including the president, and the British, French, German, Russian, Turkish, and Italian prime ministers. Various assorted kings, sultans, and heads of state had been taken with them. The number of Park Service staffers taken prisoner on the island was not known, but was thought to be fewer than a dozen.

Two Meters Under the Water
Seventy Meters off the Statue of Liberty

Eddie the Fish they called him. He was an ungraceful man on land. From the time he was a child, his real home had been the water. Growing up in Dover, he always had the ocean, and most of the year he would leave the house at all hours and swim, getting away from a father who sat in his chair and drank his way into numbness every night. He got through school, and wanted to join the army, but they had no jobs for swimmers. Eventually, he found a way to earn a living swimming.

Now, more formally, he was Major Edward Finchley, Royal Marines, and the best man in Her Majesty's Special Boat Service. The SAS guys got the glory, but the SBS knew who was the best of the best, and they sometimes proved it in training exercises. The SAS really hated it when the SBS teams got inside their perimeter and stole their commander's best whiskey. Those bottles of twenty-year-old Glengoyne were getting hard to find.

He had tasted a lot of water around the world, but only once before had he tasted water with this odd, dirty metallic flavor. It seemed to come right through the mouthpiece of the scuba gear the first time, and sure enough it was coming through the mouthpiece the same way now. He prayed that this swim wouldn't be like that other one.

That other swim was still with him. After the Americans had gotten the good pictures of the Russian carrier being built in the Ukraine's Nikolayev shipyard, the admiralty had decided they wanted some close-ups. That was nearly six years ago, and the *Varyag*, as the ship was to be called, was a 65,000-tonner, capable of projecting Russian power almost anywhere in the world. Defense budget cuts had taken their toll in the United Kingdom as well as the United States, so when the call came in, there was only one SBS team capable of mounting the spy op.

He and the other six SBS men had been inserted by submarine, riding their underwater sleds inside the Russian shipyard. Half an SBS team, one boat team, was enough to do the job, and few enough to reduce the risk of being spotted. Tempting as it was, there was no war, so they could not mine the ship; they only had orders to take pictures. The water was foul, probably from all the metal plating shops the Russians had at the shipyard. Their waste water contained everything you didn't want to swallow, like nickel, cobalt, lead, and a bunch of chemical solvents. They took pictures, all right. In the dark of the moon, they scaled the side of the hull and measured everything, including the reduction gears that had just been laid out on the floor of the drydock for installation. The pictures were turned over to the intelligence team. Eddie later found out that they were so good, the engineers could determine the ship's top speed from them.

They had gotten out, but just barely. No one spotted them, but the charts had the currents all wrong. They were swept along, far south of the pickup point, and then their sleds had run out of battery power. They had to swim for it, against the currents. It took hours, and they lost two men. There was nothing for it but to keep going. Five of them made it to the pickup point, and the sub was still there for them, almost three hours late. He often wondered whether the Russians had noticed the calling card he left. On the back of one of the engineering drawings on what had to be the construction boss's table, he had written the SBS motto, "If Not by Strength, then Guile" in English, and left a team shoulder patch on top of it. He had been sick for a month after that swim, as had the rest of the survivors. The water had gotten them when the Russians couldn't.

This swim was going to be as bad, maybe worse. The currents were real killers. They could drown you in a minute or two if your air was used up and you had to stay on the surface. The dirty flavor of the water chilled him inside.

When the call had come again, Eddie the Fish and his boat team had climbed on an RAF transport and had begun their flight to New York within three hours of the incident. They were swimming around Liberty Island as soon as they had their gear unpacked, and what they were reporting back was anything but comforting. Good information, but very bad news.

The Iraqi submarine had taken a station on Liberty's right, practically under the arm holding the torch. The frigate had driven itself against the east pier. What was worse, air ops reported that both ships had their radar scanning all around. So much for an undetected helo drop onto the island. From the helos, and the reports of the coast guard cutters and the New York fireboat, there were terrorists in each of the four buildings at the island's north end, and in the gift shop near the west pier. Undoubtedly, they were in radio contact with their friends inside the statue.

Worst of all was the statue itself. Within a hundred miles, there was no harder target for the SEALs to penetrate. The statue sits on a small fortress. Twenty-foot-high stone walls, with only two doors at the front and rear of the stone star the statue's base rests on. The base itself is more stone, ten stories tall with foot-thick walls all around and heavy bronze doors. The base was built in three levels, each of them easily defended by covering the doors, and the terrorists had seen to more cover than they needed, with machine guns all around the top of the star, sandbagged in for a real fight.

The top of the star is a terrace, about forty feet wide, with two doors into the statue. Above it are two higher, smaller terraces, each commanding a view of the island and the water and air approaches to it. Three doors in front, three in back, two on each level. No other way in or out.

Inside the statue, according to the intelligence briefs, was another nightmare for an assault team. At the star's rear entrance, a huge room housed the elevators to the top of the pedestal, and the original torch which had been replaced in 1986. Ten feet up was a balcony, which ran around the entire room. Getting above it was a problem. Stairs on the right and left lead to the next level, which also has a split view, and more stairs to the third level, where a huge square room surrounds the stairs leading to the Statue's crown. From the air and sea reports, the hostages were all—or almost all—held in the room on the third level up. There were probably twenty terrorists in the room with them, maybe more.

The SBS's nuclear detectors had picked up nothing around the frigate, so it probably was clean. The sub reeked of radiation, but that could just be from its archaic reactor. There was no word on the bomb.

Aboard U.S.S. Bayonne

That was enough for Alan Ahearn, for now. "Maintain course and speed. When we enter the harbor, get us to about 3,000 yards from the Libyan boat. XO, I want us in position due south of the island. I want to be able to shoot either the frigate or the sub or both at the same time."

"Aye, aye, skipper. Maintain flank speed."

16 March
1448 Hours

Atkins thought they were nuts, but what else was new? Tommy sat in the pilot's seat of the rented chopper. He and Cully had managed to find some civilian clothes and had climbed into the helo after Mussilli had talked the NBC guys out of a camera and sound set. All they wanted was the exclusive to the film that was taken, which Guido readily promised. Cully took a crash course on the camera, and the NBC guys thought it was a hell of a deal. They get the film without being shot at.

The scenario predicted that morning was not to be. The United Nations was still dithering over who would negotiate when the time came to leave, so the reporters went alone. Salim had decided that the hostages would participate in the news conference, but from the outside. When the three designated helos landed, the newsmen, including O'Bannon and Atkins, were searched briefly and then marched out to the base of the statue, and then inside and up to the first wide terrace. Nine of the hostages, this time not including the president or Broughton, were brought out for inspection by the media. Among them, only the French prime minister was recognized immediately. From behind his mask, Rashid introduced them, but not by name.

"Here you have Norway, Brazil, India, Belgium, Germany, and Greece. Over there are Turkey, Indonesia, and Mexico. All for you to see. We promised to keep them safe, and we have. We know that your negotiators want us to release some as a gesture of our good faith. We will not. We wait for some demonstration of *your* good faith."

Three reporters shoved forward, microphones in hand. Cully pointed the camera and kept it rolling. A built-in microphone would record the sound. Guido fiddled with his notepad and tape recorder.

Cully looked around as much as he could. The statue was as the intel guys described it. There were machine guns all around the terrace they stood on. Rock walls. Too few doors. Not much else to see. In a few minutes it was over, and the terrorists were rushing them back to the helos. Atkins lifted off as soon as Mussilli climbed in.

"Anything we didn't know, Cully?"

"Just one thing. I counted ninety-three hostages, which means that they have all of them in one place. What's your count, Mr. Mussilli?"

"I got ninety-four. The official count from the U.N. this morning was ninety-two. So either way, if there's anybody that ain't in the statue, it can't be more than one or two people."

"Yeah," said Cully. "And Tommy, they sure picked a pisser of a place to get into, and with all this press around, getting in unseen just ain't gonna happen."

"You guys wanta know how to get in?"

Cully gave Mussilli a sour look. "Mr. Mussilli, we're grateful for your help. But leave this to us."

"Pal, I've been in the news business since you were in diapers. Let me tell you, 'cause it's as plain as day. These guys love the cameras. They love being the center of attention. This is more than their holy war. They want to make a big splash."

Atkins couldn't stand it. He practically shouted into the intercom. "So tell us something we don't know. Sweet Jesus, how the hell can you make a bigger splash than they've already made? Blow up the world?"

"You missed my point. This little party we just had will keep everybody busy for a while. But being in front of the cameras is an addiction. Politicians get it all the time. If you guys want in, be ready the next time they call a press conference. There *will* be a next time, and it'll probably be late tonight or first thing in the morning. I'll bet each of you a bottle of my favorite scotch it'll be tonight."

"Why tonight?"

"Because I saw it in their eyes. These guys like it, and they won't be able to wait to get more of it. All you gotta do is dress your guys up like a bunch of network weasels and wait for an invitation."

Atkins's voice had a thoughtful tone. "Ah, Mr. Mussilli, I think we need to take you back with us. Let's drop off the camera and film. Please stay in the helo. Cully will dump the stuff with the NBC guys and we're outa here. You need to talk to our boss. By the way, have you ever fired an automatic weapon?"

They were back to the Battery Park Hotel roof. Mussilli and Atkins were on the scrambled phone with Pierson and Hunter.

16 March
1605 Hours

This was the hardest part of it. Having to trust the safety of your men, and the success of the mission, to someone not a part of the team. Pierson had spent almost an hour with Rubia, thinking out how reliable the intercept of the cell phone call was, how they could make use of it, and how to attack a seemingly untouchable target. Without some way in, no matter how good the people were, they would be lost, and the hostages killed before anyone could prevent it. And what about the nuke?

Trusting someone who wasn't part of the team was bad enough, but trusting a reporter went against everything he had believed since Vietnam. The press were the problem, right? You could never trust these guys, they were all out to screw the military. But there were, he had to concede, a few who wouldn't. A few you could talk to. Rubia insisted he could trust Guido Mussilli. Mussilli at first couldn't believe Pierson was serious, but when the commandant of the Marine Corps marched into the room and put him on the phone with La Guardia, Mussilli was all business.

Pierson had Rubia and the ops people drafting some sort of plan. They were on the scrambled phone with Cully, who was a short helo ride from the center of chaos. Other than helo, there was no way in or out of the city. The panic caused by the nuclear bomb threat was total. The streets were flooded, and there were many dead in the rioting. The New York National Guard was coming, but they couldn't be mobilized for another eight or ten hours. Meanwhile, the city was eating itself alive.

At the White House, things were worse. There had been too much debate. There were calls from every government whose leader was a captive, and from many whose leaders weren't even there. There were frantic consultations with heads of state. There were two more shouting contests with Bella Brandon. After the second of them, La Guardia had ordered the Secret Service to lock her up in the residence. They did so immediately, not without a few grins to each other.

Negotiators were offered from many governments. The FBI hostage rescue team was available, along with the FBI negotiators. But the HRT was unprepared for this situation. More than 100 heavily-armed men with a nuclear bomb was out of their league.

The negotiators all thought they could talk these people out, but La Guardia was skeptical. This wasn't a normal hostage-taking. These people had seized a military objective, which they had to hold until another objective—the destruction of Israel—had been achieved. They didn't need to negotiate. They were sitting pretty.

"All right, fellas, stack 'em there."

Cully and Wilson turned to see six men wheeling trolleys stacked with locked plastic bins into the room. Every one of them was dressed in a dark gray jump suit with "Heckler & Koch" stitched elegantly on the left breast pocket in gold. A stocky blond figure in an identical jump suit was leading them in, already tearing into one of the bins. Steve Lemoyne was the president of Heckler & Koch of America. In his factories the best small arms in the world were made. An engineer long before he was promoted to boss, he would lie awake nights thinking how to make better guns for his favorite customers, the SEALs and the SAS.

"Steve! What the hell you doing here?"

"Oh, hey, Cully! Long Tom called me a coupla hours ago and said you guys were back in the game so I thought I'd bring you a few goodies. Just a few things you might need. I have civvies for everybody who isn't already in 'em. The stuff is pretty basic, I can't run a fashion show. Grab gear from Pete there." A tall, heavy-set man raised his hand.

"I have a .45 Socom pistol for each of you. A few new Mark 8 machine guns and, ah, where's Rome? Rome, you may wanna take a look at this. I brought it along 'cause I thought you'd be here."

Lemoyne held up something that looked like a shotgun, but had three barrels. It was as short as Wilson's old pump gun, but the similarity stopped there. "Listen and learn, boys. When you guys got in trouble for taking your hands off a guy to pump the gun, I thought we needed to develop something like this for you. See, it works kinda like a gatling gun. The three barrels rotate, powered by the gas and recoil of the previous shot. Single shot or three-round bursts. It's belt fed, but we can rig it with a fifty-round box magazine. The rate of fire is only 200 rounds a minute. Can't hold it if we go faster than that. Rome, I filled it up with flechettes for you, but my guys have all sorts of other stuff if you want it."

Wilson swung the short heavy gun to his hip. "The answer to a maiden's prayer. Works for me, Mr. Lemoyne."

"Steve, this is all well and good. But we have to go in concealed. All the big stuff will have to be so buried under the other equipment, we'll never get it out fast. Whaddya have that'll fit in my sock?"

Lemoyne thought for a minute, and walked over to the only bin that he hadn't opened. He dialed a combination on the lock and it popped open. "Okay, Cully. If you want it, here it is." He picked up a short-barrelled automatic with a short, thin suppressor on it. The whole thing was smaller than his hand.

"I think you'll want to take a look at these." O'Bannon hefted the small pistol. It had a light touch and a very good balance. Just slightly barrel-heavy.

"This is something we updated from an old World War II version built when Wild Bill Donovan was the boss of the OSS." One of Lemoyne's men threw a twenty-pound sandbag into a corner of the room. "Donovan wanted to impress President Roosevelt with his R&D program. He snuck an earlier version of this into the Oval Office. Watch."

Lemoyne pointed the pistol at the sandbag. In the sudden silence, they heard only the slap of the bullets hitting the sandbag and the empty cartridges hitting the floor.

"It's a hot-loaded six-shot .22 magnum, completely silent and flashless. Donovan did what I just did in the Oval Office, and gave the Secret Service guys a heart attack. I checked with some friends in Langley. They okayed lending you a few of these. You can double-tap these guys before they know anybody's shooting. Want some ankle holsters?"

"Steve, you are a beautiful human being. Okay, guys, line up and draw your stuff. We're on the job, and the clock is running."

They stayed at it, running back at each other with ideas, checking the position of the support troops. Everybody understood that there was way too much firepower against them. There was no way to simply rush the target and hope any of the hostages would be alive after the first charge. Then there was the nuke. They all agreed that the hostages would have to be secured by a small assault team that would be inserted without being detected, to be followed by a larger assault to effect the rescue.

But how the hell to do that in a target with stone walls, too few doors, sandbagged machine guns, and radar coverage, all of it lit up by every goddamn press spotlight in the Western world? Despite the continued warnings, the press helos continued to orbit the island, spotlighting the areas where the SEALs had to land in darkness. When they started discussing the plan to pose as a big network TV news crew, some of the SEALs laughed out loud.

17 March
1748 Hours

The Pentagon's basement is a maze of tan and green corridors. Where once a tunnel rumbled with buses dropping off and picking up commuters was now a sealed-off line of offices. Lower still, and closer to the center of the building were the offices of the command staff and the Joint Chiefs of Staff operations rooms. In the center of it all was the Tank, the top-secret conference room where operations were planned.

There was news coming in from the Middle East. A day and a half into the war, the Israelis were sinking fast. They could hold out one, maybe two more days. Nobody knew how long. An attack on the statue had to be timed perfectly so that whatever American forces might be deployed to help the Israelis could be there in time. There were reports of massive movements of Syrian and Iranian tanks, with every aircraft in the Arab world in support. If America was going to move, it would have to be before about noon the next day in Israel. The intel guys said that was the best estimate of how long the Izzies could hold on.

The attacks had to be carefully coordinated. If the operation at the statue went sour, the strikes in the Middle East might have to be called off. If the nuke in New York wasn't found in time, the whole plan would fail. If hundreds of people didn't do precisely what they were supposed to at precisely the right moment they would fail.

General Stoneman looked at his shoes. He had been doing that a lot lately. The fight had gone out of him when he saw the few options that were left. *How could I have let things drift so far? How did I let the force structure slip so badly out of balance? Why don't we have our people as ready as they could be? Why didn't I stand up to the president and the others who wanted cut after cut?* His mind didn't focus on the problem at hand. Neither did his staff.

Tom Dunham didn't like this one bit. Nothing this complicated could possibly work. There were too many moving parts. Each of the operations was dangerous, but linking them like this was a recipe for disaster. Not that he had any better ideas. Long Tom Pierson was as satisfied as he ever was. No operational plan like this had ever been put into practice, and this was no time to screw up. His people would do the job and do it well. If all the pieces fell into place. The meetings and rushed conversations with the White House staff were distractions he didn't need. But it was a good sign that they were listening. La Guardia had made his orders clear. Rescue the president first, and save the Israelis if you can. Whatever happens, don't let that bomb go off in New York Harbor. Pierson knew there were no sure things in war. *And, God knows, we're at war.*

The operational plan evolved over several hours. With precise timing and a little luck, the SEALs might just make it. Then again, they might all get killed trying.

18 March
Outside Haifa, Israel
0358 Zulu

The Syrian tank columns had reached the outskirts of the city the day before, and were beaten back after a huge fight. Try as they might, they couldn't penetrate the defense perimeter that the Israelis had established. It was a final defense, like the ones around Tel Aviv in the 1950s. There were women there and old men. Like the Warsaw ghetto. Like Stalingrad when the Nazis came. The army was still fighting, but what was left of the bigger units were farther north and east. They were left with some old artillery pieces, some mortars and the like, manned by reservists and old men, women, and teenage kids. The fighting was fierce, and they serviced their guns like veterans. They knew that defeat meant death, not just for themselves, but for their families. No one would survive.

The ammunition still seemed to be plentiful, but the water was not. The water trucks had stopped running that morning, and without air cover they weren't likely to come back. And there was no air cover. The Arabs had taken huge losses, but the few Israeli fighters and bombers left were being kept for strikes into Syria and Libya. There was no airborne air defense today. Then they heard the rumbling of the tanks. They were coming again. They would come again, and again through the night. Until they broke through. The Arabs were not used to winning. They were beginning to enjoy it.

Colonels in the Air National Guard were supposed to be paper pushers. They were too old to fly, and they were managers. At least that's what the book said. Colonel John Mastropolo had never read the book, so he just kept flying. His 992d Tactical Bomber Squadron had roots back in the days of Hap Arnold and the old Eighth Air Force, which dominated the skies over Germany. Now a part of the New York ANG, the 992d flew the A-10 Warthog. It was old, it was slow, it was ugly. But it could stay over the target for hours and it carried so much armament, it seemed like it could kill tanks all day.

The night sky was never a calm place in the Middle East, but as Mastropolo led his squadron to the rendezvous point, he knew it wouldn't be very hard getting in or out. A-10s couldn't dogfight worth a damn, and the Russian pilots flying those Su-27s were good. That's why Mastropolo's squadron was joining up with two squadrons of U.S. fighters, staged out of Turkey.

Flying high and fast, the F-15s were as old as the A-10, but a good match for anything else in the sky. Anything except their other escort. Under them, only about 1,000 feet off the ground and about four miles to their left, a squadron of F-22s loafed along at subsonic speed. They were as stealthy as the A-10s were ugly. Another squadron of them was flying a parallel course on the right, about 5,000 feet higher. Mastropolo's squadron was taking the "sandwich" attack right to the center of the enemy's strength. . . . If they weren't too late. There were five similar strikes planned and two others in the air right now.

17 March
1955 Local
New York

This had to be the goddamn stupidest operations plan anybody had ever come up with, but nobody had a better idea. Seven of them were crammed into one of the CH-53s with all kinds of camera and audio equipment. The helo still smelled of fresh paint. Everybody hoped that a few minutes in the air would cure that. There were two other helos following them.

All three helos had TV equipment packed in rollaway carts. In some, below the TV equipment were the tools of war.

Mussilli had been right. Just after 6 P.M. the terrorist leader had broadcast another invitation through the big microwave dish they had set up on the front of the statue's pedestal. They were to be there by 8 P.M. to set up a live broadcast for 9 P.M. The CNN crew gladly traded their cameras and jackets, as well as their helo, an old Bell Jet Ranger, to the small group of men who showed up suddenly at their base on top of the Pan Am tower, one of the few uptown helipads in New York. Their producer had called and told them to cooperate. Something about a direct request from the vice president' s office.

The CNN guys were really pissed that this group was followed in by a group of MPs who took them into custody. Security, they said. Hadn't these guys heard of the First Amendment? The reporters relaxed when four guys who said they were from Staten Island delivered a case of wine and some amazing pasta dishes. The TV men asked who they were, and they just smiled. All of these miracles arrived by large green helicopters, which seemed to be arriving or departing every minute or two. After the first two bottles of wine nobody remembered to be mad. Spaghetti carbonara is a powerful anti-anxiety drug.

None of the team was visibly armed. In civvies, they all wore bulky windbreaker jackets or sweats, except for the two "on-camera" media mentionables in suits. Some had cameras, some had lights, some had sound equipment. Everything was in working order, and they all knew how it had to be working in about one hour after they landed. There was no room for error there. Everything that the networks had promised the terrorists was there, and they had to put it together and make it work.

All of them had the small H&K hideaway guns; some also had Walther PPKs and the like in their ankle holsters or taped to the small of their backs. The bigger stuff, including the H & K .45s were hidden in the bottoms of some very large wheeled carts and leather cases. If the guns were discovered, the SEALs knew, they would all be killed before they even had a chance to draw their weapons.

The Mark 8s and heavier stuff was packed under the TV equipment, in dozens of boxes in the back of the three helos. They had one commercial-version CH-53, painted like a CNN helo, and two Bell Jet Rangers, one painted in CNN colors and one for CBS. Mussilli wanted to paint "ABC Sports" on the side, but Tommy vetoed it. The suggestion of WDFU TV was also nixed.

They all knew that their lives and those of the captives depended on how convincingly they could act like asshole reporters. This goofy guy Mussilli with the press badges told them how to act and how to stay cool. He kept talking about it. Soon everyone in the helo had figured that he kept talking to cover his own case of the nerves. Guido Mussilli was a newsman to the core. He was unarmed except for his hip flask. He took a big swig out of it. This would either be his biggest story ever or his last. Maybe both.

Mussilli didn't know how much was riding on his plan and his ability to act it out. At that moment, hundreds of aircraft, dozens of ships, and thousands of men and women were converging on two very different battle areas. He was worried enough about his role. They hadn't told him the rest of the plan.

The SEALs took up two of the helos. In the third, the Raj and five of his men looked very unhappy. They had wanted to rope ride to the island and force an entry through the statue's back door. But this was his penance for finishing first in his television arts and sciences class at the university. The slight, quick man could really handle all this equipment. He had a long black knife taped to his left calf, and a Walther PPK .380 on his right. Throwing knives were stuck in various parts of his clothing. His sour look evidenced his thoughts. This stuff wasn't good for anything beyond arm's reach. He knew his men would probably come out of this, but how to save the hostages with such puny weapons? He resolved to snatch the biggest weapon he could from the first terrorist he killed. If they didn't kill him first.

It was a short ride to Liberty Island. The terrorists signaled them into a landing area on the broad walkway behind the statue. Cully and Wilson exchanged looks. If they got through the next few minutes alive, they had a good chance. Now or never. Time to get by the search that was sure to be made.

Cully hustled through a door, camera shouldered and running. Wilson, lugging a big battery pack and a light, followed close behind. Two other men came out with hand-held lights, the rest started wheeling large carts toward the back door of the statue. The other two helos disgorged a shouting muddle of microphone-toting people firing questions and pointing cameras. Salim looked at them and shook his head.

"Quiet, all of you. You will follow my orders now, and instantly. Pick up your equipment and follow my men into the back door. You pilots. Start your engines now and take off immediately. If you are not out of here in two minutes, we will open fire on you." Salim looked around as the SEALs scurried around, careful to stay out of Salim's way. He was very satisfied with himself, thinking that he had just shut off the only way for any of them to escape.

Atkins was not satisfied at all. "His" team was on the ground, and his role in the operation was over. He shouted out to Salim.

"Hey, you, sir. How will we be able to land when we come back for these guys and all our stuff?"

Tommy's eyes locked on Salim's, and the thug looked straight at him. Tommy was sure he had just blown the whole thing. He started to reach for his microphone when Salim shouted back.

"You will call on the radio. Your own man will relay our instructions to you. When you come, be sure to use all of your lights. We will fire on any unlit helicopter."

Atkins waved and lifted off, the other helos in close pursuit. They sped off into the darkness. "The hell with this," Atkins said to himself. While the others headed for the Battery Park Hotel, Tommy kicked his rudder pedals and pushed the cyclic all the way forward. As the ship roared forward, he pushed the collective down gently. Soon, he was less than fifty feet over the water. "This is more like it," he thought. Less than a minute later, he flashed under the Verrazano-Narrows Bridge, headed straight out to sea.

"*Iwo*, this is TV 1, over."

"TA, that you?" The officer in *Iwo Jima*'s flight control center couldn't believe his ears. He'd heard that voice hundreds of times, but not lately.

"Yeah, it's me. Request clearance to land. I have urgent reports for the boss."

"Roger, TA. You are cleared to land on aft pad 1."

Iwo Jima, with two small escort ships was circling just outside the mouth of the harbor. On her hangar deck were the aircraft for the final assault. Pierson and Stoneman had planned well. There were two Harriers, three Apache gunships, and five more big Sikorskys like Atkins had just landed. But these weren't painted for TV. They were painted in standard special ops black, and their radar and gun pods were all in place.

Tommy jumped out of his helo and saluted the officer of the deck and the colors. Without pausing, he ran to combat control and was soon talking to Hunter and Pierson on the secure satellite phone. The operations plan was just getting a small change. What the hell. The whole thing was a floating craps game anyway.

18 March
0458 Hours Local
Over the Water Outside Haifa Harbor

It had been a long flight for the squadron, coming out of Nellis AFB in Nevada, joining up with the rest of the wing coming out of Texas and all the way across the Atlantic to Israel. Being in the air for long periods was no problem in a larger aircraft. In the B-52, a guy could get up and take a walk around. But these B-1s were cramped and even with only a crew of four, there wasn't much time to loaf. Especially when the afterburners kicked in. They were a bit slow compared to an F-15, but they had all the punch of a stack of ICBMs. *It was a very comfortable ride*, the squadron commander thought. *This is a pretty cushy way to earn a living.*

Lieutenant Colonel Rene "Frenchie" Bouchard was always fidgeting around in the cockpit. F-111s, B-52s, and a lot of other complicated birds had kept him busy in the thousands of hours he had been flying them. Especially the Buff, as the crews called the B-52. Buff, like most pilot lingo, was an acronym, but one not approved in the code books. It stood for "big ugly flying fucker." It was the oldest aircraft in the inventory, and it was only ugly if you were standing in a target zone. A whole wing of them was right behind Bouchard. But his flight, and the rest of the Nellis-Texas squadron, flew the B-1B Lancer. After setting the computers, there wasn't much for him and his copilot to do but drink coffee. They had been in and out of Syrian airspace for over an hour. What the radar operators saw of them didn't matter much. There wasn't much in this airspace that could catch them.

Orders came through last night. They would orbit around Damascus until about 2200 U.S. Eastern time. Then they would get the go signal and unleash an electronic storm that would paralyze Syria. After their electronic barrage, the Buffs would saturate the field with thousand-pounders, pulverizing the Syrian tanks and infantry. The B-1s had other orders if the Syrians threatened to launch any more of their ballistic missiles. A lesson had been learned from the Gulf War. After that war, a very smart man named Chuck Horner took a hard look at his friends and former enemies alike. The message from them was clear. They had learned that to go to war with America, you need to use nuclear weapons, or other weapons of mass destruction. Horner knew that there would never be another war as easy as the past one.

Horner had been commander of the Allied Air Forces in the Gulf War. He had made plans for the U.S. Air Force to strike as the Israelis did in 1972. If the Syrians, or for that matter the Iranians or the Iraqis, lit up their missile firing systems, they would be detected. And then the B-1s would use their other weapons, the low-yield tactical nukes they each had in their internal bomb bays. And, if necessary, the cruise missiles, which packed enough punch to vaporize any one of these countries.

"Sir, there's flash traffic coming in."

Bouchard looked at his copilot, who was decoding the signal. "Sir, we have a go. We're to hit the jammers at precisely 0500 and then do a BDA for the Buffs who are gonna hit the tank formations around Haifa." The bomb damage assessment was just as important as the strike. It told you whether you'd have to go back to the same target, and the bandits were always there the second time.

"Anything on the missile launchers?"

"Negative. All quiet."

"Okay, it's a go. Prepare for low-level maneuvering." There were coffee cups being drained all through the squadron. When Bouchard wanted to, he could make this huge boat really dance, and they knew they'd have to follow his lead. From recent experience they all could testify to his fondness for low-level maneuvers in a plane that wasn't really built for them. Unsubtle power was what the B-1B was all about. The B-2 guys flew like ballerinas. The B-1 crews looked down on them. Usually from an altitude of about 80,000 feet and a speed of about Mach 1.5.

Around the city, there had been some optimism about the lack of more missile attacks, but the news reports were horrible. Missiles armed with chemical warheads had hit Jerusalem and Tel Aviv. The IAF had taken such enormous losses that the air force colonel who had come out of the city—his fighter had been shot down, and he had ejected over the city's center—said that the IAF would not be able to help them. They would fight or die alone.

And the Americans would not come this time. Their president had been taken hostage, and the price of his freedom was American neutrality. Many of the people in the city said the Americans couldn't be blackmailed like that, but who knew? There had never been a situation like this before. The American vice president was not someone the Israelis knew. He had had no role in foreign policy before. Nobody knew if the American system of government permitted the vice president to commit them to a war. And who was he? Was he a friend or not? No one in Israel was certain.

The day's fighting had been extremely close. They had taken enormous numbers of casualties. Old men, women, children were dying in the city from the artillery bombardment, which went on all day and night. There were women and old men fighting on the front lines, too. And they were dying along with everyone else. They talked in the lulls between the Syrian attacks. Why not use the bomb? Everyone knows we have it. Why not use it now, when the war may soon be lost if we don't? If we are all to die, let us take as many of them with us as we can.

The dawn brought no respite from the shelling, and the noise of the tanks' engines said they were coming again. Ammunition was still plentiful, but soldiers were not. Keep fighting. There is nothing else to do but die.

17 March
2257 Hours
New York Harbor

They had been working hard for only a few minutes, but it seemed like hours. The terrorist leader, whom others called Salim, had ordered them up to the third tier of the statue's base, where the hostages were being held. They had humped all of the equipment into the base and up the elevators, and started to set it up. The SEALs and SAS men had been familiarized with the equipment by one of the network crews and by the CNN crew they were impersonating. There were lights, sound equipment, and the all-important satellite uplink through a large telescoping tower antenna, which they had set up amid boxes and carts of equipment. Wires were run all over the place. Equipment cases were stacked neatly out of the way, but just at hand. A lot of equipment was left in them, ready for the right moment.

Mussilli wasn't nervous while they let him work. He fussed over the lights and the microphones. The microphone stands were old, and some of them couldn't be made to stay up high enough. Guido enlisted some of the terrorist guards for setup duty. He was everywhere, directing the hostages and the terrorists for their interviews. Cully and a few of the others followed Mussilli as he went among the terrorists, trying to interview them. Only the leaders would speak, and Mussilli had a hard time getting them to stop. Cully rolled the camera through monologue after monologue. They said the same things over and over. The world was unjust to their people, and now it had to pay.

After the equipment was set up, they were ready to test it. Salim was introduced to a burly blond fellow named Thompson, the "head sound engineer." Tommy Thompson looked around, taking cues from Guido and Cully. Duke Jamison was a long way from the beach at Laguna. He was lugging the lights and reflector umbrellas back and forth across the big room. His surfer's smile was permanently pasted on his face, the look of an adrenaline junkie. Jamison knew this was the biggest kick he'd ever had.

The Raj looked down two terraces below the control console he was setting up. As the "broadcast director," he would sit at this control panel and choose the broadcast from the cameras around the room, including the one Cully was carrying. One of the big plastic equipment bins had been rolled up just behind him.

On the terrace below, the terrorists' machine guns were all pointed out, and the men at them were all looking down. They had remarkable discipline, he thought. Few of these punks had any sense at all. He had expected them to be looking up at him, ranging away from their posts. And their weapons. No matter. The job would be done, no matter how much discipline they showed. Raj was the director of the show in more ways than one. In front of him, a bank of three monitors had been set up, and he ran the satellite uplink, which had two channels for TV and one which linked him to the assault force.

He was practicing cueing cameras and moving some of the equipment around. He made sure that a large black leather case was no more than a foot or two from his left arm. He was giving so many hand signals to the crew that the terrorists started to mimic his motions. There was a lot of rummaging through the equipment carts and cases.

Mike Rigazzi had been elected "producer" for the crew. He positioned everyone and cued Raj, who lit up the equipment. Inside the Pentagon Tank and in the White House, the television brought a live image from inside the statue. There were three cameras, one for the outside view, one for the temporary podium they had set up, and one on Cully's shoulder, which roamed around the big room.

Cully was busy, positioning the camera he was running and responding to orders from Mussilli. He knew the general layout, but the terrorists had moved the hostages into two groups, one on each side of the staircase. There were about 100 hostages there, sitting on the floor. The terrorists, about twenty of them, were walking nervously around the room, punching and slapping the "reporters," poking into their equipment, looking for something suspicious. They found nothing, but they kept looking. Cully glanced at his watch. An hour and three minutes until the news broadcast was supposed to start. Sixty-three minutes more. A long time to keep their weapons secret.

He looked down. The lights at the statue's base were turned off. If they were on, the machine gunners wouldn't be able to see down to their fields of fire. This plan was so much improvisation. What the hell. He yelled over to Mussilli.

"Hey, boss. We can get a better shot if they turn on the floodlights."

Mussilli took the hint. He walked over to Salim.

"My cameras can make better picture if you tell your men to turn on big lights at bottom."

Salim scowled. "You don't have to speak pidgin to me like I was some movie Indian. I speak English better than you do. We will turn on the lights a few minutes before you broadcast the news. These people of yours look sloppy. Get them to clear their equipment away from the stairs. Someone might fall."

The outside lights went on, bathing the statue from head to foot. Anyone looking down would now have a hard time seeing where the assault forces would run to the relief of the SEALs. Cully was walking around, sometimes checking shots through the camera, sometimes helping string power cords for the TV monitors they had set up for the Raj near the back door to the room. He looked at the hostages and didn't recognize anyone. He kept walking, and turned when he heard someone weeping quietly on his left.

Evelyn Broughton had noticed the lean young man across the room. There was something familiar about the way his eyes searched the room again and again. The room had been dark since the hostages arrived. Now it was as bright as the study she favored in Downing Street. At first, she wasn't sure it was the same man, but when he walked by, she knew him.

He heard the sobbing and turned to her. She gave him a blank look. The sobbing was coming from the large man leaning against her. The president had been crying for two hours and didn't seem about to stop. Broughton's eyes met Cully's. She raised an eyebrow. He held his hand up to scratch his nose and winked at her. A cold fear took her. It was him, the man she remembered, who had saved her life before. But what could he do here, against so many? If she was going to die, she'd die standing up, fighting. If there were others here, what were they going to do, and when?

17 March
2253 Hours

Eddie the Fish had had enough of New York. His team was in the water again and had the toughest job of all. There are four buildings at the other end of the island, and the terrorists could have the hidden nuke in any one of them. If those buildings weren't searched before the news broadcast began, it might not be possible to stop them from setting it off. Seven swimmers were a few yards off the beach and on time. Even through their dry suits, they shivered in the cold water. Seven minutes before 11 P.M. Time to get going. Eddie kicked forward through the last few yards of water and was on the beach and sprinting to the first building precisely at 2254 hours. Six minutes.

• • •

The Raj looked completely cool. He smiled at Salim, who had pushed him back off the director's console with the muzzle of his gun. Salim poked and prodded, but didn't open anything up. He didn't dare. If any of this equipment broke, the broadcast might not go on schedule. Petrov would be angry. Five minutes.

Evelyn Broughton looked down at Ike Brandon. He had stopped sobbing. A very husky black man had camped out in front of her. He had pushed a small cart up against the wall next to her, and was dipping into it for something every few minutes. He never seemed to find what he wanted. He was stringing wires, and seemed to be concentrating very hard. His eyes flicked from her to the young man with the camera, to President Brandon, and then to the terrorist standing nearest to her. The look on his face reminded her of something, but she couldn't place it. What was it? It suddenly came to her. It was a look she had seen before. It was the look on her father's face the time he had to shoot a crippled horse. The man was looking at the terrorist as something to be killed, remorselessly, inevitably, and sadly. He didn't enjoy it. But it was his duty, and he was going to do it. Four minutes.

• • •

Eddie the Fish and his SBS unit found only two guards in the first three of the rear buildings they cleared. Those two were quickly disposed of by two men with supressed MP-5s. Two down, two killed. One more building. Three minutes.

• • •

Cully was wearing a web belt with battery packs hung all aroung it, as well as a headset for the short-range radio linking him to the Raj. It had more than one frequency, and he flipped from one to another every minute or so. "Hammer, this is TA. We are three minutes out."

Cully couldn't believe his ears. He whispered into his microphone. "TA, this is Hammer. Roger three minutes. What the hell is going on?"

"Did you really think I'd let someone else chauffeur you assholes around?"

"Later, TA. Let's do the job."

Alan Ahearn spoke quietly to the chief of the boat. "I want the deck gunners up and ready before anybody else goes topside." The man nodded and spoke quietly through his intercom. U.S.S. *Bayonne* had been at battle stations for three hours. No time would be wasted now. Two minutes.

Cully looked around for what had to be the thousandth time. He had laid aside the shoulder-held camera and taken position behind the middle one covering the makeshift podium. His earpiece should chirp three times with the signal from Eddie the Fish. Three times meant the nuke had been found, and the attack was a go. Two chirps meant the nuke was still missing, and go anyway. Four chirps was the abort code. He looked at his watch and waved to the Raj and Wilson. The cameras were on, trained on the podium where Salim and Rashid were herding the president and a half dozen others up to the microphones. Lights burned down on them from the stands going ten feet up above the podium. Cully's earpiece chirped loudly once, twice, and went silent. One minute.

Mussilli looked at his watch and waved to Cully. "Light 'em up. We'll start with the president and work our way left around the room. That Salim guy wants to say something before we interview anybody. Here, Salim, stand here. We'll keep the camera on you."

"I will speak. You will listen. You will not ask me questions until after the hostages speak. The prime minister of France will speak first. Then Germany, then the United States, if he is able." Salim looked over to Brandon. The three heads of state had agreed to make the speeches Petrov had written for them. Each was about the same, pleading for their nations to capitulate to the Arab nations. Salim stood, looking far into the camera's lens just as Petrov had told him. Rashid walked away, back to where the steps led up to the statue's head.

"Sure, sure. Just stand here or we can't get you on camera."

One of Rashid's men waved him over to the radio. A call was coming in, and a lookout had spotted a large helicopter approaching. "Does it have all of its lights on? Has he given the password we gave him before?"

"Oh, yes. He has all of his lights on. It is the same one that brought the reporters. I recognized the pilot's voice."

"Very well. Tell him to land where he did before. Just behind the statue." The man turned back to the radio. A minute later, while Salim and Rashid were posing for the camera, Cully heard the unmistakable sound of a Sea King landing.

The Raj was holding his hand up for the broadcast signal to the entire crew. He was counting down with his fingers in the air: five, four, three, two, one. Cully had Rashid in the viewfinder of the camera, and reached down, scratching his ankle. His right hand slid behind his ankle, and he palmed the little automatic. Wilson glanced at Cully. A wild gleam had come into his eyes. Wilson thought, *Oh, shit. Here we go again.* Wilson turned around and reached deep into the cart next to Evelyn Broughton.

17 March
2300:01 Hours

Atkins felt strange flying with the big helmet on. For twenty years, it was his constant companion, but now it felt heavy and awkward. He'd never noticed that before. No, it felt good. He was flying the lead in his CNN helo. But even though it was filled to the roof with a squad of marines, every light was on. The damned thing looked like a flying Christmas tree.

The marines were as keyed up as any bunch of troops he had ever seen. The three more squads from their platoon were crammed into three helos following them. Behind was a string of helos and Apache gunships from the decks of *Iwo Jima*. Three Harrier fighter-bombers circled overhead. More helos would follow, pouring a steady stream of marines and rangers into the coming battle.

Hunter had planned to land four marine companies on the island, but the final plan called for only one, plus a company of Army Rangers. The company of marines was not hard to choose. When Dunham asked which company he would send, Hunter named them without a moment's thought. Their commander was a narrow-faced captain named Hall who would never admit there was civilization north of Virginia. Hall's Second Squad had just won the annual competition for the best rifle squad in the Corps, and the entire company was just as good. Now they rode silently in Atkins's helo. This was the point of America's spear.

Like every member of the division, they all wore a shoulder patch just issued at the orders of their new division CO. It was a reissue of an old World War II division patch. It was diamond-shaped, with a dark blue background and had the five stars of the Southern Cross in white and a big red number one down its center. Stitched in white on the number was the name of an island: Guadalcanal. Hall had said that his boys were too young to know that story, so they were going to write their own. Okay, thought Atkins. Maybe tonight's the night.

Alan Ahearn sat in a black hole in the waters of New York Harbor. Rigged for silent running, U.S.S. *Bayonne* was virtually undetectable by the best ASW people in the world. The opposition here wasn't nearly that good. Even so, Ahearn played the game for all it was worth. No one knew they were there, other than the folks at COMSUBLANT who ordered them there. And Pierson. And some guy named O'Bannon.

"Ah, Captain. Anybody figure out how it's gonna be when we blast his guy? I mean that's a pretty good-size reactor he has on board."

"No problem, XO. All we gotta do is just hit his bow, and dump it in the bay. The cooker should scram itself and shut down."

"You really believe that, boss?"

"Okay, okay. Maybe it'll be a coupla years before we can visit that side of the island again."

Ahearn sat, headphones on, listening to the Victor boat cycle its engines again and again, then go quiet through the night. What the hell was he up to? *Bayonne* had been at battle stations for too long. The crew was getting tired. Just now approaching 2300 hours. Time to quit playing with this guy.

Ahearn spoke softly. "Chief, make tubes one and two ready for firing. Set them to go active immediately. We want them both in his bow. Open outer doors."

To the sonar operator sitting beside him: "Yankee-search the bastard in five, four, three, two, one, now."

Bayonne's main sonar let out a ping that rang the hull of the Iranian boat like a Chinese gong. Commander Ali bin-Muhadi's face blanched. He started screaming orders. "General quarters. Cast off all lines. Make speed ahead. Come to course two-two-zero. Prepare tubes one through four for firing." Men were running all through the boat. They knew what that sonic pounding meant.

"Bearing three-three-five, range three-one-one-zero yards, sir. We have his solution."

"Set and shoot. Fire tubes one and two."

Bayonne rumbled as the fish left the tubes. "One and two on the way, sir. They've already gone active, running hot, straight, and normal. They have the target, skipper."

No need for quiet now. "Cut the wires. All ahead two thirds. Come to course zero-seven-five. Combat surface. Surface action port side. Reload tubes one and two. Give me a bearing on the frigate. Prepare tubes four, five, and six for firing."

17 March
2300:03 Hours

Bayonne leaped ahead, nearly level as it broke through to the surface, still accelerating through 20 knots. Hatches cracked up and down the deck as the Marines shoved past the sailors who had already manned the 30mm deck gun and pointed it toward the little island. Ahearn rested his hand on the old .45 in his belt holster. Hell, he had a nuclear submarine to fight with. But the .45 felt good on his hip.

"Sir, we have the frigate. We'll have to run 'em out a bit and dog leg around the island at two thousand yards."

"OK, give me a bearing and set the torps for the dog leg at two thousand."

"Sir, four, five and six are ready. We have his solution."

"Set and shoot four, five and six. Give me a time on the first two shots. I want the reload report right away. Let's make the rubble bounce."

The first two torpedoes reached their target only a few seconds apart. The Victor-class boat never had a ghost of a chance. The first torpedo blew its bow off, the second hitting just forward of the conning tower. The other three flashed quietly through the water, going past the southern tip of the island.

17 March
2300:04 Hours

Cully moved left around the camera. Wilson was reaching into a large bin he had wheeled up between a couple of the terrorists and Broughton. Rashid glanced at Cully and saw his face. For the first time in his life, Rashid was frozen by fear. It gripped him like a cold hand, crushing his chest. He gasped. Cully's hand came up to his face, and Rashid looked into the tiny muzzle of the .22. Wilson had finally found what he was looking for at the bottom of the bin. All around the room, the other SEALs and SAS men were reaching down into their shoes or the big plastic bins.

Rashid slumped to his knees and fell backward, total astonishment on his face as he died. Around the big room, terrorists were falling and dying quietly. His eyes flashing around the room, Salim screamed "Kill them, kill them all!" Scrambling madly past his dead and dying comrades, Salim flew through the east door and down to the second level.

All of the SEALs fired at the nearest targets, grabbing guns from the fallen, reaching into the bins for MP-5s and .45 pistols. Cully and Wilson stepped around the camera, seeing Broughton and the president, a tall man pointing his weapon at Broughton, three more pointing guns at Brandon and others. Cully fired at the ones aiming at Brandon, Wilson cutting two others in half with bursts from the three-barrelled gun. Brandon screamed for mercy, reaching for Wilson, who slammed him to the floor yelling, "Keep your head down, asshole." Cully grabbed an H&K machine gun from a bin near President Brandon, and fired burst after burst, other SEALs firing, SBS men firing from the back entrance where they had crashed through the door. Cully fired again as others advanced toward Broughton, throwing himself in front of her as one fired, grazing his head with a 9mm round, the rest of the team shooting sporadically, the giant Suleiman Semret standing, screaming, "Allah Akbar," and strangling a terrorist with each hand, grabbing a knife and jumping on top of a third. Duke Jamison's surfer's smile died with him, a bullet passing through the back of his head, three other SEALs falling with fatal wounds. Mike Scott took a round in the shoulder, but kept firing left-handed. The Raj ran past Cully, firing at other terrorists in the corner, and glancing to his left to see Tommy Thompson killing a man with a blow with the edge of his hand, cutting up under the man's nose. Then a sudden quiet. Then the best sound: Atkins's helo passing close by.

He looked left and saw Broughton inching up near where he crouched. Broughton was bleeding from her left leg, which had been grazed in the exchange. She had a big .45 in her right hand. She looked at Cully and Wilson. "You are making a habit of saving my life. But if I am to die, I will die fighting."

Cully nodded to her. "Yes, ma'am. You're not gonna die. But please stay low, now, and follow Chief Wilson. Run. Please." There was an irresistible command in his voice. England's iron lady obeyed and ran. Cully looked up and saw Suleiman Semret grinning from ear to ear. Their eyes met. As Cully gave him a thumbs up, Semret threw his head back and yelled, "Allah Akbar," with a voice that shook the walls.

Cully spoke quickly into his microphone. "TA, TA, we have secured the hostages on the third level. Repeat, the third level up."

No answer. "Tommy, do you read? We have the third level secure, but we need help fast, over?"

"Roger that, Hammer." Cully was never so glad to hear anyone's voice.

"Hammer, we are thirty seconds out from the flagpole. Can you give cover fire for the landing?"

"Negative, TA. We're getting probing fire from below. We need those reinforcements in here and right goddamn now."

"Hold on, Hammer."

Atkins swung the big helo back around and headed east over the water from the north end of the island. He looked out to the statue. No way the marines could survive the run from the flag to the base. No way to get into the base, anyway. Too many bad guys between the back door and the upper level where the hostages were. Tommy clicked the intercom to the marine captain sitting behind him.

"Ah, Captain Hall. We have a slight change of plan. Can your boys all jump out from the right door?"

"Yessir. Just get us close..."

"Captain, you're gonna get closer than you ever wanted to. Just get your people lined up."

Atkins slewed the chopper back around. The terrace area above the first level of the statue's base was wide enough to land on, but the third one up was where they had to go. It was much narrower. Too narrow to land on, too narrow to even approach without shattering the rotors against the statue. If the rotors torqued off the top of the helo . . .

Atkins hit the brakes as they neared the statue, the helo rocking back, then forward. Salim and his men saw it and opened fire just as Tommy slipped the helo sideways, level with the third terrace level. The rotors slammed into the southern face of the statue and as the marines leaped for the pavement, the big machine tore itself to pieces, and the front fuselage bounced down onto the second terrace. Atkins dived out the right side of the helo as it burst into flames.

Tommy made for the door, pulling his pistols as he ran. Salim saw him and stepped through the door.

Tommy, running toward the door, dove sideways, firing both pistols as fast as he could pull the triggers. Salim and a man to his right opened fire, cutting Atkins down hard. His body bounced off the side of the door, spun around, and went over the low wall.

One floor above, the marines swept into the big room.

"Where the hell did you come from, and where's everybody else?"

"They're a bit behind us. I'm Hall. Who the hell're you?"

"I'm O'Bannon. Where's Atkins?"

"Dunno. I don't think he got out of the bird."

"Captain, put half of your men at the west door and half at the east. We gotta hold those stairs."

By then, more helos were approaching, and one had touched down where the flagpole had been. Salim and his men knew they could either retake the hostages or die where they stood. A few ran off to the frigate. They had heard the sub explode. There was no place else to hide. Salim had heard the sub explode, too. He had also heard Atkins's helo crash land on the floor above him. He had sixty or seventy men left. More than enough to retake the hostages.

"You three, set up a machine gun on the first terrace. Kill anything that moves. You two, and those four, slowly up that stair. You others follow me." They began climbing the stairs. Cautiously. Quietly. All of the shooting would be in the west stair. He and two of the men would go up the east stair, if they could get through to the stairs which led up to the statue's head.

Cully knew they would all be rushing up the stairs in a minute. The Raj was firing down on the machine gun emplacements, tossing grenades as quickly as he could pull the pins. Inside, there was fire coming from above and below. Cully and Wilson huddled on one side of the staircase going to the crown. There were a lot of terrorists coming, and the SEALs had orders to hold until relieved. And they were damned well going to do it.

Cully looked around quickly. There were hostages scattered all over the big room, shouting and pushing to get outside. Some, the smart ones, were keeping low and sticking close to the surviving SEALs. Cully gathered his men around the hostages. With Hall's marines and the Raj's team they could hold the stairs. For a while, anyway.

The remaining SEALs, as well as the Raj and his team, split up to guard the hostages and the doors. They had to hold. There would be no second chance.

17 March
2303 Hours

"Confirm the sub kill with torpedo 1," the exec yelled to Ahearn through the intercom. "Come to zero-nine-zero and slow to headway speed. How much longer on five, six, and seven?" he yelled in return. *Bayonne* had covered the distance to Liberty Island in under three minutes. Its deck gun could now support the landing.

"Twenty seconds, skipper."

"Activate and cut the wires."

"Forward thirty mount, engage the radar dish on the flat; fire!" At Ahearn's command, the large radar deployed by the terrorists suddenly disappeared in a chattering roar.

17 March
2306 Hours
Hi Diddle Diddle, Charge up the Middle.

The big helo made a wide turn, arcing around the statue. The doors were open. No way to touch down without drawing fire. The pilot set the chopper down hard, and the first squad of the lead platoon of Delta Company, 3d Battalion, First Marines, jumped out firing. From the center of the LZ, they ran to the outside of the low wall that lines the boulevard behind the statue. They spread out, taking what cover they could.

Over the wall, the tree-lined avenue was a clear field of fire for the terrorists manning the machine guns on the first level of the statue's base. Worse yet, on the bottom level, one was firing directly down the center of the assault route. Despite the Raj's grenades, three of them were still firing, and had turned their fire down on the marines. A hundred meters is a long way to run when someone is shooting at you. More helos landed, and there was a steady stream of marines jumping into the fight. The machine gunners found the range, and the marines jumping from the helos were being cut to pieces.

The platoon commander paused, his men grouping behind him and to the left. He heard a continuous firefight inside the statue. No time to wait. He turned to one of the other platoon leaders who had come up behind. "Lieutenant, it's about a hundred meters from here to the back door. Bet you a case of Bud I can get there faster than you can."

The other lieutenant was only a year out of college. He had run the 440 at Indiana. "I'll see you the Bud and raise you a quart of Jack in the Black."

"You're on. Pass the word. We go in one minute. Everybody follow me, but don't bunch up. Okay?"

The senior platoon leader grabbed the radioman and hit the army frequency. "Delta to air. We need some help with those machine guns on the north side of the Lady." No answer.

"Delta to air. We'll never make it. Who's up there, goddamn it?" Still no answer.

"Okay, we go anyway. Thirty seconds. Ready?" The platoon leader raised his right fist in the air.

A stream of words filled his headset. Whoever it was, he was talking so fast they could hardly understand the words. "Sorrywe'reabitlateboys. ThisisFire Hose. HoldforthirtymoresecondsDelta."

The junior lieutenant turned to the senior man. "Who the fuck is Fire Hose?"

"Raise your head in thirty seconds, and you'll see."

Then they all heard it. The heavy droning of the AC-130's engines was clear, even over the din of the firefight.

The pilot's butt shifted uncomfortably in the seat. His wife couldn't understand why he stayed in the Air National Guard. His stockbroker's pay was rising so fast, she couldn't believe he wanted to do anything other than stay home and help her spend it. But it was his damn eyes. Nobody should have 20/10 vision. But he did. He and his crew had won every gunnery contest for AC-130s the Air Force and the Air National Guard had held for five years. When the call came for a gunship, Fire Hose's number was at the top of the list.

Captain Elvin "Fire Hose" Hutchison had a boring flight from the base in Florida. As usual, the flight was uneventful, loud, and uncomfortable. That was the only thing this bird had in common with the stock C-130. After Rockwell finished with it, the AC-130J had enough firepower to level a city. But it was still slow, loud, and a pain in the ass to ride. But he loved it. It was part of him, a huge suit he put on.

He had a clear view out the side window of the big ship. The two machine gun positions looked bright, the heat of their fire guiding their own doom toward them. Hutchison eased the Specter gunship into a slow, big turn, banking the left wing down.

"Firemission. ReadyontheVulcans." His copilot had long since shifted the fire control to the two 20mm cannon jutting out of the left side of the ship. The pilot aimed again and pressed his trigger. For an instant, the marines on the ground thought the big bird had turned a spotlight on the statue. Then the report of the cannon reached them, and they knew the light was the huge muzzle flash from the cannon.

The terrace where the machine gunners sat suddenly became a meat grinder that killed men, a flood of lead chewing up everything in its path. The marines looked over their wall through the cloud of dust and debris the Specter's fire had thrown into the air.

The senior lieutenant raised his right hand and waived forward with a shout. "Marines, follow me!" They all rose, leaped over the wall and ran toward the front door, firing at the remaining gunners inside the statue's base.

By now the rest of the company had been landed, and helos were dropping the Army Rangers in as the second wave. The terrorists inside the statue, realizing their danger, managed to get a second machine gun going through the back doors in the lower level. The marines were taking heavy fire from the two guns slowing their advance. As soon as the Rangers landed, they were hit hard as well.

Inside the statue, heavy fire was coming from below, but with Wilson's short bursts and the heavier weapons they had in play, they could hold. For a few minutes at least. Cully glanced back at the team. They were taking fire from the staircases where the dozens of terrorists were trying to advance back into the hostage room. The marines kept throwing grenades down the stairs, the terrorists charging up the stairs in small groups.

Slowly, one by one, the SEALs and the marines were being hit. Cully heard the helos outside and the firing by the marines and Rangers, almost to the back door.

The marines were running at top speed—ten, twenty, thirty yards. Faster as they went, firing as they ran, forty, then fifty yards. In just a few seconds, twenty of the marines were down. Of the twenty, five got up and kept coming.

One lieutenant went down, and then the other. Seeing them go down, the men paused. They stopped when the other lieutenant went down. The assault had almost failed when one officer got back up. Wounded in the leg, he climbed back up and limped toward the statue, firing his M-16 one-handed. Seeing him, the marines all leaped toward the target, shouting, shooting, and each hoping to get the bastard who shot the boss.

Faster, closer, a few more seconds and they were only twenty yards from the back door, Hall firing through the door, two platoon sergeants stopping a few yards back, shouldering rifles and firing grenades through the heavy glass doors, two tremendous explosions rocking the statue's base, the marines pouring through the door, half going to each side, forcing their way up the stairs to the first level.

Cully didn't take time to count the dead. The statue was far from secure. Rifle fire was still coming from below. He stuck his head out into a stairway, drawing fire again. As he turned around, he saw Salim slip through the door and dash up the stairs that led to Liberty's head.

Jesus, he thought. *The nuke*. Cully ran up the stairs following them. The narrow circular iron stairs didn't let you see more than about ten feet above where you were. Turn, look, and fire. Another eight steps up, turn and look. No one.

At the third section, Cully turned into a long burst from what sounded like two guns, threw himself backward and lost his balance. By the time he regained balance, Salim and the other man had reached the point where the steps branched off to the arm. He raced after them.

Salim turned to the other man. "He is alone. Stay here and kill him. I am going to detonate the bomb." He ran up more stairs, turning to the left where they branched off to the arm of the statue and the torch.

Cully slowed, moving after the sound of footsteps above. Rashid stood silently, waiting. He crouched slowly, reducing his profile in the dim light.

Cully charged up the stairs, saw the second man, and fired just as the other man did. The man died as Cully's left leg took a slug and gave out beneath him. He heard Salim's steps above. Not straight above, but off to the side. It could mean only one thing. He reached for the radio, and clicked it on. Nothing. It was useless. He started dragging himself up the stairs. "Gotta get there before he sets it off," he thought. "Gotta get there." Losing a lot of blood. Shock coming on, he weakened fast. He felt faint. Steps below him. A small figure in the dull light.

"Cully. It's me, Rajah."

"Where's the target?"

"Never mind these guys. The bomb. In the torch. Get outside and call in a strike."

"Right." The Raj turned and disappeared. In less than a minute, he threw himself down the stairs, and as he ran out the door, he keyed the army and marine frequencies.

"Movers, this is Hammer 3. The bomb is in the torch. I say again, the bomb is in the torch."

The lead Harrier pilot turned his flight back toward the statue and slowed to 250 knots. "Roger Hammer 3. The torch. We're in hot."

No radar emissions from the target. No IR signature from a statue. Nothing to shoot at for all the fancy stuff, thought the pilot as he lined his ship up. *Just one missile, and the Mark 1 eyeball. Easy, easy. Just a little more*. He steadied the gunsight pipper on the top of the statue's hand and pressed the missile button. The Maverick roared off the Harrier's left wing and accelerated toward the torch.

Salim never heard the plane approach as he took the last steps three at a time and dove for the bomb, throwing down his machine pistol. He reached for the detonator just as the missile hit the top of the statue's hand, just where it grasped the torch. He never felt the explosion.

From inside the statue, Cully thought for an instant that the nuke had gone off. The explosion knocked him back down the stairs. He managed to grab a handhold and stop his fall. As he lost consciousness, he saw an enormous light over his head and thought, *This is what it's like to die*.

18 March
0503 Local

John Mastropolo and Frenchie Bouchard, along with more than 180 other U.S. and RAF aircraft, saw the huge arrays of Syrian tanks at the same instant, but from different angles. The people at the city's edge were fighting and dying again, and the Syrian infantry supported by the tanks was at the city's outskirts, coming in from the north and the northeast.

One young Sabra girl had been firing a rifle since the war began. The sergeant came by every few hours to move her to another location or to get her more ammunition or food. She was well forward of last defensive lines, the last between the advancing Syrians and the women and children left in the city. She was only nineteen, but all the other teenagers were on the front lines, too. She knew how to fire a rifle and usually hit what she aimed at, so they made her a sniper. She was tired and wanted a hot bath. Her back ached steadily from a fall she had taken the night before, climbing among the rocks to look for a better spot. But she stared through her binoculars constantly, searching for another target.

She had managed to wedge herself into a chimney between two large rocks, in the side of a hill facing north. It was safe unless a tank got a clear shot at her. She had a canteen of water and a few candy bars to nibble. They had come around twice yesterday to give her more water and ammunition. She could see other fighters a few dozen yards away. She wasn't sure, but one of the men looked like the man who ran the dry cleaner she goes to. Went to.

She would probably die today, she thought. But she had thought that for three days now. It began as a crawling fear that reached deep inside her and almost tore her stomach out. But now it was just a numbness. If she died, she would die here, and that wasn't so bad. The sky was clear, and the rising sun was turning it robin's-egg blue. She wondered if her boyfriend was still alive. She thought of him often. He was in a tank, somewhere out there.

Her ears rang from the gunfire. She wasn't really sure what she was hearing any more. They seemed to hear a low rumble off in the southwest. It wasn't going to rain. Her ears were playing tricks on her now. She looked out, squinting into the east where the morning sun was still low in the sky. It grew louder, and she blinked. It wasn't the sound of tank engines. From the side of her hill, she could see across the plain for miles. There were tanks and infantry coming again. They were probably still a mile or two off. Maybe time to die. She shouldered the rifle and looked through the telescopic sight. The big Bausch & Lomb lens reached out at twenty power. Dust, more tanks. She couldn't see the infantry yet through all the dust. The rumbling came again, and this time she was sure it was from above. It was louder still. Syrian planes?

She looked up and thought she saw something, but wasn't sure. Then the plain in front of her erupted in flame and smoke. A rapid series of blasts stunned her, and she felt a trickle of blood coming from her left eardrum. But she looked out, and screamed, not in fear, but in joy. She would live, and so would many of her countrymen who would otherwise have died that day. The Americans were here. An A-10 roared over her, banked steeply, and went back to the fight. Higher, a black flying wing whispered by. She didn't know or care about how or why they suddenly were there. She saw the "stars and bars" of the U.S. Air Force on the side of each aircraft that passed over her. She laughed up at them through her tears. She pushed her way out of the crevice, stood up and waved with both her arms.

"Hey, boss, will ya look at that? Some babe with great knockers is waving to us."

Bouchard smiled to himself. At low altitude, people could see them coming and going, but still couldn't touch them. Electronically, they were visible, but their speed and power were too much for the bunch below. He turned the B-1 slowly so they would pass over the girl again. *Go home, kid*, he thought. She looked up and waved again. The big B-1 dipped its left wingtip, then its right, then its left again. Then it was gone.

The first two days of the war had gone very well for Pougachev. He smiled inside the oxygen mask. Every one of his pilots had three or more kills. He had eight. The kill ratio was about five to one in his favor. If the Americans stayed out of the fight one more day, there would have been no Israeli Air Force by sundown.

Yesterday, he had killed an Israeli in an old Mirage III after flying inverted and suddenly pushing forward on his stick, ending up stalling and seemingly flying backward, standing the Su-27 on its tail. His maneuver, the "Pougachev cobra," had taken its first kill. Not since World War I, not since Immelman made his Immelman turn a hallmark of air combat, had a pilot invented a maneuver that others would have to copy. The Pougachev cobra. They would all try, and remember the day over the Golan Heights.

Now, Pougachev couldn't believe his ears. The scramble alert had arrived too late. The Syrian crews on the radar had fallen asleep again. He didn't know what aircraft were coming, just that there were hundreds of them. No one could be that incompetent. He cursed the Syrians, cursed his own country for putting him here. The only thing he didn't curse was the squadron, his squadron, which had managed to get their Su-27s into the air just as the bombs started falling on his runways. They had made a run into Jordan to hide and regroup. It had only taken a few moments, but they were already getting low on fuel for what he wanted them to do.

It was a dangerous business, but Pougachev knew he was the best. Nothing could prevent them from surprising the attackers from below. The Su-27s had terrain-following radar, which could put them almost at ground level, and the

Americans never had developed the look-down, shoot-down capability the Russians had favored for a decade.

Pougachev's ten fighters stayed in tight formation. The distance from the Jordanian border to the battle over Haifa would be covered in four minutes. He reached for the master arming switch and turned it on.

"Gotcha, sucker," thought Hank Moody. He was looking at the display that rode near his right thigh in the tight Aurora cockpit. In it, he saw the images taken by the electro-optic sensor mounted in his big ship's mid-fuselage bay. It was a purely passive electronic sensor, built by a small band of crazy engineers in Barrington, Illinios. It didn't announce one's presence like radar. More than a camera, it didn't record images on film, like they did in the old U-2 days. The light was scanned over millions of electro-optic pixels, which recorded it, and the camera read out crisp digital pictures in real time, three frames per second at normal speed. More if you needed it. The damned thing was so good, he could read the tail numbers on Pougachev's fighters from his perch above them. They were at about 2,000 feet above ground level. He was at about 95,000. Nice camera.

The scrambled radio was already tuned to three frequencies, and Moody selected the F-22 frequency by a switch on the left engine throttle. "Crapshoot, Snake Eyes. You have company. Bearing zero-one-six, range two-one-zero, altitude two-zero-zero-zero, speed six-zero-zero." He pushed forward gently on the stick, and the Aurora eased itself down another 5,000 feet. All the better to see from there.

The F-22 squadron commander replied, "Snake Eyes, Crapshoot 1. Roger that." Matt O'Bannon made no signal to his other aircraft. Quietly, without radar or radios, the F-22s changed course, dropped altitude to 1,500 feet, and pushed themselves to supersonic cruise.

Going from an F-117 to an F-22 was like going from a pickup truck to a Porsche. It accepted speeds above Mach 1 with a purr of electromechanical satisfaction. It didn't try to slide out from under you; it seemed to start going where you wanted even before you touched the stick. It handled so well and so easily that all the pilot had to think about was fighting. The F-22 put him where he needed to be every time. Not the fastest, but the stealthiest, most lethal fighter ever, its prototype had been delivered with the characteristic black skunk of the supersecret Lockheed Skunk Works painted on its twin tails. Ben Rich's boys had done it again. His ghost was probably laughing its spectral ass off.

The F-22s didn't break a sweat at 900 knots, and they would close on the Russians at a speed of 1,500 knots. They were too low for the Russians to look for them or expect them.

The other F-22s only dropped down to 5,000 feet. They would all be between the Russians and the B-52s. Anyway, they would be on the Russians before the Russians got to the A-10s. But what was more important, none of the enemy radars had them yet. Nor would they until it was too late. On the Russian radars, the F-22 had a radar signature about as big as a bumblebee's. There were two chances they'd be spotted, slim and none. The high flight of F-22s veered sharply out and turned to a course that would bring them in from behind the Russians.

Pougachev looked to his right and left. The wingmen were positioned perfectly. He smiled to himself. He had trained these men, flown these aircraft. They knew they could win. No threats showed on his passive sensors. Radio silence made them invisible. No one could get to them in the minute it would take to get to the A-10s. They were showing on his long-range TV screen. Forty seconds. He reached for his missile guidance radar.

The wingman shouted the warning as the first of the AMRAAMs came in and tried to evade by pulling up sharply. The missile went with him, but couldn't stay on track and sped off into the sun. Two fighters to his right and behind him were hit and fireballed into the ground. Most of the formation was looking for an approaching dogfight, but as they turned or climbed, they came right into the sights of the F-22s. Half of the Raptors had come in below them from up-sun, slowed to 550 knots, and launched their missiles from close in. When the Russians climbed away from the attack, they ran directly into the other half of the '22s, coming in from behind at higher altitude. They didn't miss at those short ranges. It was over in seconds. Pougachev's next conscious thought was that riding the parachute wasn't so bad. His back ached miserably from the ejection. He looked down at the ground. How had this happened?

The F-22s climbed, looking for more targets. Matt thought of his little brother, and wondered if he was fighting somewhere. He said a small prayer, and then keyed the microphone. "This is Crapshoot. We are bingo fuel. All Crapshooters, RTB."

• • •

The Raj sat down on the stone path outside the statue's front door. By then, every mother's son in the American Army and Marines seemed to be on the island. There were press helicopters orbiting about a quarter mile away, pointing cameras down on every square foot of the island. He looked up at where the top of the torch had been. In its place was a bright fire from the missile's magnesium warhead. It seemed to light up the entire harbor.

From where Frank Clooney stood on the deck of his fireboat, it looked like someone had set the statue on fire. He gave the only orders he knew, and soon the *Brooklyn* had two water cannon arcing streams up to Liberty's torch. Rajiv Singh looked up. The fire reflecting off the arcs of water looked like a rainbow.

A marine lieutenant with a heavily bandaged leg limped up to him. "Are you Hammer 3? There's a shot-up SEAL lookin' for you at the back entrance."

"Thanks, my friend," said the Raj and ran off to find Cully. He found him at the statue's base, being swarmed over by medics and guarded by two very quiet SEALs. Their boss had been shot, and they wanted a piece of somebody as the price. Mike Scott and Tommy Thompson knew the Raj. They waved him over to where Cully sat, propped up against the base of the statue. Behind him lay a body which some civilian medics were zipping into a big black plastic bag. Rajiv Singh looked down at the face of Tommy Atkins. One of the medics said, "Okay, this one's bagged and tagged. Pick up that end and we'll put him over with the others."

"Please," Cully said. "Leave him here with us. He's one of ours."

"Look, fella, we can't do that. Our orders are—"

"No, you will leave him here." The Raj's hand strayed to a short curved knife stuck in his belt. Thompson and Scott were suddenly behind him, their hands pulling back the bolts of their MP-5s. A voice boomed behind them.

"What the hell is goin' on here?" The voice belonged to a marine colonel whose name tag said "Harrigan." The battalion commander.

One of the civilian medics began, "We have orders to remove the bodies, and these people—"

"You O'Bannon?"

"Yes sir. And this man they want to take away is one of us. It's Tommy Atkins, sir. He saved all of our lives today." Cully's voice faded as he looked at the body. "He's been a part of us for so long. We'd just like to sit with him, for a while."

The colonel looked at the medic. "If they say he stays for a while, he *stays*. And if you have a problem with that, you're gonna have a problem with my whole fucking battalion. Got it?"

The medic shrank away under Harrigan's glare. Raj knelt down beside Cully.

"Will you lose the leg, Cully?"

"Naw, I'll be okay. I may limp for a while, but it's the price of doing the job." They both looked up at the torch and then down at Atkins's face, calm in death. They stared at him for a long time. By now, another New York City fireboat had joined the first, their huge water cannons arcing a rainbow through the burning torch. Cully smoothed Atkins's hair back, then looked over to Singh.

"I guess it's worth it, Raj. We got to see freedom's fire."

Two Hours Later
The White House

Patched and clean, with a shave and a make-up job, the president looked ready to meet the media. At least from the neck up. But Brandon sat shivering under a blanket in his big desk chair in the Oval Office. "I can't. I don't care. I can't do it any more," he said to his none-too-sympathetic wife. "I have Rose typing my resignation letter now. They've called Rehnquist. He's on his way to swear Vinny in."

She looked at him with much the same disgust that Broughton had shown earlier. "Okay. I'm through arguing. And after today, I'm through with you. How dare you do this to me? How dare you resign? You're pathetic. You don't deserve to be president."

The chief justice was in the Roosevelt Room, about ten yards down the hall. They had waited for the President Pro Tem of the Senate and the Speaker of the House to join them. He had been roused out of his bed by the Secret Service and had thrown on a suit with a fresh shirt. He shaved with an electric razor in the car on the way into town. Nobody ever saw what was under the robe. But this was the White House, and he *was* the chief justice. Standards must be maintained. The ceremony was brief, and he congratulated La Guardia before walking tiredly back out to the waiting car.

In front of the cameras, the Oval Office looked quiet, with the new president sitting uncomfortably at the big desk, and at a much lower height than his predecessor. Dunham, Touchman, and the Joint Chiefs were all there. After hearing their briefing about the interrogation of the prisoners and what the Aurora flights had shown, there was no doubt that the feisty little guy was going to retaliate and do it right now. He issued their orders. They all had said the obligatory "yes, sir." Spontaneously Dunham and the Joint Chiefs had saluted him. La Guardia felt a bit sheepish about that, but they went ahead quickly, issuing the orders to carry our their president's decision. The green light went on on the top of camera 1.

"My fellow Americans. We have come through a great crisis tonight. I am here to report to you that by the bravery of our young men, President Brandon, Prime Minister Broughton, and almost all of the others held hostage at the Statue of Liberty have been freed and are safe. There was much loss of life, and the statue itself has suffered great damage.

"But that damage is not permanent, and we will repair it. We'll repair the damage to our nation as well. I regret to report to you that President Brandon has suffered much in this crisis, and an hour ago he tendered his resignation. We all wish him a quick recovery and Godspeed in his new life out of the public eye. In accordance with the Constitution, Chief Justice Rehnquist swore me in as president a few minutes ago.

"I also need to report to you the conclusions we have reached about this terrible incident. From the prisoners we have captured and from our own intelligence sources, we have determined that the government of Libya was responsible for this outrage. Muammar Qaddafi and his henchmen brought nuclear terrorism to our shores. There is only one remedy.

"I have just sent a message to the Senate and House of Representatives asking them to declare that a state of war exists between the United States and Libya. The Speaker and the President Pro Tem have each assured me that a Declaration of War will be passed within the hour.

"Let me make this very clear. We have no quarrel with the people of Libya. We have been wronged by the dictator who has governed them for almost thirty years. Colonel Qaddafi has conducted terrorist attacks against Americans all too often. We know of at least fifty incidents where he, either directly or indirectly, has attacked American people and property around the world. He started this fight, and we're going to finish it, and finish it right now, so help me God.

"But let there be no mistake. If the Libyan people do not surrender Muammar Qaddafi to us within twenty-four hours, alive or dead, we shall exact a just and terrible vengeance. Mr. Qaddafi, this is a promise from me to you. We *will* get you, whatever the cost. If you do not surrender today, the U.S. Air Force and Navy will destroy your country tomorrow. Destroy it utterly.

"I must also report to you on the war in the Middle East. For the past three days, our friends in Israel have withstood attacks the likes of which the world has never seen before. The enemy has used poison gas and biological weapons to attack Israeli cities, and tens of thousands of people lie dead. Men, women, and children have been killed indiscriminately. You and I have seen the images on CNN. It is a horror beyond our imagination.

"Early this morning, at the same time as the attack on the terrorists at the Statue of Liberty, aircraft from our air force and navy attacked the Iraqi, Libyan, Syrian, and Iranian ground forces, which were about to overrun the last lines of Israeli resistance. Thanks to our attacks, the Israelis were able to hold on for one more day. In that day, elements of the First Marine Division were landed near the city of Haifa, and they have pushed eastward for about twenty miles. I have given the Marines orders to keep going until the enemy forces either surrender unconditionally or have been destroyed totally.

"I talked a few minutes ago with the marine commander on the ground, General Jim Hunter. He asked me to tell you that the marines have landed and have the situation well in hand. Before dawn tomorrow, the Army's 101st Airborne Division will be there as well, to be followed by the 82nd Airborne. America stands by its friends. This, too, is a fight we didn't start. But we'll damned well finish it.

"To my countrymen, let me close by saying that what we have gone through was unthinkable just a few days ago. But the fact that we have come through it and are able to hold our heads high says that America's heart and soul are still intact. As long as there are some of us who are willing to give their lives in defense of our liberty, the rest of us can always sleep well. Whatever the danger, America can face it and overcome it with pride. God bless America, and all her fighting men and women. Good night."

The president turned to Touchman. "Freddy, you're fired as of right now. I want General Dunham retired from the marines and in your job by the end of the week. Tom, get those boys back safe from wherever they are. I want to decide what to do with them, and I want your advice."

CHAPTER 30

AT THE SOG

Three weeks later, Cully could walk on his crutches without help. The docs said he could use a cane in a few days, but he was already walking with one a few times a day, and his own private plan for recovery included jogging and swimming, starting Friday. His pals at the FBI School at Quantico said he could use their pool anytime, the cost being some hand-to-hand lessons for the Hostage Rescue Team. The call came from Captain Schaeffer to report to Admiral Pierson's office in Washington, pronto. So off he went, with Wilson, as usual, at his side.

When the Navy Gulfstream jet landed at Reagan National, there was a car waiting. Cully was surprised to see Pierson inside. He wore four stars now. The DCNO was now the chairman of the Joint Chiefs. "Pleased to meet you, master chief. Good to see you again, O'Bannon. How's the leg, son?"

"Pretty good, sir. I plan to be back to full speed in a month or so."

"Don't rush it, boy. We need you back at top speed for good, not just for a while. Did Schaeffer tell you where you're going?"

"No, sir. I brought Master Chief Wilson along. He can recount the events of the battle as well as I can. He was right next to me almost all the way through it. What's the agenda for us, sir?"

"Well, we don't have an agenda. You and Wilson are meeting with the president in ten minutes."

"What does he want with us, sir?"

"He has some notion that you can still contribute something more to the national defense. I'll let CINCWORLD tell you himself."

They drove in silence up the George Washington Parkway to the Memorial Bridge. Cully and Wilson looked out the windows at Arlington Cemetery. There were thousands of white crosses there, arrayed in neat rows up the hills from the river. Cully and Wilson went silent at the sight. Soon enough, they were at the West Gate where Cully had entered an eternity ago. They did the usual drill with the search, the metal detector, the IDs and the badges. Their dress white uniforms still looked a bit out of place.

They checked in with the reception secretary, and the president's personal secretary, Sophie Goldberg, all 200 pounds of her, bounced out to greet them. She had been with La Guardia for more than twenty years, starting in his borough president's office in Staten Island. No matter how many times people suggested politely that she be replaced with a cookie-cutter plastic blond, La Guardia just ignored them. Sophie was a good New York mama, and she watched over him like a hawk. She took good care of him, and he knew she was his wife's best friend. Can't win 'em all. At least she didn't mind cigars.

Sophie looked Cully up and down, then smiled. "If ya don't mind waitin', th' boss will be witcha in a minute. By the way, are you married?"

Cully smothered a chuckle. "Thanks, ma'am. We don't mind waiting. And no ma'am, I'm not. But I plan to be soon."

Wilson was pretending to admire the enormous clock over the reception desk and trying very hard to look down the receptionist's blouse, when a tall thin man with an Abe Lincoln beard came storming through the door, elbowing the marine guard in the stomach as he passed.

"Why are you keeping me waiting?" shouted Steven Krueger. "How many times do I have to tell you to keep these military thugs out of my way!" Krueger, facing unemployment, still had White House access and, as usual, was abusing it.

Before Cully could stop him, Wilson had stepped forward and thrown Krueger against the wall. His forearm was across Krueger's windpipe, and the thin man, his toes reaching for the floor, was rapidly turning blue. "Mr. O'Bannon, what should I do with this limp-wristed bag of . . . ?" The marine at the door was standing at attention, trying unsuccessfully to stifle a grin.

"Why not grab a leg in each hand and pretend he's a wishbone? Ah, drop him, Chief."

Wilson did. Krueger sat down hard, and Wilson turned back to him. "Next time one of those military thugs opens a door for you, say thanks, punk." Krueger just sat there, his eyes wide in shock.

Two minutes later, Mrs. Goldberg ushered them into the Oval Office. La Guardia sat there, lighting an enormous cigar. "The only thing Jack Kennedy ever did wrong was to cut off my supply of Havanas. Humph. Now that I'm the president, maybe I'll fix that problem. Welcome, men. I'm proud to meet ya, Chief. I met your boss before you were famous. Now, all I can say is that the nation is proud of you both.

"I invited you here to tell you in person that Congress has voted the two of you the Medal of Honor. I want to present it to you both next Tuesday in the Rose Garden."

Cully was sure he was going to step in it, but went ahead as gently as he could. "Sir, I don't think that would be right."

"Nonsense, boy. You earned it."

"Sir, that's not what I meant. I'm sorry to be causing a problem, but if every man in my platoon doesn't get one, I don't want one. Four of our guys died there, sir. So did the best helo driver the navy ever had. It wouldn't be right for me to take the medal and not give them one." Wilson chimed in with a quick, "Me, too."

La Guardia reached for his humidor and held it out to the two SEALs. Wilson took a cigar. It looked as big as a shoulder-fired missile. The president leaned across Cully to light it. "Okay, fellas. That's my screw-up, not anyone else's. But what you've just said proves once again that you really are the best we have."

He smiled again. "For a coupla guys who aren't from my neighborhood, you drive a hard bargain. The whole team gets the Big Pin next Tuesday. Capiche? And we'll specially honor those who were killed, including the helicopter pilot. We'll bring their parents or wives down here on Air Force One. Okay?"

"Yes, sir," they said in unison.

"And one more thing. I want you both to stay in business for a while. O'Bannon, you'll find yourself in charge of rebuilding the SEALs, and then you're gonna be commander of SEAL Forces Atlantic when the current guy retires. Okay?"

"Sir, I don't know what to say!"

"Yeah, yeah. And as for you, Master Chief Wilson. You're due to retire the end of this year. I'd like you to delay that for a year or two. Keep this guy out of trouble for me, will ya?"

Wilson smiled. "Sure thing. We'll be in trouble more often than not, but only when you say so."

"Good. Now the two a you get the hell outta here. I got work to do." He bellowed out the door as they left, "Sophie, what's next, dammit?"

EPILOGUE

2010 Hours
Little Creek, Virginia

Katie pushed her glasses back up her nose with one hand while taking the teacup out of the microwave with the other. The past year had been a complete blur. Her mother kept calling just to see what she might be reading in the paper the next day. After the initial uproar over the Battle of the Statue of Liberty, as even the staid old *New York Times* had called it, there was the call from Cully, still in the hospital, asking her to marry him. She had stood beside him when the platoon went to the White House for the Medal of Honor ceremony. Duke Jamison's mother stood on her left, leaning on Katie, both crying quietly for her son.

Then there was the navy wedding at the chapel at the Academy, with all those odd Brits in sand-colored berets who arrived at the ceremony by parachute and spent the next three days raising merry old hell. They had virtually kidnapped Cully and Katie, put them on the RAF plane to London, drinking and raising hell again. Finally Katie cornered the Raj and he admitted the flight was on Broughton's orders. The ceremonies at Downing Street and Buckingham Palace were spectacular, with the queen herself putting the Victoria's Cross around his neck. Cully smiled a lot, as did Katie, particularly when she told him she was pregnant. The navy gave him public speaking coaches, but he never seemed to get past the "Aw, shucks, ma'am" stage. As a politician, he was hopeless. But the president kept an eye on him. That couldn't be bad, could it?

There were the Senate hearings, the restoration of the SEALs as a unit, and Senator Barrett's announcement that he would retire. Then the Old Man had died of a massive stroke, just two days after they told him the baby was coming. Cully said cryptically that maybe he was waiting for that news.

She had worried about fitting into navy life, but the welcome she had received from Cully's peers, superiors, and their wives had long since wiped that fear away. Better still, Chief Wilson's wife was mothering her the same way Rome took care of Cully. Her new extended family seemed to grow every day.

Katie had joined a small law firm in Virginia Beach and had already gained a reputation as a helluva deal maker. The partners in the firm were amazed at the connections she had, and they were already talking among themselves about how soon they could make her a partner.

And then there was the baby, born almost three weeks ago. Cully kept calling him "son" with a tone of wonder in his voice that Katie loved.

She turned out the kitchen lights. Barefoot as usual, she started up the stairs to the baby's room. The base housing office had told them there was a six-month wait for houses for lieutenant commanders and commanders, but that was before. It seemed that lieutenant commanders who were promoted directly to captain by special presidential order somehow jumped to the head of the line. The house was nice, but not very big. Only admirals got the big ones.

She pushed the door to the baby's room open quietly. Cully sat in the rocking chair, with the baby in his arms, half dozing himself, with the smile she always loved. Katie tiptoed in.

Cully whispered, "Shhh, he's almost asleep. He really looks like an O'Bannon, doesn't he?"

She smiled and whispered back, "Yup. Same nose, same thick head." Cully got up slowly and gently laid the boy down in his crib. Katie padded out of the room. As he turned to leave, Cully said, "Semper Fi, son."

Without knowing why, Patrick Bart O'Bannon smiled, sighed, and fell asleep.